Praise for

*The Castle in the Forest*

"This remarkable novel about the young Adolf Hitler, his family and their shifting circumstances, is Mailer's most perfect apprehension of the absolutely alien. . . . Mailer doesn't inhabit these historical figures so much as possess them. . . . Mailer the wild empathizer, the maestro of the human ego, is keen and blunt about . . . what, in effect, are the deceptively homey psychological origins of evil." —*The New York Times Book Review*

"Saturated with a very material sense of evil: The moods, textures, auras and above all the smells that announce the entrance of the Devil into earthly affairs." —*The Boston Globe*

"Terrifically creepy . . . Mailer has an inclusive vision of evil, one that embraces nurture, nature, and supernatural demonic forces, all of which come together in that perfect storm over the spick-and-span Hitler home. . . . An icy and convincing portrait of the dictator as a young sociopath." —*Entertainment Weekly*

"[A] blackly hilarious, beautifully written book . . . [It] has vigor, excitement, humor and vastness of spirit. . . . A great book." —*The New York Observer*

"[A] dramatic etiology of modern evil . . . one of his strongest." —*San Francisco Chronicle*

"His most controversial feat . . . The Pulitzer Prize–winning paladin deftly blends fact and fiction to tackle his greatest villain yet: Adolf Hitler." —*Vanity Fair*

ALSO BY NORMAN MAILER

*The Naked and the Dead*

*Barbary Shore*

*The Deer Park*

*Advertisements for Myself*

*Deaths for the Ladies (and Other Disasters)*

*The Presidential Papers*

*An American Dream*

*Cannibals and Christians*

*Why Are We in Vietnam?*

*The Deer Park—A Play*

*The Armies of the Night*

*Miami and the Siege of Chicago*

*Of a Fire on the Moon*

*The Prisoner of Sex*

*Maidstone*

*Existential Errands*

*St. George and the Godfather*

*Marilyn*

*The Faith of Graffiti*

*The Fight*

*Genius and Lust*

*The Executioner's Song*

*Of Women and Their Elegance*

*Pieces and Pontifications*

*Ancient Evenings*

*Tough Guys Don't Dance*

*Harlot's Ghost*

*Oswald's Tale: An American Mystery*

*Portrait of Picasso as a Young Man*

*The Gospel According to the Son*

*The Time of Our Time*

*Why Are We at War?*

*The Spooky Art*

*Modest Gifts*

*The Big Empty*

# THE
# CASTLE
## IN THE
# FOREST

RANDOM HOUSE TRADE PAPERBACKS
NEW YORK

# THE CASTLE IN THE FOREST

A NOVEL

# NORMAN MAILER

2007 Random House Trade Paperback Edition

Published in the United States by Random House Trade Paperbacks, an imprint of The Random House Publishing Group, a division of Random House, Inc., New York.

RANDOM HOUSE TRADE PAPERBACKS and colophon are trademarks of Random House, Inc.

Originally published in hardcover in the United States by Random House, an imprint of The Random House Publishing Group, a division of Random House, Inc., in 2007.

LIBRARY OF CONGRESS CATALOGING-IN-PUBLICATION DATA
Mailer, Norman.
The castle in the forest: a novel / Norman Mailer.
p.   cm.
ISBN 978-0-8129-7849-0
1. Hitler, Adolf, 1889–1945—Family—Fiction.
2. Hitler family—Fiction.   I. Title.
PS3525.A4152C37   2007
813'.54—dc22      2006049389

Printed in the United States of America

www.atrandom.com

2  4  6  8  9  7  5  3  1

Designed by Stephanie Huntwork

*To my grandchildren,*
*Valentina Colodro, Alejandro Colodro, Antonia*
*Colodro, Isabella Moschen, Christina Marie*
*Nastasi, Callan Mailer, Theodore Mailer,*
*Natasha Lancaster, Mattie James Mailer,*
*Cyrus Force Mailer, and to my grand-niece*
*Eden River Alson as well as to my godchildren,*
*Dominique Malaquais, Kittredge Fisher,*
*Clay Fisher, Sebastian Rosthal,*
*and Julian Rosthal.*

# Contents

# BOOK I

## THE SEARCH FOR HITLER'S GRANDFATHER

# 1

You may call me D.T. That is short for Dieter, a German name, and D.T. will do, now that I am in America, this curious nation. If I draw upon reserves of patience, it is because time passes here without meaning for me, and that is a state to dispose one to rebellion. Can this be why I am writing a book? Among my former associates, we had to swear never to undertake such an action. I was, after all, a member of a matchless Intelligence group. Its classification was SS, Special Section IV-2a, and we were directly under the supervision of Heinrich Himmler. Today, the man is seen as a monster, and I would not look to defend him—he turned out to be one hell of a monster. All the same, Himmler did have an original mind, and one of his theses does take me into my literary intentions, which are, I promise, not routine.

# 2

The room that Himmler used when speaking to our elite group was a small lecture hall with dark walnut paneling and was limited to twenty seats raked upward in four rows of five. My emphasis will not be, however, on such descriptions. I prefer to concern myself with Himmler's unorthodox concepts. They may even have stimulated me to begin a memoir that is bound to prove unsettling. I know that I will sail into a sea of turbulence, for I must uproot many a conventional belief. A cacophony erupts in my spirit at the thought. As Intelligence officers, we often seek to warp our findings. Mendacity, after all, possesses its own art, but this is a venture that will ask me to forsake such skills.

Enough! Let me present Heinrich Himmler. You, the reader, must be prepared for no easy occasion. This man, whose nickname, behind his back, was Heini, had become by 1938 one of the four truly important leaders in Germany. Yet his most cherished and secret intellectual pursuit was the study of incest. It dominated our highest-level research, and our findings were kept to closed conferences. Incest, Heini would propose, had always been rife among the poor of all lands. Even our German peasantry had been much afflicted, yes, even as late as the nineteenth century. "Normally, no one in learned circles cares to speak of the matter," he would remark. "After all, there is nothing to be done. Who would bother to call some poor wretch a certified offspring of incest? No, every establishment of every civilized nation looks to sweep such stuff under the rug."

That is, all ranking government officials in the world except for our Heinrich Himmler. He did have the most extraordinary ideas fermenting behind his unhappy spectacles. I must repeat that for a man with a bland and chinless mug, he certainly exhibited a frustrating mixture of brilliance and stupidity. For example, he declared himself to be a pagan. He predicted that there would be a healthy future for humankind once paganism took over the world. Everyone's soul would then be enriched with hitherto unacceptable pleasures. None of us could conceive, however, of an orgy where carnality would rise to such a pitch that you might find a woman ready to throw herself into a flesh-melting roll with Heinrich Himmler. No, not even in the most innovative spirit! For you could always see his face as it must once have been at a school dance, that bespectacled disapproving stare of the wallflower, tall, thin, a youth full of physical ineptitude. Already he had a small potbelly. There he was, ready to wait by the wall while the dance went on.

Yet he grew obsessed over the years with matters others did not dare to mention aloud (which, I must say, is usually the first step to new thought). In fact, he paid close attention to mental retardation. Why? Because Himmler subscribed to the theory that the best human possibilities lie close to the worst. So he was ready to assume that promising children when found in low, nondescript families could be "incestuaries." The word in German, as he coined it, was *Inzestuarier*. He did not like the more common term of such disgrace, *Blutschande* (blood-scandal), or as it is sometimes employed in polite circles, *Dramatik des Blutes* (blood-drama).

None of us felt sufficiently qualified to say that his theory could be dismissed. Even in the early years of the SS, Himmler had recognized that one of our prime needs was to develop exceptional research groups. We had a duty to search into ultimates. As Himmler put it, the health of National Socialism depended on nothing less than these *letzte Fragen* (last questions). We were to explore problems that other nations did not dare to go near. Incest was at the head of the list. The German mind had to reestablish itself again as the leading inspiration to the learned world. In turn—so went his unstated coupling—much recognition might be given to Heinrich Himmler for his profound attack on problems originating in the agricultural milieu. He would emphasize the underlying point: Husbandry could hardly be investigated without comprehending the peasant. Yet to understand this man of the earth was to speak of incest.

Here, I promise you, he would hold up his hand in precisely that little gesture Hitler used to employ—one prissy flip of the wrist. It was Heinrich's way of saying: "Now comes the meat. And with it— the potatoes!" Off he would go on a peroration. "Yes," he would say, "incest! This is one very good reason that old peasants are devout. An acute fear of the sinful is bound to display itself by one of two extremes: Absolute devotion to religious practice. Or nihilism. I can recall from my student days that the Marxist Friedrich Engels once wrote, 'When the Catholic Church decided adultery was impossible to prevent, they made divorce impossible to obtain.' A brilliant remark even if it comes from the wrong mouth. As much can be said for blood-scandal. That is also impossible to prevent. So, the peasant looks to keep himself devout." He nodded. He nodded again as if two good pumps of his head might be the minimum necessary to convince us that he was speaking from both sides of his heart.

How often, he asked, could the average peasant of the last century avoid these blood temptations? After all, that was not so easy. Peasants, it had to be said, were not usually attractive people. Their features were worn away by hard labor. Besides, they reeked of the field and the barn. Personal odors were at the mercy of hot summers. Under such circumstances, would not basic impulses trigger forbidden inclinations? Given the paucity of their social life, how were they to acquire the ability to stay away from entanglements with brothers and sisters, fathers and daughters?

He did not go on to speak of the pell-mell of limbs and torsos formed by three or four children in a bed, nor the ham-handed naturalness of the most agreeable work of all—that hard-breathing, feverish meat-heavy run up the hills of physical joy—but he did declare, "More than a few in the agricultural sector come, willy-nilly, to see incest as an acceptable option. Who, after all, is most likely to find the honorable work-hardened features of the father or the brother particularly attractive? The sisters, of course! Or the daughters. Often they are the only ones. The father, having created them, remains the focus of their attention."

Hand it to Himmler. He had been storing theories in his head for two decades. A great believer in Schopenhauer, he would also give prominence to a word still relatively new in 1938—*genes*. These genes, he said, were the biological embodiment of Schopenhauer's concept of the Will. They are the basic element of this mysterious Will. "We know," he said, "that instincts can be passed from one generation to the next. Why? I would say it is in the nature of the Will to remain true to its origins. I even speak of that as a Vision, yes, gentlemen, a force that lives at the core of our human existence. It is this Vision which separates us from the animals. From the beginning of our time on earth, we humans have been seeking to rise to the unseen heights that lie ahead.

"Of course, there are impediments to such a great goal. The most exceptional of our genes must still be able to surmount the privations, humiliations, and tragedies of life as the genes are transmitted from father to child, generation after generation. Great leaders, I would tell you, are rarely the product of one father and one mother. It is more likely that the rare leader is the one who has succeeded in breaking through the bonds that held back ten frustrated generations who could not express the Vision in their own lives but did pass it on through their genes.

"Needless to say, I have arrived at these concepts by meditating upon the life of Adolf Hitler. His heroic rise resonates in our hearts. Since he issues, as we know, from a long line of modest peasant stock, his life demonstrates a superhuman achievement. Absolute awe must overwhelm us."

As Intelligence agents, we were smiling within. This had been the peroration. Now our Heinrich was ready to enter what Americans call the nitty-gritty. "The real question to be asked," he said, "is how does the brilliance of the Vision protect itself from being dulled by commingling? That is implicit in the process of so-called normal reproduction. Contemplate the multimillions of sperm. One of them has to travel all the way up to the ovum of the female. To each lonely sperm cell swimming in the uterine sea, that ovum will loom as large as a battle cruiser." He paused before he nodded. "The same readiness for self-sacrifice that will carry men at war through an uphill attack on a forbidding ridge must exist in healthy sperm. The essence of the male seed is that it is ready to commit itself to just such immolation in order that one of them, at least, will reach the ovum!"

He stared at us. Could we share his excitement? "The next question," he said, "soon arises. Will the genes of the woman be compatible with the sperm cell that has managed to reach her? Or will these separate elements find their respective genes to be in dispute? Are they about to act like unhappy husbands and wives? Yes, I would answer, dispute is often the prevailing case. The meeting may prove sufficiently compatible for procreation to occur, but the combination of their genes is hardly guaranteed to be in harmony.

"When we speak, therefore, of the human desire to create that man who will embody the Vision—the Superman—we have to consider the odds. Not even one in a million families can present us with a husband and a wife who are close enough in the inclination of their genes to bring forth a miraculous child. Not even one, perhaps, in a hundred million. No!"—again the upraised hand—"let us say, closer to a million million. In the case of Adolf Hitler, the numbers may approach the awesome distances we encounter in astronomy.

"So, gentlemen, logic would propose that any Superman who embodies the Vision, is bound to come forth from a mating of exceptionally similar genetic ingredients. Only then will these separate embodiments of the Vision be ready to *reinforce* each other."

Who could not see what Heinrich was aiming at? Incest offered the nearest possibility for such unity of purpose.

"Yet," said Himmler, "to be reasonable, we must also agree that life is not always ready to certify such an event. Debased males and females are the ones who usually come into the world from these family intimacies. We have to recognize that products of incest usually suffer childhood ills and early deaths. Anomalies abound, even exhibitions of physical monstrosity."

He stood there, sad and stern. "That is the price. Not only are many reinforced good tendencies likely to be present in an incestuary, but unhappy inclinations can be magnified as well. Instability is, therefore, a common product of incest. Idiocy waits in the wings. And when a vital possibility exists for the development of a great spirit, this rare human must still overcome a host of frustrations profound enough to unhinge the brain or induce early death." So spoke Heinrich Himmler.

I think all of us present knew the subtext of these remarks. Back

in 1938, we were looking (in greatest secrecy, you may be certain)
to determine whether our Führer was a first- or second-degree
incestuary. Or neither. If not, if neither, then Himmler's theory
would remain groundless. But if our Führer was a true product of
incest, then he was more than a glowing example of the likelihood
of the thesis, he might be the proof itself.

## 3

I am ready to speak of the obsession that revolved around Adolf
Hitler. Yet what brings more of a dark cloud to one's mood than
living with a question that will not return an answer? Even today,
the first obsession remains Hitler. Where is the German who does
not try to understand him? Yet where can you find one who is content with the answer?

I must surprise you. I do not have this particular trial. I live with
the confidence that I am in a position to understand Adolf. For the
fact is that I know him. I must repeat. I know him top to bottom.
To borrow from the Americans, given their rough grasp of vul-
garity, I am prepared to say: "Yes. I know him from asshole to appetite."

Nonetheless, I am still obsessed. It is, however, by an altogether
different problem. When I think of relating how I know so much,
an anxiety arises that can be compared to diving at night from a
sheer cliff down into black water.

Let it be understood, therefore, that in the beginning I will proceed with caution and speak of no more than was available then to
the SS.

For now, that may prove enough. There are particulars to offer
concerning his family roots. In Special Section IV-2a—as already

explained—we surrounded our findings with immaculate secrecy. We had to. We were the ones most ready to look into the most unpalatable questions. We had to live with the fear of unearthing answers poisonous enough to imperil the Third Reich.

On the other hand, we had a special confidence. Once we obtained our facts, even should they prove disruptive, we would still be able to choose the mistruths that would bolster patriotic feelings in the populace. Of course, it could not be guaranteed in advance that every finding would be manageable. We might uncover an explosive fact. As one example: Had Adolf Hitler's paternal grandfather been a Jew?

# 4

That was one possibility. Others were nearly as dire. For a period, we played with an inquiry into a semicomic but delicate rumor. Monorchidism. Did our Führer belong to that group of unhappy and hyperactive men who possess only one testicle? It is true that he invariably covered his groin with a protective hand whenever a photo was about to be taken, a classic gesture, understandably, if you are ready to shield the remaining testicle. But it is one thing to note such a vulnerability, another to verify it. While results could be obtained easily enough by interviewing the few women who had had intimate relations with the Führer and were still alive, how were we to control the repercussions? What if word got back to Hitler that a couple of officers in the SS were, so to speak, fingering his genital(s)? We had to give up the project. That was Himmler's decision: "If our Esteemed Leader proves to be a first-degree incestuary, then all questions of monorchidism are subsumed. Monorchidism is, after all, a likely by-product of first-degree incest."

It was obvious. We were to go back to the best explanation for the legendary Will of the Führer—Blood-Drama!

Moreover, we all detested the possibility that Adolf Hitler's paternal grandfather might have been a Jew. That would not only destroy Himmler's thesis, but oblige us to bury a major scandal. Our uneasiness derived in part from a rumor that had begun to stir among us eight years before, back in 1930, when a letter reached Hitler's desk. The young man who penned it was named William Patrick Hitler, and he turned out to be the son of Adolf's older half brother, Alois Hitler, Jr. The nephew's letter offered its hint of blackmail. It referred to "shared circumstances in our family history." (The fellow had gone so far as to underline those words.) That would have been a dangerous letter to send if the nephew lived in Germany, but at the time he was dwelling in England.

What, then, were these "shared circumstances"? William Patrick Hitler was speaking of the Führer's grandmother, Maria Anna Schicklgruber. Back in 1837, she had given birth to a son whom she named Alois. Living then and thereafter in a miserable place called Strones, a wretched hamlet in the Austrian province of Waldviertel, Maria Anna used to receive small but regular sums of money. Those near to her assumed it came from the unnamed father of her boy.

Yet that same boy would grow up to be Hitler's father. While Adolf would not be born until 1889, and would not come to power until 1933, one story did manage to stay alive among the peasants in Strones. It was that the stipend had come from a well-to-do Jew who lived in the provincial city of Graz. According to the legend, Maria Anna Schicklgruber worked as a maid in this Jew's house, became pregnant, and had to return to her hamlet. When she brought the infant to be baptized, the parish priest listed the birth as "Illegitimate," a common declaration in those parts. The Waldviertel was known, after all, as the poorhouse of Austria. One hundred years later, following the Anschluss in 1938, I was sent down to the region, and my findings proved, in fact, fascinating. While it would still be premature to explain how I learned what I did, I can,

however, offer my conclusions. For now, that must suffice. In time,
I hope to have the courage to say more.

<h1 style="text-align:center">5</h1>

The Waldviertel, situated north of the Danube, is a land of tall
beautiful pines. Indeed Waldviertel can be translated directly
as the "wooded quarter," and the silences of the forests are dark in
contrast to the green of an occasional field. The soil, however, does
not welcome agriculture. An Austrian hamlet in these backwoods
delineated the meaning of dirt-poor. In those years, the Hiedlers
(who later became Hitlers) lived in Spital, a village of sorts, and the
Schicklgrubers, their cousins, lived nearby in the aforesaid Strones,
which was deep in the mud along its one lane, no more than a few
dozen huts with roofs of thatch. If Strones was profuse in pig wal-
lows around each dwelling, cow flop was more prominent in the
town meadows, and the redolence of horse manure was valued.
This was, after all, an area where many a peasant had to pull his
own plow through various grades of mud. There was gumbo thick
as lava, rivulets of silt, gravel washes, muck and slops, clods, rocks,
common clay. For that matter, Strones did not even have a church.
The locals had to walk to another hamlet, Döllersheim. There
in the parish registry, the name of Maria Anna's son was inscribed
as "Alois Schicklgruber, Catholic, Male,"—and, as we know—
"Illegitimate."

Maria Anna, born in 1795, was forty-two when Alois was born
in 1837. Coming from a family of eleven children of whom five
were already dead, she certainly could have cohabited with any one
of her several brothers. (Himmler had, of course, no objection to
that, since her bastard Alois was, I repeat, Adolf's father.) In any

event, despite the abysmal poverty of Maria Anna's parents, she dwelt with her son for the next five years in one of her father's two small rooms. The mysterious money that came in small but dependable installments helped to support these Schicklgrubers.

While we were obviously eager to find a trove of intrafamily copulations, such a desire did not allow us to dismiss the Jew from Graz. Indeed, eight years earlier, in 1930, inquiries had already been made. As Himmler related it, Hitler, on reading his nephew's letter, had sent it on immediately to a Nazi lawyer, Hans Frank. The Führer, as some may no longer recall, did not become Chancellor until 1933, but Hans Frank was already looking in 1930 to worm his way into the inside circle around the Leader.

Frank had unhappy news to deliver, therefore, concerning Maria Anna's pregnancy. The likelihood, he declared, was that the father had been a nineteen-year-old, the son of a prosperous merchant named Frankenberger who was, yes, a Jew. It made sense. In those years, the scion of many a well-to-do family had his first carnal outings with a housemaid. Nor did she have to be anywhere near his age. Such an initiation was accepted by the bourgeois mores of a provincial city like Graz as a reasonable if undiscussed practice. It was seen as a good deal better than allowing a well-to-do lad to consort with whores or settle too early on a sweetheart from a less prosperous family.

Frank claimed to have seen some conclusive evidence. He told Hitler that he had been shown a letter written by Herr Frankenberger, the father of the young man who had bedded down with Maria Anna. This letter promised regular payments to take care of Alois until he was fourteen years old.

Our Adolf, however, disagreed with these findings. He told Hans Frank that the true story, imparted to him by his own father, Alois, was that the real grandfather had been Maria Anna's cousin Johann Georg Hiedler, who had finally come around to marry her five years after Alois' birth. "All the same," said Hitler to Hans Frank, "I would like to examine this letter from the Jew to my grandmother."

Frank told Hitler that he did not as yet possess it. The man who held it was asking too high a price. Besides, the letter must certainly have been photographed.

"You have seen the original?" Hitler asked.

"I was able to look at it while in his office. He had two big fellows standing beside him. He also had a pistol on the table. What must he have been expecting?"

Hitler nodded. "One cannot even expect a sudden end for a man like that. The letter, after all, will be in one place and the photographic copy in another."

One more concern for Hitler to carry.

By 1938, however, our search had delivered alternatives. It no longer seemed certain that Maria Anna was still receiving steady money five years after Alois was born. Following her marriage in 1842, she and her husband, Johann Georg Hiedler, had been much too poor to have a home of their own. For a time they had had to sleep in a battered old trough once used to feed cattle in a neighbor's barn. Of course, that did not prove that no money had been sent. Johann Georg could certainly have drunk up the funds. In Strones, he remained a legend due to the extent of his tippling. Indeed, his large intake of liquor had to be at odds with the assumption that they were that poor: For why would a drunk like fifty-year-old Johann Georg marry a woman of forty-seven with a five-year-old brat unless she had enough income to allow him to drink? Moreover, the extent of his boozing would hardly suggest that he had been Alois' father. Indeed, this Johann Georg Hiedler made no objection when Maria Anna asked Johann's younger brother, also named Johann (but, in this case, Johann *Nepomuk* Hiedler), to take the boy in and raise him. This younger brother, Johann Nepomuk, was, by contrast, a sober, hardworking farmer with a wife and three daughters, but he did not have a son.

So Johann Nepomuk now stood out as a likely possibility. Might he not be the father? That was certainly possible. Yet we still had to find enough evidence to discount the Jew.

Himmler sent me to Graz and I went to some pains examining

the century-old records. No man named Frankenberger was to be found in the city ledgers. I pored over the *Israelitische Kultusge-meinde* of the Jewish Registry of Graz, and this finding was confirmed. Back in 1496, the Jews had been expelled from the region. Even three hundred and forty-one years later, in 1837, at the time Alois was born, the Jews had still not been permitted to come back. Had Hans Frank been lying?

After looking at these results Himmler declared, "Frank is one bold fellow!" As Heini put it together for me, one had to go back from 1938 to 1930. At that time, when the missive from William Patrick Hitler arrived, Hans Frank was just one more lawyer ready to hang around our people in Munich, but it was clear enough now what he had done. He had invented the compromising letter in order to stimulate a closer relationship to his leader. Given the absence of the document, Hitler could not know whether Frank was making it up, telling the truth, or, worst of all, actually in possession of such a paper. It could have been the end of Hans Frank, if Hitler had sent a researcher to Graz, but the lawyer must have been ready to wager that Hitler did not want to know.

Since Himmler was grooming me to become his close assistant, he also confided that he would not use my 1938 research to tell Hitler that there were no Jews in Graz back in 1837. Rather, he told Hans Frank. We laughed in unison, for I understood immediately. Could there be one official within our ruling group who was not searching for a dependable grip on any and all of the others? Frank was now in Himmler's grasp. Given this mutual understanding, he did serve Himmler well. In 1942 (by which time Frank was known as "the Butcher of Poland") Hitler became nervous again about the Jewish grandfather and asked us to send a good man to Graz. Himmler, looking to protect Hans Frank, told the Führer that he had sent an agent and no tangible evidence was found. Given everyone's preoccupation with the war, the matter could be put more or less to rest. Such was Himmler's advice to Hitler.

# BOOK II

## ADOLF'S FATHER

# 1

The year 1942 is, however, a century and more away from 1837. For that matter, so is 1938. I mention the latter date once more because of a minor episode that occurred in Austria during the Anschluss. It does provide an insight into Himmler. If, behind his back, he was still ridiculed as Heini—ill gaited, pompous, wide assed and flat assed, as pious a mediocrity as any other man who has risen too high—the detractors were merely describing the shell. Nobody, not even Hitler, believed more profoundly in Nazism's philosophical principles.

I remember that on the first morning after the Brown Shirts marched into Vienna, a squad of them—beer-hall types with big bellies—collected a group of old and middle-aged Jews, professional class, pince-nez absolutely in place, and put them to work scrubbing the sidewalk with toothbrushes. The Storm Troopers laughed as they watched. Photographs of the event were featured on the front pages of many a newspaper in Europe and America.

Next day, Himmler spoke to a few of us. "That was an expensive indulgence and I am pleased that not one of our SS men had anything to do with such a crudity. We all know how this kind of action lowers morale among so many of our best people. It will certainly encourage rowdyism in Vienna. Nonetheless, we do well not to reject out of hand the primitive instinct revealed by the act. After much reflection, I can say it was a successful piece of mockery." He paused. He did have our attention. "There is a curious, even, I would declare, a hidden sense of inferiority among many of our folk. They feel that the Jews are capable of bringing more concentration to a task than most of us can—the Jews do know how to study—which is why so many of them have been grossly successful. It is very much a notion among these people that in the end they will win everything by working harder than the host race of any country they happen to inhabit.

"So, I would say this act burst out of the rough but nonetheless instinctive understanding of our German people. It does tell the Jews that work, if it is not attached to a noble purpose, is meaningless. 'Scrub away with those toothbrushes,' our street boys are saying, 'because you Jews, whether you know it or not, do exactly the same thing every day. Your virtuous scholarship goes nowhere but into endless contradictions.' Therefore, on second thought," Himmler concluded, "I will not condemn out of hand the deeds of these low-rank Nazis."

The story is useful if one is to understand Himmler, but does interrupt my account of how I came to learn the truth as to who, really, was Alois' father. While I am prepared to give his name and describe the occasion, I recognize that some readers will be annoyed that these disclosures will be presented without accounting for my sources. A fact is not a fact, some are ready to say, if the means by which it was obtained cannot be presented.

I agree. Nonetheless, my real means are not to be revealed, not yet. Using the assets of Section IV-2a proved insufficient on this occasion, but I did piece together an answer for Heini—I knew that if my end product could support his case, he would accept it.

Let us content ourselves for now, then, with the conclusions presented to Himmler in 1938. Once I brought back the information that the Jew from Graz did not exist, I suggested that we shift our inquiry to the actions of the one brother of Maria Anna Schicklgruber who had actually been resourceful enough to leave the mud of Strones and make a little money as a commercial traveler. What was best about this brother is that he did pass regularly through Graz, so, at first, I decided to build our case on him and ignore the actual family Maria Anna had worked for—a widow and two daughters. By study of their old bank accounts, it was clear that no extra money ever came to her from these ladies and, indeed, they discharged Maria Anna when they discovered she had made some petty thefts. Pregnancy in an unmarried maid could be tolerated, but the loss of a few coins, no! I then decided that Maria Anna might have been looking to protect this brother by telling her father and mother that the money was coming from a Jew. That would get them off the scent.

Before I passed this speculation on to Himmler, however, I concocted—or so I thought—a more promising alternative. Why not choose Johann Nepomuk Hiedler, the hardworking younger brother, as our seminal agent? While the traveling salesman, Maria Anna's brother, would offer a prima facie case of incest, this was still one step removed from Himmler's real objective, since it would posit that the father, Alois, was the incestuary, rather than Adolf.

On the other hand, if Maria Anna conceived Alois with Johann Nepomuk, then Himmler's thesis was strengthened. Significantly so. For Klara Poelzl, the young woman who would yet be Alois' third wife and would become Adolf Hitler's mother, was also the granddaughter of Johann Nepomuk. If Alois was Nepomuk's son, then Klara could be nothing less than Alois' niece! An uncle and a niece, Alois and Klara, had conceived our Führer. This would make a solid presentation. Moreover, I knew how to embellish it for Heini. My final scenario offered carnal flavor: I declared that Maria Anna Schicklgruber and Johann Nepomuk Hiedler had conceived Alois on the day she came back from Graz for a visit. Nepomuk, who lived in Spital, happened to be visiting Strones, and went to the straw for his hour with Maria Anna. She became pregnant on the spot. Nepomuk could not question the news, for the act had been out of the ordinary. Indeed, she told him as soon as she regained her breath, "You have given me a baby. I swear it. I felt it!"

As my scenario was also ready to explain, Johann Nepomuk loved his wife, he loved his three daughters, and he would never disrupt his home. Notwithstanding, he was ready to consider this matter from Maria Anna's point of view. He was a decent man. So he encouraged her to tell her parents that she was receiving money from

Graz, but he, Johann Nepomuk, would be the one to provide steady sums for the child to come. So she told her family that the money came each month from Graz, even if no one ever saw the envelopes.

Maria Anna put up with the situation, but how could she be content? After five years had elapsed, she told Nepomuk she would have to confess the real story. It was humiliating, she told him, to face the women of Strones each time she left her door holding a five-year-old by the hand.

Nepomuk proposed that his older brother Georg be installed instead as her spouse. Nepomuk did not like his brother, and Georg did not like Nepomuk, but a new source of money is life-blood to a drunk. I exaggerate, but not by much. Georg married Maria Anna for her stipend and enjoyed the knowledge that it came from Nepomuk, who worked even harder in his fields to gather the extra kronen. For Georg, it was a rare pleasure to use the hard labor of a younger brother to support his dissipations. He did possess a fund of ugly spirit. A perfect fury full of failure.

Maria Anna, wed at last, wanted a husband who was ready to say he was Alois' father, but Georg proved quick to tell her that she was interfering in a matter involving his personal honor. If he had managed in the course of many a spree to inform a few of his drinking companions just why he had gotten married—for the money, dimwit!—he saw all the more reason to make no fool of himself by legitimizing this brat who everyone knew was not his own. He might be a drunkard and a failure, but he was certainly not a cuckold. Let this bastard remain a bastard!

Such was the legend I presented to Himmler. It was buttressed by interviews I worked up with those few of the very old inhabitants of Strones who were born before our drunk, Johann Georg Hiedler, died in 1857. The links, if examined closely, were too rusty to secure the story, but Himmler liked these conclusions and so they held up. I had delivered a family history in which there was no Jew in the Führer's bloodstream, and his father and mother were uncle and niece by blood. I had thereby succeeded in making Adolf Hitler a First-Degree Incestuary One Step Removed.

Himmler had an epiphany. "This," he said, "more than anything else, reveals the incredible bravery and fortitude of the Führer. As I have often pointed out, early death or serious malformation is the most likely prognostication for First-Degree Incestuaries, but once again the Führer has shown us his incomparable powers of perseverance. Genius and Will, his unique properties of character, derive from the rare intensification found in First-Degree Incestuaries, even when they are one step removed. We have been blessed with the triumphant result. Our Führer's agrarian genes fortified through the generations have found a triumphant metamorphosis into his transcendent virtues."

Here, Himmler closed his eyes, leaned back, and exhaled slowly. It was as if he must expel every errant spirit in his lungs. "I will not speak to you of this again," he went on in a low voice, "but occasions of close incest are truly perilous. One has need of the Führer's Will to succeed in such a situation." (I capitalize Will since he used the word with reverence.) "It is my belief that in the world of numinous spirits surrounding us, there are many elements we are right to call evil. It is even possible that the worst of these spirits collect about a presence whom in earlier times we used to speak of as Satan. This embodiment, should it exist, would certainly be ready to pay great attention to Incestuaries of advanced degree. For indeed, how could such an Evil One not be eager to distort the exceptional possibilities that arise from the doubling of God-given genes? All the more power to Herr Hitler, then. He has actually been able, I would declare, to stand firm with the Vision in the face of the Devil himself."

Little did Himmler know that his remarks could be multiplied by an order of magnitude. I had not been promulgating a false legend, but an irony. For the story I had concocted out of no more than barely feasible evidence happened to be true. It was Johann Nepomuk Hiedler who did supply the money, and Alois Schicklgruber was his secret child. Yet the irony within this irony was that Alois' son, Adolf Hitler, was not merely a First-Degree Incestuary One Step Removed but had been conceived in the very center of

incest. The niece, Klara Poelzl, who would become Alois' third
wife and Adolf Hitler's mother, was not only Alois' wife but also
his blood daughter. Of that relationship, I can soon offer many
details.

<h1 style="text-align:center">2</h1>

To fulfill such a promise, I must now expand this memoir and
commence a family history much as if I were a conventional
novelist of the old school. I will enter the thoughts of Johann
Nepomuk, as well as many of the insights of his illegitimate son,
Alois Hitler, and I will also include the feelings of Alois' three
wives and his children.

We are finished, however, with Maria Anna Schicklgruber.
That unhappy mother perished in 1847 at the age of fifty-two, ten
years after the birth of Alois. The cause was termed "phthisis
on account of dropsy of the chest," a galloping consumption she
contracted after sleeping in the cattle trough through her last
two winters. The collateral cause was rage. Toward the end, she
thought often of how healthy she had been at the age of nineteen,
her body quick, her singing voice praised for its beauty when she
had been the soloist of the parish choir in Döllersheim. But now,
having suffered under the curse of three decades of lost anticipations, she was full of the added fury that Georg had brought to
their occasional couplings. He, like many a drunk before him, succeeded, however, in outliving everyone's assumption that his death
would come early. After her demise, he actually kept going for ten
more years. Drink had been not only his nemesis but his dear
medicine, and, only at the last, his executioner. He went in a day.
They called it apoplexy. Having never bothered to visit Nepomuk

or Alois, he was not missed, but by then, Alois was twenty and working in Vienna.

For that matter, Alois had not suffered unduly when his mother was lost. Spital, where he lived with Johann Nepomuk and the wife and three daughters of the Hiedler family, was a long walk from Strones, and he had come close to forgetting Maria Anna. He was happy with his new family. In the beginning, Nepomuk's daughters, Johanna, Walpurga, and Josefa, then twelve, ten, and eight, were delighted to have a five-year-old brother, and took him gladly into their bedroom. Since Spital was a full-sized village rather than a hamlet, a separation between prosperous and poor had begun to appear. A farmer could even be considered well-off—at least in his own town. There were a few such in Spital, Johann Nepomuk being the first. The wife, Eva, kept a good home. She was also most practical. If she had a suspicion that Nepomuk might actually be more than an uncle to the boy, she could not, on the other hand, forget the disappointment in his eyes each time she gave birth to a girl. It was probably better for all concerned to have a boy in the house. Yes, she was practical.

And Alois was loved! By his father, by the girls, even by Eva. He was good-looking, and like his own mother, he could sing. As he grew older, he also demonstrated that he was ready to work in the fields. For a time, Johann Nepomuk even contemplated leaving the farm to him, but the boy was restless. He might not always be there to take care of whatever unforeseen obstacle, large or small, might settle upon the daily work. In contrast, Johann Nepomuk had so much love for his labors that on the best of days he felt as if he could hear the murmurs of the earth. While he was not at ease with the long silences that hovered over the end of afternoon, a spell would often enter his dreams by evening. The sum of his fields, his sheds, his beasts, and his barn became a creature equal to a demanding woman, cavernous, haunting, smelly, greedy, needy, ever extracting more from him. He would awake in full recognition that he could never leave the farm to Alois—Alois was the child of the woman in the dream. So he gave up the notion. He had to.

Such a gift would enrage his wife. She wanted a good future for her daughters, and the farm might not provide more than two respectable dowries.

Over the years, new problems presented themselves concerning these dowries. For the first marriage, the oldest daughter, Johanna, was given only a pinched share of the land. But she had, after all, chosen to marry a poor man, a hardworking but unlucky farmer named Poelzl. When it came to the dowry for the second daughter, Walpurga, who was already twenty-one, Nepomuk was obliged to be more generous. The putative bridegroom, Josef Romeder, was a strong fellow from a prosperous farm in Ober-Windhag, the next village, and negotiations over the size of Walpurga's dowry were stiff. In the end, Nepomuk deeded over the richest portion of his land. That left only a modest tract for the third daughter, Josefa, who was sickly and spinsterish. As for Eva and himself, he kept a fine small lodging in an orchard at the border of what was now Romeder's property. But the small house in the orchard was enough. He was ready to retire. Given the length and heat of the negotiations over the dowry, the ceremony to transfer the lands proved as much of an event as the wedding that had just taken place.

Nepomuk led his new son-in-law around the property, boundary line by boundary line, and stopped before every marker that established a separation between his fields and the land of the next farmer. Nepomuk would say, "And if on any day you gather fruit from this man's orchard, even the fallen fruit, may you labor under a black sky." After which he would give Josef Romeder a clout to the head. At each of those eight separate jogs along the boundary line, he repeated the act. Johann Nepomuk was full of the kind of woe that hangs like a deadweight on one's back. He was not mourning the transfer of his farm so much as the absence of Alois. His dear adopted son, Alois, was not there because Johann Nepomuk had banished him three years earlier, when the boy was thirteen and Walpurga eighteen. He had discovered them in the hayloft of his barn, and it caused him to think of the other barn where he had gone to the straw with Maria Anna on the afternoon that Alois had been conceived. A memory of the glory of this act of love with Maria Anna Schicklgruber had never left him. He had had only two women in his life and Maria was the second, and not at all a village wench to him, coarse grained and ass-bare in the hay, but a Madonna lit by sunlight, an image he had earlier acquired by way of the stained-glass window of the church in Spital. This image never failed to enlarge his estimate of the volume of his sin. He was living in sacrilege, that he knew, and yet he would not relinquish the image of Maria Anna's face in the stained-glass window. It was reason enough not to go to confession too often, and when he did, he would invent other sins for the booth, large ones. One time, he even confessed to coition with the farm mare, a deed he had never attempted—one does not make love to a large horse for too little!—and the priest in return asked how many times he had committed this sin. "Only once, Father."

"When was that? How long ago?"

"Months, months I think."

"And how do you feel now when you work with the animal? Are there similar urges?"

"No, never. I am ashamed for myself."

The priest was middle-aged and had little to learn about the peasantry, so he could sense that Nepomuk was lying. Nonetheless, his preference was that the account be true because bestial sodomy, while as mortal a sin as adultery or incest, was to his mind less grievous. It would, after all, produce no offspring. He proceeded, therefore, to exercise his office without further questioning.

"You have degraded yourself as a child of God," he told Nepomuk, "you have committed a serious sin of lust. You have injured an innocent animal. For your penance I give you five hundred Our Fathers and five hundred Hail Marys."

That was identical to a penance the priest had given earlier that morning to a schoolboy who had treated himself to an underhanded spit-in-the-palm masturbation in class (a most stealthy act!) and then rubbed his spit and semen on the hair of the boy in front of him, a small boy.

Johann Nepomuk contented himself afterward by confessing to
the same priest upon occasion that he still had lewd thoughts concerning the mare but was careful to do nothing about it. That took
care of confession, but the continuing absence of Alois caused Johann Nepomuk Hiedler to live in an agony of love. He had wept
like a biblical father and torn his shirt when he found his son and
daughter in the straw. He knew that he had just lost the boy. The
brightest light of nearly every one of his days, that lively young
face, would have to leave. To the shock of the other women in the
family, Alois was sent away that night to a neighbor's house and in
the morning was put on a coach to Vienna.

Nepomuk did not tell Eva, but then, he did not have to, because
Walpurga, at her father's insistence, was kept at home for the next
three years. The young woman's marriage with Romeder, empty of
courtship, had to be arranged. Yet Eva, while as alert to the chastity
of her daughters as a drill sergeant studying the precision of his
platoon on dress parade, would still nag Nepomuk to allow Walpurga to walk on Sunday with a girlfriend.

"No," Nepomuk would say. "The two of them will wander into
the woods. Then boys will follow them."

On the day he stalked the boundary line with Romeder, he was
burdened each time he struck his daughter's new husband. What
an injustice he was doing to his new son-in-law. Ergo, he hit him
harder. A marriage was being founded on a lie. Therefore, no tres-
passes should be made on the land of the neighbor. That would be
a sacrilege against the earth. How Nepomuk mourned the absence
of his son!

A lois did well in Vienna. With his good and agreeable face, he was taken on in a shop that made cavalry boots for officers.

He now served young men who carried themselves as if their bodies, their uniforms, their decorations, their footwear, and their souls had been fabricated by the same awesome source. Their confidence in their personal appearance had much to offer Alois. These men, he observed, looked to be at ease with the beautifully dressed ladies they escorted. On Sundays, he would rarely miss watching their promenade. The women's hats were so finely wrought. He had the passing thought that if he met a young milliner, they could open a shop and young couples of the best and highest classes would visit their store hand in hand looking for splendid boots and stylish hats. It was the only business concept he was to have for many a year, but he did play with such a dream because beautiful ladies stimulated him. He loved young women. He had had such contentment playing with his stepsisters, which is to say, as only Nepomuk knew, his half sisters.

He met no young milliner, however, and the idea gave way to a better one. He could never be a cavalry officer, since that depended on being born into a proper family, and he came from a place where more was known about a pig's habits than the scent a man should put upon his handkerchief. Alois would not aspire to what was not there. But one thing he knew—he was able to live on good terms with Vienna. No one back in Spital had been as ready to improve himself. Early on, then, he understood his own ambition— he wanted to spend his life in a decent uniform and be admired for his posture. And his intelligence. He was certainly not stupid, he knew.

At the age of eighteen, after five years in the boot shop, he applied to the Austrian Finance Ministry for a position in Customs, and was accepted. In another five years, he had risen to the rank of Finanzwache Oberaufseher (Finance-Watch High Overseer), which was equal to no more than Corporal, but already the uniform was impressive, and for that matter, it usually took ten years to rise even to this level, especially if you joined the Service with no connections.

He had written on several occasions to tell Johann Nepomuk of his progress, and at last, in 1858, a letter came back. Nepomuk's youngest daughter, Josefa, had died, a great blow to the family, and Nepomuk hinted that he would like Alois to visit.

In 1859, he returned to Spital looking exceptionally tall for a man of medium height: In the eyes of his family, his bearing was authoritative. He actually looked wellborn.

It did not take long for Johann Nepomuk to realize that he had made a serious mistake in inviting Alois to visit, but Nepomuk was as bent by now as a tree that has faced too much wind for too many years. The death of Josefa throbbed in his side like the gash left by an axe. He felt too tired to keep watch on Alois.

Indeed, what could he do? Johanna, the oldest daughter, seven years older than Alois, had been married at the age of eighteen and for the last eleven years had been faithful to her husband, Johann Poelzl, who usually kept her pregnant. She had once been agreeable in appearance. Now her hands and feet were raw and her features had thickened from bearing six children, of whom by now only two were still alive.

If Johanna had once been cheerful in spirit, this state, long eroded, revived at the sight of Alois. He had been her darling when he first came to the house. She used to fondle the five-year-old whenever she brought him to sleep in her bed. Through the years until he left, she would pull his hair and kiss his cheek, until once when he was eight and she was fifteen, they had begun to roll together in the hay of the barn, pretending to wrestle. But he was only eight and nothing had taken place.

This time, no question. At the first opportunity, which proved to be the only one, Alois continued his father's tradition of apocalyptic intercourse in barn straw, and Klara Poelzl was conceived. There was no question in Johanna's mind. Each time, she had known the moment when Johann Poelzl, her husband, had put a child in her. But this occasion was superior. No small event took place in her body. "You have made me feel as I have not felt before," she said when they were done, and when Klara was born, Johanna sent him a letter that he received in the midst of rigorous training for an examination to bring him up to Finanzwache Respizient, the highest position available to the lower ranks of the Customs service. His attention, therefore, was not on Spital. Still, her letter lived with him through the years. It was only three words long (three words that Johanna had been certain of spelling correctly) and he read it over many times. *"Sie ist hier,"* wrote Johanna in the pride of a momentous event (although she did not sign her name), and "She is here" took its place in the guardroom of his heart, even if Alois' mind was on his career. In truth, he might not even have made love to Johanna on that visit if he had not already been with Walpurga all those years ago, and a year before that with the youngest, Josefa, his favorite back when he was twelve (his first), and so he felt he owed it to himself now to have the remaining sister— how many men could boast of knowing three sisters so closely?

If he could measure himself by such deeds, it was in relation to the accomplishments of other low-ranking officers in the Finance-Watch. His rise was remarkable for a young man with so sparse an education. Nonetheless, in four more years, he had another promotion, and still another by 1870, when at the age of thirty-three he had worked himself up to Customs Collector. By 1875, he was Full Inspector and would write below his signature, on any government paper, the full weight and address of the title: "Official of the First Class Imperial Customs Post in the Railroad Terminal, Simbach, Bavaria. Residence, Braunau, Linzergasse."

All through his rise toward the highest official rank that was open for a man of his beginnings, he never relinquished any of his good appetite for women. The first principle of Austrian bureaucracy was to do your job, but the more effective you became at such tasks, the less you had to fear for the little indulgences of your private life. This understanding he obeyed to the letter. In those years, no matter where he was assigned, he would stay at an inn. Before long, given his confidence, he would proceed to conquer the loosely defended bastions of the cooks and chambermaids in the hostelry. When he had gone through all of the available women, he would usually move to another large inn. Through the forty years of his career, his change of residence was frequent. In Braunau, for example, he moved twelve times. Nor did it bother him that his women were not elegant enough to walk with cavalry officers. Not at all! Elegant women, he had come to decide, were too difficult— no doubt of that—whereas maids and cooks were grateful for his attention and would raise no ruckus when he moved on.

In 1873, he married a widow. Having developed an eye for the social stature attached to any woman presuming to pass for a lady—his occupation demanded, after all, some ability in that direction—he was not dissatisfied with his choice. He might be thirty-six and the widow already fifty, yet he could respect her. She came from a worthy family. She might not be good-looking, but she was the daughter of an official in the Hapsburg tobacco monopoly that produced a share of the Crown's income, and the size of her dowry was agreeable. They lived well; they had a personal maid. His own salary was, by now, substantial—the principal of the highest public school in Braunau did not earn more. As his rank increased, so did his uniform generate an increase in gold trim and gold-plated buttons, and his cocked hat was entitled to sprout elegant official embroidery. His mustache was now worthy of a titled Hungarian, and his face came at you, jaw-first. His inferiors at the Customs post were told they were always to use his correct title when speaking to him. With it all, he was putting on weight. Soon after his marriage, and very much at his wife's urging, he shaved his mustache and grew sideburns on each side of his face. Given the care he afforded them, they soon became as imposing as castle gates. Now he not only looked like a Customs official in the service of the Hapsburgs, but he even resembled Franz Josef himself! There he was, a fair facsimile of the Emperor, with a full expression of duty, hard work, and an imperial face.

His wife, Anna Glassl-Hoerer, had lost, however, her appeal for him. This deficit occurred some two years into the marriage, when he discovered that she, too, was an orphan and had been adopted. In turn, she also lost respect for his presence when he (grown weary of making up stories about an imaginary and somewhat fabulous Herr Schicklgruber, his father) confessed that there was no such man on the parental side of his natal ledger, merely a blank.

She began her campaign. Alois was to legitimize himself. His mother, after all, had been married. Why could that not be taken to mean Johann Georg Hiedler was the father? Alois knew it was unlikely, but now that Anna Glassl was making it an issue, he was not averse. He had, after all, never enjoyed his last name, and Anna Glassl was not necessarily wrong when she judged that his career, despite its success, had been obliged to deal every day with the sound of Schicklgruber.

He traveled from Braunau through Weitra to Spital in order to see if Johann Nepomuk would help him. The old man, now turned seventy, misunderstood. When Alois told him that he wanted his last name changed to what it should be—Hiedler!—Johann Nepomuk's heart passed through a scalding shame. He thought he was being named as the father. Immediately he was ready to argue that at this late date, what with his two remaining married daughters to think of (not to mention his wife, Eva!), how could he declare himself Alois' father? These excuses, however, did not reach his mouth. At the last instant, he realized that Alois was only asking for Johann Georg to be named as his sire. Whereupon—old men being as ready as young girls to move on the instant from one extreme of emotion to the other—he was furious at Alois. His own son did not want him, Nepomuk, to be thought of as the father. It took another moment to recognize that Georg, having married Maria Anna, was the only one who could be used legally for this venture.

In a farm cart pulled by two old horses, he journeyed with Alois and Romeder and two neighbors who had agreed to serve as witnesses all of the miles from Spital to Strones, then farther on a few miles to Döllersheim, all of it close to a four-hour journey on a narrow meandering carriage road impeded by many fallen limbs and a few uprooted trees, but still reasonably free of mud on this October day. (With mud, it might have taken eight hours.) On arrival, Johann Nepomuk came face to face with the particular priest he had no wish to remember. There he was, a very old priest now, shrunken in stature, yet still the priest who had scolded him for traffic with the vulva of a mare.

This recollection was shared by the two men, even if there was not the smallest shift of expression between them. They were all present for the business at hand, Alois, Nepomuk, Romeder, and the two witnesses who had been brought along from Strones. Since none of them but Alois knew how to write, the others signed the document with an XXX. They said they had known Georg Hiedler and that "in their presence and repeatedly" he had admitted to being the father of this child. The mother had stated the same. They swore to that.

The priest could see that, legally speaking, very little was correct. Each of the witnesses' hands had shaken with a good bit of godly fear as they put down an XXX. One of them, the son-in-law, Romeder, could not have been five years old when Anna Maria died. Of course, she would have told all to the five-year-old! Moreover, Johann Georg was also long dead. Given such a dubious case, a more careful proceeding would be appropriate.

The priest did what he had been doing for years—he certified the paper, even as he kept smiling with his old and toothless mouth. He knew they were lying.

He would not, however, insert the date. On the yellow page of the old parish registry of June 1, 1837, he crossed out "Illegitimate," put Johann Georg's name in what had previously been the

blank space, and smiled again. Legally speaking, the document was
shaky, but it did not matter. Which church authority in Vienna
would challenge such an alteration? The word was to encourage
certified fatherhood no matter how late in life it arrived. Already in
some districts of Austria, illegitimacy was up to forty births per
hundred. Of that forty, could even half be free of one or another
unmentionable family matter? So the priest, disapproving of these
loose procedures even if he was bound to accept them, chose not to
inscribe his own name. If it ever went wrong, he could disavow the
paper.

Then he spelled each of the witnesses' names by choice, inas-
much as there was no agreement on orthography from province to
province—one reason why Hiedler eventually became Hitler.

Now that Alois had his new name, he decided to stop off for an
hour in Spital rather than continue on immediately in Nepomuk's
cart to the railroad station at Weitra. The change from Schicklgruber to Hiedler was sufficiently agreeable for him to feel an upsurge
in the happy region below his navel. This was, he knew from long
experience, one of the gifts his nature had given him. He was as
quick as a hound to sense when female company happened to be
near.

Was it Johanna who had put him on the alert? She lived next
door to her father, and at this moment Alois glimpsed a woman
looking out the window. But, no, that could not be Johanna. This
woman looked older than his wife. Now he was in no hurry to visit.

Yet his steps took him to the door. Once again, the Hound had
not betrayed him. For if there in the doorway was Johanna, prema-
turely deep into middle age, beside her was a girl of sixteen. She
was the same height as himself, with the nicest and most agreeable
features, modest, well formed, with a good head of abundant dark
hair and the bluest eyes he had ever seen—they were as blue as the
light that once reflected from a large diamond he had seen behind
a glass in a museum exhibit.

So soon as he separated himself from the powerful hug and
whole set of steamy kisses Johanna left with her honest saliva on his

mouth, he took off his cocked hat and bowed. "This is your uncle Alois," Johanna said to her daughter. "He is a wonderful man." She turned back to him and added, "You look better than ever—there is even more to the uniform now, yes?" And she pulled her daughter to her. "Here is Klara."

Johanna began to weep. Klara was her seventh child. Of the others, four were now dead, one was a hunchback, and her son, now nineteen, the oldest remaining, had consumption. "God never ceases punishing us for our sins," she said, at which Klara nodded.

Alois had no desire to hear about God. Spend a little time with Him, and the Hound might moan for shame. He preferred to enjoy the thought that he could soon see more of this niece.

He took a walk outside the village with the mother and daughter. They went to that part of Nepomuk's fields which now belonged to the husband, Johann Poelzl, who—no surprise to Alois—bore no resemblance to this rare blue-eyed Klara. Poelzl had gray, clouded eyes and a face full of lines that drooped in concert with a sad nose. It was obvious that he had given up the once-enduring hope that sooner or later he would be certain to prosper because he was an honest farmer. Nor did Alois stay. Poelzl had the expression on his face of a man who still has a host of chores. On this day, scattered in the rows of stubble, were stray ears of corn not yet too rotten to feed to the pigs, and Poelzl stood on one foot and then the other (as if to talk for another two minutes would allow more of the remaining ears to spoil). If he was also discomforted by the implicit prosperity of Alois' uniform, Poelzl's mood took no happier turn when Alois remarked that his own wife was not well and needed a maid who was pious and of reliable breeding. Was it possible—not to rush things!—that Klara might be just that person?

Poelzl could hardly say no when he was told of the amount his daughter would be able to send back. Cash not dependent on a crop was the best of crops, and, as always, he needed money. The alternative—to borrow further sums from his brother-in-law Romeder or his father-in-law, Nepomuk, was unpleasant. Poelzl could hear the diatribe that would come from his wife's family. Johanna's disposition had become so sour that he often thought (very much in private) that her blood must taste like vinegar. Nor did he wish to listen to the loud sigh of his brother-in-law as Romeder came up with some kronen. He certainly didn't want to hear the advice which was bound to come from Nepomuk. That would insult his judgment. A farmer could have fine instincts for husbandry and still be prey to bad luck—did that mean he must pay tribute twice by listening to others when he had already paid once by living with an insufficient return from his fields? So he accepted the fact that Klara would go to work for Uncle Alois, but his feelings turned over in him with the emptiest anger of them all—rage that has lost its heat.

One week after Alois' return to his post in Braunau, Klara followed with a small chest filled with a modest cache of clothes and a few possessions.

# 4

Alois and Anna Glassl had three rooms in the second-best inn of Braunau—the Gasthaus Streif. There was also a small room for Klara on the top floor where other maids and servants slept.

For a while, Alois entertained the happy notion that he might be able to spend a little time up there with Klara, but his niece did not welcome him, not exactly. It was evident to all including his wife that Klara was steeped in respect for her exceptional uncle, but it seemed no cause for concern to Anna Glassl—not yet! The girl was pious to a degree that would have seemed incomprehensible if one did not understand that death was her nearest relative. There were lights in those pale-blue eyes that spoke of angels—godly angels and fallen angels. Her face was so innocent that one could ask in all honesty what she could know of fallen angels, if not for that second sense which is there to tell us that devils hover like moths at the closing doors of life. Even the innocent do not always like to dream of the departed.

Alois could envision other dubious portals—the doors to Klara's chastity might open to an icehouse. So he was charming to his niece but made a point never to touch her. His wife, as unhappy by now as a crow with a broken wing, had put up with his yen for maids and cooks, but then, about the time she began her campaign to expunge the name of Schicklgruber, she allowed her distrust of him to take on new force. Never had Alois encountered jealousy so passionate, so far-ranging, and so much to the point. Yet he felt ready to deal with it.

While he considered his first quality as a man to be dedication to his work—to the cleanliness of his personal appearance, and the punctilio he presented in each and every working hour, he had not stood for years at a border post looking to root out the attempts of travelers and merchants to cheat the Hapsburg Crown of its tariff without learning a good deal about false presentation and outright mendacity. Now he was having to exercise such abilities himself in order to divert Anna from another girl he had taken to visiting on the top floor of the inn.

There was an old Viennese joke that to have a flourishing society, both the police and the thieves must keep improving at what they did. He thought often of the remark. It was true for Anna Glassl and himself. The more acute her sense of what he might be up to, the finer were his lies.

She had cause for distrust. There were days when he made love to each of the three women he could look upon as regulars. In the morning, full of the bounty of sleep, he would take care of his wife, and in the afternoon when Anna Glassl was napping and his off-duty time coincided with an hour when the chambermaid washed their floors, he usually enjoyed the coquetry of her hips as she, down on her hands and knees, slung a wet cloth from side to side—

truth, he rarely saw her face at such times. And in the evening after Anna Glassl had gone to sleep, there was Fanni.

So if he was ready to wait for Klara Poelzl, it was because his nocturnal and, for the present, true interest was with this waitress at the inn, a nineteen-year-old named Fanni Matzelberger, who was voluptuous but lithe, and—by every good measure—smoldering. He had learned to strip his eyes of all expression when she crossed the room, but she did have an irrepressible turn to her hips that spoke to him—Fanni was a good girl who did not want to be so good.

Indeed, as he soon learned by visits to her attic room, she was a virgin of the most tormented sort, a maiden in the old peasant tradition: She had kept the formal entrance to her chastity intact but the same could not be said of its neighbor. This was not all so agreeable for Alois. The Hound was too large to permit a good poke into "the smelly and the damned" (or so he would characterize it). Fanni would moan in a very low voice (in order that the rest of the attic not hear) but they were both suffering. All the more intense became their embrace. In the heat of the hour, they loved each other, a not uncommon reaction when the carnal ore is considered to be contraband.

He told himself that she was no more than a good-looking daughter of a prosperous farmer—she did have a decent dowry—but he also told her that he loved her. She said, "Enough to give up your wife and live with me?"

"I will give her up," he said, "when you give me something else!"

No, she must remain a virgin. So soon as she was ready to do what he wanted, there would be a child. She knew. Then there would be another child. Then she very well might die.

"How do you decide such things?"

"We have gypsies in my family. Maybe I am a witch."

"What a remark!"

"No, you are a bad man and I am a witch. Only witches put their mouths in forbidden places. Now I am afraid to go to confession."

"Stay away from priests. They are there to suck your blood. They are the ones who will leave you weak and good for nothing."

They argued round and round about whether she should or should not go to confession. She was tempted to let him win, and then, given the force of his desire, she did give it to him, she gave it up, and proceeded to tell him one month later that she was pregnant. Had the time come, she asked, to tell his wife?

He no longer trusted Fanni. He did not think she would have become pregnant if she was really afraid of dying. Besides, he had been lying to his wife with so much skill that now he did not dare to confess. Prevarication, like honesty, is reflexive, and soon becomes a sturdy habit, as reliable as truth. Anna Glassl-Hoerer Hitler was fifty-seven and looked ten years older (although to his continuing surprise she could be a virago at dawn). To lose her would reduce his financial situation measurably. Moreover, he would be giving up a lady for a farm girl, a most attractive farm girl, but then he had decided long ago that in the end a peasant was like a stone. Throw a stone high in the air—it will always come down. Whereas a lady was like a feather. A lady could tantalize you with her intelligence. He would hate to give up his ever-increasing skill as a liar.

Here is a sample from the dining room at the Gasthaus Streif:

ANNA GLASSL: I see you are looking at her again.

ALOIS: I am. You have caught me. If your eyes were not so beautiful, I would have to say that you own the eyes of an eagle.

ANNA GLASSL: Why don't you catch up with her after we eat? Just give her a good one for me.

ALOIS: Your mind is wicked. I like it when your tongue is so crude.

ANNA GLASSL: Cruder than it used to be.

ALOIS: Anna, you are exceptionally wise, but, in this case, you are wrong.

ANNA GLASSL: Look, my dear, I have put up with chambermaids and cooks. You have come to bed smelling of onions on many a night. And that is better than sniffing laundry soap. But I don't care, I tell myself. The man must remain amused. Only, why do you still try to insult my intelligence? We know the girl is beautiful. At least once in your life make love to a waitress who does not look like last night's pudding.

ALOIS: All right, I will tell you the truth. I like her looks, yes, a little bit. Although she is not truly my type. No, she is not. But in any case, I would not go near her. One hears the worst talk. I don't even want to tell you because you like her.

ANNA GLASSL: Like her? She's a tart. She's a tart in training. Your true type.

ALOIS: No, she is diseased. I have heard that she has an infectious disease between her legs. I would not go near her.

ANNA GLASSL: I do not believe you. I cannot believe that.

ALOIS: Do as you choose. But, I can promise you, she is the last girl for you to worry about.

ANNA GLASSL: Who then do you want me to worry about? Klara?

ALOIS: You have a splendid sense of humor. If we were not in public, I would laugh out loud, and then you know what I would do. You are so attractive, so wicked. You would even send me out to kiss a nun.

## 5

Finally, Fanni told Anna Glassl that she was two months pregnant and soon to show. For Anna, that was the end of the marriage. For Alois to tell her that the girl had a disease. When all the while he knew she was pregnant—unforgivable! Besides, Anna Glassl was more tired of Alois by now than fearful of living alone. It was truly exhausting to muster up her remaining arts in order to pretend to be a virago at dawn. By now she craved peace. She even decided that her jealousy had been some last inoculation against what was worse—precisely the chill distaste for a mate that seeps in even as jealousy loses heat. So she moved out. Since they were Catholic, divorce was not possible. To obtain even a legal separation, Anna, by Austrian law, had to declare not only their incompatibility but state in writing that she felt a direct aversion to him. Alois was obliged to read this. The phrase stood out in the document like a boil on one's chin. It irked so much that he showed his copy to drinking friends. "Look, she speaks of a personal aversion. This is nothing less than outrageous. If not improper, I could tell you how much aversion was there. On her hands and knees so soon as I would say, 'Get ready.' "

They would laugh and move to other subjects. He was in a state of irritation these days for more reasons than Anna Glassl's departure. Fanni and he were now living together in the same suite of rooms at the Gasthaus Streif. That was fine with him: he was the first to say that he was never attached to the past. Then he discovered that Fanni was not pregnant—she had only thought she might be. Or was it that she had had an early miscarriage? She was resolutely unclear.

He thought that was a terrible lie to have told him, but what could he do? He had never known such pleasure with a woman. Of course, Fanni was soon as jealous as Anna Glassl, and her ears had perfect pitch when it came to hearing any trace of desire in his voice for another woman. Soon enough, she stove a hole in the well-guarded vessel of his future plans. Klara, she told him, would have to go. Otherwise, Fanni would.

This was too much disruption for Alois. Fanni would soon be truly pregnant, or so he expected, given the hints he took from the declarative surge of her womb at the happiest moment, which billowed through him even as he was racing full stream into her—not the sort of conclusion he usually came to with other women. (Except once—so long ago—with Johanna.) Besides, he was certainly ready for a child, preferably a son, to carry on his name. Yes, when he was not in the midst of his best moments with Fanni, he thought often of the oncoming time when she would be six or seven months along, and it would be Klara's turn. The likelihood of future complications did not deter him. It was in the nature of his work to be able to handle more than one problem at once.

As for scandal, he did not worry. Not unduly. In Braunau, he was used to being a center of gossip. The townspeople might complain to the stars above that he was living with a common-law wife, but that would go nowhere. He saw himself as equal to an officer garrisoned in a town to which he owed nothing. He received his money from the Finance-Watch in Vienna. So long as his work proved flawless, this faraway arm of the Hapsburg government would hardly care how he acted in his personal life.

Having risen to the highest level of the middle ranks, there he would probably remain. His job was secure. The Customs needed him. After all, it took years for an official to become as practiced as himself. In turn, he needed the Customs. How could he ever find another job that paid as well? He had developed into the perfect instrument for what he did, but that was not a skill to be used for anything else. He was fixed therefore in his job, and the Finance-Watch was locked in with him. So, devil take the townspeople. What they said might rankle, but it would not interfere with more interesting pursuits. One girl would bear his child, and the niece (who trembled in front of him when he spoke) would become his mistress. Of course, she would be more than ready when the time came. Why else did she quiver? It was because the niece knew he could teach her all the things she did not know, and did not even dare to think about.

This was the secret project into which Fanni intruded. No girl named Klara was going to keep working for them.

"You are mad," Alois answered. "Can't you see? Klara would be happier in a convent."

"Your interest is not in her happiness, but yours. She must go."

"Do not speak to me that way. You are young enough to be my daughter."

"Yes, I am, and I have heard the Polish people say that a father should never make love to his daughter or she will lose all respect for him."

Klara had to go. He could not relinquish what he now had in Fanni, not for the uncertain promise (when all was said) of a transformation from angel-nun to all-compliant madly loving niece. No, that was hardly guaranteed.

# 6

After Klara left, it was Fanni who suffered the most. Gone, now, were the confidences they had offered to each other. There had been much for both to learn—they were so close and so different. It ended, however, because Klara was not good at lying. She turned beet red with embarrassment when Fanni would hint at what went on between Uncle Alois and herself. (Klara having called him Uncle, Fanni had taken on the habit.)

"Confess," Fanni would say, "you, too, want to be in bed with our Uncle."

"No," Klara would reply, and feel as if her cheeks would blotch if she did not tell the truth. "There are times, yes, when, yes, please, I want that. But you must know I won't, I never will."

"Why?"

"Because he is with you."

"Ach, that," said Fanni, "would not stop me for a minute."

"Maybe you, no," said Klara, "but I would be punished."

"This is something you know?"

"Please, I know."

"Maybe you don't," said Fanni. "I told Uncle I would die if I let him give me a baby, but now I think in this other way. I want a baby, I am near to having a baby."

"You will," said Klara. "And trust me. I would never be with Uncle Alois. You are his woman. That is my vow."

They kissed, but there was something within the aroma of the kiss that Fanni could not trust. Klara's lips were firm and full of character, but not completely. That night Fanni had a dream where Alois made love to Klara.

Before she left, Klara wept just a little. "How can you send me away?" she asked. "I gave you my vow."

"Tell me," said Fanni, "what is the foundation of this so-holy promise?"

"I swear it by the peace of my dead brothers and sisters."

It was not the best reply. Fanni had the sudden thought that Klara might also be concealing a witch in herself—she could, after all, have disliked her brothers and sisters, some of them, anyway.

By way of the Finance-Watch, Alois made proper arrangements for Klara in Vienna. She would obtain clean and gainful employment in the house of a modest and elderly lady. (Alois was more than ready to protect her chastity.) So, now, after four years of good and honest work at the inn, sleeping each night in the smallest of the maids' rooms, Klara packed her belongings into the same modest chest she had brought with her on arrival, and left the Gasthaus for new employment in Vienna.

If Fanni was now more at ease with Alois, the best of moods could nonetheless vanish in no more than the interval it took to close her eyes and open them. How could she be certain that her distrust of Klara had been honest fear? What if it came from spite as cruel as the pain of a bad tooth? She knew she was full of spite. That was why she called herself a witch.

Even as she had foreseen, she was truly pregnant now. If that offered contentment, she continued nonetheless to feel remorse. She had banished the sweetest girl she knew, and there were days when Fanni was on the edge of asking Klara to return, but then she would think: What if Alois comes to prefer Klara? Then the girl might not be faithful to her vow. How unfair that would be to the unborn child!

Fourteen months after Anna Glassl received the decree of separation, Fanni gave birth to a boy whom Alois without hesitation named Alois. They could not, however, call him Alois Junior—not as yet. The name still had to be Alois Matzelberger, and this bothered Alois Hitler. He went through a period of remembering what he had taken pains to forget—that a child could feel as empty as an empty belly when he had to walk around with no more than his mother's last name. Now Alois Senior went to bed every night cursing Anna Glassl.

He was not a man to give all of himself to a curse. He considered such an act equal to spending a private horde of gold. Nonetheless, he would deliver his curse every night, and it had venom to it. So he was not all that surprised when Anna died. And most suddenly! This curious event did not occur until fourteen months after Alois' son was born and Fanni was very much pregnant again, but Alois still reckoned that his anathema might have had some effect. He saw it as an expensive payment for a necessary conclusion— expensive because there could always be unforeseen consequences.

Indeed, Anna's death certificate stated that the cause was unknown. This convinced Alois that it was suicide. He did not like the thought. He was no superstitious fellow, not, at least, as measured by his disbelief in the near presence of God and the Devil. Rather, as he was ready to explain over a stein of beer, he placed his faith in the solid and intelligent processes of dependable forms of government. God, no matter how august and faraway, would look, doubtless, upon government in the same manner that Alois did—as the human fulfillment of divine will, provided such will was exercised by scrupulous officials like himself. Alois had not absorbed this idea from Hegel, Alois had not read a word of Hegel, but then, where was the need? He and Hegel were in agreement—the power of this idea had to be there for all to breathe. To Alois, it was self-evident.

In accord with such a premise, Alois preferred, therefore, that death have a clear-cut end. It could come from a burst appendix or by way of consumption, even as Maria Anna, his own mother, had ended. Suicide, however, left him uneasy—he liked to fall asleep quickly (as he put it to his drinking companions) "with a fart and a snore." Anna Glassl committing suicide was one thought to keep him awake. He would have gone to her funeral but he did not care to subject this new nocturnal uneasiness to the sight of her face in the coffin. So Alois stayed away. That was another tasty item for the town's gossip.

All the same, no matter how Anna Glassl had ended, she was, at least, no longer there. So he could marry his common-law wife, his new lady, Franziska Matzelberger, which he did. The second child was now a good seven months along in the womb, and Fanni's belly was beginning to look as big as the prize melon in a field. He was forty-six, she was twenty-two, and the wedding took place in another town, Ranshofen, four miles away and four more uncomfortable miles back for the pregnant bride.

She had sworn she would not have the ceremony in Braunau. It was not only the eyes of the women. Young men snickered as she went by.

Alois was annoyed. It cost extra to transport by hired carriage the two Customs officers he had invited. This was no serious expenditure, but all the same, needless. Besides, he was disappointed in Fanni. His new wife was not as ready to face other people as she ought to be.

Moreover, she was a nervous mother. She insisted on having the second baby in Vienna. A midwife would not be as spiteful there, she told him. Who, in her situation, asked Fanni, could trust any woman from Braunau? More expense.

Anna Glassl, with all her faults, had been a lady—he would, he decided reluctantly, never be able to say the same for Fanni. It was not that he expected it of her, not a farmer's daughter, but still she had once shown progress in such directions. Now it was all going backward. When he first knew her, she moved well, she was quick, she charmed the guests of the inn even as she served them. He thought she was a most witty creature for a waitress.

Now she yelled at the servants—all the fire in Fanni had gone to her temper. Their rooms at the inn were not properly taken care of. When he suggested that they might call Klara back, Fanni carried on for all of one evening.

"Yes," she told him, "then you can do to Klara what you did to me. Poor Anna Glassl."

Poor Anna Glassl! He came to realize that Fanni must now be dreaming about Anna. Could they not move forward as husband and wife? It was not the best marriage, he decided. You should not have to get into the same fight every evening.

She spent two weeks in Vienna before their daughter, Angela, was born, and in that time he had to pay for a nurse to take care of Alois Hitler, Junior. Before the week was out, Senior had seduced the nurse. She was fifteen years older than Fanni, heavyset, a hard worker once he got her to bed, but he could sleep because she got up in the middle of the night without complaint when the boy was crying for his mother.

Up until then he had been faithful to Fanni. Now the only way to make the nurse more palatable was for him to alternate her with the cook. Fanni came back from Vienna looking weak and tired and, before long, knew all about it. She did not scream at him. She wept. She was not well, she confessed, and there he was without patience to wait for sick people to mend. He was a brute, she told him.

They had been living together for close to three years before they could marry, but now, by the time Angela was a year old, Fanni was seriously ill. Signs of a deepening disorder were everywhere. She would pass from fits of temper to hysteria, then to loss of interest in her husband, plus an incapacity to take proper care of their two children. A doctor told her that she had the beginnings of tuberculosis. Klara was brought back from Vienna to be with Alois Junior and Angela even as Fanni moved out of the inn to a small town called Lach in the midst of a forest called Lachenwald, "Laughter-in-the-Woods," but neither the name nor the good forest air had the power to restore her. In Lach she stayed for the ten months before her end.

# BOOK III

## ADOLF'S MOTHER

# 1

In those months, Klara visited Fanni more often than Alois did, and the wound they had left in each other all but healed. On the first visit, Klara had fallen on her knees before the bed where Fanni rested and said, "You were right. I do not know if I would have been true to my vow." In turn, Fanni wept. "You would have been true," she said. "Now I tell you to give up your vow. He is through with me."

"No," said Klara, "my promise must remain! It has to be stronger than ever." She had a moment when she thought she might at last have a true understanding of sacrifice. This left her feeling exalted. She had been taught to search for just such a pure state of the soul. Those teachings had come from her father, that is to say, her father-in-name, old Johann Poelzl, who was sour on all matters but Devotion. "Devotion to our Lord Jesus Christ is all of my life in each and every day," he would tell her—he was indeed more pious than any woman in Spital. At many a meal, after saying grace, he would tell Klara (especially once she passed the age of twelve) that to give up what one truly desired was the nearest one could come to knowing the glory of Christ. But to attain such moments, one must be ready to sacrifice one's dreams. After all, had God not sacrificed His Son?

Klara was soon trying to relinquish her desire for Uncle Alois. That fever had not gone away during the four years she worked for Anna Glassl, nor over the next four years serving the old lady in Vienna who alternated between doting on Klara and counting the silverware. She was one old lady who had the real heat of suspicion—it irritated her when the silver count was correct (as it always was) because paranoia that cannot be confirmed is more difficult to bear than a loss from outright theft. The old lady was secretly proud of the perfection with which this young servant kept house for her—it spoke of respect for her mistress—yet the honesty made her irritable.

Years earlier, in payment for her one cardinal sin with Alois, Johanna had turned into a very good housekeeper, and Klara responded to such duties. It was as if the mother and daughter believed that what was left of the family—given the ghosts of all those dead children—depended on offering ceaseless attention to the daily skirmish against mud, dust, ashes, slops, and all crusted plates, cups, pots, and cutlery.

By now, Klara was never lax. Each household task required respect for the labor even when one knew how to do it well. Sacrifice, however, was different from such work. Sacrifice was an ache that lived next to her heart. If she wanted Alois, if she dreamed of Alois, she was still obliged to find a way (once Fanni's two children had been put to sleep) to keep him at arm's length. There was not a night in the inn, the best inn of Braunau, the Pommer Inn (to which they had moved), when Alois was not staring at her. Slightly drunk from the three steins of beer he took into himself each evening with one or another of the Customs officers before returning to the Pommer for the meal Klara had cooked in the kitchen of the hotel and brought up to their lodgings, he would eat with full gusto, saying not a word, just nodding to demonstrate his enjoyment. Then he would stare at her in the privacy of their sitting room, his eyes wide open as if to share his thoughts. The recesses of her body were soon fingered by his imagination. Her thighs burned, her cheeks burned, her breath wanted to inhale his breath. If one of the children cried out in sleep, she would jump up. The sound was equal to a cry from Fanni come to her all the way from Laughter-in-the-Woods. Afterward, a cramp of disappointment would be sure to follow.

Alois was often on the point of describing to his drinking associates how he loved her eyes. They were so deep, so clear, so full of the desperation to have him.

Why not? Alois kept to his view that he was one exceptional fellow. Whom did he know besides himself who was as ready to claim his indifference to religious fear? That was its own kind of bravery. He often made a point of declaring that he never went to church. Nor would he confess to a priest. How could a run-of-the-mill priest be equal to him? He had his allegiance to the Crown and he needed no more than that. Would God be about to punish a man who served the State so well?

Just the week before, a cousin had inquired whether his son, now of age, would be happy working on the Finance-Watch. Alois had written back:

**Don't let your boy think it is a kind of game because he will be quickly disillusioned. He has to show absolute obedience to his superiors at all levels. Second, there is a good deal to learn in this occupation, all the more so if he has had little previous education. Heavy drinkers, men who get into debt, and gamblers and those who lead immoral lives cannot last. Finally, one has to go out in all weather, day or night.**

Naturally, he felt equal to the sentiments in the letter, nor did he have to brood about "those who lead immoral lives." Immorality, Alois knew, was not to be confused with the details of your private life. Immorality was taking a bribe from a smuggler, whereas private life was too complicated for judgment. He did not know to a certainty that Klara was his daughter—after all, he did not have to trust Johanna Hiedler Poelzl's word. What, after all, was the point of being a woman if you could not lie with skill? *Sie ist hier!* True, or not true?

All the same, she might be his daughter.

Alois knew why he didn't have to go to church, nor to confession, he knew why he was brave. He was ready to take the same forbidden road that drunken peasants and adolescents blundered into while sharing a bed. But he, unlike them, would not look back in fear and penitence. He would just do it. Yes.

Which he finally did at the end of a short evening that had been much like all the other dinners when he had looked at her with no deceit in his expression and no activity but to stand up now and again with his pants in full profile, his proud bulge ready to speak for itself. Then he would poke the fire and sit down and look at her again. On this one night, however, he did not say good night as she put her hand on the door to the children's room, where she, too, was sleeping, but instead, strode forward, caught that hand, kissed her on the mouth, and brought her to his bedroom and his bed, even as she begged him in a low uncertain voice to do no more, "please, no more," whereupon he proceeded to lay a track with his hand, so veteran at insinuating his fingers through the defenses of garments and corsets, all the way to the nest of hair she had so long concealed. And there it was, much like feathers—downy—much as he had expected. Half her body was on fire, but half was locked in ice, the bottom half. If not for the Hound, he might have stalled at the approach to such a frozen entry, but then her mouth was part of the fire and she kissed him as if her heart was contained in her lips, so rich, so fresh, so wanton a mouth that he exploded even as he entered her, ripped her hymen altogether, and was in, deep, and in, and it was over even as she began to sob with woe and fright and worse—in shame for the throb of exaltation that had shivered through her at a bound and was gone. She knew that this had been the opposite of sacrifice. Nor could she stop kissing him. She went on and on like a child raining kisses on the face of the great adult beloved, and then there were other kisses, softer, deeper. He was the first man she had ever kissed as a strange man rather than as a relative of the family, yes, the wrong kind of exaltation. She could not stop weeping. Nor could she stop smiling.

## 2

So Klara was now his lover, his cleaning woman, and the nurse-maid to Alois Junior and to Angela. On many a night she was also his cook—unless (having hired one of the hotel maids to sit with the children for an hour) they went downstairs to the dining room of the Pommer Inn, there in full display as uncle and niece, the middle-aged Customs officer in uniform and his demure young mistress. No one in Braunau was fooled, no matter how often she might call him Uncle. It was enough to stir a boil of outrage in the onlookers that he could sit there as if he were Franz Josef himself, ready to claim, "In company with the Emperor, I, too, have a lovely mistress." On any night that he took her downstairs to dine, it never failed—he would make love as soon as they came back, his voice so hoarse he could hardly speak. "I am your bad uncle," he would say in the thick of the embrace, "your very bad uncle."

"Yes, yes, my bad uncle," and she would cling to him, hardly able to distinguish pain from what was seeking to become pleasure—a most unholy pleasure. "Oh!" she would cry out. "We will be punished."

"Who the hell cares?" he would growl, and that brought her closer to the unholy pleasure.

Invariably, she would weep when it was over. It was all she could command not to scream at him. Inside her was all the congestion of all that had not quite come to pass. She felt so guilty.

Now it was Klara's turn not to go to Mass. She was working for the Devil (so she knew!). She felt as if her finest impulses were now bringing her nearer to the Evil One, yes, even the loving care she gave to Alois Junior, and to Angela. The more she adored them, the worse it must be. Her tainted presence could pollute their innocence.

Then, there was Fanni. Klara had not told her but knew she must. Because if Fanni did not know now, she would certainly find out so soon as her life ended, for then she could watch from the other side. Fanni would be left with the intolerable thought that Klara never cared enough to tell her.

Yet in the last week of Fanni's illness, when Klara did confess, the answer was brief: "This is my punishment for sending you away four years ago. That is fair."

"I will take care of the boy and girl as if they were mine."

"You will take better care than I would," said Fanni, and turned her face away. "It is all right," she said, "but you must not come to see me anymore."

Then Klara knew once again that she lived in the grip of the Evil One. Because if at first she was hurt, she soon felt furious that Fanni was still ready to send her away, and the anger was present on the day that Fanni was interred, a very long day, since Alois did not bury Fanni in Braunau. He had chosen Ranshofen (On-the-Brink-of-Hope), where they had been married. This was not from sentiment but annoyance. The word in Braunau was that he had bought Fanni's coffin months before she died. The townspeople were saying no less than that he had found a true bargain in advance (a mahogany job confiscated from a smuggler at the Customs gate). In truth, he had only bought the damned crate ten days before her death. It was not as if he had sat on it for months. So he could not forgive the gossip. Moreover, the tragedy of death was overrated. So many times, it was like saying goodbye to a friend who has outworn every welcome. He did not plan to visit the cemetery too often. His eyes were on Klara for tonight. By evening, after the funeral, he could not stop looking at her. Those blue eyes—so much like the diamond in the museum!

In bed on that hot August night, Klara's life received another life. It had traveled directly to her heart, or so she felt. For her soul seemed to reside now right there beneath her heart, and she came close to falling into darkness from the pleasure—except that the pleasure went on and on. Now it did not stop. She belonged to the Devil. He had dug into her with the most evil enjoyment she had ever known, and so her guilt in the morning was as heavy as a water-logged tree. She had a dreadful moment on realizing that part of her delight had come because Fanni was gone. Yes. All the love she had felt for the long-sick friend had vanished into this unholy glee, this long-withheld and so nasty joy that she could at last release because the woman who banished her for four years was dead. Now she could be the wife.

She became pregnant. No surprise.

She never indicated that she wanted him to marry her, but he knew. "A man can be a fool," Alois liked to say, "yet even a fool must be able to learn from experience. Only by this, should he be judged." So Alois knew that he must be responsive to this new duty.

Besides, he wanted to get married. The displeasure of the good people of Braunau had gotten under his skin. Literally. An intolerable itch now bothered him and sometimes would last for as long as an hour. It had to be the thoughts of the townspeople. For the first time, he considered the possibility that any anonymous letters written to the Finance-Watch about him were not necessarily going to be thrown away by the officials who received them. Inquiries could well ensue. Such matters moved slowly, but now that Klara was pregnant, it could prove an offensive sight if, in four or five months, she could not step into the street due to the size of her belly. That would put no honey into the letters sent to the Finance-Watch.

He could also say to himself that for the first time he did have some liking for the woman he would marry. Anna Glassl had satisfied his sense of rank—no question there—but he did not enjoy the pale smell of her perfume. And Fanni, to say the least of the worst, was like a wild woman in her shifts of mood. Klara, however, was calm and knew where she came from. He had to like how she took care of his children, and if she gave him a big family, well, nothing too terrible about that. It would shut the mouths of the towns-people.

In any event, what with children dying so often, a large family was one more form of insurance. Lose a few, and you still had others.

On the other hand, technically, he and Klara were cousins. When Alois made his first inquiries at the Braunau parish house, he discovered that he would have to file an application.

Now Alois had to worry about the lie that had been certified near to nine years ago when he had traveled to Strones with Johann Nepomuk and the three witnesses. Could that stand in the way of a quick marriage? On official paper he was Johann Georg Hiedler's son, and therefore was Klara's cousin, one step removed. Might that be too close? If he would now claim that Johann Georg was in no way his father, he would have to go back to being Alois Schickl-gruber. Not to be contemplated! So he and Klara would have to take the long step of asking for an ecclesiastical decision.

In Braunau, the incumbent of the parish church, Father Koest-ler, proceeded to study the problem. After a month came a discouraging response: The power to grant dispensations in cases such as Herr Hitler's did not reside in him. Klara and Alois would have to apply to the Bishop of Linz. Father Koestler would help him to write the letter.

# 3

Most Reverend Episcopate:
Those who with most humble devotion have appended their signatures below have decided upon marriage. But according to the enclosed family tree they are prevented by the canoni-

cal impediment of collateral affinity. They therefore make the humble request that the Most Reverend Episcopate will graciously secure for them a dispensation on the following grounds:

The bridegroom has been a widower since August 10th of this year, and he is the father of two minors, a boy of two and a half years (Alois) and a girl of one year and two months (Angela), and they both need the services of a nurse, all the more because he is a Customs official away from home all day and often at night, and therefore in no position to supervise the education and upbringing of his children. The bride has been caring for these children ever since their mother's death, and they are very fond of her. Thus it may be justifiably assumed that they will be well brought up and the marriage will be a happy one. Moreover, the bride is without means, and it is unlikely that she will ever have another opportunity to make a good marriage.

For these reasons, the undersigned repeat their humble petition for a gracious procurement of dispensation from the impediment of affinity.

Braunau am Inn, 27 October, 1884

Alois Hitler, Bridegroom

Klara Poelzl, Bride

Alois had become friends with Father Koestler's housekeeper, a plump middle-aged woman with a light in her eye.

Given the matching light in his eye, he showed her the letter and said, "There is no mention of a very important reason for our marriage. The bride is pregnant."

"Oh, we know that," she said, "but it is not a good idea to leave a stone in the envelope."

After a digestive pause, Alois said, "That is fine advice. It is well seated," and he put his hand on her behind as if to test the center of her wisdom. She gave him a crack across the face.

"How could you do that?" he asked.

"Herr Hitler, don't you get slapped a lot?"

"Yes, but I also receive nice surprises. From good women who are not as high and mighty as you."

She laughed. She could not help herself. The cheeks of her face must be as red as the place where he had left his compliment. "Good luck with the Bishop of Linz," she said. "He is a timid fellow."

Word did not come back from Linz until a full month had passed. The Bishop of Linz would not grant the dispensation.

If Alois had had little liking for the Church, he could now despise it. "Churchmen wear black cassocks," he said to himself, "to cover their lily white asses."

To Father Koestler, he asked respectfully, "What, then, Father, is the next step?"

"The letter containing your plea must now be translated into Latin by the diocesan scholars in Linz. That would allow us to send it to Rome. I think the papal court will be more receptive. They usually are."

Yes, thought Alois, they will be far enough away not to worry about an Austrian man and woman. To the priest he said, "I thank you for your wisdom. I learn much from you, Father. I think in Rome they will see that the act of providing a decent mother for my two children will constitute good Catholic virtue. That is a virtue I seek to acquire."

His hints were not small. He was one sinner who might be ready to return to the mother fold.

Father Koestler was sufficiently pleased to offer good economic advice. Since translation into Latin was costly, it might be wise to sign a *Testimonium Pauperatis*.

"This says, 'a declaration of poverty'?" Alois could translate that much Latin by himself.

"It will remove the obligation, Herr Hitler, to pay for the translation."

Herr Hitler restrained himself from remarking that as an officer of the Crown, he considered himself well-to-do, thank you. Instead, he accepted the advice. He was not so removed from the wisdom of the earth as to wish to pay a tithe that he could avoid.

Three weeks later, close on Christmas 1884, Rome granted the dispensation. But Alois and Klara still had to wait. No marriages could be solemnized until two weeks after the anniversary of the Holy Birth. This further delay proved unhappy for Klara; her belly would be up to four visible months by then.

"It's a big fellow we have here," said Alois.

"I hope that is so," she said. What could come out of a mother like herself who had felt so near to the Evil One on such a crucial night? Even if the child lived, might it be marked? The thought would haunt her wedding.

Like many of the nuptials of Customs officials, the day was divided into two parts. As Klara would say: "We were standing by the altar before six in the morning, but by seven Uncle Alois was out there on duty at his post. It was still dark when I came back to our rooms."

That night they had a reception at the Pommer Inn and Johann Nepomuk, now a widower, came all the way from Spital to Braunau in company with Klara's sister, Johanna, named after her mother, Johanna Poelzl, who sent her "most soulful regrets." Just as well, thought Alois.

Johanna's daughter, serving as a proxy (and also named Johanna), was a hunchback. This occasioned some corner-of-the-mouth humor between two of the Customs officials. "Yes," said one, "the question is whether Alois will think it is good luck to rub her hump."

"Don't talk so loud," said the other. "I hear this hunchback has a terrible temper."

There was music. An accordion was played, and Alois and Klara did their best to dance, but Alois was stiff legged. To stand all those hours on duty did not make you an artist for the dance floor.

Others followed. Customs officials and their wives. One of them had a son old enough to dance a vigorous polka with the recently hired maid for the newlyweds, a girl with crimson cheeks and merry eyes named Rosalie, and this Rosalie had also prepared a roast leg of veal and a roast suckling pig to place in the center of the wedding feast.

She had also thrown too many logs on the fire. The rest of the dancers soon gave up. The room had become much too hot. Half in annoyance but half in exuberance, Alois kept teasing Rosalie, "Oh, you are the one who is in a hurry to burn up a man's goods, are you not?" and Rosalie would cover her cheeks with her hands and giggle.

Rosalie's eyes would open wide when she was teased. It was no small matter that her breasts were undeniably full, and now were heaving in the aftermath of the polka. It did not need even that much to convince Klara. Alois was ready for his next diversion. She would remember this night for all the years to come, those years of sorrow when the child Gustav she was carrying on this night and the two who were to follow, Ida and Otto, were all to die in the same year, Gustav at two, Ida at one, and Otto only a few weeks old.

Johann Nepomuk also noticed the warmth of the room and the look in Rosalie's eye. "Get rid of that maid," he whispered to Klara, but she did no more than shrug. "The next one could be worse," she whispered back.

Nepomuk had a terrible nightmare after the wedding party. His heart felt ready to burst. He could have died that night in his bed but instead he continued to live for another three years. There is no organ more resistant to rupture than the heart of a tough old peasant. Nonetheless, he never felt the same, a cruel punishment for an old widower who was trying to hold on to what was left for him. Death, when it came to him at the age of eighty-one, arrived with the same epidemic that took away the children.

## 4

Diphtheria had come into their family like the Black Death. Mucus welled up from the throat of the two-year-old and the one-year-old, an up-pouring of green phlegm, thicker, heavier than the mud of Strones. Noises rasped forth from the boy and girl, sounds uttered with the tortured authority of an old man and an old woman working their lungs like galley slaves to clear a straw's width of passage. Gustav died first, Gustav, always sickly, a two-and-a-half-year-old who looked like the ghost of Klara's lost brothers and lost sisters, then Ida went, Ida, fifteen months old, certainly the blue-eyed image of Klara, going three weeks after Gustav. Both deaths came back to the mother in the blow that soon followed. That was Otto's end—Otto, just three weeks old!—lost to a galloping colic that gutted him. The stench of a baby born to die in its first weeks of life settled into Klara's nose as if her nostrils were another limb of memory.

She had no doubt whose fault it was. Alois had been close to the Evil One. But such a matter she could understand. A boy in Vienna all alone and he always wanted so much. Of course! But for herself, there was no excuse. She had desired a family where children did not die but grew to their full age, and yet she had been unfaithful to the Lord God Almighty on the night Gustav was conceived, yes, and that secret pleasure she still looked to find on nights when Alois chose to make love as a change in his diet from the present affair with the new cook, Rosalie, at the Pommer Inn.

She hated him for such acts. But then, she also learned that this kind of hatred was treacherous. It seemed to increase her desire.

Whereas on those nights when she felt a moment of love for Alois, all such good life turned to ice below. Alois would grumble when the act was done even as she was kissing him in a fever to set things right.

"Your mouth gives promises you do not keep," he would tell her.

It did not feel as if she were married. Anna Glassl and Fanni were always in her mind. If she had begun as a maid, and then become a nurse to Fanni's children, and then a stepmother, now her own children were dead. Alois Junior and Angela had been sent to Spital when diphtheria assaulted the younger children, and so escaped infection. They were back with her now, but all of their three rooms at the Pommer Inn still reeked of the fumigation that followed each death, and the odor lived on in Klara's clothes through the three separate days of the three services at the cemetery. She knew how small a coffin could be—she had learned as much from the losses in the Poelzl family—but the miniature coffins of her own children were three slashes upon her heart that awakened the love she had not dared to feel when her children were alive. She had been too terrified of the evil she could bring to these newborn souls. It was only after the death of Gustav that she realized she had loved him.

Alois, in his turn, had decided he was not about to forgive God. To his friends at the tavern near the Customs House, especially the newcomers, young Customs officials, he would speak with the authority of his three decades in the Finance-Watch. "It is the Emperor who has the power to guide us," he remarked one hot summer night. "The real power is right there. God does nothing but kill us off."

"Alois," said an older friend, "you speak as if you are not afraid of going upstairs."

"Upstairs or downstairs, the real authority for me is Franz Josef."

"You go too far," said his friend.

By the time he reached home, Alois was usually in no good

mood. The beer wore off in a sour cloud. He would scold Alois Junior, he would upbraid Angela, he would not say a word to Klara. Now no more often than once a week (and he was furious at how much these three deaths had taken from his vitality) he would look at Klara again as he had on their first night and would try to conceive of how to introduce her to certain *spécialités de la maison*. He did not speak French but he knew all he needed to know about those few words. One of the Customs officers would brag that he had been to Paris in his youth. There, in a brothel, he claimed, he had learned more over two nights than in all the rest of his life.

Alois refused to be impressed. Some of the details were not foreign to him. Fanni, for one, liked to put her mouth into many a place, and Anna Glassl was no lady when you got down to it. And now and again, with one of the maids or cooks, he would receive a nice wet surprise.

Of course, these days he was with a frightened bird whose torso could scorch him even if her thighs were as cold as a snowbank. She made love, yes, when he could actually get all the way into her—not often—she was as strong as the Hound, yes, so much like bitches he had seen snarling and snapping at a male dog's genitals. Klara did not snarl or snap, she just jumped up on her altar, alone, always alone, she was so private that he wanted to put his mouth where she was most private, and then he could slip the Hound into her mouth. He would show her where Devotion was located. *Spécialités de la maison!*

Yet, on this hot summer night when he tried to open her closed legs, pushing harder than ever with the force of his arms, there came a moment when his breath overtook him. A startling pang! For one instant, he felt as if he had been felled by thunder. Was that his heart? Was he the next to die?

"Are you all right?" she cried out as he lay beside her, his breath going in and out with a rasp that sounded as terrible as the last winds of their lost children.

"All right. Yes. No," he said. Then she was on him. She did not know if this would resuscitate him or end him, but the same spite, sharp as a needle, that had come to her after Fanni's death was in her again. Fanni had told her once what to do. So Klara turned head to foot, and put her most unmentionable part down on his hard-breathing nose and mouth, and took his old battering ram into her lips. Uncle was now as soft as a coil of excrement. She sucked on him nonetheless with an avidity that could come only from the Evil One—that she knew. From there, the impulse had come. So now they both had their heads at the wrong end, and the Evil One was there. He had never been so close before.

The Hound began to come to life. Right in her mouth. It surprised her. Alois had been so limp. But now he was a man again! His mouth lathered with her sap, he turned around and embraced her face with all the passion of his own lips and face, ready at last to grind into her with the Hound, drive it into her piety, yes, damn all piety, thought Alois—damned church-mouse wife, damned church!—he was back from the dead—some kind of miracle, he was all there, his pride equal to a sword. This was better than a storm at sea! And then it went beyond such a moment, for she—the most angelic woman in Braunau—knew she was giving herself over to the Devil, yes, she knew he was there, there with Alois and herself, all three loose in the geyser that came out of him, and then out of her, now together, and I was there with them, I was the third presence and was carried into the caterwauling of all three of us going over the falls together, Alois and myself filling the womb of Klara Poelzl Hitler, and indeed, I knew the moment when creation occurred. Even as the Angel Gabriel served Jehovah on a momentous night in Nazareth, so too was I there with the Evil One at this conception on this July night nine months and ten days before Adolf Hitler would be born, on April 20, 1889. Yes, I was there, an officer of rank in the finest Intelligence service that has ever existed.

# BOOK IV

# THE
# INTELLIGENCE
# OFFICER

# 1

Yes, I am an instrument. I am an officer of the Evil One. And this trusted instrument has just committed an act of treachery: It is not acceptable to reveal who we are.

The author of an unsigned and unpublished manuscript can attempt to remain anonymous, but the margin of safety is not large. If, from the beginning, I have spoken of my fear at undertaking this work, it is because I knew that sooner or later I would have to reveal myself. Now, however, that I have offered this disclosure, there is a shift in the given. I can no longer be envisioned as a Nazi officer. If in 1938 I could pretend to be a trusted aide to Heinrich Himmler (by the means, yes, of inhabiting a real SS officer's body) that was temporary. When so ordered, we are always ready to inhabit such roles, such human abodes.

I recognize, however, that these remarks can hardly be accessible to the majority of my readers. Given the present authority of the scientific world, most well-educated people are ready to bridle at the notion of such an entity as the Devil. They have even less readiness to accept the cosmic drama of an ongoing conflict between Satan and the Lord. The modern tendency is to believe that such speculation is a medieval nonsense happily extirpated centuries ago by the Enlightenment. The existence of God may still be acceptable to a minority of intellectuals, but not the belief that there is an opposed entity equal to God or nearly so. One Mystery might be allowed, but two, never! That is fodder for the ignorant.

There need be no surprise, then, that the world has an impoverished understanding of Adolf Hitler's personality. Detestation,

yes, but understanding of him, no—he is, after all, the most mysterious human being of the century. Nonetheless, I would say that I
can comprehend his psyche. He was my client. I followed his life
from infancy a long way into his development as the wild beast of
the century, this all-too-modest-looking politician with his snippet
of a mustache.

## 2

As a newborn, he was a most typical Klara Poelzl product. He
was not healthy. Indeed, he terrified Klara every time a drop
of mucus oozed out of his nose or a bubble of sputum popped from
his infant lips.

It is probably true that she was ready to die if he did not live.
The attention she gave to Adolf's early days would have been seen
as hysteria in any woman who had less cause for concern, but then,
Klara was living at the edge of the abyss. Recollections of her
nights with Alois were pervaded now by the penetratingly corrupt
smell of the sickroom as Gustav, Ida, and Otto had been lost one by
one in the same few months of the same year. She had prayed de-
voutly to God to save each of her three babies, but the prayers were
unavailing. As she saw it, God's rebuke could only confirm the sin
of her condition.

After Adolf was conceived, she formed the habit of washing her
mouth every morning with laundry soap. (Alois was now full of a
predilection—especially in late pregnancy—to force Klara's mouth
onto the Hound and keep it there, one big hand on her neck.)

No surprise then if her love was for the baby. So soon as Adolf
gave some real indication of living—he would soon smile with delight at the approach of her face—she began to believe that God

might be kind to her this time, that He could even be ready to forgive. Would He be ready to spare this child? Might she think His Wrath had lessened? Had He even given her an angel? Such is the nature of pious hope. Then she had a dream that told her to have nothing to do with her husband. Such is the nature of pious obligation.

Alois soon had to face the possibility that a will of iron, when forged by prayer, can be quite as powerful in a wife as a highly developed biceps on her mate. At first, Alois could not believe that her refusal to let him touch her was more than a whim, a new species of enticement. "You women go back and forth like a kitten chasing its tail," he told her. Then, deciding that rebellion such as this was to be mercilessly crushed, he seized her buttocks in one hand and her breast with the other.

She bit him on the wrist hard enough to draw blood. Whereupon he cuffed her, leaving Klara with a bruised eye. *Gott im Himmel!* He was obliged next morning to beg her not to go out until her eye was no longer discolored. For a week, his hand bandaged, he shopped for food after work—no tavern on those nights. Then, with her bruise gone at last, he still had to give up what he considered irrevocable rights, and was obliged to sleep in a huddle on his side of the bed.

Since this state would be maintained over quite a period, I choose for the present to stay closer to Klara. An intensity of emotion is always attractive to demons and devils, even as farmers dream of black soil for future crops.

It need hardly be underlined that the death of Otto, Gustav, and Ida proved useful to us even if death is still in God's domain, not ours. Their loss intensified Klara's adoration of Adolf past any usual measure of large maternal love. When he began to scream every time she kissed his lips, she came to recognize that it was the odor of lye on her mouth. But since Alois had been driven to his side of the bed, there was no longer a need each morning to use the disinfectant. So she could kiss Adolf again even as he gurgled obligingly.

We expected that this would prove useful. Excessive mother-love is almost as promising to us as a void of mother-love. We are keyed to look for excess of every kind, good or bad, loving or hateful, too much or too little of anything. Every exaggeration of honest sentiment is there to serve our aims.

However, we would wait. When it comes to turning a child into a client, we follow a reliable rule. We move slowly. While an incestuous procreation followed by swarms of mother-love will offer rich possibilities, particularly when the event has been fortified by our presence at conception, and we have, therefore, every reason to expect exceptional potentiality to be present for us, still we wait, we observe. The child may not live. We lose so many. All too often, God is aware of our choice and, heartlessly—I will say this about Him—yes, God can remove certain children *heartlessly*, no matter the cost to Himself. The cost to Himself? A curious calculation is present. The Lord is not insensitive to the hopes of those who surround the young one. The early death of an exceptional child can demoralize a family. Even when He knows, therefore, that a given individual has been in good part captured by us, He hesitates. Sometimes He does not wish to take on the collateral damage to the family. Besides, His angels can always look to steal the child back from us.

So the Lord is respectful of mother-love even when it is all-embracing. It can come as no surprise, then, that many artists, ogres, geniuses, killers, and an occasional savior live to maturity because God chose not to dispose of them. The first element of mutual recognition in the struggle between the D.K. (as we shall now often call Him) and our leader—the Maestro—is their mutual understanding that no single splendid human quality is likely to prevail by itself, unaltered by His powers or ours. Even the noblest, most self-sacrificing and generous mother can produce a monster. Provided we are present. All the same, this is not a game where we can count on the end result. That is why investing in the newborn is an unbalanced gamble for both the Maestro and the Lord.

But I can see that further explanation of the conditions, limitations, and powers of the world I inhabit must be presented or too little will be understood.

I will attempt, then, an explanation of these Two Kingdoms, the Divine and the Satanic. I could speak of them as two antagonisms, two realms, two visions of existence at odds with each other, but Two Kingdoms has been the term used by us for countless centuries. Needless to add, we devils are confronted daily by a formidable array of angels. (We call them the Cudgels.)

While these warring forces will not be unfamiliar to anyone who has read *Paradise Lost*, I would note that many of us are well versed in literary classics. I cannot speak for the angels, but devils are obliged to be devoted to good writing. Milton, therefore, is high in our arcana of those few literary artists whom we do not have to look upon as unforgivably second-rate (because of their sentimental inexactitudes). Milton, after all, did provide his intuitive understanding of the contest between the Two Kingdoms. No matter how inaccurate were his details, he did present a pioneer demonstration of how such armies might have confronted each other at the commencement of that great estrangement which occurred when the earliest squadrons of angels divided into opposed camps and each was convinced that they were the ones to direct the future of human beings.

One can offer respect, then, to that great blind man, even if his descriptions are out of date. Devils who serve the Maestro do not go to war in phalanx against angels any longer. Rather, we are artfully installed by now in every corner of human existence.

To bring, therefore, a first explanation of the sinuosities, salients, dead ends, and recesses of our war, I am obliged to offer an outline of the forces we look to exert now on human society. I would start by remarking that there are three aspects to reality—the Divine, the Satanic, the human—in effect, three separate armies, three kingdoms, not two. God and His angelic cohorts work upon men, women, and children to bring them under His Influence. Our Maestro, and we, his representatives, look to possess the souls of many of these same humans. Until the Middle Ages, human beings could not bring much of an active role to the contest. Often, they were pawns. Hence the notion of Two Kingdoms. By now, however, we are obliged to take the individual man or woman into account. I will even say that many, if not most, humans are at present doing their best to be beholden neither to God nor to the Maestro. They seek to be free. They often remark (and most sententiously), "I want to discover who I am." All the while, we devils guide the people we have attracted (we do call them clients), the Cudgels contest us, and many a particular individual does his or her best to fight off both sides. Humans have become so vain (through technology) that more than a number expect by now to become independent of God *and* the Devil.

This, it can be repeated, is but a first approach to the perversities embedded in existence, a sketch of the true complexity of events.

For example, I can recover, if necessary, the concealed, even long-buried, memories of a client. Such power, however, consumes Time. (Time is a word I capitalize since for us, as well as for the angels, it is a resource comparable to Money's power over humans.) We are always calculating the Time we can afford to give each of our clients. My need to acquire more insight in a given situation must always be balanced, then, against the investment required at working our will upon a particular person. For this reason, the average human is not usually of interest to us. Their powers of insight, memory, and ill intent are limited. Rather, we look to find men and women who are ready to transgress a few large laws—whether social or divine.

Such men and women are, I fear, no longer common. Often we have to be content with mediocrities. In our company, provided we are sufficiently patient, we can improve them. That can produce promotions for oneself. I have had clients whom I was able to develop to the point where they could serve in one or another of our larger projects, and my own situation prospered from that. The average client, however, caught in the back and forth between a guardian angel and a directing devil like myself, often ends by producing little that is useful to either Kingdom, and I can certainly recall a few unhappy situations where the guardian angel who was my opposite number came away with the spoils.

At one unhappy period in the past, as a result of such losses, my position did suffer. For a time, I was assigned clients of petty origin or modest achievement. I encouraged common soldiers, for instance, to injure the morale of their company by desertion, I encouraged workers and peasants who looked to stir up revolutions but turned corrupt. I knew a few priests in small towns who got into trouble with little boys, and more than a few estate managers who pilfered funds. I indulged petty barons and counts as they gambled away the last of old holdings, and I might as well list petty thieves, drunken louts, and unfaithful husbands and wives of the worst sort. I had a horde of clients, but only a few could stimulate my developed skills. So often, I had to serve as proctor for clients born with little who soon proceeded to have less. While I could rarely know whether the Maestro was safeguarding my talents for some future purpose or continuing to relegate me to various backwaters, I took hope on one occasion when he chose to remark that I might yet be given a post comparable in its challenge to some of the epic encounters of our Kingdom during the first three centuries of the Church in Rome. Yes, that might still be there for me, provided I was ready to pay unremitting attention to my humdrum duties with wretches, thugs, and drunks. I did, and eventually was selected to oversee the work of a number of minor demons who were keeping watch on an Austrian family whose developed potentialities might yet prove astounding. Insignificant at present was this embryo, and his parents equally so, but he had ancestral fault-lines full of the intoxicating stink of our old friend blood-scandal. So I was to stay close to him after his birth.

I did not dare to ask, but at this point, the Maestro chose to

speak directly to my curiosity. He said: "Why have I been so interested in this creature not yet born? Can it be that he will yet possess a mighty ambition? I may propose that you take him on
full-time. At present, however, it is no more than a project. It could
certainly fail. In time, if he develops the greater part of his promise,
he could, as I say, become your only client. Must I say more?"

All this was uttered by the Maestro with characteristic irony. We
never know how serious he might be when he speaks to our mind's
ear. (His voice is a cornucopia of humors.)

In any case, I dared not ask: What if I fail? Many projects do. On
the other hand, I soon learned how he was conceived.

Some readers may notice that I first spoke of that exceptional
event as if I were the one in the connubial bed. Now I state that I
was not. Nonetheless, in referring to my participation, I am still
telling the truth. For even as physicists presently assume to their
scientific confusion that light is both a particle and a wave, so do
devils live in both the lie and the truth, side by side, and both can
exist with equal force.

The explanation—provided one is ready to follow—is considerably less difficult than, let us say, Einstein's Special Theory of
Relativity.

# 4

Spirits like myself can attend events where they are not present. I was in another place, therefore, on the night Adolf was
conceived. Yet I was able to ingest the *exact experience* by calling
upon the devil (of lower rank) who had been in Alois' bed on the
primal occasion. I must say that that is always an option for us—we
are able to share a carnal act after the fact. On the other hand, a

minor devil can, on the most crucial occasions, implore the Evil
One to be present with him during the climax. (The Maestro encourages us to speak of him as the Evil One when he does choose
to enter sexual acts, and on that occasion, he was certainly there.)

Afterward, once I began my assignment to young Adolf Hitler,
the moment of impregnation was repeated for me by the devil who
had been present. It came into my senses with a completeness of
odor and physical impact that can be termed absolute. Thereby, it
happened to me. Among us, to be given an exact recollection is
equal to being present. So I also knew from the incomparable intensity of the occasion that the Maestro had actually joined with
the attendant devil for one instant (even as Jehovah offered His immanence to Gabriel during another exceptional event).

While I would not be attached exclusively to Adolf Hitler for
some years, he was always in my Overview. So I am ready to write
about his early life with a confidence no conventional biographer
could begin to feel. Indeed, it must be obvious by now that there is
no clear classification for this book. It is more than a memoir and
certainly has to be most curious as a biography since it is as privileged as a novel. I do possess the freedom to enter many a mind. I
could even say that to specify the genre does not really matter since
my largest concern is not literary form, but my fear of the consequences. I have to be able to do this work without attracting the attention of the Maestro. And that is possible only because in these
latter-day American years, he is more attuned to electronics than
to print. The Maestro has followed human progress into cyber-
technologies far more closely than the Lord.

I have chosen, therefore, to write on paper—which can offer a
small protection. My words may not be picked up as quickly. (Even
processed paper still contains an ineluctable hint of the tenderness
God put into His trees.)

While the Maestro has no desire to use up any part of his resources by monitoring every last one of our acts—there are too
many demons and devils for that—he is also not inclined to let us
go on ventures he has not selected. Years ago, I would never have

dared to embark on this written record. My fear would have been absolute. But now, in the inundations and engulfments of technology, one can try to steal a bit of secrecy, a private zone if you will, for oneself.

Ergo, I feel ready to continue. The assumption is that I can succeed in concealing my output from the Maestro. Intelligence work can be understood as a contest between code and the obfuscation of code. Since the Maestro is heavily engaged, and his present existence is more arduous than ever—I believe he deems himself closer to eventual victory—I feel free to venture out. I have grown more confident that I will be able to conceal the existence of this manuscript until, at least, it is finished. Then I will feel obliged either to print it or—destroy it. This second option has always offered the safest solution (except for the near-mortal blow to my vanity).

Of course, if I publish, I will then have to flee from the wrath of the Maestro. There are options open. I could choose to enter the equivalent in our spirit-life of the Federal Witness Protection Program. That is, the Cudgels would hide me. Of course, I would have to cooperate with them. Conversions are their stock-in-trade.

Ergo, I have a choice—treachery or extinction.

I do, however, feel less dread. By revealing our procedures, I can enjoy the rarefied pleasure (for a devil) of being able not only to characterize but to explore the elusive nature of my own existence. And should I be able to finish, I will still have the choice of destroying my work or going over to the other side. I must say, the latter option begins to appeal.

Since I am unfaithful to the Maestro, I must show no sign. My modest duties in America are being performed impeccably, even as I offer these further details of the work I accomplished in the early upbringing of my most important client.

# BOOK V

## THE
## FAMILY

# 1

By the time he was a year old, Klara called the boy Adi, rather than Adolf or Dolfi. (Dolfi was much too close to *Teufel*.) "Look," she would say to her stepchildren, "look, Alois, look, Angela, isn't Adi an angel, a little angel, isn't it so?" Since the baby had a round face, big round eyes as blue as hers, and a small mouth, and therefore looked to them like any other baby, they nodded with easy obedience. She was a good stepmother and that was all right with Alois Junior, and also with Angela, especially since they had been told by their father that Fanni had been crazy.

Klara did not plan to speak with such open enthusiasm to her stepchildren about the newborn, but she could not help herself. The beatitude was in her eyes. Adi was giving every indication that he would still be there tomorrow.

Breast-feeding fed this certainty. She was putting her own strength into him, her ready nipple never far from his mouth. Some of our minor devils, who passed over Braunau at night, would report that her prayers were more heartfelt than those of any other young mothers living nearby. Devils, obviously, have minimal attachment to the sentimental, let alone the heartfelt, but one or two were bothered. Klara's prayer was so pure: "Oh, Lord, take my life if it will help to save his." Other women, being more practical, complained to God about what was missing in their days. The most greedy were always looking to own a better house. The stupid were looking for a surprisingly good lover, "yes, if you permit it, Lord." There was rarely a sweet for which they did not pine. Klara's prayers, by contrast, yearned to give long life to the child.

While the Maestro was not often sympathetic to breast-feeding since its absence could stimulate ugly energies we could later employ, he was more tolerant in cases of first-degree incest. Then he wanted the mother to be close indeed to the child. All the better for us! (A monster is most effective when it can call on mother-love with which to charm new acquaintances.)

Excretory dramas also offer advantages. A dirty butt on a baby can send a signal—the mother may be a potential client for us. The opposite is also of use. Klara proves a fine example here. She always kept a clean house. Her rooms at the Pommer Inn were now as spotless as any home tended by several good maids. The furnishings gleamed. So, too, was Adi's pip-squeak of an anus kept as immaculate as an opal, small and glistening, and of that, too, did I approve—an incestuary must always be kept aware of the importance of his or her excrement, even if it comes down to a little asshole that is forever being polished.

# 2

Not long after Adolf was born, Alois decided to leave the Pommer Inn. This move amounted to his twelfth change of address in Braunau over fourteen years. But Alois had good words for the Pommer: "It has *elegance*. I don't know that I would use the word for much else in this little city." He had a dozen such remarks to enliven a hundred situations of small talk. "Women are like geese," he was ready to say. "You can recognize them from behind." Heavy tavern laughter would follow, even if none of them could explain what was so particular about the rear end of a goose. Or, when speaking to fellow professionals: "To pick out a smuggler is easy. Either they look like the wretches they are, or they are too good to be true. They dress too well, they speak too well, and the amateurs always work very hard at looking you in the eye."

When asked, however, why he had moved from the Pommer Inn after a residence that had lasted for four years, he would shrug. "I like a change," he would say. The truth was that he had used up the waitresses, chambermaids, and cooks at the Pommer who were not too old or too ugly, and he could have added (and did to one or two friends), "When a woman goes dry on you, change your house. That can put a little oil in her."

On the day when the Hitler family left the Pommer Inn, he had, however, a most uncharacteristic thought. It was that fate could yet choose him for high position. I will remark that his idea of high position was to become Chief Customs Officer for the provincial capital of Linz. Indeed, fate would yet give him exactly that post. Never superstitious (except when he was), Alois decided that the shift from the Pommer Inn to a rented house on Linzerstrasse was a good move. He and Klara both agreed that they needed more room, and now they had it. Of course, there were no females in the attic, but he could manage with that. He had nosed out a woman who lived on his route home from the tavern. He had to pay for the privilege by purchasing a small gift from time to time, but then the rent on Linzerstrasse was low. It was a dreary house.

All the while, he fought against falling in love with his wife. She infuriated him. If ants were like bees and had a Queen for whom they labored, then Klara was Queen of the ants, for she commanded his skin to crawl, his crotch to itch, and his heart to toll in his chest—all of this coming from no more than Klara keeping to her half of the divided bed. He had to think of how lovingly she had looked at him on the night of her wedding. She had worn a dark silk dress, rose colored with a white collar—that much white she allowed herself as a bride—and on her white forehead, she had teased some charming curls. At her breast was pinned the one piece of jewelry she possessed, a small green cluster of glass grapes looking real enough to mislead a man into reaching for one. And then there were her eyes—no mistake! He had to fight against falling in love with a woman who kept the cleanest house in Braunau just for him and for three kids—two of them not even her own!—a woman always as polite to him in public as to an emperor, a woman who never complained about what she had and didn't have nor nagged him about finances, a woman who still had only one good dress, the one worn at her wedding party, and yet if he had laid a finger on her, she would have bitten it off. He wondered if the difference in their age was what it was about. Better than marrying her, he should have put her in a convent. Yet his skin itched at the thought of how she would not let him near.

Drinking at the tavern, he would look to regain some pride. His dislike of the Church had by now become a conversational grist. At home, he would glean further material from an anticlerical volume he had found in an antique bookshop in Braunau. Indeed, the store owner, Hans Lycidias Koerner, would meet him on many an evening for beer. While the bookseller kept himself at a scholarly level above more mundane discussions by offering no more than a nod of his head from time to time, his wise presence, his shaven chin and shaven upper lip, his full muttonchops, his peephole spectacles, his half-bald head of burgeoning white hair offered a slight but legitimizing resemblance to Arthur Schopenhauer and thus gave support to Herr Koerner's smallest assent, just enough to carry the other Customs officers around the more bruising turns of Alois' argument. While they were hardly to be counted as churchgoers— "No good man wants to be neutered," most were ready to admit— still they were officials. So they could hardly feel at ease when a prestigious institution was mocked, let alone the Holy Roman Church.

Not Alois. He showed no fear in declaring that he had no fear. "If there is a Providence larger than Franz Josef's power to provide for us, I have not encountered it."

"Alois, not everything comes up to a man with a printed sign," said the officer closest to him in rank.

"It is all a mystery. Mystery, mystery, mystery, and the Church keeps the keys, they are our caretakers, *ja*?"

The others laughed uneasily. But Alois was thinking of Klara and how her piety left a hot rock in his stomach. He would grind this rock to powder. "In the Middle Ages," he said, "do you know? The whores, they were more respectable than the nuns. They even had a Guild. For themselves alone! I have read about a convent in Franconia so stinking bad the Pope had to investigate. Why? Because the Franconia Whores' Guild complained about the illegal competition they were receiving from the Franconia nuns."

"Come now," said two drinkers at once.

"True. It is true. Absolutely true. Herr Lycidias Koerner can show you the text." Hans Lycidias nodded slowly, reflectively. He was a little too drunk to be certain on which side his authority should fall. "Yes," said Alois, "the Pope says, 'Send a monsignor to look into it.' I ask you: What does this good monsignor report? It is that half the nuns are pregnant. This is the sober fact. So the Pope now takes a real look at his monasteries. Orgies. Orgies of homosexuals." He said it with such force that he had time to take a long swallow from his tankard.

"That, of course," said Alois, once fresh breath had also been ingested, "need not surprise us. To this day, half of the priesthood are mama's boys. We know that."

"No, we don't," muttered one of the younger officers. "My brother is a priest."

"In that case, I tip my hat to him," said Alois. "If he is your brother, he is different. But that was then. And I assure you: The priests who were real men did worse. You ever hear this saying by the Pope? From the same Pope. He said, 'No priest needs to marry so long as the peasant has a wife.' "

The unspoken demand of his voice was that the junior officers be ready to applaud with laughter. So they laughed. "It was exactly like that," he said. "The poor merchant has one wife, the priest has ten, and the bishop cannot enter heaven—too many wives to bring along."

"Which bishop?"

"The Bishop of Linz, don't you know?"

Alois had not forgotten the Bishop of Linz, who, six years ago, had refused his application to marry Klara. He certainly recalled how, in order to defray the expenses of translating his letter into Latin, he had been forced to declare himself a pauper. That still rankled.

On the walk home he came, however, to an unhappy conclusion: His tirades against the Church might have to cease. He was fifty-four years old, and for many years had not worried about his position in life. He knew that he would rise in the ranks open to him, but no higher.

Now, however, a well-placed friend up in the Finance-Watch had told him that there was talk of a promotion for Alois Hitler up to Chief Customs Officer at Passau. Given his lack of formal education, this would be a true rise in rank. "However, you must now watch yourself, Alois," the friend said. "All this is still a year away. Keep a good name if you want to be moved to Passau."

He had always seen himself as exceptional, afraid of no one (except for certain superiors in uniform), and possessed of a genuine magnetism for women. (How many men could say that much for themselves?) Moreover, he had never been timid about public opinion. Nobody he knew could say as much. In that department, he was no coward.

But now this respected friend (by way of his confidant in the upper councils of the Finance-Watch) was saying, "Watch out for the townspeople in Braunau."

This caution traveled into his digestion. Because Alois could not decide whether to trust his friend. The man was a practical joker. In fact, he was the same one who had once told him: "The townspeople of Braunau are nothing. You can put your thumb to your nose at them." Alois had indeed put together a good many habits around that remark, but the truth was he had certainly said too much tonight if there was any ground to the rumor concerning Passau. Of a sudden, he was learning how much ambition he had, a real ambition which he had never admitted to himself. He couldn't. It would have been like a river breaking through a levee. But now he knew this much: He had to stop pissing on the Church.

Yes, his wife might be a cold tit to him and a jug of warm milk to the baby—what a guzzler! never off the tit. Yet he must get by all that—she was a useful wife. Good for the children, good cook, very good with the Church.

Now, he, personally, was not going to be caught at a High Mass except for State occasions, holidays. He did not wish to live with a new itching attack, no, he did not see the confessional box for himself. His skin prickled. A serious official of the Crown like himself should not have to bare his soul to a priest.

Women, however, should be seen in church. So, yes, he admitted to himself, Klara was an asset concerning his new professional goals.

## 3

In our ranks, we look upon excessive ambition as a force at our disposal. We are ready to attach ourselves to any urge that mounts out of control. Of no passion is this more true than outsized ambition. Yet ambition is also related to the Lord's purposes. After all, God designed ambition for humans. (He wanted them to strive to fulfill His Vision.)

Of course, the Lord's supposition was a folly. As the Maestro is never loath to tell us, a human who suffers from too much ambition succeeds only in exemplifying the Creator's own lack of anticipation. The D.K., wishing His Vision to be innovative, had created the human will as an instinct all but free of Him. Once again, God had miscalculated. Ambition is not only the most powerful of the emotions but the most unstable. So many of the most ambitious choose to blame God for a run of bad luck.

Large appetite for success has, therefore, to awaken our interest. The D.K., a prodigious optimist, had not foreseen that the men and women who intended to promulgate His Vision had better possess the selfless ambitions of saints. In contrast, the Maestro has always been alert to the lodes of perversity to be found in human flesh.

Consider the case with Alois. Many people guard their ambition as the most sequestered part of their emotions (guarded even from their own awareness). For so soon as ambition becomes excessive, it is ready, if necessary, to shred a good many long-held convictions about the inviolability of one's honor. Or one's loyalty to friends. All too often ambition can become as blind as a scythe.

No surprise then if Alois was not the only one in the Hitler family to suffer such a disruption. Ambition, being a true germ, is infectious. If Klara now had a child who was actually giving signs of staying alive, her breasts, in consequence, were suffused with joy, the most generous joy she had ever known, and now she wanted everything for Adi. To such a degree, indeed, that she was ready to allow her husband to cross the middle of their bed.

A second courtship began. She was still breast-feeding Adolf. So there was no question of a pregnancy. What inspired the return of some carnal interest was her growing appreciation of Alois. He had built strong foundations, after all, for the good future of Adolf. Even as her husband had risen from the mud of Strones and Spital to the honor of an officer's service to Franz Josef, she, in turn, was ready to dream of the heights to which little Adolf could ascend should his ability prove equal to the vigor of his father.

For that, however, he would need this same father to love him. Once, in her gentlest voice, she said to Alois, "Sometimes I wonder why you never hold Adi."

"It will just make the other two jealous," he answered. "Jealous kids are not to be trusted with babies."

"Alois and Angela hold him all the time," she said. "They are not jealous. They like him. Sometimes you could say they love him."

"Let us keep it that way. Maybe they are happy because I do not hold him."

"Sometimes I am afraid he is not very important to you," she dared to say.

She had gone one step beyond where she had thought to go. Bad enough for him that he had only half a bed, but now she was looking to scold him? "Important to me?" he said. "*That* I can answer. He is not important to me. Not yet. I want to see if he will live."

She did not weep often, but here she burst into tears. The worst had happened, and once again she felt weak before her husband. She was not free of loving him.

At that moment, the dog began to bark. Alois had bought a mongrel for a few kronen from a farmer he knew. Since they were living in a house, rather than at an inn, the purchase could be considered protection worth the cost. But the dog, whom he named Luther, proved disappointing. While Luther worshipped Alois and quivered before his master at every shift of tone, he did not seem otherwise alert. Moreover, he had nervous habits. On this night, as Alois shouted at him to stop howling, poor Luther watered the floor.

Afterward, Alois had his regrets. The dog, after all, did adore him. First, however, he whipped him. Even as Luther tried to crawl away, the poor bottom of the beast became soaked in his own outpourings. All the while, he was yelping in full terror. The uproar woke the children. Alois Junior came out first, then Angela, and Adi at the last, not yet two years old, but agile enough to get out of his low bed and walk into the midst of this. Klara leaped up to seize him. She was ready for the worst, she hardly knew what—that the child would step into the urine, that he would cry for her breast, that Alois might strike them both—she had seen the look in her husband's eye when Adi became too greedy with her nipple. None of this happened, however. To the contrary, the child looked with solemn interest at the whimpering dog, then at the flailing hand of the father, and the boy's blue eyes had a gleam, a look of remarkable intensity for one so small. She had seen it on his face when suckling him. He would stare at her with the tender expression of a lover overwhelmed for a moment by the implicit equality of flesh to flesh, soul upon soul. At such instants, she felt as if this child was closer to her and knew more about her than anyone.

Now, as Adolf stared at the wet dog and then at the overflushed face of his father, there was no tenderness in this look, but much comprehension.

Klara felt an odd panic, as if she must now startle the little boy into weeping so that she could give him her breast and thereby remove him from the room. And she succeeded. Adi burst into a rage as she took him up, bore him away, and force-fed him. Indeed, he nipped her enough with his young teeth for Klara to cry out, whereupon he stopped bawling long enough to give a deep and hearty chuckle.

From the room she had just quit, she could hear Alois bellowing.

"That dog can't learn to control himself!" he cried out of his own pain at the awful turn the evening had taken. Luther was bleeding at the mouth from blows he had received full-face on his muzzle, but in turn, Alois' palm had a small but ugly laceration from raking one fierce slap across a broken incisor in the middle of Luther's sad front teeth.

# 4

While I delight in writing about these people like any good novelist, and so am ready by turns to observe them sardonically, objectively, ironically, sympathetically, judgmentally, even compassionately, still I must remind the reader that though I do not present myself as sinister (since I have no desire to gratify a casual reader's notion of how a devil is supposed to behave), I remain a devil, not a novelist. My interest in character is, however, genuine. From the onset of our service, the Maestro instructed us to make humankind an ongoing study. He even encourages us to feel close to what is godly in people. If one is to be alert to the spoils that may be there later, it helps to comprehend the subtle differences between genuine and counterfeit nobility. If we had religious orders in our muster, I might be the equivalent of a Jesuit. I share with them a fundamental understanding. I am always ready to acquire a sympathetic comprehension of an opponent—I see it as my duty to be ready, indeed, to know more about godly sentiments than all but the most gifted of the angels.

That may be why the Maestro encourages us to speak of God as the D.K. (At least those of us who work in German-speaking lands. In America, it is the D.A.—dumb ass! In England, the B.F.— bloody fool! For France, A.S.—*l'âme simple*. In Italy, G.C.—*gran cornuto*. Among the Spanish, G.P.—*gran payaso*.) So D.K. stands for *Dummkopf*. It is not that we look upon God as stupid—never so! Moreover, we know from experience (and lost battles) that the Cudgels can, on occasion, be as bright and incisive as ourselves. Our use of the word Dummkopf comes, I expect, from the Maestro's determination to wean us from our greatest weakness—the unwilling admiration we feel for the Almighty. As the Maestro never allows us to forget, God may be powerful, but He is not All-Powerful. Hardly so. We, after all, are also here. If the D.K. is the Creator, we are His most profound and successful critics.

All the same, we have to recognize that the angels have succeeded in convincing most of humankind that our leader is the Evil One. So our best recourse, the Maestro suggests, is to take pride in the term. When I write E.O., or speak of the Evil One, it is with full knowledge of the irony of the concept. The Maestro has given us so much, our subtle master. "Leave excessive reverence to the God-worshippers," he tells us. "They need it. They are always on their knees. But we have work to do, and it is tricky. I recommend that you keep thinking of Him as the Dummkopf. For, indeed, given what He could have achieved, this is what He is. Remember:

It is our universe to gain. It is His to lose. Keep calling Him the Dummkopf. He has not accomplished as much with his men and women as He intended."

## 5

The reek of the urine, the shit, and the blood of Luther became the first in a series of episodes remarkable for their powers of *transmogrification*—that is to say, dramatic and thoroughgoing metamorphosis.

So, for example, Adolf's bowel movements now began to dominate Klara's life in the house on Linzerstrasse. Before the episode with Luther took place, she had certainly been alert, no matter how often Adi soiled his wrapping cloths, to keep the child clean; indeed, the act, as I have remarked, became a dalliance between mother and boy. She wiped him so carefully that his eyes gleamed. He discovered heaven. There it was, right up in his anus next to the gas and the cramps. All the while, his mother subtly, tenderly, delicately expunged the soil, wet or dry, from his *rosebud* (which was, of course, Klara's secret name for her dear baby's incomparably dear little hole—*die Rosenknospe*). She was so proud of its pink sheen that she could not even suppress her joy when her stepchildren were watching. Indeed, unlike other good mothers in Braunau, she barely bothered to teach Angela how to substitute for her. She was, after all, wholly superior to the unhappy elements in the procedure. His stool (which could be as rank as any other colicky child's) did not occasion her disgust. If the voiding had been outrageous in smell, or what was worse, gave a hint of the empty cavern that lurks in the odor of grave illness, her breath remained calm. In truth, she preferred the stink to be rich. The stronger, the better. A sign of health. Such was her love for Adi.

Yes, love sparkled between them. His eyes danced as she dredged his cheeks with feather-smooth wipes of the rag, and her eyes—whether she knew it or not—were so full of admiration that his little penis stood up. She, in turn, would giggle and coax it back (most properly) as they both laughed. For, of course, it jumped up again. Whereupon she wished to kiss the tip, and then blushed. Be assured! She did not. Such innocent joy.

All this had to change after the episode with Luther.

She lived again in high fear of Alois. Now she was always in fear that Adi's swaddling cloths might bag open. What if Alois came upon a plop on the floor? Once, stepping out of the parlor to start a dish in the kitchen, she returned in the next minute to see the child playing with his spoil, and shuddered at the thought of Alois coming through the door.

So, training began. It was like trying to teach a bright but willful dog. In the beginning, Adi might even tug at her skirt, or take her to the closet that held the chamber pot and cry out for her to remove his cloth. After which, as she complimented him for his prowess, they would go, two spirits in one, through the wiping. For such intelligence, she offered full praise. His eyes would glow.

She became, however, too hopeful—which is to say—too ambitious. She wanted Adi to learn how to unsnap the safety pins that held his cloth. Indeed, he was able to. Day by day, success followed success, until one morning, he pricked his finger. After that, he would not go near the pins again. She lost patience. He had come so near and now he refused to continue. Finally, she scolded him, and that was certainly the first time he had heard such a tone issue from his mother. He rebelled. Knowing how important he was to her, his response was keen—he felt the same clarity of mind with which he had watched Alois beat Luther. At that moment, the boy had been illumined by new knowledge. He did not measure the difference between a dog and a man, for Luther was still as much a person to him as his father, but he could see the instant result: Luther had collapsed into abject terror, and yet the dog still loved his master.

So would Klara love him, he decided, even when he would not

obey her. Taken out of his cloth and allowed to run naked from the waist down, he began (never when his father was at home) to leave his product right next to the chamber pot. Which brought Klara so close to screaming that Adi could hear every sound she did not make. In consequence, he felt masterful.

He went too far. One day when she was in the midst of waxing her kitchen floor, he spread his spoil over the upholstered arm of the parlor couch, studied it, knew by a new tumult in his chest—so curious in sensation—that this was different. Risk was present. All the same, he would show it to her. He did.

This time she stood stock-still. She sensed that he had done it on purpose, and so did not say a word, merely cleaned the sofa, by which time he had an attack of diarrhea and began to laugh and to bawl, but she did no more than sigh and clean him soundlessly in listless loveless fashion. This made such an impression on him that he awoke in the middle of the night and went to her bedroom. Alois had been called to Passau for preliminary interviews and the house had not seen him for a week, but just before midnight he had come home. Since the boy enjoyed going to his mother's bed whenever she was alone, he was surprised, even as he cracked the door, to hear a little gasping, and wheezing, and then the bull-roar of Alois' voice. Beneath were his mother's cries, soft, and full of the oddest torture, cries that spoke of joy soon to come, so soon to come, yet still, beyond reach, yes, now, almost! No, not yet! Through the half-open door (kept open particularly for her to hear him should he cry) he saw a sight his mind could not take in. Something looked like four arms and four legs and two people, but one of them was upside-down. He could make out Alois' bald head and side-whiskers pressed between his mother's legs. Then, without a word his father sat up. He was now sitting on her face!

Adolf walked away as silently as he had entered, but he had no doubt. His mother was betraying him. Just then he heard a final set of cries intense enough to turn him back toward the room. From what he could see by moonlight coming through the window, his father had begun to belabor Klara with all of his body, his big belly slapping on her belly. And she was grunting like a dog. So full of contentment! "You beast, you are an ugly man, you are an animal, you!" and then again, "You, yes, you, *ja, ja, ja*." There was no question. She was happy. *Ja!*

He would never forgive her. That much the two-year-old knew.

This time Adolf went all the way back to his room. He could, however, hear them still. In the bed next to him, Alois Junior and Angela were giggling. "Goosey, goosey," they kept saying back and forth.

## 6

He began to bawl for his milk not thirty minutes after Klara had sunk into the best sleep she had known for years.

Must one suppose that because a child's deepest reactions seem to have a half-life of no more than thirty minutes, they cannot be profound? Because of that betrayal, he might never love his mother as much again. Yet his feelings were heightened. There was pain in his love now, and an anger which revealed itself by nipping at her breast with his teeth. Indeed, for a few days, he felt close to Luther, and when drowsy, would sleep beside the dog through an afternoon. Truth, he saw the hound as a sibling, and this brotherly affair went on until Adolf began to take too much advantage, punching Luther in the belly, trying to poke his eyes, and sometimes trying to kick him in the ribs. When the dog began to growl at his approach, Adolf would whine and run to Klara. There was a period when her delight in breast-feeding was gone. The nipping at her breast had done it. The days of weaning were at hand.

In those private councils of her mind that would never be available to her child, her stepchildren, her husband, nor even to the confessional box, she had come to the conclusion that she must have another child. If this came in part from the old fear, even now, that Adolf might not live, she also feared that she would never love him as much again, no, not as once she had, and so maybe there should be another child.

Besides, she was entering a new time in her marriage. She looked forward to being with Alois in their bed. For on such evenings—after all these years—desire came alive again, desire was there!—down in the marrow, deep!

We may remember that the last time we saw Alois, he was burying his nose and lips in Klara's vulva, his tongue as long and demonic as a devil's phallus. (Be it said: we are not without our contributions to these arts.) Alois was certainly being aided by us. Never before had he given himself so completely to this exercise, and quickly he had become good at it, and so quickly that no explanation is possible unless we are given credit as well. (Which is why we speak of the Evil One when joining in the act—we do have the power to pass these lubricious gifts to men and women even when we are not attempting to convert them into clients.)

By morning, Alois could not believe he had done it. To lower himself to such an extent! To make her pay for such bottoming on his part, he had, we must recall, clumped his buttocks once more over her nose and mouth—precisely the frightful sight that drove Adolf back to his bed and caused him to bawl for milk not a half hour later.

Yet, by morning, Alois also felt tender toward Klara. This unexpected gentleness in concert with the astonishing pleasure he had given her by way of his tongue, a joy whose unexpected preciosities had conducted her up to, yes, all-but-occult regions, had also left her ready enough to forgive the rotten part. (Indeed, his heavy behind smelled better than Adi's.)

As a devil, I am obliged to live intimately with excrement in all its forms, physical and mental. I know the emotional waste of ugly and disappointing events, the sour indwelling poison of unjust punishment, the corrosion of impotent thoughts, and, of course, I also have to engage caca itself. It is true. As devils, we live in shit and work with it. So, we often look to comprehend a marriage through the eye of the cloaca—and I will add, that is not the worst way, since parenthood is not only the crown but the outhouse of marriage. As St. Odon of Cluny stated so unforgettably in a remark worthy of the best of devils: *inter faeces et urinam nascimur*—between shit and piss are we born. That leads me to say that the proper study of marriage resides not only in partnership, congeniality, affection, boredom, predictable habit, daily annoyance, verbal scuffles, and daily despair, but in the guts and smear of it all—the comradely knowledge of all the forbidden tastes, smells, and bodily nooks. Indeed, if all of that were absent, the sacrament would have less foundation. On caca, is marriage based. So I would assert. You, in turn, are free to reject my opinion because I am a devil, after all, and we do look for the lowest common denominator to any truth. Small wonder if the condign properties of waste are part of our province.

# 7

Alois' promotion came through. The Finance-Watch named him to the post of Chief Customs Officer at Passau, and Klara was pleased, so pleased. She was married to a man of achievement.

On the other hand, they could hardly move before Alois was due to work at his new post in Passau. That was a full day's travel from Braunau which meant there would be weeks at a time when Alois had to live apart from the family. In consequence, Adolf could loll in the big bed next to his mother.

If it was grievous that Klara would put him aside whenever Alois came home, so did the child also learn that the loss of such happiness would be regained so soon as Alois was off again to Passau.

This condition lasted for a year. Even when the family did finally rent a place in Passau, Alois had to oversee other border towns. In consequence, he was absent nearly as much as before—which permitted Adolf to sleep again close to his mother.

As for Alois, the new position gratified his vanity, but introduced a threat to his confidence. In Braunau, a less important station, the smugglers rounded up had usually been petty individuals. Since most of the product crossing was agricultural, weighings were tedious. Braunau might be nicely situated on the river Inn, but even its architecture was humdrum.

In Passau, Austrian Customs, by mutual agreement between the countries, operated on the German side of the Danube. The difference was visible. Passau had once been ruled by a Prince-Bishop, and so could boast of medieval towers. Some of its churches dated back to the onset of the Middle Ages. Passau's walls reflected the grandeur of dedicated duty, ancient crimes, torture chambers, dark secrets, bygone glory, and—much to the point for Alois—criminal smugglers with imagination enough to be something of a match for him.

So, he was not without discomfort in the new position. If, until now, his uniformed presence had been a full warning to would-be malefactors, he knew that much depended upon the rigor of his professional manner. So he took pains to present a personality of monumental official calm, a man who had set an incorruptible seal on himself. Let travelers know that he was not the fellow with whom to play games. He had studied many an upper-class Customs officer—those with university learning, some with livid, invaluable dueling scars. They were the ones to model oneself after.

Taking up his command in Passau left him feeling, however, less inside his own good Austrian skin. His tone, in consequence of being on the German side of the border, became a touch too harsh. Occasionally some trifle would provoke him unduly. Once he went into a tirade because an underling addressed him as "Herr Official" rather than "Herr Senior Official Hitler." He could sense that his

new subordinates were better educated than the ones at Braunau.
Could these new faces be growing critical of him? Now and again,
looking down from his post at the rush of the Danube below the
Customs' bridge, his eyes would sparkle with tears. He would find
himself thinking of Braunau, and of the two women buried in the
region, dear carnal-spirited Franziska, yes, and for an instant he
would also mourn Anna Glassl. No beauty, but she had known
what to do under the sheets.

He smoked all the time. His nickname, unknown to him, was
"the Cloud of Smoke." (Here, the German is good enough to offer:
*die Rauchwolke!*) "And today, what is the mood of *die Rauchwolke?*"
one young officer might ask another as he came on duty. Alois
knew these juniors were resentful because he did not allow them
the liberty that he enjoyed—nonetheless, the very injustice of it
would enforce his authority. While a good officer had to be fair for
the most part, he could still exercise a few inequalities. Done judi-
ciously, that proved effective. One's inferiors were reduced a notch.

Now that Klara and the children had joined him in Passau, he
also became more severe with his offspring. Alois Junior and Angela soon learned not to speak to him unless they were asked a direct question. Otherwise, they were not to interrupt his thoughts.
If Alois Junior happened to be outside, the father would put two
fingers to his lips and whistle. It was identical to the call he used
to summon Luther. In turn, Alois Junior, fresh cheeked, strong,
stocky, and with a face like his father's, had driven Klara and Angela
into hysterics one afternoon by picking up a monumental turd that
Adi had chosen to deposit on the parlor rug. When stepmother and
sister began to scream at the sight of it in Junior's hand, dark,
doughty, and as forbidding as a primeval club, he chose to stalk
after them, his eyes wild. What a mischief! Klara and Angela were
crying out in terror. Then Adi joined the chorus and screamed with
the rest even as he chose to prance right behind Alois Junior, keeping on with it until his big brother, tiring of the sport, tore off an
inch of the stuff, whirled around, and planted it on the tip of Adolf's
nose.

That evening Klara told Alois Senior. The beating that ensued was comparable to the attack on Luther. Next day, Alois Junior could just about crawl off to school. Profound, after that, was the discipline in the house. When Alois came home from his duties, the children dared at most to whisper. Klara, unwilling to upset him, was also quiet. Supper was eaten in silence. The smell of Alois' breath, rich with meat and sour from beer, mingled with the aroma of red cabbage.

After dinner, he would take to the armchair, select one of his long-stemmed pipes, tamp his tobacco into the bowl with all the authority that is ready to ensconce itself in the thumb of a man of official importance, and then proceed to overpower the air with his own smoke. Alois Junior and Angela went to their room once permission was given. But Adi was called forward.

His father would cup the three-year-old's head in his hand, and with a divided grin—50 percent affection, 50 percent pure meanness of spirit—proceed to blow smoke into Adolf's face. The boy would cough. The father would chuckle.

As soon as Alois let go of his head, Adolf would smile and run off to the water closet. There, he might throw up. Sometimes, head bent over the pail, the three-year-old would remember the sounds of Alois making love to Klara, and such groans accompanied him through the lurches of his stomach. He kept asking himself why his mother never complained about the smoke.

She did not dare. She sensed that the greatest provocation to her husband would be to comment on his pipe.

Moreover, Adolf had provided her with new cause for fear. Cleaning his bottom one day (and she did not make this large discovery until he was three—such were her curious proprieties) she came to notice that he had one testicle, not two.

A town doctor reassured her that this medical phenomenon did not have to be fearsome. "Such boys often grow up to be men with large families."

"So he will not be different from others when he goes to school?"

"Boys of his condition are sometimes active. Highly active. That is all."

Such kind words did not soothe Klara. The missing testicle left one more stain on the Poelzl family. Her sister Johanna was not only a hunchback, but there was a first cousin—a true imbecile. Not to speak of all of Klara's dead brothers, her dead sisters, her own dead children. There was not enough, she decided, of Alois' strong constitution in Adolf, no, none of the strength Alois had so obviously passed on to Alois Junior. This was also her fault. She had loved her husband on the night that Adolf had been conceived, but only on that night, and in a way—was it unholy?—such a night!

But now—could it be too late?—she would say that she loved her husband again. She came to this conclusion slowly, step by step, over many months, but on one fine night in June, a year and a half after his transfer to Passau, she felt a new respect for him. For just that afternoon he had learned that in another six months, he would be transferred to Linz, the capital of the province, there to serve as Chief Customs Officer. It was the most important assignment you could find in all the Service between Salzburg and Vienna, and it came at a fine time since he would be ready to retire in a few years and this promotion would increase the size of his pension.

On that night, they conceived. Perhaps there was never an hour when she loved Alois more simply, or realized she wanted a second son so much. Little Adi with his one testicle had put a small but yearlong horror into her heart. She did not dare to think any longer that Adi might live a long life. On the contrary, they needed another child. She dared to pray for a boy. The new one, she decided, must belong to Alois as much as to herself.

# 8

Edmund was born on March 24, 1894, a few weeks before Adolf would be five. Klara had told him that he would soon have a brother or—if God so desired—a sister, and Adolf was ready either way. He looked forward to playing with the baby on arrival. He expected to meet a child half his age, at least as measured by size, a living creature ready to speak, but in any event, certainly able to listen. On the approach to Klara's bed, however, he was aghast, for there he saw no more than a cloth bundle on her breast with a face inside the wrappings as wizened as an old apple.

Having been sent the night before to a neighbor's house, where he went through the discomfort of sleeping on a small bed between Angela and Alois Junior (who kept pinching each other over his intervening body), he knew that changes were coming. This perception turned into his first large sorrow when, next day, as he rushed to his mother's bed, the midwife put out a hand as large as his face and said, "Don't hurt the baby."

Klara made it worse. She put a hand on his head. But it was passing in its touch and he could feel no love. Tears came to his eyes.

"Ah, the poor little one," said the midwife and led him out of the room. "In a few days," she said, "you can get nearer to the new brother."

"Will he talk to me?"

"Oh, you will be the first to understand him." With that, she laughed and returned to the bed where his mother lay.

He rarely got near enough to Klara. Yet just a few weeks ago, he had been able each morning to enjoy the same conversation with her.

"Mommy," Adi would ask, "are you the most beautiful woman in the world?"

She would tease his hair. "What do you think?"

"I think you are the most beautiful."

She would hug him to her breast. The love her breasts held for him was not so complete as it used to be. Yet she would pretend that it was, even if a year had passed since she had stopped feeding him. Now he not only would gorge on the cream puffs she often prepared for dessert but would wolf them down at such a rate that Alois Junior would complain audibly if Klara was present, or, in her absence, rap a knuckle on his kid brother's head. Klara, prey to new uneasiness at how little attention she gave to Adi these days, would defend his right to the cream puffs. "He is so little," she would say, "he needs them more than you."

Following the birth, Klara was often too fatigued to cook. The temporary servant made cream puffs that tasted like sour milk. Klara, in her turn, was breast-feeding Edmund all the time. So it seemed to Adolf. He experienced a new sorrow that blended with the sad undertone of the church bells in Passau, so many bells, so frequent.

Now, when he tried to ask if she was the most beautiful woman in the world, she would laugh unhappily. "Oh, I am an old worn-out girl," she would say. "I am not beautiful, Dolfchen. But your sister Angela will be."

Adi did not agree. Angela was undependable. Angela was always ready to pinch him. She was nice, at times, but treacherous. "No, you are more beautiful than Angela," he would say, and his mother would shake her head.

Meanwhile, much of the time, his father was in Linz. One week after Edmund's birth, Alois took up new and full-time duties there. Since Linz was fifty miles east of Passau, Alois did not bring back the weight of his strong voice more than twice a month. Now, when Angela and Alois Junior were away at school, Adi would be alone with his mother and the infant, yet Klara still did not have a lot of time for him. And at night, he no longer could be certain where he would sleep. Alois Junior would often take over his cot, and Adi would have to move to Angela's bed. Sometimes she would tell him that he did not smell good. "So, Adi, your breath is rotten," she would say. Often, he would put a blanket on the floor to escape her.

He was also afraid to go outside. There were boys his age and older playing on the field in back of the house, and their yells were fearsome. He spent his time looking at the illustrations in a book his father had bought about the Franco-Prussian war of 1870. He decided he would like to be a brave soldier. Could he be? He was so afraid!

One afternoon, after school and much at Klara's bidding, Alois Junior pulled Adolf out of the house and led him to the field behind the house. Yes, he had known it would be so. A dozen small boys were playing at war.

Alois Junior studied the group, then selected the leader of one army, a stout five-year-old. "This is my brother," Alois told him, "and if you let anyone on the other side hit Adolf, you will hear from me." He punched the boy on the arm hard enough to certify his words, and departed.

When Adolf came home that evening, Alois Junior told him, "From now on, I eat the cream puffs first. As many as I want. If you cry to your mother, mama's boy, I will not protect you on the field."

"I won't cry," said Adi, holding his breath as tightly as if he were clinging to a rope.

Next day, he went to the game by himself. He was more afraid of Alois Junior's derision than of any blows he might take in the battle.

Actually, there had been little enough punishment on the first day. The fat boy was quick to use his own body to shield Adi from every attack. Besides, it did not take long to grasp the basic principle. Divided into two teams, the boys took turns chasing each other. It was really not a war. More like tag. Once you were touched, you were dead. And each melee lasted but a few minutes. After which, the boys, close to breathless, would count the losses, take a breath, and start up again. On the first charge across the field, somebody would always get knocked down. Once, when the fat boy whom Alois Junior had chosen was waylaid by two kids from the other team, it even happened to Adolf. A rude shove on the shoulder and he was slammed to the ground. Earth was driven up his nose.

He did not cry. It took a considerable effort by his will. He had to negotiate with himself in order to keep from weeping, and then was hurt that no one applauded his newfound stoicism. His feelings were as bruised as the scrape on his cheek. His nose burned from the outrage to his nostrils, but he managed not to cry.

He also managed to get through the rest of the battles that day without another collision. He was quick to dart away whenever an enemy soldier came near. To his delight, he even tagged one boy.

On the next day, his face was in the dirt again. The fat boy was rueful about it and begged him not to tell his brother. Adi had the pleasure of patting him on the back. No cause for alarm, he announced, not a word would he say. Yet that night he could hardly sleep. He felt that in time to come, the fat boy, Klaus, would be his lieutenant, while he would be captain.

To accomplish such an aim, he came up with a new set of rules. War, he reasoned, was not two armies charging at each other all the time—war was also maneuvers from side to side. He did not know the word as yet, but he had an instinct for the concept.

To his new mates he now proposed that they shift over from the flat field to a hill in the next meadow. Each army could now begin at the base of opposite slopes, and so would not be visible until one or the other crossed the summit.

Once he had convinced the boys of this change, he brought in an amendment. The leader on each side, he insisted, must not be touched. "The highest officer," he argued, "must always be respected."

To gain his point, it did not hurt that stout, sturdy Klaus was always by his side. All the same, Adi was a little amazed at how well he could deal with these matters. So was I.

# 9

Following young Adolf's first war games, I was instructed to take a more direct interest in his development.

Be it understood that further investiture is never routine. Each case is unique. The average man or woman assumes that one can lose one's soul to the Devil on an instant, and permanently, but the premise is so false that the sermon is repeated in church every Sunday as an active threat. The real situation, however, is that we do not appropriate people by way of a lightning flash. Nor does Satanic entrapment brand a man or woman forever as our vassal. Rather, it is an ongoing tug-of-war. So soon as we seek to invest our powers in a client, the Cudgels are likely to appear. Complete possession rarely occurs. Indeed, after a series of such battles, the odd soul actually captured by the Cudgels or ourselves can bear more resemblance to a throwaway than a prize. (Schizophrenic people can be the victims of such contests.)

Entrapment, then, is not free of paradox. The clients that we find most difficult to approach are those with the greatest potential. Conversely, individuals who are easy to pick up rarely offer real skills. It takes so little to traduce a drunk. We do, however, polish what is left of their charm. That helps to consume a little more of the compassion of their families, especially if the mother, father, or any of the siblings are obsessed with not losing the last of their charity. In effect, we injure that family's God-loving hearts. But such is simple work. Gains are small. Ultimate ends are not served. Our final aim, after all, is to draw the majority of humans away from allegiance to the D.K.

There is, however, another factor in every contest—an economic factor. It concerns the separate resources of Divine energy and of Satanic energy. They differ.

I can allow that even in the higher cadres of devils and angels, we hardly know who has more Time to allot to a contest once we vie for possession of a particular man or woman. Of course, this does not involve immense happenings. The D.K. can, for example, disburse whole bonanzas of Divine substance into His sunsets, which, it must be admitted, bolster human morale. There, I would call Him a spendthrift, but then, we devils devote our attention to the expenditures of Time involved in securing a new client. To give years to a promising varlet who eventually goes over to the Cudgels leaves a budgetary blemish on one's record. When choosing a target, we try, therefore, to exhibit more acumen than our opponents.

For example, we rarely fail to attend the couplings of rich and powerful people (so full of infidelity!). As has been noted, we do not ignore incest, whether among the rich or the poor. Sex acts, however, particularly those illumined by angels, present a more demanding task—it is not routine to slip through their blockade. But we try. It seems—I dare to speak here only for myself—as if the E.O. has never been able to accept his failure to be present in the hour when Jesus Christ was conceived.

Fortunately for us, Jesus proved to be a not untypical Son. The record we are furnished informs us that He was often at odds with His Father.

I stray from my point. The prevailing fact of our existence is that we are obliged to live within a limited budget, and so, our projects are chosen with discretion. Except in special instances, we do not take large interest in the early development of children. "Over the first few years," our Maestro will remark, "a child is caught between the need for love and the development of its will. These inclinations are so naturally at odds with each other that an early approach is rarely necessary."

Except for unusual cases like Adi's, we exercise no intervention until the age of seven. Well into the nineteenth century, a very young child was always in danger of being carried off by one disease or another.

Past the seventh birthday, it becomes easier for us to assess the prospective health of young clients. On the other hand, our Maestro terms the next five years the Age of Clods. "They are now encountering the world in its basic form—their school years. Nearly all of them rush toward habit, routine, and stupidity as the most immediate forms of protective insulation." More often, then, our selections commence with adolescence. Now the energies invested by the D.K. are there at last for us to mine.

I have spoken at this length of our cautious process of selection because I wish to emphasize how uncommon was the special attention given to Adi for his early years. That his name was Adolf Hitler was, after all, of no importance then.

All the same, I had lived (by proxy) in the demonic instant of his conception, and then had been assigned to review the work of the devils who would oversee his family's activities. It was light surveillance. Our jargon for this kind of action was *milk runs*, an expression we employed long before it was adopted by Army Air Force pilots in the Second World War. Any one of our devils might pass by a house in the hours before dawn, and by way of the small and large family storms that had transpired since the last visit, new information was acquired. It required no large expenditure unless the abode was guarded by a Cudgel. Normally, however, one could make a quick pass by the house and sweep up the findings. While humans slept, we did our work.

I had been able then to keep up with a close history of the Hitler family over all the years since Adolf had been born. (Be it understood that my devils also kept track of numerous other projects in that region of Austria.) If what my agents had offered up to now was modest, it had, nonetheless, sufficed. Reviewing Adolf's early years, I confess that I saw no vast promise in the boy. He was outrageously in need of love and damnably vulnerable. The odds were that he would creep through life with a self-protective ego. At least, so I would have judged if the Evil One had not been present at his conception. That event, however, had to enter my judgment, and so even during the busiest nights the Hitler family was included on every milk run.

This routine of careful but passive observation was overturned altogether for me on the day that Alois Junior dragged Adi off to the boys' afternoon game of war. The Maestro intervened. I received a direct message: "Take closer care of him now. Stiffen his spine. We can lose much of his potential if we don't take steps."

# 10

When given a direct order, I had no room for deviation. I did what I was told to do. I stiffened the boy's spine. Indeed, I will make the claim that the task was accomplished with finesse. For I did not inject any special funds into his courage or his will; rather, I provided him with enough wit to carry out the job himself, since he had been the one, after all, who chose not to weep when his face was in the dirt. Afterward, he had also displayed his own cunning at finding ways to avoid physical punishment.

I was aware again of the superior insight of the Maestro. Adi showed a few signs that he was worth the work. The child might even be as much superior to an average five-year-old as a young racehorse to a run-of-the-mill mule. I enjoyed working with him, and that was just as well, since the order had come during a period when I could not afford new inroads on my budget. Improving a child's courage usually demands the disbursement of precious stores, precisely those funds we have managed to steal from the Cudgels. Of necessity, we have become skilled at impersonating angels. Even an adult, feeling our infusion of love, tends to believe it is bona fide. I suspect Kierkegaard had just that in mind when he proposed that people had to be wary of feeling too saintly, since they could not be certain of the source of such feelings. They could be working for Satan.

I might as well add that we devils are human to this degree—a fine return on our investment puts us in the best of moods, so I had come to enjoy being with Adi as he showed his capacity to improve the war games.

He soon saw, and I believe this came as much from his perception as mine, that outposts were necessary. It was wrong to send soldiers over the hill with no knowledge of what they might encounter. A scout from each army had to attempt, therefore, to work his way up close enough to the summit to gain a look at the dispositions of the other side. Following in logical sequence came another change in the rules—an advancing army had to be free to move its forces from flank to flank, even as it climbed the hill. The defense could also shift. Of course, this called for larger forces on each side, but Adi was soon able to convince his regulars that more boys should be invited from nearby streets and fields. Of course, they, the originals, having been first on this hill, were entitled to promotion in rank. Let me offer one of his speeches to his troops.

"Why are we here?" he would ask. "Is it because we need to know more about war? Yes. Because, my friends, when we are big men, we want to be heroes. Is that not true? Klaus, do you want to be a hero?"

"That is what I want."

"Of course. It is what we all want. All of us. But for that, we must learn more. So, we need more soldiers. How are we to do this?

"I will tell you. It is by talking to all who are willing to join us. We, who are here now, can then be given high rank. And we who command will be very high in rank. Not just captain, or major, but a general.

"Klaus, here, will be my colonel."

Those are the words he used. I will admit I took the pains to inspire him. We have that power just as much as the angels. Under

our influence, clients can speak with more wit, confidence, and insight than when they are on their own. We use such a technique,
however, sparingly. It does require the use of special funds.

On this occasion, it was worth it. While I had certainly helped
to endow him with an eloquence no ordinary five-year-old could
muster, some of those good turns of speech came from him. A few!

Before long, he and his troops were engaged in hour-long contests. There were endless alterations of the rules. The numbers increased to fifteen and twenty a side.

Word came from the E.O. "Enough for now. Let us see how
much of this endures after the move."

That was not uncharacteristic of the Maestro. We had to be
ready to accept quick changes. In this case, the family's situation
had altered. Alois was going to move Klara, Angela, Alois Junior,
Adi, and the baby Edmund up from Passau to dwell on a farm some
distance from Linz.

While the war games are now done for a time, I feel the need to
soothe what might be a growing uneasiness in the reader. Good
readers are an unprotected species—their allegiance moves in advance of their judgment. Some may have felt uncomfortable, therefore, to discover that they were enjoying these first successes of the
child, Adolf Hitler. Be assured. To read about the skills or triumphs
of any protagonist is bound to elicit happiness in just about all who
follow the story, especially if there is a suggestion of the sentimental, or even better, the magical—useful tools for any author who
wishes to arouse quick emotions in the reader. That is why so many
popular writers come looking for us. We love them. We do not dis-
abuse them. We enjoy them. Popular writers usually believe they
are working both for God and their own prosperous selves. All the
while, we are encouraging them to steep their readers in baths of
misperception. The profit comes to us. Misperception of reality
will, at the least, waste God's Time, and that is a form of compound
interest in our economy.

# BOOK VI

# THE
# FARM

# 1

Yes, Alois was going to retire. He would buy a farm. In the last year of his Customs work, he had begun to look about, and by February of 1895, he bought what he deemed might be the right property in a town called Hafeld, thirty miles from Linz. So, in April, Klara and the children made the move from Passau to this newly chosen abode. It was, indeed, a rural retreat. The closest school was in the nearest hamlet, Fischlham, a mile away, and there, after the summer, Adi would enter the first grade. Meanwhile, over the next few months Klara could live on the farm with their four offspring while Alois completed his service in Linz.

Of course, retirement could not come without opening a few cracks in what had been a most impressive edifice. I speak of Alois' ego. When we consider the meager materials out of which he had had to nourish this stalwart of his psyche, he may even have been entitled to taste a little meditative nectar.

He was not able to enjoy it, however. Too bad! If only he had enjoyed working at his final post in Linz, his last title, Chief Customs Officer, would have left a deposit of real satisfaction. But any problems with personnel that he had encountered at Passau were now magnified. Linz was a major center of attention for the Finance-Watch. It was the capital of a most important province, Upper Austria, and Customs was stocked, therefore, with ambitious junior officers who seemed never at a loss to show their subtle contempt for the failings of senior officials less wellborn than themselves. Most of these young men were ready to take for granted the future attainment of high office, and such confidence in junior officers left Alois feeling out of joint. For the first time in all the years that he had been wearing a uniform, he did not always strike the passing eye as an immaculate official. (That now demanded too many pains.) Nor was he as punctual as once he had been. Sometimes, at the point of issuing disciplinary reprimands, he would hesitate long enough to contemplate the possible repercussions. Worse. There were one or two occasions when he forgot what he was next about to say.

For just such a reason, he eased up on smoking restrictions. He no longer enjoyed confronting the in-held wrath of younger officers. But, in consequence, he enjoyed his own tobacco less. He also began to feel as if all his associates, young and old, were now impatient for him to retire. He had put in, after all, near to forty years of service. While he had the right to continue for another twelve months, he did not deem it wise. Small, steady inroads on his vanity kept lowering him into a modest dream. What if he chose to become a gentleman farmer? That would not be so bad, no, not out there in the autumn sun of his last good years. What the hell! Born a peasant, he could end as a well-to-do fellow who had gone back to the earth.

He had money enough. He could buy a decent farm outright. He would have his pension, and his savings—he and Klara had certainly exhibited thrift. Besides, he had in hand the sum and interest of a large part of three wives' dowries. It could be said that the first two had brought real money to the union. If Anna Glassl had succeeded in recovering, through law, half of her large dowry due to their separation, still, the half remaining was not small. Franziska, while hardly up to that measure, was nonetheless the child of a prosperous farmer. Even old Johann Poelzl, Klara's father, had come forth with some long-saved kronen when they married.

On the other hand, Alois understood money only too well. Not all coin was equal. Deep in one's conscience, one had to pay a tithe for money that was not earned properly. Money gave back its reflection of how it had been acquired. Sometimes this thought gave him a passing chill. A good part of his prosperity could be seen as the flower that sprouted from the coffin-soil of dead wives' dowries.

During this last year of service, while Klara took care of the children in Passau and he was free in Linz, he had begun to feel too old for other women. That was when he told himself to go back to the earth. It was what he had always heard from Johann Nepomuk—"the real woman is in the fields." The old man had to take but one drink and would repeat it over and over. "The real woman—look for the real woman in the fields. Respect the fields."

It was an adage Alois could enjoy even if his present plans did not include heavy work with the soil. His aim, rather, was apiculture. He was looking to develop beehives. He would market the honey. That would be his crop. All the same, owning a little land might be equal to acquiring another limb, a fifth appendage so to speak, as important to a man with peasant roots as a trunk to an elephant.

Five years ago, about the time Adolf was born, he had bought a farm. In many a way that purchase had been more exciting to him than the birth. Unlike the first three of Klara's babies, land was not going to die.

The reverse had occurred. The land did not perish, but his ownership did. The holding had been near Spital, about a hundred miles from where he was then working in Braunau, but he had had, even then, some notion of retiring there later. In the interim, it might be a good way to take care of his sister-in-law, Johanna Poelzl, in preference to having her dwell with them as a maid. He did not want Johanna in the parlor every night, not with that dome on her back. Poor hunchback!

All the same, he did feel some admiration for his sister-in-law. Johanna was not in the least afraid of God. She would put no trust in Him. "God," she would declare, "did not have to kill off so many of us in the Poelzl family." Alois could tip his hat to that. "She's not like my wife," he was fond of telling the tavern. "Klara is ready to kiss every cross she meets."

All the same, Johanna did not run the farm very well. Sooner or later, every hired man who worked there was antagonized by her sharp tongue. Finally, she decided to live again with her father and her mother—also named Johanna. If we recall, this Johanna was the one who had been Alois' mistress on an unforgettable occasion. (*"Sie ist hier!"*)

Alois was able, however, to sell that first farm at a modest profit and so was not ill-disposed now to taking on the property in Hafeld. Here was a farm he could work himself. It was called the Rauscher Gut (which can be translated as the Wind-Blown Estate) and it offered nine acres of pasture plus a two-story wooden house under a thatched roof with good views of the mountains of the Salzkammergut. In addition, there were fruit and oak and walnut trees. A hayloft was in the stable, and stalls for two horses and a cow, plus one prize sow.

It seemed perfect. After the purchase (and only *after* the purchase), neighboring farmers were ready to hint to the new arrival that the land might be beautiful, but it was not necessarily going to be famous for its crops.

He looked upon these comments as exactly the kind of hazing that resident farmers would visit on a newcomer. Oh, he assured them, it did not matter. The land would be given a rest. He was there to raise bees. That was his element. Good honey could become the most prosperous crop of them all.

Indeed, in the last days before his retirement ceremony (which was acceptably eulogistic to Alois and most impressive, even thrilling, to Klara) he did have a series of drinking nights as a closer way of saying farewell to his staff and to the decades of his work. Since he had no desire ever to be seen as a man who would moon over the past, he dwelt on his future, he bullied his junior associates, plus a couple of old cronies and a few respected town officials, to drink more than one stein with him on the merits and mysteries of beekeeping. Indeed, he belabored each table on each night with so much concerning "the mysterious psychology of these little creatures" that the junior officers would warn each other, "Tonight, let's try to keep the Cloud of Smoke from smoking us out with his bees."

In truth, Alois did see himself as something of a philosopher on this subject. What an achievement for an untutored peasant from the Waldviertel to be able to give a lecture equal to a university savant!

In these last weeks, then, before retirement, in the same Linz tavern he had frequented each night after his Customs House shift, Alois spoke more and more of the higher concepts of apiculture. Honeybees formed an amazing world, he would inform his drinking cohorts. "With rare exceptions, these tiny creatures offer up their lives to one purpose: It is to build a future for the generations who will follow. The honey they convert from nectar and pollen is not only for their own consumption, but, gentlemen, it is also produced to feed their larvae." He nodded. "These larvae are installed in the tiniest hexagonal cells, a wonder to behold, because they are constructed symmetrically out of the very beeswax these insect workers make from pollen, which process, gentlemen, is so mysterious that it is not yet wholly understood even by the most modern chemists."

His company nodded, their spirits glum. This was not lively beer talk. But Alois, on these last nights, had become the kind of lecturer who is always ready to exhibit an incorruptible lack of sensitivity for his audience. "Some bees," he now remarked, "the heftier ones, become guards to watch over the entrances to the hive. Do you know? They are ready to go into battle at the cost of their lives. They will even fight off such powerful raiders as wasps or spiders or termites. Yes, all the insect world, you see, is looking for a free meal in the honey. But that is only one of the obstacles to a peaceful life for the bee. All through the summer, many of these worker bees are constantly engaged in keeping the interior of the hive cool. How? By means of tireless activity. They never stop fanning their wings. A good many even wear out their wings. After which, they are ready to die. They give up their lives in this hard labor of creating a draft to cool the hive. Why? Because the larvae cannot survive in too much heat. Think of it. Thousands of wings all fanning away, even as others go out to forage and bring back more supplies from the fields of flowers. They collect the pollen in pods on their legs and then, flying back to the hive, they manage to stay aloft under the weight of loads of pollen and nectar that weigh more than their own bodies. I tell you, they create a society that is not unlike ours, but it is certainly more hardworking."

None of the junior officers were ready to argue. (If they did, he might go on for another hour.) It took one of the older town officials to reply. Taking several portentous sips of smoke from his pipe, he said, "Come, Alois, they are only insects."

"No, good sir! With all due respect, you are mistaken. There is much more to them than one would think. Some, I believe, live to finer purpose than the average human dolt. Let me say, they are one of the wonders of our universe."

# 2

I was not prepared for Alois' interest in these matters. Here was not the man I knew. While I could see his practical purpose, since the product was eminently salable, apiculture also had its risks, including the peril of receiving a serious number of bee stings. On the other hand, it might be reasonable to engage in such efforts rather than endanger his long-used heart by plowing a field.

I was plagued, all the same, by an uneasy suspicion. Alois was too sincere in this enthusiasm. He was not sufficiently concerned with profit. That was what disturbed my understanding. The desire for money is the taproot that usually drives men like Alois into new activity. So the relative absence of this desire suggested that Alois was ready to undertake this venture because it satisfied something I had not yet perceived in him.

I did recall that he had dabbled at keeping bees in one small town near Braunau, but soon saw a better reason. In these last few months, he had taken the pains to write a short article for a beekeepers' journal and the piece was published. Alois had acquired a degree of book knowledge on the subject that provided him with a point of view on new modes of cultivation. Beehives made of straw, he declared, would soon be outmoded. *Skeps* they were called, squat-ribbed domed objects about the size and shape of big-bellied human torsos, and these old skeps had their drawbacks. To harvest the honey, beekeepers had to keep the population of the hive stunned with smoke. That left the hive in a near-comatose condition. It was a harsh and imprecise process. Sometimes, the skep had to be ripped open in order to collect the product. Despite the smoke, some honeybees were still active enough to sting the collector.

A new and much-discussed innovation was, however, being developed in England and in America. That was the point of his article. Even in Austria, there were beekeepers ready to do away with the old skep. For its time, the skep had been an improvement over the more barbaric practice—common through the Middle Ages—of chasing the bees out of their hole in a tree, but advanced beekeepers were speaking these days of hives that could become the equivalent, or so his article proposed, of a metropolis for bees. This new housing, no greater in size than a wooden cabinet you could set on a bench, would be filled with wax trays installed vertically. The worker bees could then build their minuscule wax cells on both sides of each tray. And in a most orderly fashion! Since this cabinet could hold a number of trays, and each tray had room for thousands of cells in a grid of rows and files, some keepers calculated that each hive now bore resemblance to what might yet be giant apartment buildings in the future.

That had been the point of his article—visionary indeed—but to explain this venture to Klara, Alois chose to emphasize the pecuniary promise. Good money would come back from clean work, and Alois Junior and Angela would help, he told her. Adi as well. He convinced her that the new project was eminently practical.

I was more than bothered. Klara might believe him, but I did not. I had decided that Alois was looking to find a way to come nearer to the Dummkopf. That was not a matter I could afford to ignore.

## 3

Alois had never been one of our clients. He was by our measure an average man, which is to say, sufficiently corrupt to be available for our use should we be in true need of him. The assumption was that he would then be open. The Cudgels would hardly be guarding the fellow. To what end? What was there to protect? Whereas, when it came to Klara, we did not choose to go near. It would have proved punishing, and again—to what end? We did not need her directly—as I have already remarked, evil children can issue nicely from the most loving mothers. Of course, average men and women find the thought repulsive. It rattles their faith in the Dummkopf. How could God allow it? A standard lament.

Alois was directly useful to us. He was so dependable in his strengths and habits, his productive contributions, his built-in cruelties (not to mention his crudities) that one could, if necessary, intensify or reduce the heat of Adolf's hatred for his father in such a way as to mold the boy. Depend on it—we depended on Alois.

But now, his outsize love for bees seemed out of character. Atheists like Alois, who attempt to go all the way to the grave without being challenged by the intimation that God may have created their universe, are not unlike pious virgins who fear the temptation of unholy heats. Such ladies can only accept their pinched carnality through a variety of counterfeits. So, too, do atheists have their substitutes by way of paganism, service to others, or, by now, technology—usually seen by them as the best possible solution to humankind's problems. Occasionally, they feel an exceptional allegiance to some phenomenon of nature. In Alois' case, it happened to be the recognition that a collaboration could be possible between the mighty and the minuscule, himself and the bees.

Sufficiently concerned, I penetrated one night into his mind, a costly move, since he was not a client, but necessary if I was to comprehend his motive, and, indeed, I now knew more. Alois saw bees as living a life with parallels to his own. That gave me cause for apprehension. To Alois, bees in search of new fields of flowers were intimate little creatures he could understand.

On any warm day, such foragers know the heat of the sun and the intimate yearning that the sun can arouse in flower petals. Alois was not about to throw open the door he had bolted to the mystical side of himself, but he did keep picturing the honeybee on its entrance into the caverns of the flower. Under the burgeoning heat of the sun, the flower would surrender its nectar to the bee's tongue, even as the hairs of the honeybee became covered with pollen. In another moment, the same bee would separate from one passionate lust to dive into another, whichever fine flower of the same species was beckoning in the breeze, the creature ready again to gather more nectar while strewing pollen picked up from the first flower to the second. Hard work and satisfied desire!

He could feel close to that bee staggering back in flight, with its pollen bags heavy, and a stomach full of nectar. Had not Alois given much to women and yet brought back much for himself—much accumulated wisdom on how to deal with his Customs House corner of the world. By the end, he invariably knew what was true and what was false in declarations offered by strangers, particularly women who might wish to deceive him, yet could not, because he was wiser. He possessed the true honey—wisdom. That was the knowledge of what others were up to, all those secrets held by passing travelers and commercial people, secrets as sweet as honey, all those little goods travelers looked to steal and keep for themselves. But he was there to capture their secrets. He could work as hard and long as any honeybee on the hottest and most productive day of summer to protect the glory, centuries old, of the exceptional

Empire of the Hapsburgs. Not all of them had been great, he would admit, not all were even very good people, but the best of them had been, like Franz Josef, good, very good. As we know, Alois could find a resemblance to Franz Josef in his own features—the same sideburns, the same dignity. It was said of the Emperor Franz Josef that he could work for endless hours at his necessary and near-to-endless duties. When necessary, he, Alois, was also ready. And yet they knew enough, both of them—the Emperor and himself—to comprehend that it was not enough to amass the honey; one must keep a taste for oneself.

Some people in Linz, he knew, fools for the most part, had been shocked when gossips spoke of the actress, Fräulein Katharina Schratt, whom Franz Josef had taken for a mistress. How could this be? The Emperor's wife was so beautiful—Empress Elizabeth. The news had spread like a spill of oil. But it had not been shocking to Alois. He understood. Men had to keep some share of the honey for themselves.

Let me not be carried away altogether by the voluptuous swells of Alois' meditation. In truth, he had some fear of bees. Once, in previous years, he had been stung so ferociously and apocalyptically (if I may put it so) that he never forgot the attack of vertigo it caused. Such power to create pain! That it could exist in creatures so small! It could not have come from the honeybee alone, he decided. Such pain must express the rage of the sun. With that, Alois was familiar. He had worked through many an August afternoon, stuffed into his uniform. Of course he knew the rage of the sun, and honeybees were agents of the sun even as he was an agent of the Hapsburgs, and thereby close to the greatness of ultimate power.

Could these epiphanies be the product of his approaching retirement? I looked forward with my own trepidation to the changes I could not anticipate once he began to live with his family on the farm.

On the very night in April when they slept in the house at Hafeld for the first time, Klara became pregnant again. Until then, she had remained with the children in Passau. Edmund had been ailing, and it was winter. Moreover, Alois would not be able to join them permanently at the farm until his retirement at the end of June. By April, however, Klara decided to brave the difficulties and, right after Easter, accompanied by Angela, Adolf, Edmund, and the sum of their possessions, she accomplished the move to Linz. It was made even more difficult since she was without Alois Junior to help her with the luggage—he had had to stay behind and board with a neighbor until the end of his school year. Angela, however, was of great help to her. She had insisted on not finishing her term, but coming along instead to help Klara.

"School is not so important," she said. "I will make up what is lost in the next year, but for now you need me at the farm. I want to be with you there."

She was right. Klara knew as much, and was moved. I would say that is the moment when she began to love Angela as a true daughter. Klara was wise enough in her innocence to know that Angela's feelings were genuine. She liked school well enough but she cared more for Klara's well-being, and so Klara in turn had become more than a good stepmother, much more.

Whatever the difficulties, they embarked by train from Passau early in the day and her husband was at the station in Linz with a large wagon and two workhorses to carry their trunks, valises, packing crates, and packages over the last thirty miles to Hafeld.

This portion of the trip lasted from noon to dark, but the day had been warm, and Alois, to everyone's surprise, entertained the children with one song after another—his voice was rich, and Klara, who had a clear if delicate soprano, would join him when she knew the words. Alois was in a rare mood, and proud of his skill with the horses and wagon. It was some years since he had gotten up on a buckboard, and he had almost hired a driver, but given his oncoming responsibilities as a farmer, he took on the project himself.

The previous owner had—as was local custom—stocked each fireplace with logs and kindling, and so the rooms, before long, were warm. What with a jar of potato soup, and bread, and liverwurst, they had enough to eat. They went to bed happily. Alois would spend the next day with his family before driving their rented wagon back to Linz.

By the first night, however, Alois was also ready to establish his investiture of the premises. By the light of the gas lamp in their bedroom, he could see that Klara looked in fine color, not pale at all, and when he said as much, she laughed in true merriment.

"You, too, Uncle," she said. "Your nose is very red from the sun."

"*Ach,*" he said, "you are still calling me Uncle. It is almost ten years that we are married and still, what am I to you? Uncle Alois? Do you mean Old Uncle Alois?"

"No," she said, "we are very proud of you. Today, so much. The horses and the wagon. You did it all. And so well. Something you never did before."

"Well, I can do a lot of things you do not know. I am never so simple as you think."

"I do not think you are simple," she said. "No, that I do not think."

"Yes, you can tell me. What do you think, my little niece?"

It was not often that she was ready to speak to him so directly, but on this night, an exceptional night after all, she said, "I wonder why you never tell me that you love me."

"Maybe," he replied, "it is because you still call me Uncle."

To his astonishment, her answer was the nearest she had ever come to speaking in a manner that most certainly belonged to other kinds of women. "Maybe I call you Uncle," she said, "because you are such a big, healthy fellow of an uncle."

This was not about to pass him by. The Hound was straining instantly at the leash. "How would you know what is the size of a healthy fellow?" he asked.

"I do not know. But I am free to guess. You are a very big uncle."

That was what made her pregnant. He was excited enough to take her by the side of the bed, both of them standing, half-dressed, and then he took her again in bed. He was full of love—for himself, first, and his prowess—such a fine power at his age. Then, he felt a degree of love for her—plus a good deal of love for the farm. It was a beautiful piece of land. He even took pleasure in the notion of coming a little closer to his children, which is to say, he had an image of working along with them in the fields. Then, about to fall asleep, he thought instead of summer bees searching the meadows. He was unusually delighted with how much power had been in his loins. To have it all there on this night, just when he had begun to wonder.

He even held Klara in his arms, which was seldom his habit, and when he woke up to honor the alarms of his bladder, he almost kicked over the chamber pot. In the dark, what with his unfamiliarity with a new bedroom, he was stumbling around, and Klara was giggling. Then she wrapped her arms around him as he came back to bed. "I am happy," she said. "I think this will be the place for us."

"Silence!" he growled. "Don't be a goose! One does not make silly predictions." Yes, he could feel the earth of the farm, all those nine acres to the rear and to the front of them, and felt just as superstitious as any of the peasants of his childhood. A person should not be as ready as Klara to speak out with good feelings to the empty night air. In any event, not aloud! Was the night so empty after all? Who knew what might be there to listen?

In the morning, she could sense his impatience to be done with the unpacking. It was obvious. He wanted to go out and walk his grounds. So she took over the larger part of the immediate tasks while he gave the children a tour of the barn, Adi and Edmund huddled close to him before the animal immanence of the two horses, the cow, and the prize sow that had been part of the purchase price. Those animals were huge, and the sow was close to overpowering in odor.

Now Alois told Adi and Edmund to go back to the house and help their mother. That was a joke. Klara would have to milk the cow, feed the pig, curry the horse, and attend to the henhouse, but he needed to walk his lands alone. He had to make more than a few decisions. So, once again, he studied the condition of the fruit and walnut trees. When he had last seen them, there was more than a little snow on the ground, but the trees looked healthy, and the large branches did appear to have integrity—strong, reasonably straight, not too many tortured shapes to suggest the aftermath of crazy storms when the trees were young.

In truth, he realized now, he had hardly studied the place before. Enough that the price was reasonable and the house owned a fine view. He had had to be in a hurry—he could not expend days in travel back and forth from Linz.

All the same, he was not so much at ease with his purchase as he had anticipated. Walking the meadows and mounting the one small hill of his new domain, he found the land was less extensive than he remembered, no larger, really, than what it was, nine acres, a good-sized parade field. On the other hand, three or four of those acres would make a decent but manageable potato field. Should he give another acre to beets? Could he plant this year? That would be the question. He could not get going until the end of June, the beginning of July, but Alois Junior would be back with them, his school year finished, and, yes, maybe they could take on some late plowing.

All this while, he felt disappointment. He had to recognize—once again—that he could not cultivate his bees, not this summer. The brunt of the project would have to wait. Honey gathering began in April and hardly lasted into September. One had to be there at the beginning. So he must wait. All right, he would have nine months now to prepare, counting at least from the time when he would be back here again, *permanently*, in June, late June, and an unexpected and most unpleasant shiver of anticipation came to him at this thought. Did he know what he was doing? That was one thought he needed to force to the back of his head. He had been in control of his feelings for many years, and he was not preparing to let go now.

5

By the first of July, Klara was visibly pregnant. In seven months, assuming the baby was born without incident, there would be a total of eight kids alive or dead who had come into existence because of Alois. Of course, if he so desired, he could add a few not exactly accounted for—he had known a number of cooks and chambermaids who had managed to conceive with what might be called mixed male parentage. And yes, whenever one of them said she was pregnant, he had agreed that he could be the true father, but then, hadn't she also been with Hans and Gerhardt and Hermann and Wolf? With rare exceptions (like Fanni) those women were not in a position to argue. It was enough to give them a decent gift.

Here in Hafeld, he was face-to-face with the other side of such achievements. Through the heat of July, in this farmhouse up on the hill, he had to look at five faces every meal, from Klara all the way down to Edmund, sixteen months old and already starting to talk. By January, there would be another child. He was used to living with people's faces in front of him, more new faces than most people had to encounter every day, but now, it was always the same mugs. He was not used to dwelling with such questions as whether Edmund, for example, had come up with a new phrase or was just gurgling out old globs of sound.

Managing the farm was another matter. He could take pleasure in Angela's work. For a twelve-year-old who had been putting cold cream on her hands ever since she was eight—a little city girl, ready to be spoiled—she was now, to his surprise, decent help. She was always currying the two horses, and washing down the cow even when that hefty lady didn't need another bath. She would also get Adolf and Edmund to laugh at the hearty contentment to be heard in the full-gutted sound of the sow every time they approached with food. Rosig (Pinky) was large for a pig, large even for a prize pig, and seemed happy in her smelly wallow with its pink rosette tacked above the stall, a prize from the summer before they bought the farm. By next winter, when all the new work wouldn't be weighing on them, Angela wanted to prepare Rosig once more for local competition. Yes, his girl, Alois decided, was a prize herself. Angela even took pains to keep the manure of the farm animals separate. She made a point of carrying each collection to a different pile. Why? Because, she declared to Klara, "My father would want it that way. Nice and neat." She even succeeded in getting Adi to take up a part of the slack. While he could be counted on to throw a tantrum, Angela would ride it out. Then the boy would follow her, his nose up to heaven in horror, but nonetheless carrying a second manure pail.

His school year over, Alois Junior arrived at the farm by the beginning of July. For a short period, no one could surpass him at work. Right off, he was splendid with the horses, particularly Ulan, a stallion five years old. Alois was proud of how quickly Junior took to the saddle. The youth was always ready for the joy of a quick canter up the hill and down, accompanied by full screams of excitement from Angela and Adi. Yet he was also available to work the plow with the dray horse, Graubart. Before too long, they had turned up three acres of hard soil pasture for the potatoes, the same sprouting seed potatoes Klara had bought and stored in the root cellar a week after her arrival. Alois Junior worked harder for two weeks than his father would have believed.

Of a sudden, this flurry fell off. Bad news arrived in a letter from the school in Passau. Alois had failed half of his courses. He would have to take those studies over again.

"I won't go back," he told his father. "The teachers are so stupid that we laugh at them."

Yes, the boy must have been brooding for these two weeks over the bad school news but had not said a word, just kept working hard. In that time, they had tilled ten inches deep into the three acres chosen, a stubborn, resistant soil, after which they laid the seed potatoes in those shallow trenches and covered them lightly, each of the sprouters a foot apart, each furrow less than a yard away from the next, but that had been only the commencement. Next came the labor that went into weeding and fertilizing. Bad memories, fifty years old, came back to Alois. He now encountered white grubs and wire worms, and had to watch as the earliest potato leaves were nibbled into green lace by aphids and beetles. Every day one had to go back for more weeding. Soon enough, watering became an ongoing problem. One could only dig a few inches down for the irrigation canals. Go deeper and potato roots would be mangled by the shovel. These shallow trenches soon filled, however, with silt. Hours had to be spent carrying pail after pail of well water up the slope to the meadow. On one of those afternoons, Junior disappeared. He was out riding Ulan. Alois put Angela to work in his stead, and for the rest of the working day, she carried the water, heavy duty for a girl her size.

That night, Alois gave his son a tongue-lashing in front of the others. "You are," he said, "very much like your crazy mother. Only with you, worse. You have no excuse. Your mother, by the end, was out of her mind, yes, but at least she had once been a hard worker. You are lazy." If the episode had happened even a year earlier, Alois would have given him a beating, exactly the apocalyptic variety that leaves a scar on the heart, but now the boy was wild enough by the look in his eyes to offer Alois pause. So he did not strike him.

Which, he came to decide, was a mistake. The boy's head should have been ringing from one hell of a wallop. Now Junior might be able to think that his father could be a little afraid of him, maybe a little, yes. For a fact, Junior kept reducing the total of his hours—a true city lad doing summer labor. Well short of sundown, he would ask Alois to let him take Ulan for a ride.

The trouble, Alois told himself, was that as a father, he was not hard enough. Under all the bite, he had a soft heart. The truth was that he adored Alois Junior. The boy was so attractive. Restless, yes, and like his mother, victim to terrible moods. He was much too prideful, and in full flight from getting a decent education. Yet he could be as charming as Fanni when he chose to be. He reminded Alois of how well she used to move. He even felt pride at how quickly his son had gotten on good terms with the stallion. Alois himself hesitated to ride him. It was truly a long way to the ground for a heavy man. But Alois Junior could saddle up with all the éclat of a prize cadet—the sort who used to promenade along the best streets of Vienna wearing the boots that Alois had made for them in those years, all the way back when he had so admired such well-turned-out young men. Memories returned of those officers strutting on the Ringstrasse with their handsome ladies, even as he, the apprentice, had dreamed of finding an elegant and lovely young milliner for himself, yes, the old dream! They would start a shop offering the finest handmade hats and most exceptional boots, a stupid dream, but now Junior reminded him of those cadets. Such a striking young man. He was not at all like little Adolf, full of hysterical temper, or tiny Edmund, full of snots.

So Alois could not bring himself to refuse when Alois Junior would ask for an hour off. Ulan, after all, had to be exercised. And the horse did love his young rider. But not the father—whenever Alois approached, the beast would show his teeth in an unmistakably evil grin.

# 6

On one warm evening in August, Alois Junior took another unpleasant liberty. This time, Klara was infuriated. The youth was at table ready for their evening supper, but Angela was not. She was in the barn currying Ulan's wet hide after her brother had put the charger into a gallop on the way back from the woods and then provided too brief a walk-down to allow the animal to cool. Klara could not believe such selfish behavior. It was one of the few times in their marriage when she spoke sharply to her husband. She was now in her sixth pregnancy, and he was no uncle to her, not at this moment. "You allowed your son to leave such work to Angela? That is certainly not right."

Alois Junior spoke up instead. "Angela likes wiping Ulan down," he said. "I don't."

"I may not know horses so much," said Klara, "but I am still ready to say that he who rides the animal has the duty afterward. The horse sees a difference. Even if you don't."

"You know nothing about the subject," said her stepson. "When it comes to horses, you are ten degrees less than zero."

"Silence!" shouted Alois. "And keep your mouth shut for the rest of the meal. Not one word."

Coming into the fray several steps behind Klara, he had to show mastery. "Yes, silence," he repeated. "I call for it."

"*Jawohl!*" shouted Alois Junior.

Now Alois had to ask himself whether he was being mocked or obeyed. "I will repeat," said Alois. "You are to be silent for the rest of the meal. Not one word."

Alois Junior stood up and left the table.

"Come back," said Alois. "Come back, sit down, and be silent."

There was a pause, and then he did come back, but in the pause was all the suggestion of what might be yet to come.

They finished the meal without another word. Angela came in flushed from currying, started to speak, and then did not. She sat down, her face still moist from the quick wash she had taken with the dipper, and put her face to the food. Sitting next to her, Adi was so full of excitement and foreboding that he was stiff with fear he might soil himself. And Klara? She ate slowly, pausing often, her spoon in the air. She was filled with an unruly desire to upbraid her stepson again, and then—no small impulse—upbraid her own Alois as well. She said nothing, however. To interfere with two men who were in such a rage was no territory to enter. Edmund, little lip-dribbling Edmund, began to cry.

That offered a solution. Klara picked him up and left the table. Then Alois rose and quit the room. Angela and Adi gathered the plates for washing, and Alois Junior continued to sit at the table, poised within his silence, gravely poised, as if he had converted his father's order into a species of reverence addressed to himself.

That night, Alois Senior could not sleep, and by the end of the next afternoon he quit his labors early. For the first time in quite a while, he went to the only tavern in the area, a full mile away at Fischlham.

He had hesitated whether to go. The company was certainly less to his taste than the old beer cronies in Linz. Besides, he knew enough about farmers to anticipate the nature of his reception. He could hear certain thoughts in advance. "The peasant who tries to act like a millionaire," they would say behind his back. Or, as easily, the opposite—"this rich idiot who wants to play at being a peasant."

He had visited a couple of neighbors in January, when he first looked at the house he was to buy, and had asked a few questions. They had not trusted him much. He expected that. They were not about to talk to a stranger who could choose not to buy the farm, yet might repeat enough of what he had heard to leave the owner offended by their gossip. So Alois was only told the good news: land good, just a few animals but excellent livestock, prize sow, good orchard—yes, and walnuts, that was easy money once a year.

Alois had not bothered to believe them. Nor to disbelieve them. He had wanted the farm. He had assumed it could not be as good as it looked, and, of course, it wasn't. Already the big cow who had been giving fine milk every day had come down with udder trouble.

He did bring this matter up at the tavern in Fischlham. He needed to. He was looking for a few opinions on the respective merits of the veterinarians in the district, and used it as a calculated opening to stimulate the farmers into a bit of candor about other things as well. Maybe he would not be perceived forever as a retired fool. So he listened to their guarded opinions about the local veterinarians and learned nothing he could count on. Next, he talked about his land.

When he told them that he had planted potatoes, they looked uneasy. In the most indirect manner, it did come out that he might have been wiser to consider beets.

"I planned to put in one acre like that, but not this first year. Too much at once."

They nodded. Farming and work. Yes. The oldest marriage. One must never do too much at once.

They were certainly slow-spoken. It took an hour of staring at the unadorned wooden walls of the tavern, fretting all the while over the one spike of a splinter in his behind (a gift of the dried-up wood of the tavern bench), before one of them would come forward with the muffled hint that this land on which he had planted potatoes should have been given to beets. That was because last year's crop had been wheat. Now they spoke of a variety of wheat whose species was unfamiliar to him, but that was what the previous owner had been planting these last three years. Who knew? The soil could now be depleted. They did not say as much; they just drew on their pipes and drank their beer and looked sad. Worst of all, as he could tell, the sadness was hardly for him, no, it was offered to the outrage done to the earth now owned by another rich man, an interloper trying to be a peasant.

The smell of the tavern became unpleasant. He could not locate the odor that mingled with the beer, but it was impure—sour milk? Old manure? A compost pile outside the door? What he resented most about this quiet dun-brown wooden den was that there was not even a hint of schnapps in the air, no, not even one good town drunkard.

The evening did not prove, however, to be a loss. He learned the name of an apiculturist who lived in Hafeld. And, for further consolation, the walk home was agreeable. The late summer moon was out, full and orange, a harvest moon. He began to feel some pleasure from his beer. Tonight those pints must have stored themselves in his stomach, ready only now to dispense some goodness. He had a long splendid urination by the side of the road.

Next morning he was back in his gathering gloom. He had to live with the disappointment of his three acres of potatoes. He would probably end with half a marketable crop. His drinking companions of last night (who in memory now smelled just like the Fischlham tavern) were right. The earth had been injured by three years of wheat. He knew as much whenever he dug up one or another early potato. And now he felt a few twinges in his gut. Was his heart acting up? Sometimes he felt as if this long-trusted organ—such a hearty companion—was forcing itself up into his brain. Yes, headaches.

Given the work yet to be done of digging up the potatoes and carting them to market in Fischlham, he ended by hiring a day laborer for the week, a stupid fellow, yet, on balance, the man probably offered up as much useful service as Junior. How was the boy going to end? Would he yet be a criminal? Alois could certainly conceive of him in something like the French Foreign Legion. Dark thoughts, but they had their appeal. When he was young, he would have made a good soldier of that variety, ready for anything. Or was that nonsense? There was something in the boy that was wilder than himself. Was that why, these days, they always had to speak to each other as if they were up on tiptoe?

The day laborer was stupid, but proved capable of putting a number of those potatoes aside for himself. Alois could not even be certain there had been a theft. Feeling not too well one afternoon, he had let the laborer take the produce to market, and the man returned with fewer kronen than Alois had estimated. A little fingering at the edges. Doubtless.

Then there was a miserable end to the prize sow. It died. Angela was disconsolate. Alois was amazed at how long and how hard a twelve-year-old female could cry.

It started with that big and pretty pig feeling grumpy. Then, day to day, it grew worse. Angela was so upset that Alois broke into his own reservoirs of pride and actually turned to his three nearest neighbors for advice. It was then he had to recognize that he had forgotten one of the laws of his childhood received from Johann Nepomuk before he was even ten years old. When it came to farming, there were no rules you could count on, no, not if you had the bad luck to meet an unexpected problem. Even your wisest friends could disagree on the solution. Of course. Every farmer, he now learned, had his own idea of how to cure a sick pig. Of course.

The three neighbors suggested, in turn, an emetic, a binder, and a diuretic. All were wrong. The sow stopped breathing, began to hemorrhage, and was gone. All three had assumed the trouble could only be in the stomach or the bowels. Where else in a pig? Who had ever heard of consumption in so big a pig? Perhaps it was something else. Even the veterinarian he called in after the demise was unsure. Probably the lungs, but he would not say.

Nothing could have aggravated Alois more. To pay good money after the animal had died! Why? Because he had to know the cause. What an idiocy! He wasn't going to raise any more pigs, not now, but still he had to know. And then he found out that the veterinarian—if you could call him that—remained no more sure of the cause than his neighbors. It would take, he told Alois, the expense of laboratory tests they could do in Linz. To hell with that! Such an expenditure would be obscene. On top of it, he had to bury the animal whole. He was tempted, but he did not dare to carve away at the beast looking for good meat. Left to himself, Alois would have searched for some choice cuts—how much did the hams have to do, after all, with the lungs? But, no, the vet was definite. "Do not take a chance, Herr Hitler, on any part of this animal."

Yes, that is what the vet told him, but only after he had been paid! And there was Angela going on and on with her hiccups and her sobs, "*Ach, ach, ach!*" Not to mention his own labor of digging a hole for the carcass.

Yes, these were losses to calculate. What kind of profits could he point to from his mediocre potato crop? When he added the cost of the seed potatoes, the compost he had bought for the three acres, and then subtracted the wages of the hired hand, the loss of the sow, and the fee of the vet as well, how could he claim to have made any respectable sum? If not for the walnuts, which had, as promised, been easy money right off the ground, he would have had no profit at all.

He could reassure himself. It wasn't that he was in real financial trouble. His pension alone was six times the income of any day laborer like the poor fellow he had hired. All the same, that hardly extracted the real thorn from his gut. One of his strengths had always been the confidence that he could know when people were cheating him. And now he had discovered that the land he bought was nothing to brag about. Once upon a time, he might have been a peasant. Now he might just as well call himself a town idiot, fooled on a deal involving land. Could he feel any worse if Klara took up with a farm boy? That was impossible, but then, how had it been so possible for himself, Alois Hitler, to be gulled on this deal?

By October, he was well settled into gloom. Even the Hound was a doleful puppy. How was he to look at himself—a man in his late middle age who dangled a wizened pup between his legs?

Klara, seven and a half months pregnant, tried to explain it to him. Now that the potato crop was in, and so much hard work was finished, it was not unnatural to feel a little unhappy. Women, she could tell him, were that way after a child was born. So much had gone into the womb, so much hope and effort, but now one was empty again. The baby might be there and beautiful, but for a time the woman had to feel empty. For a little while. It was natural.

She had never waxed so philosophical before, not to him, but he was ready to take her head off. "What am I, a woman?" he wanted to shout.

## 7

Changes occurred, however. Alois' depression lessened. Junior was no longer around. Klara had taken it upon herself to suggest that he should be sent to Spital, where he could work with her father, Johann Poelzl, who by now had certainly become old enough to need a family hand. It developed that Alois Junior was also in favor of the move. His father's depression, with all its muted threat of more despotism, lived like a fist in the midst of the son's thoughts.

So it was settled. Alois' cart, driven by the hired man, would take the fourteen-year-old to Linz. Then he would travel by train to Weitra, where he could get on another cart that passed through Spital. The boy was gone, and a cloud of dark presentiment could lift.

In September, Adi and Angela began school in Fischlham, Angela in the fourth and most advanced grade for twelve-year-olds, Adi, at six, going to first grade.

His first school days proceeded through a bright and mellow September, a fine walk with his sister over hills and meadows. There was only one peril—a full-grown bull grazing in a fenced-in pasture. Depending on the bull's mood, they could choose to go around, or dare to cross the field. On most days, they did not dare.

Soon enough, Adi learned that it was unwise to shame Angela

when she was afraid. She knew how to pay him back. She could always inform him that he smelled awful. Sometimes it was his
breath; as often, his body odor.

Probably she did not know to what depth down in his quick-
beating chest these accusations entered, but deep they went, and
for good cause. They were true. He did have an odor—a touch of
sulphur and an unmistakable hint of something rotten—and of that
I may soon choose to speak. Such off-odor is one of the constant
problems besetting our clients. The Cudgels are quick to pick up
such a clue.

From Angela's point of view, it was simple. Whenever Adi was
teasing her, she would tell him he smelled. She did not really mind.
Bad smells did not bother her. She was accustomed to sour milk
and horse manure. A passing wind reeking of pig wallow from a
neighboring farm even brought real sorrow to her heart—poor
dead Rosig!

"What are you crying about now?" asked Adi. "You tell me how
I am bad-smelling and I am the one who should cry."

"Oh, shut up. It's not you I cry for."

That meant she was thinking of Rosig, and he did feel sad for
her. This was not because he had liked the sow so much (in fact, he
had been jealous of Angela's affection for the beast) but because he
did like his older sister. She was good most of the time. Besides,
she was the brightest girl inside the four walls of the one-room
schoolhouse, just as he was the smartest boy.

Depending on weather and the immediate needs of the neighboring farms for additional labor, there were sometimes fewer than
forty boys and girls, sometimes it was down to thirty, even twenty-
five, but the schoolroom contained seating divisions for these four
grades; and each child, first to fourth, six to twelve in age, was able
to listen to all that took place in every other class. This was a routine matter since there was only one teacher, a middle-aged lady,
Fräulein Werner, who had a large nose and wore spectacles.

Adi was soon able to follow the lessons for all four classes. His
introduction to German history came by way of the senior grade,

the fourth, where Angela and the others were studying the exceptional deeds of Charlemagne. An hour later, in first, Adi would be asked in company with the other beginners to decide which pictures of animals should be connected to printed words on a big card that Fräulein Werner would hold up. In the beginning, it was wondrous—all those wiggling letters that made a word. At first, the drawing vibrated in his eyes, but before long, it turned into no more than a puzzle. By the time he had reduced it to a solvable problem, he took care not to make the same mistake twice. Indeed, he soon grew bored waiting for others in his class to catch up. Then, he could barely wait for the lessons of the third, who were studying the geography of the Hapsburg domain, the Great Hapsburg Empire, as Fräulein Werner would always say. If permitted, he would have been ready to speak out to those students who were simpletons and could not find any of the places on the map that he had already noticed, Braunau and Linz being the first to catch his eye. Plus Passau, just across the Danube.

So, by the age of six, he was absorbing the lessons of the eight- and ten- and twelve-year-olds, and it pleased him that Angela was the brightest in her class. He could see the approval in Fräulein Werner's eyes each time they entered the room, but then, they were also the neatest brother and sister. That was Klara's doing, and that helped to put them up high in Fräulein Werner's favor.

His neat clothing did oblige him, however, to keep away from the other boys during recess. Soon enough he had to deal with a bully who kept daring him to wrestle.

"Are you crazy?" he would answer. "I am in my good clothes. My mother will kill me if I get them dirty." The daily wars of Passau had enriched his voice with just enough assurance to deter the other. But then that boy was nothing. If Adi could manage to live with Alois Junior, how much had he to fear from a fool like this, also named Klaus? It was big sister who bothered him with all this teasing.

## 8

These days Angela had come into her first period, and Klara was doing her best to allay the girl's distress. She could see that it was connected in Angela's mind with Rosig, who hemorrhaged blood all over her hams before she died.

To bring some calm to such outraged feelings, Klara spoke for the first time of intimate matters. She adored her stepdaughter. The twelve-year-old was by now the equal of a close friend, and so Klara spoke not only of this new condition, but went on at good length about odor in general, and its peculiar subtleties in nature. Odor was part of nature. Casting about for happy examples, she presented a piece of information Alois had provided her in passing. Once, Klara had asked how he could be sure his own bees (once he started his hives) would know how to find their home. As she understood it, he planned to acquire a couple of hive boxes, each a full colony in itself. There they would be, sitting side by side in the shade of the big oak near the house. "How will these thousands of bees know to which box they belong?" she asked.

He was sufficiently pleased by her curiosity to explain that he would paint each of his boxes a different color, green for one, sky blue for another, even pink, possibly, for a third. Bees, he explained, liked to return to dwellings that could be close to the color of the flowers whose nectar they brought back.

"But you tell me that each day these little creatures go to a different kind of flower. They are faithful only for this one day at a time to each variety of flower. Is that not so?"

"Yes." He wasn't certain he liked the conversation. Would he be able to answer all her questions without slipping and sliding into other matters?

"So it could be a flower of one color on one day, and another color is what they like tomorrow?"

"Yes."

"How do these bees not get mixed up?"

Yes, he was reluctant to tell her. It was not something to talk about. Not necessarily. Still, he chose to proceed. For Klara to be interested in apiculture might, on balance, be better for him than if she showed indifference. "Each Queen has her own odor," he informed Klara. "Since she will fertilize every cell in every comb and so puts tens of thousands of eggs into separate wax cells for their beginning in life, so she is certain to pass her own odor into each of her thousands of larvae, yes, her eggs, her future children."

"That is remarkable," said Klara. "How do you know this, Alois? So much you know."

"I have read about these discoveries in books," he said grudgingly.

"You have never smelled it yourself?"

"Do I look so stupid as to put my head into a hive in order to give a dozen bees the opportunity to fly up my nose?"

She began to laugh. In certain ways, she knew him well. He might read his books on the subject, but, at bottom, he did not like to admit that he had not learned the subject by way of his hands, his feet, his strength, his five good peasant senses.

Indeed, Alois had told her a little too much. Now she had to know more.

Before the conversation was over for the night, she actually prodded him into explaining how the Queen was fertilized. She was, after all, curious about any Queen who could give birth to so many thousands of children and still remain a Queen. There was such admiration in Alois' eye when he spoke of this. Everything depended on *the Queen*—the success of the hive, you could say.

So Alois did choose to lead Klara through a few descriptive steps. Given her evident excitement, he could sense it would be to his advantage on this night. She was clearly full of ardor at the thought of so female a creature, so tiny, so extraordinary.

He explained then that this young Queen, very much a virgin, not twenty days out of her own wax cell (which was no larger in width and depth than the eraser tip on the end of a new pencil), would, so soon as she emerged from that cell, be fed by Queen-bee nurses and Queen-bee attendants. Yet just three weeks from that first day, she would be ready to take her virgin flight out of the hive. Usually this would happen on the first warm day in May. Up she would lift into the heavens, flying higher than all but a few male bees who would attempt to follow.

"The ones who are called drones?" asked Klara.

"Yes, fat spoiled fellows. They jam their corner of the hive. They live to eat, and on a good day they fly around like fools. For the fun of it. They do not even bother to bring back pollen. It is only when this virgin Queen—who you might say is still a Princess—comes out for her first flight that they are able to justify their existence. On this day, they have been flying around waiting for her. They know she is coming. This Queen who flies so high, who is so beautiful compared to all her sisters, those thousands of worker bees, yes, workhorse females always looking for more nec- tar to bring back—those poor girls do not have full ovaries, so they go out and forage, except when they are attached to other duties for the hive. Clean-up duties. Chores. But this Queen, she is differ- ent, still a virgin, she is not yet really a Queen, more, as I say, a Princess. Then, she chooses to fly so high that only a few of these drones can follow. It comes down to two drones, to one, but, oh, this last strong one, he reaches her, he puts what he has, yes, you know what I mean, his very own organ which he has kept inside himself until now but suddenly it comes out, springs up, you could say, into, yes, yes, springs into—call it her vagina—why not? It is so, and she takes it all in even as they are up in the air so high, just the two of them."

"It is a wonder," said Klara. Her eyes had begun to shine. She actually said, "A miracle of love."

"No, not exactly," said Alois. At this moment, he did not know how to continue. If he said too much, he could spoil what he was looking for on this night. Still, his shrewd side was ready to speak, and he knew, yes, the best was most likely to come from telling it all.

"This drone," he said, "this one good brave drone, sticks it in so far, which is exactly what nature demands, we must suppose, that then he cannot get it back."

"What?"

"No! *Donnerwetter*, he can't pull out! The Queen has hooks, or something of the kind, very sharp hooks, and that keeps him there. She likes him there. He is stuck. When he does insist, when he has to pull away, you won't believe it, his good organ is ripped right out of him. He is obliged to leave it behind. His manhood! Gone. All gone."

"And him? What happens then? To him?"

"Oh, he dies. He is gone. He falls to earth."

"The poor creature," she said. But she could not help it. Against her will, Klara's mouth pulled into a smirk, then slipped over to a smile. Once begun, she had to laugh. Then she could not stop. Never before had Alois heard her laugh so long.

"What a life," she finally said, and Alois had been right to tell her. She was over six months into her pregnancy, but they made love that night. Alois had known more than one woman who could even give you a good piece of the real business in that very last week before she would pop out someone else's baby. But that had hardly been the case with Klara. On this night, however, she was different. It was equal to her best.

Of course, he certainly did not go on to tell her of two other things. The first was that the Queen was perfectly capable of having other lovers after that first fabulous flight. Over the next few weeks and into June, she could have five or six more lovers. That would store more semen in her ovaries, enough to lay thousands, then tens of thousands of eggs, one each for every cell among those thousands of cells, and she would continue to do so until cold

weather came. Then this cycle could be repeated each spring for
the next three years to come. All that wealth of impregnation derived from no more than five or six copulations! This meant that
for the rest of her life, the Queen would have no more to do with
drones but would be feeding honey and pollen to the pupae she
had created while her court, her worker females, followed her with
devotion, capping the cells of larvae with a mysterious wax substance they were able to make from the pollen of the May flowers,
a wax that no chemist could duplicate in the laboratory. No, he did
not describe how devotedly the Queen would have to work for the
rest of her life, and he certainly did not tell Klara that when mating season was done, these female worker bees would evict the
drones from the hive. When it came to dealing with the laziest
bums who would not stir, the worker bees would sting the drones
to death. (Nor did the worker bees lose their stinger on such occasions. The belly of a drone was softer than human skin.) After the
slaughter, these same worker bees would sweep the carcasses out of
the hive. Nor did he speak of other complications. There was always a tendency, once real warm weather began, for as much as half
of the colony to be ready to swarm, that is, to fly away, desert the
hive, go back to the way they used to live in the hole of a tree. You
could lose your profit in a hurry. Nor did he tell her of Princesses
who were often extinguished by the court of bees who surrounded
the Queen. He left such details alone. It was better that Klara
should remain sympathetic to what would be his oncoming enterprise.

Klara had not only been engrossed by what he told her that
night, but now thought it might divert Angela from her woes, and
so decided to tell her about the wrenching end of the brave drone
who did succeed in reaching the Queen. This time, Klara had company in her laughter. They carried on as if they were both of the
same age, and as Klara divulged more and more of what she had
learned from Alois, the topic turned not only to odor, but to the exceptional power of the Queen. There she was, this creature, hardly
larger than her own nursing bees and certainly smaller than any

drone. Nonetheless, she had the power to impregnate the air of the hive and the thousands who dwelt within it. All of them would know their own hive, since they all smelled the same. "It is," said Klara, full of a new set of giggles, "as if all Russian men and women have one kind of awful aroma, and those Polish oafs another. Maybe there is a good decent smell of tea for the English, and we Austrians, we have to be something special, we are warm like strudel." Again, she had Angela full of giggles. "And the French, yes, a shameless ugly scent. So harsh! Worse than rotten onions and old gravy. Italians—nothing but garlic." They were hugging each other by now. "Maybe the very worst, the Bohemians. I shouldn't describe them. Stinking old cabbage."

They wiped their eyes. Adi, hearing their laughter, came to join them. He was annoyed when they explained nothing, merely kept laughing at the sound of each country.

All this talk of good and bad smells gave a special tingle to Angela's nose. In school, she was now most aware of Fräulein Werner, with all her talcum powder, and then there was her own little Adi. He was absolutely smelly at times, especially when he ran up and down too many hills. She was always coaxing him to use more soap, or on those nights once a week when Klara boiled enough water for each of them to bathe in the big washtub, Angela would insist on lathering his back and his armpits before returning the bar of soap to him. Then, with a wholly mischievous grin—"You have the soap now, so put it where it can do some work, you careless boy."

Adi would scream with anger at such incivility, and made certain to be loud enough for Klara to come running in. Yet he would not repeat a word to his mother. He was in turmoil. Did he smell as bad as Angela kept saying, or was his sister crazy? Who could know? He could barely sniff a thing on himself.

Angela, however, would begin to brood once again on the death of Rosig. The prize sow had indeed been full of a strong odor, not unlike Adi at his worst, or was it Rosig at her worst?—enough! Angela began to cry for both, the boy and the pig together. Full of remorse for teasing him, she tried to make amends by telling him a few of the wonderful secrets Klara had told her, all of this new knowledge about bees, and on many a morning as the two walked to school, she would take up the topic again—her head was so full of what she had been told that Adi's imagination was soon inflamed by the mysteries of the Queen.

Ever since they had come to the farm in April, he had been most aware of the nearness of bees. In May and June, there had been hours in full daylight when the sky was full of tiny lights, glints of light whipping about, flying in so many directions. His mother was always warning him that he must not try to touch any such tiny creature should he see one on a flower. Worse, he must never dare to kill one. That same bee could give him something to remember! Then one fine morning in July, Edmund got stung and couldn't stop screaming for the longest time. So Adolf, in his turn, had been most respectful of the perils of their presence.

Now, however, to hear that the Queen shared her odor with every bee in the hive, yes, that did excite his thoughts.

The night after he heard that his father might be going to talk to a neighbor about purchasing what Alois called "the first materials"—an announcement he made on a Saturday evening at dinner—Adi had a vivid dream. He saw an army of bees flying in circles above the farm. Standing near their house was an old man who was dressed differently from anyone Adi had ever seen. His shirt remained outside his pants and came to his knees, and he wore an old knit wool hat over his white hair, a hat as long as a stocking. It hung half down his back. He was not short, but he still looked like a dwarf because he was bent over. In this dream, Adi knew his name. The man was called *Der Alte*, and the boy woke up on Sunday morning to learn that his father was actually going to visit a beekeeper named Der Alte.

How could he not ask his father if he could go along? Alois was surprised, then pleased. Every Sunday until now, Klara was picked up by another farm couple in their wagon to go to Sunday Mass in Fischlham's small chapel. She would travel with the three children, even as Alois stayed at the farm. "In truth, in good conscience, I cannot go," he would tell her, and he would be left alone to walk his fields. This morning, therefore, he was all the more pleased that Adi asked to join him.

I can say that I was directly instrumental in shaping the boy's dream. It had been my first active participation with the family since the night I entered Alois' mind just after his beer-soaked sermon in Linz about the beauties and wonders of apiculture.

Now I feel that I must address the reader again on an unappetizing matter. It does concern Adi's bad smell.

# 9

It is curious, yet, after all, not so curious that few matters concerning men and women are so uncomfortable to discuss as bad odor. I will add that humans who labor for the Maestro can hardly avoid that libel.

Enough! Stinks do not make for happy devils. At this time, approaching the end of the nineteenth century, our problems could often be traced to one phenomenon. Many human beings in whom we invested found it necessary to remain exceptionally fastidious in their personal habits. Otherwise, they would at varying times smell rank enough to arouse distrust.

How this condition began, I cannot say. My recollection of earlier eras is highly imperfect and usually is no more available to me than the stunted instinct a human might have of previous incarnations. It is probably not in the Maestro's interest to have us know any more than we need to know. Rather, we are asked to deal with problems directly before us. We do not have to call, after all, upon Judas or Bluebeard or Attila the Hun to encourage a drunken client to go for one more tot of booze. In consequence, we can have almost no definitive insight into the beginning of the war between the Dummkopf and the Evil One. Whether they were both gods or, as Milton proposed, the contest was between God and an angel as important as Lucifer, is beyond my province. Nor can we dismiss the possibility that the Dummkopf, in early command (and disarray) of this earth and this solar system, may have been in sufficient difficulty to address Himself to higher powers out in the galaxies. It is possible that the Maestro was sent here by those greater powers because they were dissatisfied with the progress of the D.K. Evolution had already enmeshed itself in numerous cul-de-sacs. Nonetheless, these matters can only remain questions for me.

Yet, if I must offer some conjecture as to what might have taken place during the aeons of time already consumed, I have to assume that the D.K. is Creator of the world of weather, flora, fauna, and all human beings, and that evolution was His laboratory—the signs of His Folly as well as of His Genius are to be found among the myriad of His creations, and the obstacles He encountered. One needs only to think of the interminable ages that passed before He could induce a few of His creatures to fly. Add to this the breadth and bulk of His earthbound and marine species, or the godly hopes that went, for example, into the brontosaurus (only to discover that this particular overenlarged beast was simply too big to survive— that is one failure). Leave it at that. The Creator had His relative successes and His abysmal failures. While it must be admitted that He never gave up, even if He was not always in firm control of the earth He had fashioned, it is also incontestable that earthquakes and ice ages brought many an interruption to His experiments and savaged many of His pursuits. Why? Because He had incorrectly designed this globe of earth in the first place.

Of one relatively small matter I am certain: By the time His most ambitious concept, men and women, had entered existence, there came a shift in the importance of odor. Concerning that, I believe I have some rudiments to offer. It is that in the long-gone era of primitive man, odor must have been one of the Creator's assets. How could He not have used its signals to aid the development of many species? In large part, humans were often drawn to one another or repelled by the messages that reached the nose. So simple and elegant a solution. Presumably their smells were ready to reveal the depth of each creature's courage, perseverance, fear, treachery, shame, loyalty, and—not least—their determination to propagate. Odor enabled the D.K. to take creative steps in evolution without having to oversee each and every mating.

I think by the time our Maestro was ready to contest His progress, the Lord could no longer believe in Himself as All-Good and All-Powerful. The presence of a colleague (probably unwanted in the first place) had to reduce His sense of His own stature. So the D.K. began to search for a method whereby His Cudgels could determine which men, women, and children had gone over to the adversary. Indeed, I would propose that the D.K. was able to mark each of our clients with a touch of condign odor, a process chosen for its simplicity and relative lack of cost. From the Middle Ages on, therefore, our Maestro had contested this obstacle to his intentions by encouraging many of his alchemists to develop perfumes whose subtleties became a means whereby rotten odors could be topped with sweeter, earthier, more untraceable, and finally more appealing fragrances, even exotic in their hint of a bit of reek beneath the bouquet. (It is, for example, impossible to keep track of the promiscuity of court life in France during the reign of Louis XIV without pondering these royal redolences, these carnal aromas so full of camouflage. They proved a boon to all of our clients who were rich enough to afford good perfumes.)

By the end of the Enlightenment, matters had altered once more. Soaps, developed by us, were able to nullify mephitic aromas. By the twentieth century the increasing erasure of human odor contributed vitally to our progress. Bathtubs, cleansing oils, and the development of plumbing all came into being, due in large part to the support we gave to such entrepreneurs.

Toward the end of the twentieth century, God's dependence on unpleasant personal odor as a means of warning His Cudgels that our clients were near had been rendered obsolete. Deodorants dominated the day. By now, in the twenty-first century, it is rare to find a husband or wife who possesses much sense of the odor of their closest partner. (This is certainly true in the more developed nations.) The loss of such cognitive power has not only lessened the dominance of the D.K. but has given impetus to us.

Back, however, toward the end of the nineteenth century, obliteration of human odor was not nearly so complete, and the meeting between Alois, Adi, and Der Alte was characterized by a curious but immediate intimacy between the boy and the old man. In part, indeed, it was aromatic.

But I must not ignore the walk to Der Alte's farm. On the way, Alois had a real conversation with his son for the first time.

# BOOK VII

## DER ALTE

### AND

## THE BEES

# 1

I will speak first, however, of the dream I installed in Adi's sleep. That was on the Saturday night which preceded Alois' meeting with the beekeeper on Sunday, and the dream was delivered in response to a direct order from the Maestro. I will add that creating a dream, especially one that has no connection to the dreamer's previous experience, is not routine. While we can, on special occasions, insert whole scenarios into our client's sleep, it is also true that dream-works produced ex nihilo make serious inroads on our budget. It certainly demands disproportionate outlays of Time!

Moreover, when the client is young, there is risk involved. Cudgels who might be involved with the client can be more than troublesome if they become aware of what we are attempting. Delicate manipulations calculated to alter future reactions in a subject's psyche should not be undertaken under battlefield conditions. Few people prosper from a nightmare.

It has been my experience that the installation of dreams that are as intense as nocturnal visions can deliver many desired effects, but success is best when one can proceed in small steps over many a night in order not to arouse the Cudgels. Count on it, the angels react with fury to any dream we initiate. This has been true from the commencement of human existence. The D.K. feels it is paramount for Him to command all dreams. Looking to control those primates whom He was inspiring to become humans, He inserted hallucinations into their sleep, and these proved essential. They sped up the process.

Much later, during what the Maestro calls the Jehovah Era

(which is—forgive these rough historical estimates—from 1200 B.C. to the advent of Jesus Christ), the D.K. disbursed a host of awards and punishments (occasionally by way of miracles, but more often through dreams). He would succeed in arousing visions in prophets and plebeians alike. Thereby, He could drive His wards on many a chosen route, often, I suspect, on not much more than an imperious whim.

Our entrance, however, into the developing life of humankind reduced such powers. No longer could Jehovah employ dreams so effectively. Now, given our copious use of such a medium, dreams rarely appear as visions. Rather, they invade sleep as jagged, broken-backed narratives. Intrusions from one side charge into the aims of the other.

The D.K.'s once-imperious use of dreams has, therefore, been nullified. Rarely can His commands be delivered forthrightly any longer. Instead, the modern nocturnal episode provides the sleeper with a hint of oncoming disturbances. If a trusted friend is likely to prove treacherous in the near future, a dream can alert one to such a possibility. On the other hand, if it is the dreamer who is ready to betray a close friend, the consequences of such an act can be dramatized by way of an imaginary scenario. Thereby, the D.K. has found a means to guide some of His human beings. The mock situations created by the dream may not be wholly comprehensible, but they do test the subject's ability to withstand intense anxiety. Even when a dream is incompletely interpreted, the subject does retain some clouded awareness of how he or she possesses less courage, less loyalty, less devotion, less love, or less health than previously assumed. The dream can now serve as a species of imperfect protective system to warn a man or woman away from situations they cannot dominate or even tolerate.

To the degree, however, that we are able to interfere with real impact, the average dream becomes a whirligig, a strew, a chaos left by the melee between the Cudgels and ourselves.

So the task of creating a clear dream for a child required special attention. As I have remarked, the Maestro did not, for the most

part, encourage such ventures with children. It will be recalled that
when the Hitler family made their move from Passau, I was instructed to cease paying attention to little Adolf. He and his family
would now be monitored via milk runs by my assistants. Except for
the sole occasion when I had slipped into Alois' brain long enough
to delve into his fascination with beekeeping, I had been working
with other clients in that region of Austria. The information about
the Hitlers of Hafeld provided by my assistants had proved ade-
quate.

Now a direct communication from the Maestro had arrived—I
was to implant a particular dream into the head of our six-year-old.
*Etch* was the salient verb. "I want you," he said, "to etch Adi's brain
with a permanent notion. You can probably gain open entrance.
We have been quiescent in that direction for so long that I expect
no interference from the Cudgels."

# 2

The act itself took no more than a few minutes, but the prepa-
ration had not been simple. *Etch*, I will repeat, was the opera-
tive word. A fixed notion, once successfully installed, can attach the
client closely to us. But etching is not there for any devil to practice. It must be done with incisive strokes. Misapplied, it can unbal-
ance the recipient.

I will go so far as to say that on this occasion, I was deft. Given
the knowledge absorbed from the milk runs, I knew that Alois
would soon be visiting this neighboring beekeeper, Der Alte, also
known as *Der alte Zauberer*—"the Old Sorcerer." Or such was the
name given him by neighboring peasants.

The term was an exaggeration. This old man was a hermit and

highly eccentric. Provoked, he could be as mean as a winter wind, but on special occasions he might seem as agreeable as any other purportedly warm old fellow. The peasants in Hafeld, having known him for decades, knew better. Nonetheless, he was the only apiculturist within a day's walk in any direction and commanded more than a little erudition about beekeeping.

What was most comfortable about Der Alte was that he had belonged to us for decades. In effect, he was an old pensioner. Moreover, he and Adi would be kin in odor, and so were likely to be unoffended by each other. The magnetic thrust of the dream soon suggested itself. Before they met, I would etch the boy's mind with a clear image of Der Alte.

As a matter of style, when it comes to dream-work, I have always been inclined to avoid baroque virtuosities. Modest scenarios are usually more effective. In this case, I satisfied myself by producing as close a presentation of Der Alte's face and voice as I could manage before placing him in Adi's dream. For the setting, I used an image of one of the two rooms of the old man's hut, and made the yard visible through the window. The action of the dream could not have been more direct. As Der Alte led them inside his quarters, he fed Adi a spoonful of honey. I made certain the taste was exquisite on the boy's tongue. Adi awakened with wet pajamas from navel to knee and a whole sense of happiness. Stripping his wet night-clothing, a not-unusual event, he went back into slumber, replaying the dream with his own small variations, looking to taste the honey again. In his mind, he was certain that he would soon meet Der Alte, and this emboldened him to ask his father to take him along next morning. Alois, as I have remarked, was pleased.

Their conversation on the walk to the Sorcerer's house is yet to be recounted but I will choose to delay that long enough to say a little more about the Maestro's concept of etching. For example, we now knew that when Adi met Der Alte on this Sunday, he would feel a new sense of personal importance, for he would believe he had the power to peer into the future. Indeed, I balanced both sides of this oncoming relation, since I also instructed Der Alte to give the boy a taste of his finest honey, and to do it directly on meeting him.

Be it said again, this man, Magnus Rudiger, spoken of as *Der alte Zauberer*, was in fact not much of an old sorcerer. His curses were neither remarkable nor effective. Whenever a sense of dread came to him from forces he could not name (usually from one or another branch of the Cudgels) he thought it was sufficient to lay a circle of salt around the table where he sat by himself in the kitchen. That, for all its picayune effect, was more effective at nudging *us* away than the Cudgels. Such minor clients can become an annoyance when they grow old.

Still, no neighbor was in a hurry to attack his self-esteem. Indeed, by way of his dress, his odor, his resonant, even reverberating, voice, and his compendious knowledge of bees, he did suggest that he was a magician. In this manner, he was able to safeguard his pride. On the other hand, he had little power to resist our occasional employment of him.

No surprise, then, that Adi, etched by the dream, was marked by the visit. His expectation that he would often be able to picture in advance people he had not yet met would become an asset for us.

We would exercise this device often during Adolf Hitler's service as an Army courier over the two years and more when he had to carry messages up to the trenches, then work his way back to Regimental Headquarters. Since his duties incurred real danger, his belief that he could anticipate the future proved of no small assistance to his courage. Too soon to speak of that, however. His experiences as a soldier—a most complex amalgam of our magic, and his desperation and dedication—remain eighteen years away. For now, I will leave this discussion of dream-etching until it is necessary to discuss the practice again.

Rather, I will follow the conversation he had with his father on the walk to see *Der alte Zauberer*. Alois, of course, did most of the talking, and was anticipating the meeting with no great confidence. It was never routine for Alois to encounter a man who knew more about a subject than himself.

As they strode along at a good pace, Alois proceeded to supply Adi's head with so many new names and thoughts that before long the boy was twice breathless. He did not dare to lag behind by a step or a word. In turn, Alois, rarely in the habit of spending time or thought on this little Adolf, was a hint short of breath himself. Over the years, he had packed enough rheumatism into his knees and enough smoke into his lungs to move as a rule with more deliberation. But now the discovery that he could actually talk to the boy offered a stimulus to his legs. It was not Alois' habit to harbor many sentiments toward his younger children, indeed, he never found fatherhood a subject of personal interest until Alois Junior and Angela worked with him on the farm. Now, most unexpectedly, he did feel a sense of something not ordinary coming to him from this little one.

Adi, in his turn, was more than excited. To be in the *company* of his father! He had barely learned to spell but Alois stood before his eyes as MEIN VATER. Just so large was his recognition of the immanence of the heavy man beside him. Alois aroused in him the same kind of awe that came over the expression of his mother when she would speak of *der gute Gott*.

How the boy wanted to please Alois! At the start of the walk, their mutual silence had been formidable, and it remained so until Adi found the words. "Have there always been bees?" he asked at last. It was a simple question but fortuitous.

"Yes. Always. Bees," Alois amended, "have been on our fine earth for a long time."

"They go very far back, Father?"

Alois gave him an encouraging pat on the nape of his neck. The boy's obvious desire to keep the conversation in flow now served to activate Alois' funds of exposition. "Yes, far back. Maybe even for a longer time than us. And there has never been a day when we didn't look to steal their honey." He laughed. "Back in the time of the Bronze Age, already we were eating honey, yes, and I can say for certain that I have seen old drawings in glass cases right there in the old Linz museum, going back into the Middle Ages, that show how beekeeping had already become a serious activity. Although wild, very wild then."

Despite his touch of rheumatism, Alois was certainly walking fast. Adi's breath was now seizing his lungs in a unique mixture of happy fervor at the fact of the conversation itself and the desperation that he might not be able to keep walking (half running) at his father's pace. So many unfamiliar words were coming into his mind at once. This past August, while he stood under the walnut tree nearest their farmhouse, a gale of wind came by like the crack of a whip, whereupon three walnuts, hard as stone, had pelted his head with such authority that he did not even dare to cry—it was as if the walnuts told him to be silent. Now he was buffeted by "the Bronze Age," and next, "the Middle Ages"—maybe he had heard "Middle Ages" before. He felt as if he might know it. Charlemagne, maybe. No question of stopping to ask—he strode along as fast as he could, the air burning in his lungs.

"They had," said Alois, "no hives in the Middle Ages. They had to go out hunting to where they could find a swarm of bees gathered together. Where? In hollow trees—where else? Locate such a tree, and then grab what you can of the honey before the bees sting your head off. That was how good men must have done it then. Only, that was not enough. They also had to scoop up the wax. This beeswax was just as important. With beeswax, you could have light for your hut. Every night. Candles! But, oh, they had to pay. So many bites. Then along would come their Duke or their Baron. If he heard about your honey, you had to pay up. A good share he took. Imagine. What do you think he gave you back?—a bow, a nice strong crossbow. Why? Because the bears in the forest were also looking for honey. Think how crazy those bees must have gotten when a bear stuck his nose right in to lap up their hive. It is one thing to sting a man, but how do you stop a bear? A bear with his thick skin! They had to go for the eyes. It didn't matter. The bear would still come looking. So a man needed a crossbow—to kill the bear. Not so easy to go near honey if the bear got there first, but you could have compensation. Sometimes you had bear meat. Once in a while, you had bear meat *and* honey."

By now, Adi's breath was on fire. Their path was passing through a small wood, and he was on the lookout for a bear. One more fear to lay on the tumult in his lungs.

"Sometimes," said Alois, "on a cold day this time of year a man would find a tree ready to fall, a dead tree with a big hollow in it, and a swarm of bees clustered right there in the hollow, trying to stay warm against the cold. Well, an enterprising fellow might dare to take the tree down. He would have to do it carefully. Don't stir up too much! He would have to do it in the evening, when bees are more quiet, especially when it is cold, and then he and his son, or maybe his brother, would carry the tree back near their hut, where they could manage to extract the rest of the honey."

"What about the bears? Would they come?"

"Yes. The kind of man we're talking about had to be ready to kill the first bear and hang him up near the bees. That kept other bears away. This is exactly how it began. But now, what is it? What has it become? A hobby! A little risky, maybe, but profitable."

"Hobby," the boy repeated—another new word.

"Soon," said Alois, "it will be a business."

They walked in silence. *Das Steckenpferd* was how Alois had put it—a horse-on-a-stick, a plaything, a hobby. Soon it would be a business, he had said. The boy was confused. Their rapid pace was now pinching his breath past the point where he could ask even one more question.

Abruptly, Alois stopped. He had become aware at last of his

son's discomfort. "Come," he said, "you sit down." He pointed to a rock, then sat next to him on another rock. Only then did he feel the pain in his own knees.

"You must understand," he said, "this beekeeping will not be fairy tales for us. Honey is sweet, but bees are not always so sweet. Sometimes they are cruel to each other. Very cruel. Do you know why?"

"No," said Adi. His eyes were, however, alight. "Please, you must tell me why, Father."

"Because they obey one law. It is so clear to them. This law says: Our colony must survive. So nobody can dare to be lazy. Not inside this hive of bees." He paused. "Nobody, except for the drones. They are there to serve their one good purpose. But then it's all over for them. They are gone. Goodbye."

"Are they killed?" The boy knew the answer.

"Of course. All of those drones. Once a year, right about now— just after summer, they are gotten rid of. No charity." He began to laugh again. "In the home of the bees, there are no good Christians. No charity whatsoever. You will not find one bee in any hive who is too weak to work. That is because they get rid of cripples early. They obey one law and it sits on top of everything."

But as they rested, Alois drew back into silence. He was feeling some dread. The neighboring peasants had praised Der Alte, they had echoed each other concerning his vast knowledge of this subject of apiculture. Yet Alois could hear no allegiance to the man himself. Now he was afraid of being cheated by Der Alte.

This was but one hint of his fear. If the attractive location of the farm rather than the land had been his good reason to purchase, he did not wish to be half-cheated again. Indeed, he had kept putting off the decision to go into beekeeping. Now August was lost. It might even be too late to start a winter colony. He must buy, and buy soon. He might even have to pay an unnatural price. He certainly did not enjoy the thought of these peasants laughing at him, but that was not his prime uneasiness. He could not quite admit it to himself, but the last time he had been in the bee business, he had

gone at it as a horse-on-a-stick, just one hive, a skep he kept in a little town at walking distance from Braunau, a place he could go to
in the evening as a respite from the tavern and his fellow officers,
or visit on Sunday in order not to have to watch everyone going to
church. But then he had a near disaster. On a given Sunday, because of no mistake he could recognize, he had been stung quickly
and repeatedly by so many infuriated bees that he decided afterward he must have been poking about in the Queen's quarters.
Who could tell with a skep? Straw has so little shape! He realized
his ignorance of the real stuff. In the course of working with that
straw hive, he had been open to ambush.

But he knew. He could tell. He was preparing in advance to recount to this man, Der Alte, that he had once taken many stings on
his hands and his knees and that the event had actually proved beneficial to the stiffness in his joints. For certain, he felt ready to impress Der Alte with his understanding of bee venom. He would
speak of the degree to which diseases in ancient Egypt and Greece
had even been treated in that manner. He would speak of the Romans and the Greeks, Pliny and Galen. Great doctors. They knew
how to make ointments from bee venom and honey. Charlemagne
and Ivan the Terrible could also be cited. He would speak of these
monarchs' afflictions of the joints and how they had had such pain
eliminated, or so it was reputed, by bee stings.

But was he really prepared to enter such a conversation with
Der Alte? When you got down to it, this might not be the correct
step to take. What if Der Alte happened to be more knowledgeable
on this matter than himself?

# 4

As I have indicated, Der Alte has been one of ours. I have called him a pensioner, and that is also accurate. Over recent years, we hardly used him, and any benefits he received from us were small. From time to time, we offered a new insight to one of his old perceptions, a species of gift-giving practiced by angels and demons alike to revive the faded confidence of the client's mind. In return, we expected to be obeyed. Certainly, the old doctor was there with dispatch to put a spoonful of exquisite honey on Adi's tongue even as father and son came through the door.

Now, I may yet refer occasionally to Der Alte as Herr Doktor, but I considered it one of his more unseemly vanities. He would insist that he was an honored and learned university graduate. I have heard him refer on separate occasions to his years at Heidelberg, Leipzig, Göttingen, Vienna, Salzburg, and Berlin, none of whose eminent universities he attended. Indeed, only Heidelberg and Göttingen ever saw him, and that was for a brief visit. Our old and learned doctor was a fraud, a half-Jewish Pole of no certified higher education, who, nonetheless, much through his own efforts, had acquired some of the verbal skills and superior manner of a tried-and-true Doctor of Philosophy. If he had chosen in his old age to look like a confirmed drunk, an odd choice, since in fact he did not drink, he was attracted all the same to many of the slovenly habits of old sots. His clothes were filthy. Even his long woolen cap managed to be full of soup stains (for he wiped his mouth with the tail of it) and his white beard was discolored with nicotine. He not only smelled of the unhappy scents we look to reduce in our clients but, to put no pretty word on it, was incontinent. Even his furnishings, let alone his garments, retained the harsh persona of old urine.

Nonetheless, he was striking. That long stocking cap which he wore even indoors in summer did serve some devoted image of himself as a court jester. And indeed, there was an old cape full of faded bright colors, a fool's motley. One could hardly expect him to be impressive in his person, yet he was. Undeniably. His eyes were extraordinary, as blue as the coldest skies of the north, yet full of lights that offered a clue to many a trick he had learned.

For forty years Alois had encountered hundreds of people a day, and so was hardly to be surprised by an unorthodox appearance. Moreover, he had developed an ability to capture the first moment in just about every passing exchange. Travelers were not prepared for the phenomenon of meeting a Customs official who possessed such a degree of authority, and few were prepared for the intelligence that stood out in his immediate glance. "Try to fool me—you will fail!" was the unmistakable sentiment offered by his eyes.

This was a prime reason for my direction to Der Alte that he must meet the father and son at the door with a spoonful of honey, and insert it without leave into the boy's mouth. Whatever Alois had been preparing for, it could hardly have been this. So rude. So gracious. And both at once! Nothing was offered to Alois but a superior smile from Der Alte, as if his piss-soaked den, worse than an abode of fifteen cats, was nonetheless Der Alte's realm and he was happy in it and, I may as well add, diabolically unembarrassed.

Der Alte won the boy on the instant. It took no more than this one move placed on top of my dream-etching. Adi's eyes were alive with the same intensity of admiration that Alois had been receiving from his son during their walk together.

They sat down. The old man fussed a little (albeit most skillfully) at preparing tea. To Alois' further discomfort, the procedure was courtly. A very old gentleman, or even a very old lady, might have been demonstrating to an unsophisticated visitor the putative elegance of a tea ceremony.

All the same, I did not approve of Der Alte. For all his gifts, he

had never accomplished much for us, not as much as I had anticipated. For a time I had expected he would become one of my prize
clients. He certainly did not have to end as a bizarre, impossibly
smelly hermit with an immense reputation for dealing with hives of
bees in a pretty little corner of Austria, a country already filled with
pretty little corners. I had lost standing with the Maestro by remarking decades ago that I saw promise in this young half-Polish,
half-Jewish Magnus. Of course, he was at that time a satyr with the
ladies. As far as I was concerned, he had turned by now into a client
who settled for too little.

Der Alte took his tea in little sips, Alois in three scalding gulps.
That enabled his host to pour him a quick second cup (a most subtle reproof). Only then did they begin to talk about the purpose of
the visit. Alois did begin by citing Pliny and Galen, then Charlemagne and Ivan the Terrible. He spoke in a most moving manner
of the afflictions of the two great monarchs and the dedication of
Pliny and Galen—two medical geniuses who had known how to
deal with ailments so grievous that others could find no cure. It was
not, he would vouchsafe, that he, personally, had suffered inhu-
manly from gout or from rheumatism, but he had indeed received
a few intimations that there could be future miseries. Nonetheless,
he had learned a great deal on one particular occasion when he had
been prey to an unprecedented attack, "just the one time, but with
many bites to the knees which subsequently provided considerable
easement against the early pains of rheumatism. I admit that I
would have given much to be a medical scientist, for then I could
have begun research on just this subject. I am even sufficiently confident of myself to believe I would probably have made significant
discoveries."

"Just so," said Der Alte, "you might, you might very well have
done just that. Because, dear sir, what you at the time believed was
there to be discovered had been detected by no less a figure than
Dr. Likomsky back in 1864, thirty-one years ago when you were
still a young man, and I might also mention Herr Dr. Terc, who put
the crowning cap on what could have been your thesis. Yes! Herr

Dr. Terc came forth with serious chemical studies on the nature of bee venom and its as-yet-undeveloped potential for precisely these valuable cures. Rheumatism and gout might both be seen by now as ailments of the past if not for the innumerable obstacles that stand in the way of administering treatment. We are still looking for more precise positioning of the bee sting onto the affected body. It is rumored that the Chinese"—now with a melting look designed to add to the mutual delight that existed already between him and the boy, he added, "the Chinese who live on the other side of the earth from us. Have you heard?" he asked.

Adi nodded solemnly. He had heard of the Chinese, heard of them in his one-room schoolhouse during the hour when Fräulein Werner instructed the geography class on the specific placement of India and China upon the great continent of Asia.

"Yes, in that far-off near-mythical land, esteemed Finance-Watch Chief Officer Herr Hitler, it is said that some Chinese can employ the power to puncture possessed by sharp needles in order to alleviate gout, an excellent solution I would think, since the least attractive aspect of my beloved bees is their eagerness to sting, yes, we love them for their honey, but not necessarily for their haste to provoke us even as they surrender their lives."

Alois sensed that he would do well to leave this topic. The tea had left a penetrating aroma in his nostrils which, to his surprise, was compatible with the urine. Needless to say, he would have preferred a good swallow of beer to pump a few of his prepared remarks up into more forceful delivery, but as of now, this conversation did belong to Der Alte. At what length he went on!

"I cannot," he remarked, "begin to call you my good friend as yet. For I do not know you. Except, of course, by way of your fine reputation. Word of your former most respected position precedes our meeting.

"Your father," he now said to Adi, "is well regarded by all, but"—and he was now back, once more, to Alois—"I am still ready to call you my friend because I feel in myself an imperative to counsel you, for, oh, I must say, there is, dear sir, so much to learn about these bees and their good keeping." He sighed with a sound of woe physically intimidating in its resonance.

"Let me note that I would not wish in any manner to impose on your pride." He stopped. Since a man's pride was involved, he would proceed no further without a *laissez-passer.*

"No, tell me, good Doctor, you must tell me what you think," said Alois, his voice normal (to the degree he could command it) but his nostrils were near to quivering. He hardly knew if he was at the onset of an intolerable sense of woe or whether a true burden was about to be lifted. What could be this imposition on his pride?

"Given your gracious permission, I would say that I must caution you about your honorable and honest desire to enter the endless vagaries of apiculture. It is, you see, a vocation." He nodded. He turned again to Adi as if the boy was one more equal, yes, all three sitting there quite alike in implicit stature. "You, little fellow," Der Alte said. "You, who look so smart, are you smart enough to know what a vocation might be?"

"No," said Adi, "but maybe I do. Yes. Almost."

"You do. You know it even before you are aware that you know it. That is the first sign of a truly intelligent person, not so?" Der Alte's voice vibrated into the tender pit of Adi's stomach.

"A vocation," said Der Alte, "is not something you do because others tell you that this is what you must do. Not so. With a vocation, there is no choice. You give all that you have to doing whatever has become important to you. 'Yes,' says the vocation, 'you must do it.' "

"I would not wish to dispute your learned words," said Alois, "no, I do not wish to commence a dispute, but surely one can keep a hive without building a monastery. For myself, I foresee no more than a modest investment for a retired man like myself."

"Dear sir, it cannot and will not ever be that way," said Der Alte. "That much I can promise a strong person like yourself. Heartbreak or happiness. Nothing between." He nodded with all the profundity of the decades he had continued to present himself as a great and learned doctor. "Herr Hitler, I cannot allow you to consider such a project until you are made fully aware of the risks that await you, the diseases and mortal enemies that surround our delicate sweet-seeking bees. After all, the honey they make is to the world of nature an exact equivalent of gold. So many of the creatures of nature, large and small, are jealous of the life of these remarkable little creatures who are not only able to make honey but dwell constantly amidst that golden and intoxicating presence. In consequence, honeybees are hated. They are pursued and entrapped. I can inform you of one species of spider who is evil, nothing less. *Die Krabbenspinne*, it is called. So soon as it finds a promising flower, this creature ensconces itself deep within the small perfumed cavern of the bloom. There the crab spider waits. I would suppose he even feels at home. He proceeds to activate the scent of this flower by stirring about in those blessed folds of the corolla; soon, the spider's own awful odor is concealed by the intoxicating elixir of the petals. What then? The crab spider waits. When the forager bee, our sweet hardworking female with its undeveloped ovaries—only the Queen, as we know, is completely in possession of that most mysterious avatar of female existence!—*ach*, these other females are there to work for the length of their short lives. So here, contemplate this poor little forager. Our honeybee smells the inimitable redolence of the flower's cavern. She enters, full of greed, to pick up her lusty store of nectar and pollen and, at once, she is done in. Cruelly! Sadistically! For the poor bee is not killed but is certainly paralyzed by a sting from the crab spider, and so must stay there, numb and incapable of saving herself, whereupon the spider, altogether without mercy, proceeds to sup on the vital liquids and subtle constituents of the bee's internal elements. When nothing is left but the dry whisper of a husk, this crab spider goes to the actual labor of ejecting the remains from the flower, after which, it lingers in all the bliss of sleep, yes, a successful destroyer's slumbers, sated, all sated, in the corolla. There, it nestles."

Adi would dream for weeks of the bee, the flower, and more than one evil bug. More came his way. Der Alte went on to describe the bee wolf, a wasp who would strike at the honeybee just as it was alighting on a flower. The bee wolf would always go for the throat. "Always. The honeybee has a soft throat. So once again, our forager is paralyzed. The wasp is now in complete command. She proceeds to squash the belly of the honeybee in order to disgorge all the nectar that hardworking little being has already taken into herself. This nectar squeezed up from the belly overflows out of the bee's mouth into the maw of the bee wolf. Is that enough? No. This female brute is now ready for the labor of flying off with her stricken victim. She transports this paralyzed and ruptured little creature to a nest most specially prepared. There, she lays her capture down next to as many as six or eight still-living but wholly stricken other honeybees caught earlier. Then the wasp deposits into this same crypt one egg, one solitary egg that will soon feed on these live, but unmoving bees. After which, this larvae, now well fed, is ready to come forth as one more bee wolf. While it is apparent that the stricken bodies served as nutrients for her growth, and were ingested, limb by limb, how were these bees able to live long enough to serve as living food, piece by piece, sip by sip? And the answer is to be found in our so-called good and wise system of nature which also demonstrates here the cunning of the cruelest maniac. The venom in the wasp's sting has preserved the flesh of these paralyzed bees. It has kept them alive for days while one hungry little wasp-to-be became a bee wolf.

"I have offered these two exceptional cases as lively examples of the perils to the life of any colony you may hope to protect. There are so many enemies. A rat will fret his claws on the front wall of a hive until the guardian bees within must come forth to repel him. These soldier-guards are heroic, but futile. They are swallowed en masse. Toads wait beneath to pick up the droppings. Another variety of spider will wrap cocoons about each bee that happens to fly right into its web. Ants may invade your hive. I have seen colonies where the bees are obliged to tolerate the ants, and will even surrender a portion of their territory in order that these indefatigable invaders do not attack the combs that hold the future brood. With mice, it is worse. In summer, they loot the combs directly for the honey. In winter, they move into the hive seeking warmth, then proceed to construct a mouse nest in one or another corner. The most valiant of our home guard attack the intruder and can on occasion succeed through the force of sheer numbers. It is not impossible. They can sting to death the invading monster. A glorious victory. But what can they then do with the carcass? For them, it is larger than Leviathan. Just so soon as the mouse begins to decompose, the hive becomes intolerable. So the bees proceed to cover this rotting presence with disinfectant. Contemplate their fabulous skill. They have managed to manufacture this now-necessary substance from pollen plus a few chosen green buds. Have you heard of it? Propolis?"

"Of course," said Alois. "They also know to use propolis for mending cracks in their walls." He was pleased with himself again.

"I see," said Der Alte, "that I have failed to discourage you."

"I live by the law of averages," said Alois. "I prefer to think of the ongoing possibility of profit rather than of the intermittent perils that surround all activity."

"Does the bee-wasp frighten you?" asked the old man of the boy.

Adi nodded, but then was quick to say, "If my father is ready to do this, then so must I be."

"You have a splendid son," said Der Alte.

Alois was ready to agree for the first time that this might be a possibility. How nice it was to learn that his little Adolf was more than a bed wetter. Might he even be the equal of Alois Junior one of these days?

But thoughts of Alois Junior invariably reminded him of all that was not yet in place. So now Alois wondered why Der Alte had been seeking to discourage him. It made no sense. Given the state of his hut, the old man could use the money. To what purpose then was he scorning a potential customer's desire to invest?

For the first time, he felt as if he had a grasp on Der Alte. The hermit understood him better than others, decided Alois. "He knows that I am a man who looks to keep his pride intact. I do not give way to the first warning. So Der Alte must know that the more he discourages me, the more I will be ready to begin my colony. He will have his money after all."

Alois now gave Der Alte what he considered his largest and most confident smile. "I respect your cautions," he said, "but we must move now to the other side of the question. Can we speak of what you will do for me, and what I can do for you?"

"Not quite yet," said Der Alte. "If you wish to remain a man with a modest little hobby, I will, of course, be available for necessary materials. But I see in you, Herr Hitler, if I may speak on a more personal level, the possibility of a true vocation. So I would propose another consideration, a better approach. To learn my metier, I put in an apprenticeship that continued for three years, but provided me with an advanced license. What I would propose to you is a more collegial relationship—may I put it so? I am prepared over the next few years, for the most modest fees, to have you associated with me as I work on my colonies. It could prove an agreeable arrangement. You will learn much, and I will have the pleasure of an intelligent man's company. It is sad to say, but in all these verdant fields that surround our Hafeld, we are the only two individuals of outstanding intelligence."

Alois kept a smile on his face but his nostrils were paying their own tithe. "Work for years with you, you foul-smelling old goat?" was the speech he did not utter. There was, after all, the need to come to an arrangement with the old mountebank.

In turn, I was horrified. No professional has a greater desire for competence than a devil. I had been incompetent here. Der Alte might have been a pensioner, but I had neglected him for too long. The loneliness revealed in these last remarks was like the chill of an unoccupied house. How intense was the old man's yearning to see more of Adi. No bold move is ever free of unplanned turns. Calculated mischief might be our province, but such indulgence should not be there for a client. Not if we can prevent it. We look to direct the romantic habits of our fold, rather than to correct them. Any future episode between the old man and the boy would not be to the Maestro's liking. Too many indeterminables!

At this point, Alois said, "I am honored by your personal interest in me, but I must explain. In my family, we are blockheads. All of us, blockheads. We are even proud of that. So, I must work alone. That is how I am. I look forward, therefore, to enjoying a mutually agreeable commercial relationship."

Der Alte nodded. He, too, had his pride. He would not repeat his suggestion.

"Yes," he said, "we will make arrangements. I will put together a couple of colonies for you and supply those tools and products you do not have in hand already." He turned to Adi. "Soon your father will be very busy. Are you able to count to one thousand?"

"Yes," said Adi. "They do that in the Upper Class at school, and so I know."

"Good. Because this spring your father will be master of many, many thousands of bees. Will you be afraid of them? Are you ready?"

"I am afraid," said Adolf, "but you know, I am also ready."

"A wonderful boy," said Der Alte, and his expression was full of love. Tears came into Adi's eyes. His mother would soon have another baby, and again it would be the same as when Edmund was born. He would not see the love he wanted to find in her eyes when she was looking at him. Not for a while.

# 5

I must now inform the reader of an unexpected summons from the Maestro that removed me from Alois Hitler and his family for close to eight months. Indeed, it took me out of Austria altogether. I can add that this alert arrived on the same evening early in October of 1895 that Alois completed his apicultural negotiations. Two colonies of bees installed in two Langstroth boxes were purchased from Der Alte, as well as a variety of tools, together with enough sealed jars of pollen and honey to feed his newly acquired inhabitants through the winter.

So soon as purchased, the goods were transported by Alois to the Hitler home. It was to prove an exciting trip for Adi, who sat beside his father in the dray and could not sleep that night in anticipation of morning, when the hive boxes would be set up on a bench under the shade of an oak tree some twenty paces from the house.

If there is some curiosity concerning how much these purchases cost, I have no dependable way to carry a calculation forward from the kronen of Alois' era to the present American dollar—certain products are priced one hundred times higher today than a century ago; other increases are more restrained. I will offer one rough estimate: Alois' pension in 1895 may have been the equivalent of sixty or seventy thousand dollars a year in the present era, and so I can say that he found the new expenditures dear. What Der Alte charged him might be the equal today of a thousand dollars. Alois, fully anticipating that he would pay too much, was weary, nonetheless, of dealing with the old man and so did not press beyond the small satisfaction of acquiring a few extra tools at no cost.

It was at this point that I was ordered to leave Adi and the other members of the family as well as my other clients in that area of Austria. They were, however, numerous enough for me to deputize three of my agents to remain while I left for St. Petersburg with my best assistants, all of us eager to embark on a massive oncoming project. We would attend the Coronation of Tsar Nicholas II, scheduled for May of 1896 in Moscow, an event still many months away.

Off to St. Petersburg. Leave it that I was obliged immediately upon arrival to commence my study of the late-nineteenth-century Russian soul, all of it—vices, beliefs, harmonies, and inner disharmonies. Once in that Slavic realm (which is so much nearer to God and to the Devil than any other land above the equator) I stayed for all of a winter in the capital prior to coming down to Moscow on a cold April morning one month in advance of the Coronation that May.

During these months in St. Petersburg, I did receive news regularly of Alois, Adi, Klara, and Angela. There were even reports on the temperament of the dog, Luther, and the horses, Ulan and Graubart. In any event, none of that was of great interest to me, not at all, what with our Russian venture approaching. The Maestro was obviously in the first stages of mounting a major and mighty mischief.

I will now make an apology, although I will do my best not to re-peat it. (Good readers do not read fiction, after all, to put up with the author's regrets.) I will say that having read the best and worst of novels for many years, which is, to remind you, part of a good devil's education, I know by now that not even a loyal reader can stay true to an author who is ready to leave his narrative for an ap-parently unrelated expedition. Until now, I have spared the reader, therefore, any reference to other cases, particularly the month I spent in London back in May of '95, when I attended the trial of Oscar Wilde and was in the courtroom on the day of his conviction for "sodomy and gross indecency"—a matter where I certainly took a hand in the jury's deliberations, since my instructions were to do my best to get him convicted. It is likely that the Maestro was looking to stimulate a rabid sense of martyrdom among many of Wilde's intimate associates, particularly those who were of good family.

# 6

I have yet to describe the disorder we planned to wreak in the wake of the Coronation of Tsar Nicholas II, but I would prefer to stay somewhat longer with an account of the small events and minor adventures of the Hitler family in Hafeld during the period while I was away. Only then will I feel free to recount our activities in St. Petersburg and Moscow. I will say that the eight months from our departure in October 1895 until my return to Austria in June 1896 were of personal importance for Adolf Hitler, and so I feel bound to tell what took place during my absence.

There is, however, a difficulty. During this absence, reports of the various experiences of Alois, Klara, and the children were passed on to me by low-level agents—the three I had left behind to oversee my portion of the province of Upper Austria. Given the import of our mission to Russia, I had, of course, taken the best assistants along. So my knowledge of what was taking place in Hafeld had to suffer a loss. Lesser devils, like lesser humans, can be insensitive to significant detail.

While I can obtain a good notion of what is happening to my clients even when I have to rely on what is given to me by mediocre agents, the work can lose tone. Nonetheless, my narrative will not suffer too critically. Long in advance of my departure, I had succeeded in bringing all my aides up to a reasonable level of perception. I say this with pride. They had so little to offer when they first came to me. I am, however, not eager to explain our means of recruitment. It would bring us immediately into a more sacrosanct question: How do devils come to be in the first place? Is the Evil

One on the alert for superior humans who might be ready to work for us, or, as is more usually the case, do they arrive as a brood of rejected humans? How this arrangement was negotiated between the D.K. and the Maestro is, as I have already indicated, beyond my knowledge. I cannot declare why or when it happened, but I would suppose from my experience that the Maestro, looking to make his way up onto a plane of equality with the D.K., had to be ready to accept a good deal of exudate—all these spoiled human possibilities. Over the centuries, perhaps even over the millennia, the Maestro had to disburse a very large share of his resources on the Time needed to train the disturbed material we do receive. It is analogous in difficulty to working up a symphony orchestra from applicants who have yet to play an instrument.

I will not pursue these difficulties here. I will only say that the agents I left in Hafeld did their best to report on Alois' ongoing efforts at beekeeping, but since they did not have a close enough sense of his difficulties, they could not always satisfy my understanding of what went on with him, his bees, his wife, and his children from the end of 1895 until the following summer.

# 7

In late October, if I had permitted it, the agents left behind would have overwhelmed me with detail. To my complete lack of surprise, Alois was having obsessions concerning his new venture.

I had no time to attend to this while in Russia. Short of forcing a direct entrance into Alois' waking thoughts, which, it may be remembered, is rarely done with men and women who are not our clients, my agents had to work by way of their milk runs. In what our Maestro chooses to call "the marketplace of sleep," most dreams of men and women are reasonably open to devils and Cudgels alike, and so their daily thoughts can be picked up in superficial degree by no more than passing through the night chamber.

We also learn a good deal through the simple expedient of listening to a family's chatter. To be sure, a plethora of superficial information arrived, more than enough to be annoying, for it was a biased portrait. My agents perceived Alois as weak and much too worried, but they lacked insight for dealing with men or women who possess strength, yet are being studied during a time of anxiety. It is easy to comprehend people who are weaker than ourselves, but it is not as simple to be ready for the true feelings of those more powerful. Respect is demanded, precisely what my locals were lacking.

Being of no great stature themselves in their former lives, they tended to pick up all that was second-rate in Alois. I was left, therefore, with the burden of discounting such improperly weighted materials. I would admonish the reader not to forget that the boy who later became Adolf Hitler emerged from a childhood with this father and mother. So it has to be obvious that we would do well to take measure of Klara and Alois' strengths as well as, needless to say, their significant weaknesses.

Very well. Here then is my developed if secondhand account of Alois' woes now that he was becoming a beekeeper.

His first concern (which I find comic, since he has spent his life in uniform) is that he has to remind himself constantly to put on light-colored gloves and a beekeeper's large hat and veil, always of the whitest material. Since he must avoid dark coats or trousers, when that is his customary dress, he is always concerned in these first days to remember to change his garments before going out to the hive boxes. Deep and somber colors, he knows all too well, do irritate bees. He knows that by experience. On the particular occasion some years ago when he had been gravely stung while working with the little colony he then kept near Braunau, he had made the mistake of inviting an attractive woman out with him one Sunday afternoon. As an element in his plan of seduction, he thought he would demonstrate not only his competence with the hive, but his elegance. Therefore, he was in full-dress dark blue uniform. That twilight he was stung so fiercely that the recollection still rises from the pit of his stomach. Alois' hopes of fornication were obliged to remain unsatisfied that Sunday, since the lady was stung as well, and on no less than the exposed flesh of her ample breast. Only a passing romance was lost, but a blow was delivered to his best opinion of himself. As we see, he continues to pay the price. Dressed in white, he feels shoots of fear. Bright as rockets, they fire off in his stomach as he approaches the hive boxes.

In some part, however, Alois remains a good peasant. He has not forgotten that one must remain on the alert after any small disaster. Unexpected value can be gained at times from an unexpected misfortune. His interesting medical theses, for example, were stimulated by the alleviation of his rheumatism on the following day— bee stings did seem to be good for his knees. When their meeting occurred, Der Alte, we remember, was ready to agree.

This confirmation could have been part of Alois' decision to accept Der Alte's opinion that imported Italian bees were superior to the Austrian variety. While Alois had his suspicion that Der Alte might be selling exactly some stock that he wished to get rid of, still, the telling point was that Italian bees were easier to handle. They were gentler, Der Alte assured him. Moreover, their rich yellow tan, not unlike the mellow glow of the best shoe leather, made them more beautiful. Alois had to admire the three golden segments of their bodies, each set off by the sharpest edging in black. Chic! That was the word that came to mind. Whereas the Austrian honeybee was gray and hairy. It did not gleam like these gilded Italians. Afterward, Alois felt as if he had been disloyal. He should have taken the "Franz Josefs," the graybeards.

What added to his unease was that he kept wondering whether he would have done better to wait for spring. Now he had to keep his colony warm enough not to perish in the cold.

Through these months, therefore, temperature within the hive had to be measured every day. Yet he must not open a hive for more than a few seconds. "No matter your curiosity," Der Alte had confided, "do not allow yourself to extract any of the movable frames for study of the combs. The cold draft that could result from lifting the large lid of the box might so lower the temperature that your bees would need hours to warm the interior again. Such a chill could decimate your population. Take no chances, Herr Hitler. Until now, from what you have told me, I assume that in the past, you have lived with bees only in June and July. Any tourist can do that. But to be the Skipper of your little people through the ice-cold air of all the winter months to come, that takes character, my friend." And then, as if to enrich the assumption, he added, "My new friend."

# 8

If Alois had stood in the dock before himself as judge, he would have found the defendant guilty. How could retirement prove so enfeebling to a strong man? He had bought the farm on impulse and now, to double such a bet, had purchased two beehives in their Langstroth boxes. Why, so suddenly, had he committed himself to apiculture over the winter? Hadn't that also been done on too quick an impulse? Der Alte had had the consummate nerve to say to him, even as Alois left, "You will soon see how much work I have saved you."

What Alois saved in work, he spent in worry. He was still under sixty, damn it, not yet sixty by a year and more, but he had such a sense of inner weariness before these new responsibilities. His two populated boxes were now set under the oak tree with tarpaper underneath for warmth, and more tarpaper above, all kept in place with stones. Two populations housed in two boxes. Each day he read the temperature in each box, then did a weighing once a week. Part of the problem was that he had more worries than work. Should the colonies look weak when spring came, he would combine the two boxes into one, and, if necessary, buy more bees, undertake more expense, more of Der Alte, who would be smelling up his pants, no doubt, from laughing so hard at the great esteemed High Customs Officer Herr Hitler with his ten thumbs all ready to be stung by what he didn't know about advanced apiary matters. Already, in November, Alois was lecturing Angela and Adi, even Klara, on the need in apiculture for immaculate hygiene once warm weather arrived. No matter how warm the day, they must certainly not leave the hives open. Above all, they must never spill honey outdoors. If they did, they must mop it up instantly, for the bees could be drawn to it and might begin to fight for free honey, easy honey, as it lay in a pool on the ground. If the puddle was deep enough, they could drown en masse.

So his fears were enough for him to harangue his family on what might or might not occur in summer. So much depended on what he read each night on how to keep a winter hive.

He did build one new hive box, which he did not need as yet, but he was proud of the skill demanded, even if his box was not the equal of the Langstroths.

Yet such work eased his worries. His chest puffed up with an old truism. "Good German blood understands," said Alois to his wife, "that blessings do not come from God, but from hard work." Still, it was not such a very good remark. Why not speak instead of Austrian blood?

That question soon came to bother him. Did a particular blood possess its own virtues? Why, indeed, praise German blood? Why not Austrian? He had an Emperor who could live with the huge (and often) idiotic problems of keeping Czechs, Hungarians, Italians, Poles, Jews, Serbs, plus Gypsies, living in peace under one Hapsburg Empire. Germans couldn't do that. Germans were always squabbling. Without Bismarck, they would be nothing. Petty principalities. King Ludwig I and Mad King Ludwig II, both crazy Bavarians. And Prussians were worse. Prussians had a ramrod up their ass. Why speak then of good German blood? "Because," he said to himself, "I know what it means."

Yet what did it mean to decide you knew something when you didn't. Although in some way you most certainly did. A nice enigma. Alois decided that he was now thinking like a philosopher. Not bad for a boy who was once a peasant. He was tempted to bring up the question at the tavern in Fischlham, but didn't, after all. They were dolts. He resented the time he spent with them. By November, he had even found himself drinking there in the afternoons, a proof, if he needed it, that there was not enough work. For that reason, he had chosen to stay away for a few days, and hang some netting near the hives in order to keep birds away in the spring. He even debated whether to visit Der Alte, but recollections of the high odor put an end to that.

Before long, he was back in the tavern. There was one pleasure he did find there. The dolts now saw him as an expert on apiculture. Every bit of advice Der Alte had offered, plus whatever nuggets he had picked up of late in the literature, could now be presented as his own well-acquired lore. Alois would be the first to say that honesty and modesty were excellent virtues and should be employed when dealing with superiors. An inferior mind, however, always wanted to feel that it was listening to a wise man. Since he was more available to the locals than Der Alte, he stood in, therefore, as the resident expert. A farmer even walked over one Sunday afternoon to seek his advice on how to get started. Alois proceeded to overwhelm him with the details of feeding a hive through the winter.

This discourse allowed him to feel like the fine fellow he had once been before his retirement. "The trick," he told his visitor, "is to master the technique of your special feeder. Because you not only put in the liquid nourishment, and cover the mouth of the jar, as I just explained, using the fine mesh, but you must then hold the vessel upside down over the bunghole above the brood that is waiting to be fed. Do you follow?" Alois could see that he didn't. Before long, this Sunday visitor, thoroughly disheartened, said goodbye—he was not likely to be competition next winter.

My agents kept providing me with these petty episodes. They were missing the depth of Alois' new anxieties. So soon as his visitor left, Alois felt so alone with his project that he began to wonder whether disease might strike the colonies.

He spent an evening reading his books, but the anxieties remained. He had dreams of living in one of his boxes, himself a bee, no more than part of a cluster living in deepest and darkest obscurity. How could these bees guide themselves in that world, so stygian, so bereft of light?

By the end, Alois had raised this dream to the level of a nightmare—now I could feel more interest in what my agents were transmitting. Alois' hive multiplied in the darkness, then escaped from the box and flew far away. They could not be found.

When spring came, would he lose his hive? In the dark, he felt for Klara, and his hand came across her belly. She was so big now, yet the new one wasn't due until January. Would he be a giant of a fellow?

She came awake with his hand on her, and would have nestled into the embrace of his arm, but in the middle of this darkness, he felt a need to discuss a worrisome matter. She was soon wide awake and unhappy.

"I hope," Alois said, "that you haven't spoken to Herr Rostenmeier."

She knew immediately what was coming next. Herr Rostenmeier was the owner of the country store in Fischlham, where once a week, on Saturday, she and Angela would buy a few foodstuffs not raised in their garden. Klara liked Herr Rostenmeier, and had begun to talk to him about the sale of their honey. Alois had told her not to make any deals, not yet, because the possibility was still there that he would do business with Der Alte. Nonetheless, she had taken pleasure in the thought that it might still be Herr Rostenmeier, and in that case she could serve as the person in between, and bring a little money back to the house. Her fingers tingled each time she thought of such a transaction.

But now Alois had decided to go to Der Alte. She knew it. "I thought," she said in the darkness, even as he patted her belly, "that you didn't like that man at all, yes, I remember you said you would have to smell him."

"He will be good to consult," Alois said shortly. The tendrils of the nightmare were still with him.

"Yes, yes," said Klara, "but you told me you don't trust Der Alte. Yes?" She was close to becoming hysterical. To be torn out of an agreeable sleep for this! "Yes, you say you don't trust him, and yet you are still ready to choose this Der Alte over an honest man like Herr Rostenmeier?"

"Klara, this is all because you feel embarrassed," he told her. "Maybe you had a little too much conversation with Rostenmeier already. Something you haven't mentioned, could it be? A real commitment. Without speaking to me first."

"No," she said, "not at all. I am not embarrassed. I made no commitment." She was tempted to add, "But this I will say, I must say, I will never understand the thinking that goes on in a person like you." However, she was silent. He would have ridiculed her for such a stupid remark. She would have been up half the night explaining those few words, "A person like you."

**9**

No surprise. Alois decided to go back to Der Alte after all. Why not? He was a realist, he told himself, and so was used to bad odors. After all, one had to deal now and again with the Devil. (My devils snickered as they told me this.)

Alois paid his visit on the next Sunday and, once again, took Adi with him. This time the boy paid attention to the route. It was but a mile away, and so he knew he would be able to find the hut again by remembering the forks of the path. All the while, he was filled with uneasy excitement. A woe as large as a loaf of bread had settled in his stomach, yet perched above such heaviness, his heart felt most alive. He knew he would not tell his father that he planned to visit Der Alte on another day and very much on his own.

"Yes," he kept saying to himself, "I will not be afraid to walk there. But not in the night, maybe not. There are too many spirits in the woods then."

For Adi, the second meeting between Der Alte and his father turned out to be even better than the first. If, at the start, they spoke about the marketing of honey and Adi could hardly follow, the conversation grew interesting once business was done. That was because the old man could not stop talking about the mysteries within the mysteries of bees. "Yes," said Der Alte in a most resonant voice, "I never weary of contemplating these tiny creatures, with their immortal honey and their near-to-immortal sting. There are such subtleties to their keeping."

A rich discourse ensued. If Alois was hardly able to speak, he was nonetheless not too displeased, for he would use it tomorrow night at Fischlham. A gift for the dolts! Adi, in turn, listened with care. The words he could not understand lived in his mind by way of their sounds.

"Can we," asked Der Alte, "ever pay enough attention to this work of Creation? It is so full of genius. These little devils come to us from the Good Lord's divine and curious aesthetic—nature's wisdom expressing itself in this most bizarre form."

Der Alte went on. He could go on! References to God's ballet, God's gymnastics, God's investiture in wonder and awe. Der Alte was like many of our clients. We encourage them to praise God. In the highest. Always.

For that matter, he went on for so long that Alois was, once more, repelled. Too much time had elapsed without exercise of his own voice. Moreover, he did not like the look in his son's eye.

Those blue eyes, so similar to Klara's, large and alive. There was reverence in them now.

Alois managed finally to interject a word.

"Why don't you take us into the kitchen, and show the boy your viewing box?"

It was obvious that Der Alte would prefer not to—even as Alois had expected—but Adi spoke up. "Oh, please, sir," he cried out, "I have never seen the inside of a bees' home. They have been with us back at the house for so long"—he tried to count quickly—"for seven, no, I think it is eight weeks, and I have not seen even one of them. Must I wait until summer? Please."

"Spring," said Der Alte. "It is necessary to wait until spring." Then, given the disappointment on the boy's face, he shrugged. "All right," he said, "but you must be prepared. It is winter. Bees are sluggish during these months."

Indeed, they were. In the kitchen, bare but for a small stove, a sink, a hand pump above the sink, and a pail beneath for the runoff, was also a table. At one end had been placed a narrow glass box, perhaps two feet long and one foot high, its interior concealed on both sides by black curtains. When the curtains were pulled back, two glass walls were revealed, not three inches apart, and a vertical frame stood in the space between, filled with small wax cells, an uncountable number of them.

Adi was disappointed. A cluster of pullulating things, no larger than dark pills in a bottle, kept climbing over each other, startled by the light, a poor gang, crammed, jam-packed, an assembly of what looked to be squashy little creatures about as ugly as roaches. (Their wings were folded.) Adi had not been so disappointed since he had first seen Edmund's homuncular face squeezed up on Klara's breast.

Now these bees could just as well have been beans bumping around in a heated pot, except, no, beans did not look so nervous. What an awful way to live! They miss the sun, the boy thought. Now they were just shoved up against each other. He sighed in preference to bursting into tears.

"At this moment," said Der Alte, "they are the poorest of the

poor, no better than sodden creatures in a slime of their own making. Yet their lives will span the extremities of existence. Now they
do nothing, but in summer, you will see them dance in the air, as
wonderful as drops of dew in early morning light. So fearless. How
they will strut as they enter into the golden petals of the flower-
blooms that are waiting for them."

"Hear, hear," said Alois. No matter the drear aspects, Der Alte
did have a manner. Give that much to the stinkpot.

And Adi was thinking, "These bees can sting you and then you
are dead." He shivered in the old man's kitchen before the incom-
prehensibility of dying. Yet, right in the midst of this chill, he felt
as close to the old man as to his father, for he could listen all day
and all night to the wonderful words that came forth.

"Come and visit me," the old man managed to whisper before
Alois gave the signal to leave.

# 10

I do not know how powerful an influence this last murmured
message could have had on Adi, but I will say that at no moment
up to this point did I feel more regret at being obliged to rely on
my Hafeld agents. Not long after (on Christmas Eve, no less!),
while the rest of the house was asleep, Adi got up from bed, bun-
dled himself into his warmest clothing, and went out to sit on the
bench under the oak tree where the two Langstroth boxes had
been placed. There he remained for a considerable time, growing
colder by the minute. Yet he stayed, and having placed himself between these two boxes, he kept embracing the back of each. He was
praying for the continued life of the bees.

This was of signal interest to me. I queried my agents more than once about what they could glean from the boy's thoughts, and some of it seemed of value. That night, Adi had heard his father complain that the screen protecting the hive entrance had been torn. The entrance was small, but all the same, a mouse might have come into the hive. Alois soon decided that this was unlikely—the hole was simply not large enough—but Adi was not convinced. Since his father had repaired the screen that afternoon, Adi no longer knew as he sat between the boxes which one might be occupied by the mouse. Ergo, he set a hand on each.

What with it being Christmas Eve, the boy was full of his mother's spirit of celebration. "On this night, one thousand eight hundred and ninety-five years ago," said Klara, "the Son of God was born, and he was the nicest human being ever to walk on earth. The loveliest, the sweetest. If you love Him, He will love you."

Adi was certain. This was one night when you could feel free to breathe the night air, no matter how cold. For the Son of God was present. Would He grant the power Adi needed to kill the mouse by the force of his thoughts?

To kill the mouse by the force of his thoughts? I knew the limitations of my agents. They could not have conceived of such a notion. This had come from Adi. It was his. His alone. If I had been present, I would have raised the stakes. I might have gotten the boy ready to believe that he could save certain lives by exercising the special power he possessed to destroy others. That is one of the most useful suppositions we can implant in clients, but it does call for a sequence of dream-etchings.

Since I was not present, I did my best not to brood over the lost opportunity. There was more than enough to occupy me in St. Petersburg. In company with my assistants, I was facing considerable opposition to my activities. I had never encountered a group of Cudgels as determined as this Russian crew. Nor as brutal. Over the last few centuries, these Russian angels had developed a powerful ability to contest the many demons we had installed within Russian Orthodox churches and monasteries. In consequence, these Cudgels—fully as rough as the meanest Russian monks—were in command of considerable zeal. During these months, they were wholly ready to defend the Coronation of the young Tsar-to-be, Nicholas II.

When the Maestro consulted me, as would occur now and again, I was bold enough to tell him that I did not like our chances of disrupting the Coronation itself. Too much would be arrayed against us. It should, however, not be difficult to create a mighty disorder a few days after the event.

I had dared to speak my mind, but then, the Maestro does not look kindly upon a lack of opinion among his close subordinates. "Allow me to muse upon the perceptions that some of you are able to offer. That is signally more useful to me than silence. I won't allow your fear of being wrong to leave you mentally inactive."

Enough. It is easy to see that these Russian matters were temporarily, at least, of more concern to me than the small events of Hafeld.

All the same, whether I was interested or not, Klara gave birth on January 21 to the new infant. That brought minimal joy to Alois. The much-anticipated strongman of the future had not arrived. A little girl was in the maternal bed. Now the ruckus of baby feeding at night and baby yowling in the day would go for naught. He had been counting on a powerhouse of a son to sweeten his old age, yes, offer an improvement over the three boys he could not, at present, boast about—the wild one, the mama's boy, and a crybaby snot. So Alois was unready to celebrate the new birth, yet he did— at the tavern in Fischlham night after night for quite a few nights until the beer began to smell as sour as infant spew. There were now six human beings in his home. Come the end of spring, when Junior returned from Spital, there would be seven. The tumult of voices in the bar was becoming comparable to the childish noise at home.

My agents gained nothing from Alois' visits to the tavern. Let men drink in a crowded room, and solidarity rises among them. They soar on zephyrs of grain spirit, a brotherly defiance against the inroads of angels and demons, a certainty that as men, they are at this moment equal to external forces.

These are not good conditions for our work, but openings do present themselves when the drinkers are staggering home. We are ready then. Sometimes, disgusted at the hours lost, we slam them to the ground. They usually take it personally, their lament most characteristic. "Somebody shoved me," they often cry out. Nobody believes them, but they know better. Wrath had struck between the shoulder blades, and it was not their own rage, not at all.

# 11

On his return, Alois may have been staggering now and again, but he was also feeling too alive to enter his house. Instead, he sat by the hive boxes and fished out a rubber tube he had been keeping in his pocket. Next, he placed one end of it against a wall of the Langstroth and thereby was able to listen to the thrumming of the tenement dwellers in his little city. A fine sound was there, almost a tune, rich with little swells of contentment. But then, why should his bees not be content? Come morning, hundreds, then thousands, would be in a cluster ready to suck on the mesh cloth of the wide-mouthed jar, gorging on honey-and-water. So, in this dark and nicely drunken hour, separate thoughts passed through Alois like horses on file, one large thought at a time. He tried to count how many bees might be inhabiting the box. No matter how drunk, he could still make an intelligent guess. Call it twenty thousand. That was bound to be the answer. Despite himself, knowing he should not really disturb the hive, he knocked sharply on the side. Because then, through the tube, he could listen to the shift in sound. Were they issuing alerts? The calls had gone up in pitch. Like the strings of a crazy violin. Then quiet again. Soft. Like cats who sheathe their claws. Purring while asleep.

He roused himself long enough to go into the house and get his shirt off and his pants. Then he fell into bed. But he was still hearing the chorus. Strange sounds. His breath lifted over a small hesitation and down he went into slumber. He had one final thought as splendid as a fine horse on parade—it was that he certainly enjoyed these hymns of the bees a good deal more than the caterwauling of an infant.

His dreams, however, were not so good. He had entered a large and cavernous interior where, to his lack of surprise, he found himself among his bees. They were defecating, and there he was, one of many, suffering just like his brother-creatures—no, sister-creatures—wasting away in the contractions of a severe bowel disease, all of them defecating into the narrow aisles of the Langstroth box—what a filthy vision.

He looked to rouse himself. Because this was a dream. Healthy bees did not soil in their own habitat (except perhaps for the worst and laziest of the drones), no, he had listened to the bees in one hive, and their sound was honorable. They would wait until the weather was warm enough to go outdoors.

But now he was awake and painfully aware of all the excrement that had been accumulating in his colonies all these months. How could the little buggers hold it in?

It was warm next morning, the first warm morning of a February thaw, and as Alois came out of the house, his horde was everywhere above, hundreds of them, thousands—who could count? They were leaving their droppings all over the place, fifty and then more than a hundred feet away. It all smelled like ripe bananas, and the snow was a field of white dotted with innumerable yellow spots out there in a large circle around the hive bench. Buttercups in the snow! Hanging on a clothesline, Paula's diapers were spotted. What an immense shower of defecation had taken place. Alois stepped it off. Yes, you could even find yellow spots one hundred paces away from the hive boxes.

Klara was as furious as she dared to be. "You never told me to be careful," she said to her husband.

"It is too bad," he said, "that you will have all this laundry to do again. But how can one apologize? It is, after all, an act we have received from that Good God you are so sure is yours." She walked away. A half hour later, water churning in two huge pots, she took the diapers off the line and set out to boil them again.

Alois was not about to tell himself that he felt sorry. Rather, he was happy for the bees. What delight they had shown while they flew about. Since it was a Saturday, Adi was nearby in the meadows and Alois, on impulse, decided to call him over. Let him hear some real talk.

"Everybody shits," he told the boy. "Everything shits, all things living. That is as it should be. What you keep in mind is that you learn how to get rid of shit or it will shit on you. Understand? You keep yourself clean, do you hear? Look at these bees. They are wonderful. They hold it in all winter. They are determined not to dirty the hive. We can do the same. We are good people. Where we live is where we keep everything spotless."

"But, my father," said little Adolf, "what about Edmund?"

"What about him?"

"He still does it in his pants."

"That is your mother's concern, not yours."

Later in the day, Adi remembered the time when Alois Junior had stuck a dab of excrement right onto his nose, and even the recollection brought forth the oddest cry. He still felt so humiliated, yet so full of glee. Nor could Adi get over his excitement at the cleansing flight. Those bees had been dancing in the wind. That was because there had been all that caca in them, and now they were free. He couldn't stop his giggles. It had all made his mother so angry.

Now he remembered what Angela had whispered to him one morning. "Your mother has a saying," she said. " '*Kinder, Küche, Kirche.*' " He nodded. He had heard it already. He yawned in her face.

"Oh, you think you know it all already," Angela said, "but you don't. There is a secret word as well."

"Who told you? My mother?"

"I can't say. It is a secret word."

"Who told you?"

She could see he was ready to burst into a tantrum. "All right. I will let you know," she said. "I heard it, yes, from your mother, your dear mother, who loves me even if I am not hers."

"Tell me or I will yell and she will hear."

"That is you. That is just as mean as you." She held him by the ear. "Remember," she said, "she told me in secret that the real saying is, '*Kinder, Küche, Kirche, und . . .*' "—she started to giggle—" '*und Kacke!*' "

Now, he was giggling as well. Oh, those bees, worse than babies. He had a crazy picture of every bee with a diaper, the tiniest diaper. He was laughing so hard that he felt like urinating, and that made him think of Der Alte who came into his thoughts so often, especially when he had to urinate.

Now Adi realized that he would like to visit Der Alte, yes, he wanted to, so much.

Next day, Sunday, was warm again, and once more the bees were out. After Klara left for church and Alois dozed, Adi started to run up and down the meadow, as if to use up the impulse to visit the old man, but in his mind he kept seeing each fork in the forest road, and knew he could find the hut. The desire to make such a trip by himself was as compelling as a rope tugging on him.

He went. And Der Alte, prepared for the visit (by the same message, for certain, that Adi had received), was there once again at the door, but the tablespoon of honey was not yet in his hand, no, for that, Adi now had to sit on his lap. "Yes, you are such a good boy," Der Alte said. "I can love you like a grandson, and you will never need to be afraid of me. Yes, you are so nice and strong." Der Alte laid a hand upon the boy's thigh, but with only the lightest touch, even as he fed Adi the honey.

The boy was not afraid, or, yet, perhaps a little. In school, they had fairy tales to read, and sometimes there were ogres in the forest and evil spirits could make little children turn into pigs or goats. However, it did not feel so risky sitting on the legs of Der Alte. It was better than his father's lap. He never knew when his father would blow pipe smoke into his face.

And indeed, they sat there long after Adi had tasted all of the spoonful of honey, and he felt happy with Der Alte's old hand resting on his knee.

After a considerable part of an hour had passed, he began, however, to feel less comfortable. Would his father begin to wonder where he was? Yet, when he stirred, Der Alte said a few words which aroused the same sense of surprise as turning a page in a book and there before you was a nice picture.

"Do not tell this to anyone," said Der Alte, "but I am trying to make one little bee very happy. I have chosen this bee to live by itself close by me. I will tell you. I keep it in the kitchen."

"Does it try to talk?"

"It does make sounds. For certain!" Der Alte smiled. "But no, dear boy, I do not try to encourage this little bee to speak our language. That is certainly too much to ask. I just try to make her happy. Which is not so easy. Because now that I have selected her, she must live alone in a small queen box I use for her, even if she is not a Queen."

"My father says that bees live only for other bees. They are"—he searched to remember the expression—"they are dedicated to the community."

"Your father is correct. Yes. Bees live in a hive. They do not seek to live alone."

"Even if they are fed good things all the time?"

"You are the smartest boy I know. You are full of understanding. I did want to see what would happen if I were to select one bee and keep her warm and most well-fed, and think about her all the time with all the good feeling that is in my heart. So when I go into the other room, I take care to speak to her. That is twenty times a day. She cannot comprehend what I am saying. But I want her to know that I am thinking of her. Sometimes I even take her out of the queen box."

"Doesn't she fly away?"

"Oh, no. I prevent such a possibility." He touched the boy's head tenderly. "When I remove it from its little box, it jumps around, it is so merry, but it knows it must not try to fly."

"Does it have no wings?"

There was a pause. "No longer does it have wings."

Adi knew. No need to ask. His happiest feelings were now trying to lift themselves above the bad ones. He asked to look at the bee.

It was little and frisky and jumped about in excitement when Der Alte opened the box. Indeed, it hopped onto the tip of the old man's finger that had been dipped into honey.

"I do not know how much more will happen," said Der Alte. "What I am attempting is difficult, and I see little chance for success. But how wonderful if I can brighten the feelings of this little creature. After all, before my intervention, she was insignificant. Can I lift her now to a level her sisters cannot attain? I feel for her. She is so lonely. She misses the horde. She is loneliness itself. But I try to bring the sweetness of relief. That can come when terrible loneliness is replaced by comradeship. Yes," he said, nodding his head.

"Oh," said Adi, "I hope you are able to do that. It is so sad to be lonely. Sometimes I, too, am lonely. But I feel afraid for this bee. Will it die?"

"Sooner or later, it must. It will. But I would like to see if I can make her happy for a little while."

"Yes," said Adi, "I understand. You love this one."

"Maybe," said Der Alte. He sighed. "Next time you visit, we will see if I have made progress."

Was Der Alte entering his senility? No! This outlandish pursuit of "well-being" for one isolated bee, an obviously stupid procedure—particularly after it has lost its wings—is not without purpose for the Maestro. The oddest experiments reveal much. Freaks can be a fount of information.

I will say one outcome became clear. Our wingless embodiment of loneliness died before Adi saw her again. What is also to the point: Der Alte and Adi had tears in their eyes on the boy's next visit and were closer than ever. Count on it. Der Alte had decorated a small matchbox to serve as a coffin for the bee, and the old man and the boy then laid it into a small hollow before covering it with a spoonful of dirt.

# 12

Early in March, a week arrived that brought the sun to Hafeld every day. The hives began to stir, and the hardiest of the winter bees came out to forage. It was likely that the Queen was now laying eggs out of her well-kept store of semen from fornications consummated high in the air last summer. Now one hive began to weigh more each morning. That worried Alois. The other should be doing as well.

He decided to open the top of each Langstroth box and look in. Whereupon he discovered exactly what he had been fearing. The two colonies might have sat on the same bench through the winter, but only one was thriving, the other could not be termed healthy. While a few dead bees lay on the lowest platform of the good box, a tumble of minuscule carcasses covered the floor of the other.

Just before the warm spell, Alois, by way of the rubber tube, had heard a great deal of restless humming in this second colony. It had worried him. Now, open to examination, many of the brood combs were empty. Had the Queen died? He did not really know how to locate the lady—she was, after all, only a bit larger than her own worker bees, smaller, indeed, than the drones.

He would have been dispirited, but his acumen had also been confirmed. He had not worried for too little. It looked like some dread disease had laid waste to the hive.

So Alois decided that all the remaining bees of this colony had to be gassed. The good hive had to be protected. He was even ready to call on Der Alte for assistance but decided that he would not. His winter-long worries had engendered their own kind of fortitude.

He chose a Saturday. Adi and Angela, home from school, were his assistants, and the process was not difficult. He took a small cake of sulphur, part of the equipment he had purchased five months ago, lit it, and left it to smoke on the floor of the bad hive. The entrance was plugged, the hive lid at the top was laid on again, and the gas did the job quickly. When Angela began to weep over the death of the poor bees, Alois sent her inside. But Adi watched, sitting beside Alois on an adjoining bench, his eyes alive in response to his father's lecture. "Your big sister is silly," said Alois. "To become so upset! In nature there is no mercy for the weak."

"I am not bothered," said Adi.

"Good," said Alois. "Now let us empty this box and clean the combs."

Adi found himself thinking of Der Alte's one lonesome bee, now dead, and that did bring tears to his eyes.

But, of course, there was no comparison. He blinked back his tears. Der Alte had loved one little bee, but the sick ones here in this bad hive dirtied the place where they ate and where they slept. No comparison.

That night, by way of a suggestion from the Maestro, I prepared a small dream-etching, simple enough to be installed by the best of my local Hafeld agents. It was a repetitive dream in which his father asked Adi to count each and every one of the dead bees. To make sure of the number, Adi was told to lay them out in rows, one hundred to each row—a tedious dream to be certain. All the same, he was proud of the high number he had managed to count. There had been forty rows of one hundred bees, all laid out on an immaculate white cloth. He had not realized until now that he could count to four thousand. No one in his class would come near. His only regret was that he had not finished the dream. There had been more mounds of dead bees to count.

Here, I would warn the reader not to make too much of the gassing nor the body count. It is not to be understood as the unique cause of all that came later. For a dream-etching, no matter how artful, leaves but a dot upon your psyche, a footprint to anticipate a future sequence of developments that may or may not come to pass in future decades. Most dream-etchings are not unlike the abandoned foundations one can see on the outskirts of Third World cities. Left to molder for lack of further funds, they lie there, excavations on a scraggly field.

It would be a gross mistake, then, to assume that this dream-etching determined all that was to follow. I assure you we would be the first to applaud if matters were that simple.

# 13

The good hive was another matter. It was thriving. The weight of the colony increased each week, and the honeycombs began to fill up. From his books, Alois had learned that each of these minuscule cells was capped with wax by the worker bees only when the water content in the honey had been reduced to less than 20 percent. To blow off such surface water, the bees had to fan their wings for hours every day. Alois felt intoxicated all over again by the dedication of his newborn creatures to such never-ceasing chores. To sweeten his mood even further, the first honey was ready, and so his bees were capping the cells—just as they were supposed to!

Out in his white garments with the big boxlike white veil over his head, protected by his gloves, Alois began to feel as if he was acquiring a bit of real technique. It was, after all, not so simple to pull combs out for examination, then slide them back again. He certainly didn't want to be such a lummox as to squash his Queen. Indeed, the confidence he gained from these results took him over to Der Alte's hut long enough to purchase a new Queen to replace the one who had been gassed in the other Langstroth box.

Der Alte even gave him a lesson on how to spot an active Queen. It was not too difficult when she was laying her eggs into empty cells, for she would be followed then by a retinue who hovered over each deposited egg long enough to discharge their own enzymes onto the larva. "Magical fortifiers," Der Alte said.

Alois had to submit to the lecture but was able to return with not one but two Queens (both impregnated in the past year). One would establish a colony for the box that had been fumigated, and the other could be installed in the box Alois had built last fall. Some of his combs of new brood together with combs of new honey would now be transferred to the two empty boxes. Thereby, all three would be partially filled, so there would be space for each colony to build wax cells for their new brood as well as storage cells for their new honey. If he had lost one colony to gassing, he would soon be able to consider himself the master of three, all flourishing—could that be? Of course, he had had to lay out good money in the hope that he could yet speak of such success.

All the same, he did feel a cautious optimism. April had come. Flowers were sprouting, the walnut trees, the oaks, the plum trees, the beeches and cherry trees, the maples and apple trees were in bloom. There would be a host of flowers in the meadow.

He liked to sit by his hive boxes with Adi beside him, the boy carefully covered and veiled in an outfit Klara had put together. Father and son now delighted in keeping watch at the entrance to each hive, where guard bees stayed on post. Every last bee that came back with pollen and honey was carefully sniffed by one of the guards before she could enter. On occasion, Adi would begin to hoot because the guard would drive a visitor away. "Look, Father," he would say, "she doesn't smell right."

Yet, with all these incoming riches, Alois still kept feeding honey to the colonies. "That," Alois told the boy, "is so that they will make even more honey." Five trays filled with combs sat in each of the three hives. And three Queens were working in three separate hive boxes to deposit their eggs in cells, while foragers were flying missions from morning to dark. Each forager would return with its load every few minutes, and then be off again. Alois had read that it took forty thousand such voyages to accumulate two pounds of honey.

Sometimes he would look at the old bees who had lived through the winter in the healthy box. They were now battered relics with frayed wings. Worn out from overuse, the hair was gone from their bodies. They were expiring. Each morning a team of newborn worker bees would collect whichever bodies had fallen to the floor of the box and sweep them out of the guards' entrance, then off the ramp. Alois could hardly mourn their passing. Young stock was taking their place. He felt as if he had finally begun an ongoing venture into apiculture. The new bees would be his, not Der Alte's. He did not dwell on the fact that all three of his Queens had been fertilized a year ago and so, in that sense, were Der Alte's children.

# 14

Given a splendid morning in May, with a host from each of the three colonies in the air, Alois began to notice a pattern in the movement of one bee. This scout—or whoever she was— kept making figure eights in the air.

"She is signaling to the others," Alois said to himself. "She is trying to show them something."

He was right in this observation, he knew it, because a good number of other bees had joined the first, and off they flew toward the head of the meadow. On the other side of that rise, as Alois soon discovered on his walk, wildflowers had sprouted overnight. The bee he had observed was indeed a scout.

An old lust came back then. If there was one thing Alois had always wanted from life (even more than a new woman), it was to be the discoverer of a new concept. He dreamed of discovering something so startling and so valuable that his name might even be honored across time.

The desire still resided in him. It gave him considerable happiness to think that he had just discovered a new concept. And by the use of his eyes alone! He had seen what he would call a bee's signal. Up above, he could swear that one bee was trying to excite the others to fly to a place where flowers were full of nectar. In none of the books he had read so far had he seen any mention of this little dance, this wig-wag in the sky. He was twice afraid to mention it to Der Alte—once, because for all he knew it might be already an established concept among apicultural cognoscenti; and if, to the contrary, it turned out to be brand new, might not Der Alte know better than himself just where to publish the observation?

Nonetheless, he still had to learn how to locate the Queen, so he decided to visit Der Alte after all. The man was skillful. That had to be said. Der Alte opened one of his hives, scanned the racks, located the Queen, reached in with a bare hand, and grasped her wings carefully and most delicately between thumb and forefinger. "In a few years," he said, "you, too, will be employing this approach to capture, but for now, I will show you a safer method." Of course, he proceeded then to discourse on all the methods and modes of discerning just where the creature might be, whether depositing eggs, or fertilizing them one after another in their new cells, or, sometimes, resting in her court.

"Once located, it is simple," said Der Alte, "to capture our Lady."

"This, as I understand," said Alois, "will be most necessary when I look to collect my honey."

"Exactly," said Der Alte. "That is a time when you are moving many frames, and scraping the wax covering away from the honey cells. A careless move can crush her." To Alois' annoyance, Der Alte wagged a finger at him. "So," he said, "we do not go first for the honey, no, we locate the Queen like the good fellows we are, and then we use a queen catcher." He took up a glass tube with a concave dome at one end. "This is what you lay over the Queen," he said, "and then you slip a little queen cage"—he held up just such a small flat container, two inches long—"underneath and blow the Queen right into the cage, *punkt!* Now she is safe. She can stay in the cage until the honey has been removed."

We can be certain that Alois practiced catching the Queen. Indeed, he spent an afternoon apprehending and releasing each of his three beauties, finding them, putting the domelike end of the tube most carefully over one or another, and then blowing her right into the little queen cage.

Performing this task over and over, he came to recognize that what he had perceived that morning in the dance of a bee would hardly seem a secret to someone so knowing as Der Alte—once again he would have to give up a fine dream—he would not be remembered as a discoverer.

# 15

Alois' fine spirits also waned with the loss of warm weather. A cold spell arrived, cruel to the expectation aroused by early spring. Alois now girded himself for all his gains to be lost by this out-of-season chill.

An old axiom returned to him. Johann Nepomuk used to say, "Spring is the season that will betray you most."

So there were days when he came close to exhausting himself through the to-and-fro of removing tarpaper from the top of each hive, only to put it back again if the light at high noon might go dim in the sky. Soon after, he had to run back to strip the tarpaper away, for the sun was out again and the day had returned to warmth.

During one near-freezing cold spell, he caught a cold. That offered a collateral worry. Was it impossible that one of his Queens might also catch a cold? In sympathy with the overlord? He scolded himself. Such nonsense!

Then it occurred to Alois that this return of his fears might not be so silly. What if it were a reflection of how he felt about the condition of his true health? Was he coming nearer to his end? It was the worst thought to have. His imagination now entered a matter he had never allowed himself to approach. All through the years, so far as he could remember, death had not seemed threatening to him. A dull end to a good life, maybe, but nothing to do with hell.

Now, however, one damn question was following another. What if death was not as he had assumed? He had been certain that religion was there for a very good practical reason. It couldn't be simpler—you had to keep the weak and unruly in order. But a man of pride (such as himself) could do as he chose.

Now he was feeling panic of a new sort. His heart took a leap at the thought, one fearful leap, as if his chest had been pummeled. Could guilt be real?

Poor Alois. He was now there for the taking. No Cudgel would bother to protect him. I could have the tried-and-true pleasure of appearing to him in a dream. I could offer an impersonation of a guardian angel. I did not even have to be present. It would be easy enough for the best of my three agents to bring it off.

But to what end? Would Alois be worth the maintenance?

The sober fact, which we do well not to ignore, is that people of Alois' age are rarely a prize. Their utility is limited. They are too fixed in their nature to warrant much molding, whereas flexibility is what we look for in exciting new clients. Ideally, we can redirect their aims with ours.

On those rarer occasions when we choose a man or woman over fifty, we look for a serviceable warp in their psychic framework that can be employed for a specific purpose. Repetitive irritations are one example. A mean old lady who keeps asking everyone whether they want something to eat when she knows that they don't can unhinge a good family. They grow uneasy at their increasing desire to smother her with the nearest pillow.

Alois, however, was too average a human product. There was little need to pick him up now. Milk runs would be enough. Let my agents hover just above his dreams.

# 16

Early in May, the weather turned warm again, and many of Alois' woes eased. In part he had already recovered some of his good spirits by cleaning and oiling the tools he had bought in the fall from Der Alte, and this chore he performed in much the manner of a good soldier who takes his rifle apart in order to oil it and put it back together again.

My Hafeld agents, having little to report, filled their latest communications with lists of his tools and did this so assiduously that I grew irked at their enumerations of pollen feeders, hatching cages, bee smokers, a water sprayer, a mating box (whatever that was!), a hive tool, even a honey stirrer made by Alois himself out of beechwood. And then there was a spur-wheel embedder for preparing the foundation of the insertable frames, as well as a capping fork— a slew of particulars which provided no interest for me.

Klara, in contrast, knew how to make better use of spring in Hafeld. She was not always counting how many of the brood nests were filled with new pupae, nor was she worrying about the temperature within the hives. Now that it had turned warm on a second wave of sun and undulant air, she was ready to loosen some of the knots that had coagulated in her limbs that winter. "God, too, is taking His rest," she said to herself even as she drew in a breath of air through the open window of her kitchen, and then, on impulse, with much left to do in the house, she picked up Paula, four months old, and went out into the meadow. The loveliest of silences prevailed, wholly without sound, a silence that took in the lightest caress of air. It was as if she could even hear the swaying of tall grass in the field and all but hear the curtsies of the flowers. It was as if the sum of these tender sensations supported the silence of the hills. "Listen to how quiet it is," she said to Paula. "Listen, little angel, and you will hear the flowers whisper." It seemed to her as if the nearest petals had heard what she said, for indeed their stems began to incline toward her, the most cheerful little daisies she had ever seen.

She knelt in the grass, the infant in her arms, and spoke to them. "You are beautiful, all of you," she said, and, yes, there was no mistaking, these flowers were stirring for her. "Yes, Paula," she said, "these flowers like you and like me because we love them. Is it not so, you little dears?" She was ready to vouch that they had heard her, and once again, they did bow delicately. "Yes, they are little ladies," she said to Paula, and had to laugh at herself for feeling— was this pure madness itself?—that the daisies were not only dear to her, but that she was dear to the daisies. "Oh, I am one big silly," she said aloud. But she could not help herself. She still believed that these white petals were listening. The balm of the air was like love, yes, exactly like the love she felt for the four-month-old in her arms. Klara's body was returning to her, or so it felt. The old poked-out, wounded, bruised, and stupid body of all those winter months after Paula had been born now felt sweet with the beginnings of true repair. She told herself that it was spring, and nature herself was enjoying a party. How could it be otherwise? Each breath was full of balm. God was near and He was in the air, her Good God, full of radiance. Yet the air was at peace. Could it be that God was resting on His laurels? He deserved as much. He deserved so much. She wanted to pray to Him then, but did not know how, since she did not wish to ask for anything at this moment, merely to praise Him for being so good, and that was better to do in church. There, everyone else would be doing the same, so it could be understood as humble, not vain, whereas here she was all alone with Paula and the flowers, and full of such happiness. For she was thinking of all the young boys and girls of her childhood and of those rare occasions when they would romp and play just like these sweet crazy bees flying around the house now and so happy to be out in the sun after living in a dungeon all through winter, crazy now with the joy that they could turn somersaults in the air, free of all duties, free of their tasks for a little while. Indeed, like Paula they were new to sunshine.

And Klara thought of the years to come when Paula would be ready to play, and that left her full of love for little Edmund, who was so kind to the baby, the only one of the children who was. Angela couldn't really care (although she was dutiful enough), and Adi was a worry—once she had seen him pinch Paula's cheek hard enough to make her cry. Klara had spanked him for that, one sharp slap across his little seat, but she wouldn't do it again in any kind of hurry. For who would think? He had glared back at her—the prince of princes, so strong a look that she had to use all the strength of her eyes to stare him down.

It was too beautiful a day to think of that moment of misery—so intense it had been—no, she would rather thank God for having given her so sweet a baby, a daughter who would yet grow up, so she knew, to be her own good sweet best friend. And she even said as much aloud to Paula. "May the angels hear me," she whispered to her child before she turned back to the house and her duties.

# BOOK VIII

# THE
# CORONATION
# OF
# NICHOLAS II

# 1

If I am now ready to disrupt the narrative by my move to Russia, I would remind the reader that I, too, am a protagonist. Since I will continue to be Adolf Hitler's guide for decades to come, his future development will, to a great degree, be dependent on my own, and I can vouch that the eight months I lived in Russia from late 1895 to the early summer of 1896 became a prominent element in my development as a high devil. Afterward, I was considerably more ready to foresee the outcome of large events—which is an instinct that only the highest devils are able to develop. Needless to add that by the 1930s Hitler had developed similar talents. What I learned about Russian Grand Dukes over my eight months in Russia proved convertible to my later understanding of German tycoons. While such gentlemen are usually more powerful in essence than royal figures, they prove equally narcissistic, and Adolf's developed gifts were able, when necessary, to play to their vanities.

I also learned how to manipulate the will of the people. I speak of the blind will of the people. When properly incited, they rush to enter the ranks of the mad. It need not be debated whether this was of use to Adolf.

I also learned a good deal about God's strengths and His increasing weakness. In 1942, a decision had to be made whether to activate the gas chambers in the concentration camps—a daunting move even for Himmler and the SS, but Adolf was ready. God would not be equipped to punish him. So he saw it.

If there are readers who still will say, "I would rather go on with what is happening in Hafeld," I have a reply. "That is your right," I can tell them. Just turn to page 261. Adolf Hitler's story will pick up again right there.

2

The beauty of the spring day when Klara felt so happy holding Paula happened to coincide (even to the hour) with the Coronation of Nicholas II. Indeed, the same early summer warmth was in the Moscow air. Even after I came back to Hafeld in June, this fine period continued across much of Europe, and these long sunny days were compatible with my recollections of the Coronation and the days that followed.

As I have stated, I was the one to suggest to the Maestro that any direct attack we mounted on the crowning event was not likely to succeed. We could, of course, initiate many an episode. Nowhere in Europe could we field as many agents and clients as in Russia. A number were of high rank. We possessed more than one Grand Duke and Duchess among the several branches of the royal family. We infested the Okhrana. We certainly had more agents among these secret police than did the Cudgels. We also had government ministers who were as loyal to us as hounds slavering over kibble. We were well installed among all the royal families of Europe, not to mention the nobility and/or the generals. Nouveaux riches lay before us like open whores. Tycoons were among our most valued and protected clients. We also had our share of anarchists, nihilists, and terrorists. When it came, therefore, to calling upon such actors, we knew that if we were ready to accept the cost, we could bring off a major disruption on Coronation Day.

Nonetheless, I was opposed to such ventures. The Cudgels

would be expecting our attack that day and so our losses might be
severe. That is why I proposed that we postpone our attack until
the Peasants' Festival which was scheduled to take place four days
later. When the Maestro accepted this suggestion, my delight was
mixed with woe. What if I was wrong? Did I begin to comprehend
the monumentality of Russia? Never had I felt the D.K.'s presence
so directly. It was obvious—God wanted this Coronation to succeed! This lay upon my judgment with all the weight of a hard
fact—a stone too heavy to lift, and so a large source of my dread remained. How to explain God's immense commitment to this Coronation?

In recent years, the Lord had invested in a variety of Russian
people and Russian causes. Attention had been paid to Monarchists
and to Republicans, to the most established aristocrats and to revolutionaries who were ready to die for the honor of overthrowing
these overlords. Nor for that matter did He ignore the Pope and
the Vatican (but then, neither did we!). He was open to the calls of
liberty and the demands of autocracy. As the Maestro once remarked, "It is not difficult to hear the workings of His Mind. 'I
may make My mistakes,' He says, 'but I do pay attention to who
wins. That is the best way to discover what works.'

"Why, after all," added the Maestro, "did He give liberty to men
and women? Obviously, the Dummkopf wanted to obtain some
notion of what He had actually put together."

The Maestro might be enjoying his irony, but what if God had
decided that His best prospects now rested on the need for a
Tsar who could enjoy a close alliance with the Russian Orthodox
Church? Could He be encouraging, thereby, a monumental ceremony to fortify Crown and Cross? Guided by Him, the new young
Tsar might even obtain some purchase on the vast if inchoate energies of the Russian people.

If true, this was an amazing decision. To depend on Russia—so
invested with corruption. So teeming with injustice! It was what we
looked to find. Injustice was a yeast to inspire hatred, envy, and the
loss of love. For rare was the man or woman who did not possess an

intense sense of the injustice done to them each day. It was our tap-root to every adult. It was a fury in every child. Our work would fall apart if humans ever came to brood as intensely upon the injustice others might be suffering.

I concluded, therefore, that an answer might be found in the young man who would soon be crowned. Was there something an-gelic about him? I made a request to the Maestro: Could I devote my efforts to learning as much about Nicholas as was possible? "Do what you can" was the reply. I could hardly decide whether I was being promoted or abandoned.

As I soon learned, it would not be routine to approach this Nicky—which is how everyone in his large family referred to him. Nicky had a beautiful Danish mother, Empress Marie, the widow of his recently dead father, Tsar Alexander III, plus four Grand Dukes for uncles, as well as brothers, sisters, cousins, and in-laws. So far as one could discern, these relatives seemed surprisingly fond of him.

But I could not, as I say, come near. I had never encountered a human being so well guarded by squadrons of angels. Usually, I can call upon keen senses that enable me to take in the spiritual weight of a human being. From the far end of a large room, I can perceive flaws of character in the corner of a nostril or the ridges of an ear. Yet I do not look to muster these fine senses for every occasion. Sa-tanic existence would be enervating if we were always obliged to operate at our highest level. Instead, we call upon these gifts only when our need is to learn a good deal about a particular man or woman, and most quickly.

I was not able to approach Nicky, however—too many Cudgels. Once again, I had to rely on materials that our Russian devils had picked up from royal valets working in the palaces of St. Peters-burg or serving in the churches and offices of the Kremlin. They were able to provide copies of numerous letters and diaries. It seemed as if everyone in every royal family of Europe was ready to write letters to parents, children, aunts, uncles, cousins, and inti-mates. In addition, most of them kept diaries. The Tsarevitch, soon to be Nicholas II, had made an entry in his embossed little book every day from boyhood on. By the time of the Coronation he felt so close to Alix (his soon-to-be Tsarina Alexandra) that she was always by his side. Literally. His diary was not only open to her perusal, but she even added her entries to his pages.

I was fascinated. These two young people were related to the highest monarchs in Europe. Alix might be only a princess from Hesse, but her mother, Alice, had been one of Queen Victoria's three daughters. When Alice died, Alix was only seven years old but Queen Victoria brought Alix to England on frequent visits.

There was also Wilhelm II, who would yet become the much-reviled Kaiser Wilhelm of World War I. He happened to be the son of Queen Victoria's oldest daughter. So he was Alix's cousin. The English prince who would yet become King George V of England was Nicky's cousin. In time, King George's oldest son would become Edward VIII until he abdicated his throne to marry Wallis Simpson. Surrounded by our devils, that couple would live on for decades as the Duke and Duchess of Windsor. (The D.K. did not even bother to assign an angel to them.)

If I list all these family ties, it is to emphasize how royal in their roots were Nicky and Alix. I can add that these august relatives seemed to agree that they were very much in love, a rare and bona fide love.

The Maestro had his doubts. To me, he remarked, "The Dummkopf presents Himself as the Almighty Avatar of Love. He is Love, and those who love Him are full of Love, and Love itself will solve all human problems. With this noxious pomade, He not only gulls a good three-quarters of humankind but deludes Himself. No one believes in Love so much as the Dummkopf."

Could this account for the number of Cudgels here? Had God retreated to His medieval assumption that monarchy was there to provide the best foundation for society? Did He actually suppose that if a handsome young king and attractive young queen remained magnificently in love with each other and were wholly devoted to belief in His Goodness, why, then, He, God, would be ready to underwrite a bold experiment? Might it turn out better than some of His other ventures? Previous monarchies had for the most part been notably void of love between the principals.

I was relieved. I now had a premise. The D.K. was no longer in full possession of His Faculties. Could that be true or was it false?

3

A ll the same, how could the Lord be seen as senile? When, on occasion, I find myself near the sea, it is difficult to believe that He is suffering any loss of His Capacities. For that matter, similar uneasiness can be aroused in me by a fine field, a rocky crag, a peerless sunset, or the retort of the heavens as lightning is followed by thunder. One can even cite the dazzlements of grass when dew is on the ground.

Of course, He could have fashioned all this aeons ago, back at the peak of His Creative Powers. In that case, did He now brood on the possibility that His Force might be slackening, which could be why humankind had become His least successful Creation? Were we now awash in the dithering of an old divinity? This Nicky and Alix—they seemed so naïve, so unfitted for any vast project. While I had not been able to get near to their living presence, I had certainly absorbed the tone of their love, their piety, their innocence. I had read hundreds of communications between them. If I now choose to present a few of those missives, it is to provide a sense of how young they were.

In June of 1894, when their engagement was just two months old, Nicky wrote to her in English, a language they could share:

**I love you too deeply and too strongly for me to show it: it is such a sacred feeling, I don't want to let it out in words that**

seem meek and poor and vain! But now I will try to break the habit of hiding my feelings, because I think it wrong and self-ish in some occasions. Darling primrosy-mine, I love you my darling!!!!!

Be it said, I took pains to count the exclamation marks. Is that not, after all, a point of kinship between us? The observant reader may have noticed that I am fond on occasion of such emphasis at the end of a parenthesis. (Interruptions of attention should pretend, at least, to be vital!)

Four months later, Nicky's father is grievously ill. Alix, always ready to add her sentiments to Nicky's diary, offers this:

> *Tell me everything, dushka, you can fully trust me, look upon me as a bit of yourself. Let your joys and sorrows be mine, so that we may be ever drawn nearer together. My sweet One, how I love you, dar-ling treasure, my very own One.*
>
> *Only yours, quite your very own little spitzbub, Pussy mine!*

**Nicky's diary, 20 October, Livadia**
My God, my God, what a day! The Lord has called unto Him our adored, dearly beloved Papa.

My head is going round, I cannot believe it—it seems in-conceivable, a terrible reality.

It was the death of a Saint! Lord, help us in these terrible days!

Later I learned that Nicky was recalling the hour in his child-hood when a nihilist had managed to plant a small bomb in the railroad car where the royal family was traveling, but in the event, the roof was blown upward by the blast. As a result, no one was in-jured. Then, however, the roof began to settle down on them. Alexander III, a giant of a man, used the holy and unholy strength of his arms to support the collapsing structure long enough for his wife and children to be rescued. Only a saint was capable of such strength, declared Empress Marie, a small and beautiful woman.

Nicky, being short like his mother, would also revere Alexander's powerful chest. Through his adolescence, Nicky had worked, therefore, at bodybuilding. He also excelled at horsemanship and at hunting—a point of honor to him. He grew a fine brown mustache and beard, yet he never became hefty enough to look like a Romanov.

**21 October, Livadia**
**After luncheon we held Prayers for the Dead and again at 9 o'clock in the evening. The expression on Papa's face was wonderful, smiling as if he were about to laugh!**

**22 October**
**Last night we had to carry Papa's body downstairs, as unfortunately, it has rapidly begun to decompose.**

Indeed, they soon had to cover the Emperor with an imperial cloth. His hands and face were turning black.

The marriage to Alix came just a few days after the funeral—it would not do for the new Tsar to remain an unmarried man. While the event took place a full year before I arrived in Russia, I was offered detailed accounts by our resident devils sufficient to inspire the confidence that I had been standing in the Winter Palace with ten thousand of the gentry. All of us were without chairs. The Russians seem to believe that devotional services should exact a penance on the body. The mighty had to remain on their feet for three hours while liturgies were recited. All the while, choral music continued, sad in its way, but majestic, due to the length of the occasion. It was as though the deepest groans of Jesus Christ had to be heard again and then again before the Bride might be proclaimed Empress. All were quick to comment on her dignity, her beauty, and on the manner in which her head bowed whenever she greeted anyone. Our devils, being not in the least generous about such matters, remarked that this bobbing of her head was reminiscent of a pigeon.

On a stay at Tsarskoe Selo, Nicky told his diary:

**Such a dear place for us both; for the first time since our wedding we have been able to live alone and live truly soul-to-soul.**

Alix added:

*Never did I believe there could be such utter happiness in this world, such a feeling of unity between two mortal beings. I love you—those three words have my life in them.*

On the next day she wrote:

*At last united, bound for life, and when this life is ended, we meet again in the other world to remain together for all eternity.*

I was intrigued by her confidence that they shared the same passport to the Eternal. Rarely had I encountered newlyweds who seemed as infatuated. Yet Nicky was twenty-six, and no neophyte in these matters. Since Alix had been a virgin, I was disposed to look upon her entries as much too concerned with demonstrating how much she was in love.

Moreover, I could not be certain of Nicky's feelings. Whenever Nicky passed by a fine forest, he would be able to remind himself that this loveliness was his land. He had been chosen by God. Would he not see Love as a vertiginous ascent where you could only maintain your balance by climbing upward?

Still, the damnable question remained. It was certainly conceivable that in His Desire to nourish their marriage, God was enriching them with physical ecstasies. How could I know? I had only the language of their letters, and the reasonable assumption that if God was going to choose a Tsar, He would be ready to support him with Wisdom and Strength—against, of course, the not-small skills of the Maestro.

## 5

On the other hand, one could also ask how well had God prepared this young man to be a Tsar. It is certain that the court had not. Everyone had supposed that Alexander III would rule for at least another generation, and so Nicky was poorly prepared for public life.

**17 January 1895, St. Petersburg**
**An exhausting day. I was in a terrible state about having to go**
**to the Nikolayevsky Hall and deliver a speech to the represen-**
**tatives of the nobility, and the town committees.**

He had been closeted with the Grand Dukes before delivering the speech. They assured him that he must follow in his father's footsteps. "Nicky, you must be *absolute*!" His grandfather, Alexander II, had been assassinated. His father had had that close call on the train. Absolute allegiance must be proclaimed.

From Nicky's speech:

*I am aware that recently in some* zemstvos *there have arisen the voices of people carried away by senseless dreams of taking part in the business of government.*

*Let everyone know that I will retain the principles of autocracy as firmly and unbendingly as my unforgettable late father.*

Despite such promises of unrelenting strength, his official duties oppressed him. He kept lamenting that he could not spend enough time alone with Alix.

As the first winter of their marriage came to an end, she began, however, to develop *symptoms*. We counted on that. Symptoms were our stock-in-trade. Victorian women were never easy to invest, but we could always send a shiver into their corseted defense of personal virtue. It called for no more than tainting their dreams with one or another smelly thought. Symptoms soon followed.

**9 April 1895, St. Petersburg**
**Unfortunately, dear Alix's headache continued all day. She did not go to church nor to luncheon.**

**10 April 1895, St. Petersburg**
**Dear Alix still has an unbearable pain in the temples and she was obliged to remain in bed, on my advice.**

An ongoing headache! When intense enough to be characterized as migraine, these headaches speak of a clear desire to commit murder. I did not believe Alix had such sentiments toward her husband, but it could be another matter with her mother-in-law. The Empress Marie had adored her huge husband for the best of reasons, and one of them was that she had been the Empress. Animosities were developing.

By June, Alix was free, however, of her worst headaches. She was also pregnant. I suspect that her mother-in-law was, in consequence, able to exercise less pressure upon her temples. In an entry to Nicky's diary on June 10, Alix wrote:

*My sweet old darling Manykins, Wify loves you so deeply and*
*strongly . . . what intense happiness . . . ours . . . our very own . . .*
*what happiness could be greater; only Wify must try and be as good*
*and kind as possible lest another little person suffer for it. A big kiss.*

This is June, but the baby will not be born until November. Is
Alix suggesting that manykins and wify have no contact down
below until the baby arrives?

My comprehension was not advancing. None of us was ready to
admit this to ourselves (and never, certainly, to the Maestro) but
the presence of real love blurred the clarity of our analysis. We
could penetrate every aspect of false love, and be demonic at converting the sensitivities of love to the imperatives of lust. Of
course, there are special occasions when God decides that lust will
be beneficial for one of His chosen, yes, there is Godly lust as well,
and so the issue can offer ambiguity.

It is a curious contest. The angels have powerful sweets to offer,
but, in turn, I would say we possess more improvisational skills
than the Cudgels. We also lack a quality I do not wish to confess,
although I must, or what I offer will make no sense. It is that I
know everything about love but Love itself. I do not like to make
this confession. Yet, it is true. I recall nothing of my existence as a
human, nor even whether I was, to the contrary, always a spirit.
This, however, I can say—I have never known Love. I can expati-
ate upon its properties and tendencies, its dilemmas, its dissipations, I can delineate most of the reasons for its presence or
disappearance, I can inspire jealousy, doubt, even periods of revul-
sion toward the beloved, I can tell you everything about Love
except that I cannot distinguish true Love from its artistic substitutes.

Witness, then, my confusion concerning Alix. I could comprehend that Nicky needed Love the way others require drink. But
Alix? Could it be that her amorous hysteria was the best way of believing that she felt heights of passion, pleasure, and devotion?

Given, however, one curious line in her letter, "Wify must try
and be as good and kind as possible lest another little person suffer

for it," I came to a conclusion. She was, indeed, declaring a temporary moratorium on sex. Over many a milk run, I had watched pregnant women enjoying the act in their eighth or even ninth month. Of course, this might be different. Alix was preparing for the next Tsar, and one wouldn't dare to bruise the development of that royal head, but still!—was there to be no sex scheduled until November? She was writing this in June! I now leaned to the hypothesis that Alix had strained mightily to rise to the passionate heights she deemed necessary for this first essential of their marriage to be accomplished but now that the heir-to-be had been put in place, she was ready to enjoy a rest. Yes, we must not do it "lest another little person suffer."

# 6

Alix was more than pregnant. Her belly was huge. The Romanovs were full of anxiety awaiting the birth of that young bouncing male baby who would soon be Tsarevitch to Nicholas II.

It is the mark, however, of good breeding that no disappointment was mouthed by them when a strapping ten-pound *female* came forth.

It did not matter that much to Nicky—Alix, at least, was safe!

**3 November 1895, Tsarskoe Selo**
**A day I will remember forever. At exactly 9 o'clock P.M. a baby was delivered and we all breathed a sigh of relief. With a prayer we named the daughter from Almighty God "Olga!"**

Two days later, Nicky is fascinated by some unexpected aspects of infant nutrition.

**5 November 1895, Tsarskoe Selo**
**The first attempt at breastfeeding took place and ended up**
**with Alix successfully feeding the son of the wet nurse while**
**the latter gave milk to Olga. Very funny!**

**6 November 1895**
**Thank God, all is well, but the baby does not want to take her**
**breast so we had to call the wet nurse again.**

I was not surprised. A few of us are able to discern the sentiments of an embryo during the final months. During the last tri-
mester, they express their uterine sentiments through their mothers'
dreams. So we knew that most infants come into the light of the
birthing room feeling affection or antipathy toward the benevolent
caretaker (or the surly warden) who so recently constituted the
walls of their womb. That is exactly why women feel desolate when
their milk is refused by their babe.

Nonetheless, these two, the wet nurse and the young Empress,
were doing their best to avoid such a recognition. So was Nicky. I
expect he was ready to tell himself that huge little Olga had the
sturdy instinct to wish to smell and taste the paps of a strong Russian woman. And I, from my funds of cynicism, think that the two
women, so profoundly different, were ready to enjoy this open (if
still surreptitious) connection of the flesh.

In any event, less than half a year later, Alix has certainly re-
sumed relations with Nicky.

*29 March 1896, St. Petersburg*
*. . . sweet precious Nicky mine, no words can express how deeply I*
*love you—more and more, day by day, deeper—truer. Lovy sweet*
*do you believe it, do you feel hearty throb so quickly, and only for*
*you, my husband?*

Nicky had been so good about the birth of a princess rather than
an heir that Alix to her sweet surprise felt a "hearty throb" on the

moment he entered her, a novel event, or, at least, I assume it was novel. Besides, fleshy determinations can shift. Olga, for example, has come to accept the given. Now she feeds at her mother's breast even as Alix is taking morning coffee with the Emperor.

Our closest attention, however, was on the Coronation of Nicholas II. It was approaching. It is safe to add that there could have hardly been a devil present who was not experiencing his share of elation and dread. There is never a time when the presence of crowds can feel as demonic to us as at a great occasion with a massive ceremony.

# 7

Festivities for the Coronation would take place in Moscow on May 14, and everywhere one saw two large letters, *N* for Nicky, and *A* for Alix. Countless numbers of platforms had to be erected for the spectators, as well as false fronts to hide the ugliest buildings on the route. Moscow was awash in visitors coming from many a nation. Those who lived on the route of the parade were renting their abodes to spectators. A window on the street could be leased from dawn to sunset for 200 rubles. Carriages accompanied by coachmen cost 1,200 rubles for the month. Useless to argue that one only wanted the coach for a week, or that one could buy ten good horses for 1,200 rubles! Even to acquire a limited view in a narrow space on a flimsily built platform came to 10 or 15 rubles— woe to the obese. To afford a balcony you had to spend 500.

Nor were hotel rooms easily available. The government had taken over whole floors for foreign princes, diplomatic representatives, noblemen, honored artists, nabobs, moguls, tycoons. The French, determined for reasons of state to leave an imprint on the occasion, proceeded to spend 200,000 rubles, a way of proclaiming themselves as the great and good ally of the Tsar. Since that had once been Germany's role, their diplomats responded by renting a palace in the woods outside Moscow that cost only 7,000 rubles, a modest gem, but then the Germans did not give a ball, just a musicale. They may have been gambling on bad weather. If so, they lost. The opening procession on May 9 offered beautiful skies.

The parade had to be comparable to the most splendid royal occasions of the past. Nicky and Alix would make their way to the Spassky Gate of the Kremlin from their temporary residence in Petrovsky Park, some six miles away. Since it was no secret that this event was hoping to equal the majestic entry of Louis XIV into Reims in 1654, the procession would look to exhibit to the world how exceptional were the resources of the Russian Empire. First came the Cossacks, with scarlet tunics, silver epaulettes, blue trousers, and black boots; on came Asian princes from unpronounceable regions, exhibiting costumes never seen before in Europe, but then they were representatives of far-off barbarian lands which the Russians had conquered over several centuries.

They were followed by the Arch Grand Master of the Coronation Ceremonies, twelve Chamberlains, twenty-five Gentlemen of the Chamber, Marshalls of the Court, and members of the Council of Empire, who were then succeeded by the regiments of the Royal Army.

Early in this progression came Nicky himself, born, as all too many were whispering, on the sixth of May. Thousands of Russians were passing such information to each other, for May 6 was the Orthodox Feast Day of St. Job the Sufferer, one of the most sinister dates on the calendar. No one would ever wish to repeat the sufferings of Job.

Nicky was most aware of this. In the first weeks of their betrothal, he had seen it as his duty to warn Alix, who replied that it would be her duty to stand beside him. In union with each other, they would overcome such a bad omen. This had to be a test given to them by God. So she saw it. God wanted them to love each other so well that they would not have to suffer like Job, not if they were ready to love God even more than had St. Job.

Just so much did I learn on the day they entered the Kremlin. I had been able at last to enter Nicky's mind, and never in my experience were so many angels surrounding a human being. Yet, on this day, as he paraded his pale English mare along the six miles from Petrovsky Park to the Spassky Gate of the Kremlin, I was able to approach his thoughts. Be certain, it was a small entry, but the approaches to his mind were not wholly barricaded. Hosannas to the Maestro! Ten years ago when the Tsarevitch was an eighteen-year-old cadet, he had had a lustful set of encounters with one of our devils. She had appeared in the form of a Gypsy prostitute. Since the affair occurred years before the Cudgels had begun to devote their massive efforts to protect him, the Maestro had succeeded in finding an unprotected if narrow ingress into Nicky's mind.

Now, chosen to use this hard-won passage, I was there for the length of the march up Tverskaya Street to the Kremlin, and so could pick up some of the thoughts passing through the royal head.

There were surprises. On this ride, his memory took him back to the years when he had been a young Colonel in the Life Guards, and he did recognize—for one moment, no more—that his days might be happier now if they could be spent in that rank. The enthusiasm of the troops, their roar of joy at the sight of him, had left a pang.

Nicky's recollections now turned libidinous. The devil who had been installed into his young experience was one whore who was still calling to him. Each cheer from the troops stirred his groin. The English mare, so elegant, so pale, must also have been alert to such arousal, for she began to offer new steps. How she pranced!

After no more than another minute, however, the fine spirits shared by horse and rider sank back into gloom. Born on the Feast Day of St. Job the Sufferer. What, indeed, had God intended?

Just as quickly, however, did his good mood return. I did my best to follow. Nicky's thoughts came pell-mell, full of clatter and echo, and even a dark mood could not prevail for long in the face of this promenade. The decorations hung upon the façades of the homes on Tverskaya Street. Moscow, on this morning, had the radiance of an old lady who had never been as beautiful before, and the glory of the light occasioned Nicky to think of his best hunting days, when Alexander III had seen fit to compliment his prowess. Nicky had blushed on receiving so rare a compliment from his father, and proceeded immediately to give the credit to his hunting dogs. Whereupon Tsar Alexander III had said, "One can measure a man by his dogs."

Yes, let the Almighty see him as the most loyal of His dogs. He knew animals, he knew them. Almost always, when drinking the blood of a stag just hunted down, the echo of the last shot still alive in the forest, he would feel close to God. The stag, so immaculate in form, had just lost its existence. Why? For whom? To Nicky, the answer was simple but profound. The death of this beautiful beast would bring a closer understanding between God and man. For it was God who had given human beings the right to take the lives of these exquisite creatures. Now Nicky remembered a blasphemy that once had burned in his throat. It came as he drank his first cup of stag's blood. He had thought: "This blood must be like Christ's blood. How else can it taste so pure?" Remembrance of such a blasphemy made him wince. It also made him think of obligations yet to come. He might feel close to God, he could certainly feel close to beautiful animals, but now there were always ministers around, eager to see him, looking to use him. The loyalty of those ministers was most attached, however, to the aggrandizement of their office. Deceit was at their fingertips. Self-interest was in their skin.

He could withstand them. So he told himself. He had a trinity of values with which to protect himself, his father's guide—Honor, Tradition, Service. Yet, to remain faithful to three such principles would demand unyielding strength. Honor could fall into dishonor, Tradition grow stiff, and Service wear one out. He was not the man to deal with endless intrigues. To keep up with such ministers was like falling through a stairwell. Whereas to kill an animal yet know compassion for the beast—marrow for the soul!

At this moment, his mare reared up. Had she just had an image of the stag's blood? A cry of fear rose from the spectators. The mare was standing on her hind legs. But then the crowd applauded. On the streets, at the windows, upon the balconies, from the roofs of Tverskaya Street—out of the tens of thousands who witnessed this moment rose a great wave of applause. Nicky, most gracefully, had kept his seat and calmed his horse. The sound of the crowd's elation traveled all the distance up to the Spassky Gate of the Kremlin. Other tens of thousands of spectators still ahead on the line of march did not see this episode and so did not know why they had heard such applause, but they too began to applaud. Nicky was flushed with pleasure.

Not for long—his future duty was still before him. He was doomed to work with his ministers, and they would never respect him. They were accustomed to the force of his father. Gloom came upon him again.

In five days he would receive the Crown and be overwhelmed with duties. Their opinions would override his own. They knew more. He had not even planned this procession. They had. They had told him that this prolonged entrance to the Kremlin would be his triumphant introduction to the world. That was why there must be so lengthy a parade. It was crucial that he be seen at the front of these many miles of procession. Yet to keep expectations alive for the onlookers, his mother and Alix would only be seen in their two golden coaches at the conclusion. This arrangement, the ministers insisted, was the most dramatic way to demonstrate the amplitude of Russian power.

Alix had wanted, however, to be nearer to him. Nicky tried to explain the intentions of the ministers. She was silent. It was one matter for Nicky to feel like a dog before God, but quite another to suffer such a sentiment before one's wife. Nothing is worse for an animal who would be brave than to be told by the eye of his beloved that he is no more than a timid and conceivably ignoble creature.

# 8

To precede the Coronation on May 14, Nicky and Alix had been caught up, after the opening procession on May 9, with ceremonial receptions that required them to offer a good welcome to many a high official from home and abroad. This ability to remain affable while not shifting one's feet, nor indicating strain, was seen as one more measure of royal competence. As he complained afterward to Alix and to his mother (with a smile), his cheeks were sore from being kissed by plenipotentiaries with stiff mustaches.

On May 13, sacred ornaments were transported to the throne hall of the Kremlin Palace and a host of anxieties rose into his mood. The ceremonies were, by now, familiar, but he felt as if hell itself were waiting. He wanted nothing to go wrong. For he saw the fourteenth of May as deliverance. By its end, he would no longer be acting Tsar, but consecrated as the Tsar. Done with that at last—if nothing went wrong.

I suspect he knew that something was in the offing. But he had no instinct for when it might happen. Each day from the tenth to the thirteenth seemed as dangerous to him as the next.

For that matter, he was not alone in such anticipations. Given the firm Russian expectation that nothing good can prevail for long, many were certain that all good weather would disappear by the morning of the Coronation. Instead, on the fourteenth of May, Moscow was alive with early morning sunshine. Morose predictions had to be postponed. Any number of women who had been quick to predict floods of downpour were still convinced something would yet go bad. Since Alix had converted to Russian Orthodoxy immediately after the demise of Alexander III, these women now said, "She comes to us behind a coffin." Given, however, the beauty of this exceptional day, a countersentiment soon arose. Many were now saying, "We are close to the end of the century. Maybe the new one, this twentieth century, will be different. Let miracles of beauty and comfort come to us."

# 9

I am not able to offer much concerning the Coronation itself. The Maestro did not include me among those devils who were going to work during that event. I did not protest. The most dependable route to his favor was to accept without comment the position you had been assigned. Besides, he even told me, as if by now I might be developing into one of his intimates, "Across the grand scheme of things, the Coronation will yet be seen as a petty event. You will miss nothing."

I was not present, therefore, in any of the cathedrals, not the Assumption, the Archangel, nor the Annunciation, but I was told over and again of the unspoken scandal of the event at the Cathedral of the Assumption.

Soon after the Tsar and Tsarina had mounted their thrones, the Chain of the Order of St. Andrew broke even as the Tsar was bending his head to receive it. Given the number of Cudgels surrounding this ceremony, was it possible that we had accomplished this? Or was it a gift of chance?

It is not routine to be precise about these matters—there is a labyrinth of relations, after all, between the Maestro and the Dummkopf. I could list an endless register of compromises, brutalities, games, and deceits on both sides. So there is much to contemplate about these Russian ceremonial procedures, fortified as they are with their relics, their icons, such instruments of Monarchical ascension as the Chain, the Cross, the Crown, the Scepter, and the Orb. Then there is the Throne itself, resonant with blessings and curses, that same Throne upon which Tsar Michael Fyodorovitch sat in the year 1613. Of course, some of the faithful believe that the ceremony itself emits an indispensable Godly power which enters the pores, the flesh, and the heart of the Tsar. But I would suspect that this magic did not emanate entirely from the Dummkopf. The Maestro took pride in smuggling his wares into God's gifts.

We were not wholly unsympathetic, therefore, to the intensity with which Nicky believed in the Lord Almighty. The Maestro would look to turn such sentiments to our advantage. So I also knew many of us would be present when the procession set out from the palace at half past ten, each step buried in the peals of a thousand church bells, some as light as the rustle of leaves, others as heavy as the groans that issue from the heart of heavy metal. The priests inside Assumption Cathedral came out to welcome the Monarchs and give them the Holy Cross to kiss. The Trinity was invoked—three times were prayers repeated, three times were the holy icons embraced. Nicky and Alix then ascended the steps of the dais in the center of the cathedral. We knew it well. We were present when Michael Fyodorovitch, the first Tsar of the Romanov dynasty, had ascended to this same Throne, so I will not elaborate on how the Imperial Regalia were placed, nor repeat the address of the Metropolitan of St. Petersburg as he importuned Nicholas II to make his public confession. And Nicky did indeed make such a public confession, but in a voice spoken so low and with such brevity that no one could hear. After which, the Tsar read the prayer for the day, and the Metropolitan said, "The blessing of the Holy Spirit be with thee. Amen."

I can say that we are always ready to feel the approach of the Holy Spirit. (On many an occasion, His Blessing is infiltrated with our spirit.) Indeed, it was at this point that the Chain of the Order of Saint Andrew broke. Of course, the priests ignored this startling event. Among them, it is a rule of order never to indicate that some element in a sacred service has gone awry. Without pause, therefore, the Metropolitan made the sign of the cross, laid his hands on the Tsar's head, and said two prayers, after which Nicholas II was able to take up the Crown, place it upon his own head, and proceed to hold the Scepter in his right hand and the Orb in his left. He then placed his royal hindquarters once more on the seat of the throne of Tsar Michael Fyodorovitch. Whether or not he felt any residual resonance from such ancient contact, he rose but a few moments later, handed over the Regalia to his attendants, and beckoned to Alix, who knelt before him on a crimson cushion, its border of golden lace. Again cannon sounded from one hundred and one guns.

The ritual continued. Orthodox service on such occasions is never brief. Many who had felt some inner illumination at the commencement now settled into the weariness of their limbs. Boredom entered the Divine Liturgy. I have to wonder if that is not part of the genius of Russian worship. For the length of the service captured many in the congregation who were without real interest at the start. Ergo, there is no need to enumerate every step taken by the Tsar and the Tsarina once they descended from the dais. A measured three paces here, three there, the Trinity to be commemorated again and once again. Indeed, the Maestro always spoke well of the Trinity, as if he knew something others did not. I have seen the best man at a wedding who, unknown to all but the bride, has had carnal knowledge of the lady, and there is a subtlety in the posture of such a fellow that I do not find dissimilar to the nuance of appreciation our Maestro is always offering to the Holy Ghost. That is always the point of his attack. Since the Holy Ghost is the embodiment of the love of the Father for the Son, and the Son for the Father, so is it always a point of attack chosen by the Maestro in order to weaken that quintessential integrity.

I believe therefore that it was the Maestro's act which broke the link in the Chain of the Order of Saint Andrew.

# 10

The Tsar and his retinue would move from Assumption Cathedral to Archangel Cathedral, where, with a few variations, the service would be repeated before going on to the Annunciation Cathedral.

I was told that the Tsar and Tsarina were in need of rest but were facing a ceremonial meal in the Palace of Facets. In his diary, he would write, "All that happened in the Assumption Cathedral, though it seems but a dream, is not to be forgotten for life." To that he added, "We went to bed early." Whether this was from fatigue or a resurgence of lust from the good and happy sense that it was done and they would never have to do it again, I cannot say. I would certainly have liked to have been in their room. At the least, I would have learned how much the corrupted sanctity—I use precisely those two words, the corrupted sanctity—of these holy Metropolitans had to do with Nicky and Alix's raptures. Had these endless ceremonies served some sweet bubble of concupiscence? I suffered all the pains of exclusion.

If it seems strange that I am always hungry to learn more, let me dispel the common assumption that God and the Devil have all the knowledge they need. I would suggest that the easiest approach to comprehending my powers is to assume that I am about as much endowed beyond an accomplished scholar as he in turn is more knowledgeable than a clod from a poorly endowed school. Since I hardly command, however, every answer to questions that bedevil humankind, I, too, can be unmanned by what I do not know.

That night, occupied with my own preparations for the Peasants' Festival which was going to take place in four days, I also missed the banquet in the Palace of Facets. It was the event of the season for Moscow and for Russia, one of those social occasions which can offer great advancement to one's future if one has been invited—an orgy of putative achievement, therefore, to the richest of the nouveaux riches.

Of course, there was also much curdling of expectation among many of these ambitious souls. They were not always happy with where they had been seated. Studying other placements in the room gave them too close a measure of their present status in the world. Had it just been lowered? Indeed, only the most elevated of the guests were in the same room as the Tsar and Tsarina. The cream of the diplomatic corps was there, and the Holy Synod, as well as the Grand Marshal, the Grand Master of Ceremonies, the highest ministers, and some of the exceptionally wealthy. The remainder had been assigned to the Hall of St. Vladimir.

A blunting of one's sense of self-importance is, however, the last punishment a monarch would care to arouse among rich, celebrated, and powerful guests—nor does it require much wisdom to be aware of this. So Nicholas, in company with Alexandra, made a point of visiting every table in both rooms, followed by the Dowager Empress Marie, the Queen and Prince of Naples, the Duchess of Edinburgh, the Crown Prince of Sweden, Duchess Elisabeth and Grand Duke Alexey, all of them proceeding to table after table through the Hall of St. Vladimir, and were in turn greeted at each seating with the kind of ovation that issues from the parched throats of people who had been all too ready to assume that no matter what trials they had suffered to obtain an invitation, their efforts had been absurd. They were about to be ignored. What relief and what applause, then, to see the Tsar and Tsarina approaching.

I will not describe the meal. It would give me no pleasure to carry on about the gold plate, the French dishes, the categories of caviar, the wines (French and Crimean), the vodka, the champagne. Banquets succeed almost always in generating the same gastric acids, but here the guests were personally served by three waiters in red coats with gold trim. The menus were illustrated, the Imperial Band played throughout dinner, and the Palace of Facets sparkled.

In that era, journalists were not encouraged to speak ill of the great and mighty. So they all declared that this occasion would never be forgotten by posterity. The Palace of Facets was, after all, renowned for the rarity of its celebrations. Only the most important events in Russian history had the power to open such ancient doors. Ivan the Terrible and Peter the Great had held their Coronation banquets here. One of the reporters from America, obviously bewitched by the occasion, concluded her piece by saying:

> *So ended the greatest day of our lives, the one to be remembered for years. We all felt that we had seen the grandest sight that could possibly be imagined and we were pretty lucky mortals, everything had gone so beautifully.*

Another reporter from America stated that he not only believed now in Russia's immense potential for grandeur, but in Nicholas' legitimacy. Russia was more prosperous and more peaceful now than she had been for years.

> *. . . Nicholas II begins his reign with the good wishes of the entire world. Monarchies, empires, and republics alike united to wish him "bon voyage" on his momentous journey. From Germany, from France, from a venerable Queen who has reigned longest in the history of England's throne, from our own President, and from many other rulers of nations great and small, he received messages of warmest greeting, and above all, the great heart of the common people with a single impulse felt that it has in the kindly, smiling face of this youthful Tsar the promise of a reign beneficial and just.*

## 11

I could understand why Nicky's ministers considered it mandatory that this Coronation surpass every grand European celebration of the past. They were facing gigantic problems. If Russia was immensely rich, it was also extraordinarily poor. For the country to become an economic power comparable to Great Britain or to America, the rapid completion of the Trans-Siberian Railroad, begun years earlier, was now paramount. Ever in need of a large inflow of foreign funds to complete work on the track, Russia had been obliged five years before the Coronation to export most of its grain to the West. The Minister of Finance under Alexander III had declared that there was no other choice. Grain was the only commodity Russia could offer in bulk. So the largest portion of the harvest had been exported. That brought on the famine of 1891. Millions of peasants died.

Now hundreds of thousands of the relatives of these peasants had come to Moscow, where they congregated at various railroad stations in the city. Many slept on the floor. This occasioned a comment from the Maestro: "Of course these peasants are looking to stay in railroad stations. Five years ago they watched their grain being taken away on freight cars. Now they wait at the depot to see if it will come back."

The peasants were certainly of interest to us. Without their loyalty, how could Nicholas II exercise his rule? He could not count on the cities. The proletariat, recently peasants themselves, now lived with their diseases—cholera, typhus, syphilis, tuberculosis. Housing was desperately overcrowded. Alcoholism was an immense social problem, prostitution another.

The sale of the grain in 1891 had, however, served its economic purpose. Investment in heavy industry had tripled over the next ten years. To balance such growth, the sewers of Moscow, now glutted, would flood slum streets in summer even as workers froze to death in winter.

Those who remained in their villages still lived in one-room log cabins, their interiors blackened by smoke. Cheap reproductions of icons were on the wall, but any visitor who came into a peasant's cabin felt obliged, nonetheless, to bow before them. Only then could he greet the master of the house, who, as master, had the best place to sleep—which was on top of the oven, still warm from the remains of the fire that had heated the evening meal. The rest of the family slept on the dirt floor. To undress was unheard of, but if the room was not too cold, the men would take off their boots before lying down. They had a saying: "The reek of your feet will scatter the flies."

Nonetheless, I respected the peasants I watched at Moscow's railroad stations. If they were old before their time and had few teeth, they were as strong, nonetheless, as draft animals. For that matter, these men and women rarely moved—they had the patience of cattle. Yet my study gave me an intimation of why the Dummkopf was devoting so much attention to Russia. These poor, ugly, big, strong, dumb men with their plain, sturdy, and often misshapen wives might be mean, small-minded, ignorant, bewildered, even stupefied, but all that could amount to no more than protective wax over a fine jelly in a jar. Beneath their torpor, I could sense a capacity to be strong, wise, generous, fair, loyal, yes, even understanding, or so, at least, had Tolstoy and Dostoyevsky harangued their readers. If future genius was to be found in the peasantry of Russia, this was of grave concern to us. Our aim, after all, was to keep reducing human possibilities. We were looking forward to the point in time when we could take the reins from the Dummkopf.

## 12

My day was arriving. An immense gathering, scheduled to take place in Khodynskoe Field on May 18, would honor all the peasants now in the city. It would be a convening for those who had traveled hundreds of miles by railroad, by wagon, even some on foot, in order to be in Moscow when the Tsarevitch became the Tsar.

The event on the field had been planned to demonstrate Nicky's love for his people. It would celebrate their value. It would entertain them. Circus performers, singers, and dancers would appear, and at numerous stands and kiosks, gifts from the Tsar and Tsarina would be distributed. The great open stretches of Khodynskoe were ready to receive half a million souls. Four hundred thousand iron mugs, painted in red and gold, bearing Nicky's initials, would also be given out, as well as silk scarves for the women, ten thousand gallons of beer, and free packages of food containing Russian bread, walnuts, sausage, cookies, and jam, accompanied by a small book about the Coronation bearing the Tsar and Tsarina's initials.

To face the horde, Nicky, Alexandra, and members of the court were to arrive by midday and sit in state on a Royal Pavilion recently erected at one end of the parade ground. It would offer places to a thousand notables. Nearby would be another pavilion with seats for an additional thousand who were ready to pay for the privilege.

Among a few officials, there was, however, a good deal of concern that there might not be enough police. Only three officers had been assigned to oversee a company of one hundred and fifty Cossacks who would be brought in to serve as enforcers. One hundred and fifty Cossacks to control half a million Russian souls? Their commander applied for more guards but was told there was a shortage of police. Many other areas of the city had to be protected against demonstrations by rowdies or revolutionaries. Moreover, the government had already spent large sums maintaining security for the Tsar during the ceremonial week. Now there was no money available for more security. The hand of the Maestro was obvious to me in all of this.

We were ready to take advantage. Thirteen years ago, following the Coronation of Alexander III, Khodynskoe Field had also served as the site for a peasants' festival. While several unhappy episodes took place, and thirty peasants lost their lives, it had been considered an acceptable loss. One was not to be held accountable for every mishap in so large a gathering.

Indeed, it was Nicky who decided to hold the Peasants' Festival in the same place again. He wished to initiate a new tradition. "From what you tell me," he told his ministers, "we need more traditions."

One problem that was not examined, however, was the field. In 1891, a large exhibition had been held on its ground. Temporary construction had been thrown up, but no funds were available afterward for filling the excavations. This immense field was now scarred with sand pits, small gulches, uncapped wells, and abandoned foundations. Broad paths had been laid out to skirt these hindrances and it had been assumed that people would move prudently. There was, after all, enough level space for half a million visitors.

In truth, there had been more immediate concerns than Khodynskoe Field. The multitudes who were coming to Moscow had to be sheltered. Some peasants might have family members who worked in factories, and so could stay in their lodgings. The grease of sheepskin jackets and sweat-ridden capes, caftans, and black woolen coats would hardly be unfamiliar odors. And, of course, there were the railroad stations. They certainly did serve as housing. What was not anticipated, however, was the great number of peasants who decided to arrive at the field on the night before. By evening, multitudes were already encamped. There was drinking, there was singing, there were bonfires. Balalaikas were played. Through the city, word had gone out. Gifts would be distributed early. We had disseminated that rumor. Yes, the best stuff would go first. Thousands of peasants moved up, therefore, and started pressing on the wooden barriers that shielded the huts and kiosks and counters housing the gifts. Others began to push forward from behind. Then, hours in advance of first morning light, the working populace of Moscow started to arrive. The slums were marching in. They, too, had heard the rumor.

On this night of the seventeenth, a gala also took place at the Bolshoi Theater. Many ladies were wearing their diamonds, so many that the glow of the gems—as a good number remarked— might be ready to compete with the footlights. Yet most of the gentry were talking about the field. It was said that by late morning one million souls would throng to Khodynskoe. One million souls! "Yes," was the word at the Bolshoi, "never before have so many of the common people been ready to offer their reverence to the Tsar."

That was said at the gala. At the field, there was a most uneasy restlessness. Some peasants began rocking the posts that supported the barriers. "The good stuff is gone," our agents were there to say. "The mugs are gone. The beer is gone." "No," went a counter-rumor, "the beer is not gone, but there is little left." The barriers began to tilt. When the first one fell, the kiosks were at once over-run. But even as some were reaching for gifts, they were knocked down by throngs pushing up from the rear. Thousands jammed into the thousands already up front. A man had no more than to stumble and another would trip over him. A third would crash, a fourth was stunned. More bodies pushed forward. Women screamed. Children wailed. Masses of men, women, and children were now being driven pell-mell into the largest of the sand pits, and there they thrashed about in a hurly-burly at the bottom,

searching for a grip on someone else's body by which to climb out
of the pit even as others fell over them. Suffocations commenced. I
had never heard such woe. Thousands of throats were roaring with
rage. As many others were shrieking in terror. Smaller men and
women were thrown upward like spray. Children moaned under the
weight of boots clambering over them. The sounds were unearthly.
Who was to count how many hundreds of heels were grinding
down now upon hundreds of torsos? Or noses. Or eyes, or teeth. A
few even escaped. Some! A few children were lifted and passed
backward overhead. Adults able to reach the edge of the crowd collapsed like minnows in the shallows, not able to breathe nor stir,
then able to breathe, or just about. Others were braying out the
names of family members. Faces were already petrified by grief.

Yet, in the manner that a storm dies down, it came to an end.
Those who had broken through to the booths and trampled over
the kiosks were forced to keep moving forward by the ongoing
pressure of those behind—until finally they reached one end of the
field. Others squeezed their way off to the side. Some in the rear,
hearing screams ahead, drew back and pushed no longer. As the
frenzy abated, people moved off in four directions. The dead lay in
the pits and on the flats.

In these early hours of daylight while some of the fallen were
still quivering, disorder spread to the streets of Moscow. Tens of
thousands of Muscovites who had been planning to be present at
the official opening later that morning had chosen to leave homes
at an early hour to avoid the crowds. Now, as they approached on
foot, wagons were coming toward them, and these bloody wagons
were accompanied by men and women wailing in grief. Some were
hysterical. They would laugh for one moment, groan at the next.
Not knowing whether to consider themselves blessed for having
escaped, they also had to fear they were in peril of losing their
souls. So many felt an unholy readiness to laugh. How could they
not, when the smallest part of them had secretly despised the dead
relative for years?

Those who were still coming toward Khodynskoe had to be bewildered by all the screaming faces coming toward them from the field. Every wagon carried bodies clothed in various stages of ruined peasant finery. Many of the dead still lay on the field with shattered noses, bloody faces, broken limbs, cockeyed jaws, twisted bodies near to nude. On the wagons, more than a few had been covered over in the remnants and rags of other people's clothes, torn from one corpse to protect the dead modesty of another.

Later came estimates of the number of lives that had been lost. At first, Nicky was told that the number was three hundred, but that minister was well known for reducing bad news by 90 percent. Later, Nicky was told that it all came to thirteen hundred people. The final toll was three thousand. He could hardly have an idea of the count. The first impulse following the arrival of higher police officials was to get the bodies off the field before the Tsar arrived. Time later to count the dead.

Meanwhile, the morning was reaching into its full glory. It was the tenth fine day in a row. The onion domes of the forty times forty churches of Moscow were resplendent in the sun. The domes, covered with gold leaf, glowed as if they were children of the sun, and their bells, celebrating this event, came forth in a variety of clangor, loud or delicately toned. But to the ears of those walking away from the field, the sound of wailing was still in their ears, a cacophony of whimpering, howling, bawling, blubbering, sorrowing, and lamentation in unholy disharmony to the bells.

I, however, aroused by the extent of our triumph, felt as if I could see into the failings of half the people I passed. So many were sick in heart, sick in soul, sick in stomach, slime clinging to their spirit, lost in the vortex of a dream. Meanwhile, the sun reflected the gold of the onion domes above each church. For the past half year, laborers in high peril of slipping off the steep pitches of church roofs rimed in winter ice had labored nonetheless at fastening new leaf to these gilded domes.

# 13

At noon, before the Tsar and Tsarina arrived, most of the litter on Khodynskoe Field had been cleared. There was still torn clothing on the sand and in the pits, but the bodies were gone. Several companies of soldiers had been brought in to move the last of the dead out beyond the outlying kiosks. There, laid in orderly rows, they would remain until the wagons could transport them to a cemetery or relatives came upon their remains with shouts and screams of recognition. Of course, Nicky and Alix, on their arrival, were seated far enough away not to hear such sounds. Instead, a chorus of a thousand young men and women had been installed in front of the Royal Pavilion, and their voices prevailed. The viewing stands were filled with distinguished foreigners and Muscovites in their best uniforms, the ladies in afternoon finery. The social principle that one must never recognize unpleasantness during a formal occasion was in force. I have been present at galas when a guest, usually one of ours, breaks wind. The repugnance felt by those nearby will sit in the air for a few moments. Sometimes longer. No one remarks on it. For the social record, it has not happened. This ability to ignore the repellent has always been the ingrained strength of the upper classes.

Now, hearing this gifted chorus of one thousand heavenly voices offering a vocal collation, who would be in a rush to recognize that a few hours ago horrors had raged? No, the well-dressed Russians in the pavilions, given their desire to ape the best manners of the British upper classes, now carried themselves like privileged onlookers enjoying a notable day at the races. The ladies and gentlemen in the stands would have looked near to perfect, but for one contretemps. An unbelievably strong wind blew up without warning and scattered clouds of dust across the parade ground. This noxious whirlwind soon reached the pavilions at the edge of Khodynskoe. There should have been no such wind on so glorious a day. All had been still. Yet the gust had come. I hardly knew if I was witnessing the fury of the Dummkopf or the rage of the dead.

On the tail of this wind, the Tsar and Tsarina arrived. Everything changed. It was as if the gale were ready to be dispelled by one more uproar of cheers so loud one could barely hear the band, that immense orchestra of national brass that played the anthem with stentorian exaltation. Khodynskoe Field was now only half-visible in the fresh dust roused by the carriages of the latecomers arriving after the tumult of the morning. Soon enough, Nicky and Alexandra waved to people flocking in and, shortly after, left the pavilion to step into their carriage and be driven a few hundred yards over to Petrovsky Palace, where the Tsar would receive selected groups of chosen citizens. In the glimpse I caught of him, he looked exceptionally pale, and I wondered if he knew what had happened. I suspect his information was still highly imperfect but, in any event, the prearranged ceremonies were maintained. Not a quarter mile from Khodynskoe, Nicky and Alix now stood at the Petrovsky gates to receive these new delegations. In all, there were fourteen groups bearing gifts. A special offering from the Cathedral of Christ the Savior was presented to Nicky and Alix first—a large platter for ceremonial bread and salt. Nine months had been spent by eight men carving this platter out of crystal. Nicky screwed up his buttocks to force a little gratitude into his expression and then proceeded to thank the eight workers for the splendid niceties of their work. Next came a Cavalry regiment, the Georgiyevskys. A delegation of peasant women was followed by distinguished artists of the Moscow Imperial Theater. After which, a delegation from the Moscow coachmen paid their respects. There was even a gift from the Moscow All-Believers, who offered a silver platter on which Nicky's initials had been laid out in diamonds. They were soon re-

placed by an army of contractors who had decorated Moscow with
lights and false fronts for the Processional on May 9. Representatives of the caterers, plus the Society of the Hunt, the Moscow
Racing Club, and even (for their centuries of service since the time
of Peter the Great) a few leaders of the long-established German
colony in Moscow came filing by. After this, Nicky and Alix were
able to enter the palace and preside over a feast for the honored
representatives of the common people. Inserting his remarks between choruses of cheers, Nicholas II spoke to these plebeian el-
ders: "The Empress and I heartily thank you for your expression of
love and dedication. We do not doubt these feelings are shared by
your fellow villagers. Care for your welfare is close to my heart."

I happened to look at the time. To me, this is no more than a
phrase. I do not need a watch. No devil is ever without a clear sense
of the hour, the minute, even the second. So I can state that as the
Tsar was making this speech, a simultaneous event occurred at a
morgue—a devil reported the exact time of the other occasion.
Two of the corpses that had been laid out on morgue tables happened to rise up out of their comatose state. They even cried out in
unison. From opposite ends of the room! They had appeared to be
dead, but now they were obviously alive.

If I mention these upstarts, it is to emphasize the conjunction of
the two occasions. I would even learn that Alix was suffering her
own climax of foreboding at what had to be close to the same moment. To each of the guests who came forward, she had smiled and
bobbed her head, still a pouter pigeon. She was, however, living in
terror. She was filled with a thought that her own death was near
and so was Nicky's. In what danger was her husband! She even allowed herself to feel some open wrath against the Russian people.
Why, she asked herself, had they felt so obliged to riot? She even
said to her husband, "There is little courtesy among our Moujiks."
Nicky did not know whether to be offended or pleased that she
spoke of *our* Moujiks. (These thoughts I received at second hand
from a special Russian devil who maintained his entrée to one of
Alix's ladies-in-waiting.)

A half mile away from Petrovsky Palace, some soldiers were laying out the last of the victims, and on those far fringes of Khodynskoe Field, other hundreds of peasants and Muscovites were searching for lost family. Meanwhile, Nicky proceeded from table to table offering greetings to the villagers as they ate their Poltava Borscht, their veal with fresh greens, cold whitefish, roast spring chicken, duckling, fresh and pickled cucumbers, dessert, fruit, wines.

Back in the stands, jugglers and Gypsy dancers were performing for the gentry. Ice cream was being sold. And behind the hutches, corpses were still being laid out in rows while distraught relatives kept staring into the battered faces of those cadavers who had perished hours ago but might, despite all disfigurement, still retain a recognizable feature. A few of the disappointed even laid a copper coin on the cold chest of a stranger. In some places, piles of bodies remained in a heap, fifty here, twenty there, arms and legs at outraged angles, filthy clothing. Doctors knelt in the dust to see if anyone stirred. All of a sudden, one of the dead was no longer to be counted as dead. He rose up. His wife, who had been weeping beside him, began to beat herself on the breast. "God is here!" she screamed, "God is here! God has saved you!" But another family, just fifty feet away, engaged in false mourning for the demise of a long-lived family patriarch, were now shrieking. For that old tyrant had also opened his eyes. "The Devil sent you back, you monster!" his aged wife cried out.

## 14

I was not a leading actor during the riots just described. The Maestro had stated it directly: I was not sufficiently familiar with Moscow to command the local devils. Instead, I was to continue my watch on Nicky. I had to recognize that I had not been seen as pitiless enough to lead on the field. That pinched my vanity. I saw myself as capable of any task, high or low, but I should have known that my assignment to study the letters and diaries of the Romanovs would remain my basic role. Nonetheless, the knowledge proved of use for years to come. The Romanovs did not perish in a bloody muck of broken bones on that day, but they would certainly suffer depredations in the aftermath.

An immediate result was the lowered efficiency of the Cudgels. There were now gaps in the circle of protection they formed around Nicky. I was able, for example, to approach within reasonable distance of the Tsar when he and Alix showed up at midday to sit in the viewing stands. By grace of the passage which the Maestro had succeeded in keeping open to his thoughts, I could detect that Nicky was not only unseemly pale as he approached the pavilion, but that this pallor came from an unruly passion. I could feel its intensity. Some turn red with rage. He was pale with unspoken fury. Like Alix, his primal displeasure was directed toward the peasants. How could they have been so ungrateful, so self-destructive? Yet—heavy as chains lying upon his heart—it was his duty to forgive them. Could he call upon such a noble sentiment when he was marooned in anger? There were so many aspects to his fury. For he was equally enraged at the ineptitude of the police.

And, soon enough, was furious at himself. He had not paid attention to the arrangements for security. Much of this could have been prevented. Or was that true? Had the event been inevitable? Were his fortunes cursed? He did not know. He could hardly know. That night, he wrote in his diary:

> **Up till now, thank God, everything went perfectly but today a great sin has taken place. The crowd spending the night on the Khodynka meadow broke through the barrier and there was a terrible crush, during which it is terrible to say about 1,300 people were trampled.**

I kept studying the phrase "a great sin has taken place." Was it the rioters or himself to whom he referred? For on the afternoon of May 18, Count Witte, who was the particular statesman Nicky listened to most, had sent word: "In respect for the dead, all festivities should be canceled immediately." Then, Witte added, "Most particularly, the French Ambassador's Ball." That was scheduled to take place on this very night, and it had been planned as the grandest evening of the Coronation.

Disagreement with Count Witte came quickly. Nicky's uncle, the Governor General of Moscow, the Grand Duke Sergey Alexandrovich, married to Alix's older sister, Ella, had taken over, among his other duties, the position of Director of the Peasants' Festival. By messenger, Sergey Alexandrovich sent a reply to Witte: "The Tsar considers Khodynka a great disaster, but would inform you that in effect it was not so great a disaster that it should darken the Coronation holiday."

The older Grand Dukes, brothers to this Governor General, were in accord. Their sentiments, however, were revolting to Nicky's cousins, the younger generation of Grand Dukes. Indeed, Nicky's dearest friend—his first cousin Sandro, who was married to Nicky's sister Xenia—declared that the attitude of his uncles, these older Romanovs, this senior level of Grand Dukes, could only be described as "monstrous." And Sandro's brothers, the sons of Grand Duke Mikhail, were in passionate agreement. Under no circumstances should Nicky attend the French Ball tonight. What an outrageous insult to the dead! Where was Russia's honor? The Tsar, four days into his Coronation, was ready to agree with Sandro, but just then came Uncle Alexey into the room, and this Grand Duke was the oldest remaining brother of his dead father.

"Nicky," said Uncle Alexey, "surely you are aware that your cousins, these Mikhailovichi, and Sandro most particularly, are not people you can afford to listen to. They are young and inexperienced. They are radical. They are silly. They are worse than silly. I tell you, they will never admit it to themselves, but they are siding with unholy forces. They wish to depose Sergey Alexandrovich so they can put in one of their own as Governor General of Moscow. Think what that will do to Sergey Alexandrovich and to Ella. Your wife will be distraught that her beautiful sister Ella has to suffer this disgrace."

I was near enough to hear these opinions. Again, the Cudgels were not about. A host of just-perished souls must have been in need of succor—perhaps the Dummkopf had dispatched the Cudgels to the morgue. This once, at any event, it was not at all difficult to stay close to Nicky.

So I heard Sandro's brother Nikolai Alexandrovich. So soon as Uncle Alexey marched off, he was ready to speak. "Nicky, I beg of you, do not go tonight to the French Ball. Recognize what I am saying. Whether we like it or not, we are still living in the shadow of Versailles. Louis XVI and Marie Antoinette could dance all night because they were naïve. They had no sense of the approaching storm. But we do. We know!

"Nicky, search into your heart. What happened, has happened. The blood of these men, these women, and these children will remain forever upon your reign. That is unfair, because you are good, you are kind. I know, if you could, you would revive the dead. But you cannot. So, Nicky, you must show your sympathy to their families. Your allegiance to them. Your respect. How can you allow the enemies of this regime to be able to say that our young Emperor was engaged in dancing through the night while his slaughtered subjects were still unburied?"

His eloquence succeeded. Nicky now knew that he did not want to go to the Ball. But his cousin was unable to maintain the high level of his argument. He soon surrendered to rage. "Why, I would ask," he went on, "didn't Sergey Alexandrovich anticipate how great was the need for police? Any fool could have told him." Soon enough, he was suggesting that nasty tricks had been played. Could he have been listening to the same rumors we had generated? In Moscow, the word was out. Many were being told that the Governor General had siphoned off Coronation funds to pay his gambling debts. It was not true. Sergey Alexandrovich was not guilty. It happened to be his assistant. (The fellow was not only in debt to gamblers, but to us—one of our Russian agents. Indeed, it was this assistant to Sergey Alexandrovich who had initiated the rumor that the Governor General was corrupt.)

Poor Nicky. If he had one weakness, it was that he could not hold two opposed ideas in his mind long enough to decide which might have more to offer. Just as he was in the midst of giving real attention to cousin Nikolai's fine speech, so two of his uncles came back to the room. They proceeded to explain, and in the sharpest terms, that it would be an international insult should Nicky not be present at the Ball. The French Embassy had made expensive preparations. The absence of the Tsar and Tsarina would affect relations between the two countries. "Nicky, we depend upon the French alliance. For that alone, you must attend. The French take pride in measuring themselves by the sanity they can muster in crises. They detest sentimentality. They are proud of their *froideur.* If you are absent, they will see you as a womanly creature, swayed by compassion, exactly when we are in need of sound diplomacy. Foreign policy must not be affected by accidents."

Nicky attended. He had the first dance of the evening with Countess Montebello, who was the wife of the French Ambassador, and Alix danced with the Count. In his diary, Nicky left this comment:

**The Montebello Ball was very magnificently done, but the heat was unbearable. We left after supper at two o'clock.**

Meanwhile, the Governor General of Moscow was smiling. He was enjoying the Ball. Grand Duke Sergey Alexandrovich had a favorite saying: "It does not matter how awful the day has been. One must possess the character and the wit to be able, when the music is lively and your drinks inspire, to enjoy an evening to the full. That is also our duty."

Sandro and his brothers had long been aware of Sergey's credo. So, on this night, they found his presence doubly intolerable. They made a point of leaving at the moment that dancing began. Uncle Alexey spoke out loudly: "There go the four imperial followers of Robespierre."

I was content. The Maestro would be pleased. He would also be amused, I was certain, when he learned that I had been able to insinuate myself into the Royal Chamber that night. Yes, I had reached the Bedroom. The Cudgels were in more disarray than I could ever recall.

For a few minutes (just before the Cudgels returned and I hurried to decamp), I was able to insinuate myself a little further into Nicky's mind, and I can report that he felt doomed. Doomed and damned. He knew this with certainty. It would take more than two decades to confirm what he knew on this night, but this night he knew. He was truly appalled. He told Alix that it might be his duty to retire to a monastery, where he could pray for the victims. It was no way to speak to a wife on a night so full of a sense of doom. It may even account for the letter Alix would yet write to her friend the German Countess Rantzau.

> **I feel that all who surround my husband are insincere. And no one is doing his duty for Russia. They are all serving him for their career and personal advantage and I worry myself and cry for days on end as I feel my husband is very young and inexperienced—of which they are taking advantage.**

How much more she might have wept if she had known what the ladies in Moscow were saying about her.

Before the Coronation, she had made a critical mistake. She had confided to her closest Lady-in-Waiting that she adored Nicky. "I love him so much. I call him secret names."

"What are these secret names?" asked the Lady-in-Waiting.

"Oh, I cannot tell you. They are so secret. I call him many sweet words, usually in English. For me, that is a warm language. Most hospitable."

It came out. Bit by bit. At last, it was in the air—her secret. The big secret that the Lady-in-Waiting swore she would never pass on to a soul. And the Lady-in-Waiting did not—not for a day or two. Then she told it to her dearest friend, and in turn this lady swore that she could be trusted altogether and forever.

In the event, the dearest friend did not feel free to give the secret away too quickly. It took a few nights before she told one friend and then another. They, too, took a vow of silence but did not wait as long before transgressing their oath. Moscow's society was soon snickering over the Tsarina's much-avowed love of English. Anyone who had a reputation for knowing what others did not know was now familiar with Alix and Nicky's secret words to each other. "Lovy, Boysy, Sweet One, My Soul, Manykins-mine, Sweetie, Pussy-mine."

After they finished laughing at Alix, one of the ladies felt bound to remind the others, "She comes to us from behind a coffin. She carries misfortune."

For that matter, the Governor General of Moscow was now called "the Prince of Khodynka."

# 15

I n the week that followed, there were eight days of fetes, dances, receptions, state visits, and musicales. On May 19, there was a banquet in Alexander Hall in the Kremlin, and on the twentieth, the Governor General of Moscow gave his own ball. The twenty-first brought the Moscow nobility together at the Hall of Columns, Prince Trubetskoi as host. Four thousand guests appeared. On the twenty-second, Nicky and Alix made a state visit to the Troisky-Sergeyevsky monastery, and on the morning of the twenty-third, Nicky gave twenty thousand rubles as a first installment on a children's home for the orphans of Khodynka. That evening, there was dinner with the English Ambassador at a palace ball in the St. Andrew Hall of the Kremlin. Thirty-one hundred guests. The Germans, laying low, gave no more than a musicale at their embassy next evening, which was followed by a palace dinner for all the ambassadors on the twenty-fifth. For conclusion, they were back at Khodynskoe Field on the twenty-sixth to witness a military review. The pits had been filled by then. It was another brilliant day, and Nicky's carriage was drawn by six white horses. Thirty-eight thousand five hundred sixty-five enlisted men marched in company with two thousand officers. Sixty-seven generals watched.

By now, I was awaiting orders to leave. I did not know if I could acclimate myself to Hafeld after these exceptional days in Moscow, but the Maestro was quick to tell me: "Respect Hafeld. It is important." There was no reason to believe or disbelieve him—his real opinion was, after all, concealed within his impenetrable bearing, but I can say that on my arrival back to Austria, I did feel better than I had in years. Khodynskoe Field had been the largest operation in which I had participated for a long time. Or so it seemed.

It is sad that few devils are permitted to retain much memory, but the Maestro employs the same principle as Intelligence agencies. No one in Intelligence is supposed to know anything about a project until there is a need to know. We, in turn, are not encouraged to remember whatever we will not use for a new project.

Since I believe that I have been a devil for many centuries and have risen in rank and been demoted, it could be asked why, with such a history, I still learned a good deal while in Russia. It is because a newly gained sophistication fades once a venture comes to an end. So we develop many new qualities of mind, but soon lose them. What is curious here is that the Maestro allowed me to keep these recent experiences intact. Khodynskoe remained in my memory and my morale stayed close to excellent. Returning to the Hitler family, I could, given our success in Russia, believe again that the Maestro's aims were not small for this client, this young Adolf Hitler.

Filled now with a lightness of spirit altogether apart from the heaviness that is requisite to being loyal when there is no choice, I felt elevated upon my return to Hafeld. Soon enough I no longer thought about Nicky or Alix. Where was the need? If in future I was to be called back to Russia, the necessary recollections would be reconstituted.

In fact, it is interesting that I had such thoughts, for, indeed, I was sent back in 1908, and would remain in Russia intermittently until the murder of Rasputin eight years later—that incomparable Rasputin, a most exceptional client. He was able to work in the closest union with me, but did insist upon continuing as well in the service of an astute and elevated Cudgel. What wars we had over Rasputin and the exceptional ins and outs of his soul.

I may yet look to portray these exceptional events, but that is not for this book. All large interruptions concluded, I now wish to record what happened to Alois, Klara, and Adolf over the next nine years. That will bring a close to this literary venture. For the present, then, we are back at the farm.

From here, I can see the path that leads to Der Alte's house.

# BOOK IX

## ALOIS JUNIOR

# 1

There was an odd matter waiting on my return to Hafeld. It was to convince Der Alte to burn one of his hives. He had been stung so severely by his bees that I found him in bed with a cruelly swollen face. Several of the stings had come close to his eyes.

Given Der Alte's skills, he could not comprehend how so embarrassing an event had occurred during the course of looking into one of his better hives. While attempting to replace the Queen—she was showing the first unmistakable signs of final fatigue—he had been attacked by her escort. Der Alte was able to subdue this revolt with the cigar he happened to be smoking at the time, but so drastic a revolt of his creatures had not visited him in years. It aroused my paranoia (which is always there in ready supply, since it is preferable to poor powers of anticipation). I had to assume that this attack by the bees was inspired by the Cudgels, and so the hive had to be destroyed.

Upon receiving my order—which I passed into him as he slept—Der Alte did not obey quickly. A few days went by. Again, I sent the thought into his sleep, but now with emphasis enough for him to recognize that it could not be construed as a dream but as an imperative, which left our old fellow full of dismay. "Do it," I repeated to him in his sleep, "it will be good for you. Tomorrow is Sunday. That will augment the good effect. Sundays provide double value. But do not employ a sulphur bomb. Too many could survive. Rather, soak the hive with kerosene. Then light it, box and all."

He groaned in his sleep. "I cannot do that," said Der Alte. "The Langstroth cost me dearly."

"Burn it."

Der Alte followed my orders. He had to. At his age, he knew how deeply we were infiltrated into him. He did not wish to live with the terrors we could arouse, fears as real to his flesh as an ulcer. Death was close to his thoughts, sometimes as close a caged beast in the next room. All of this, however, left me indifferent. It is hard not to feel contempt for old clients. They are so submissive. Of course, he did it. What facilitated the act was that a good part of him was still enraged by the attack from his bees. His sense of the given had been upset. Old habits are willing to afford few shocks.

Sunday morning, he laid the hive on the ground and doused it. Staring into the commotion that seethed up in its flames, he did feel better. I was on the mark. It *had* been good for him. But he was perspiring like a horse. He was, after all, full of woe at the incineration itself—that did violate his professional instincts. He expected to weep for all those innocents now scorched into extinction with the guilty, but to his surprise, a rare sweetness returned to his loins. This was the first such sugaring of his body he had felt in years. As with many an old man, his lust had been confined to his head. It had been a long time since any accompaniment to a libidinous thought had been more memorable than a twinge of his groin.

I will mention that Adi happened to be present at the burning. He, too, had been given a message in his sleep which he had no difficulty in accepting. He slipped away from Klara and Angela even as they were preparing to go to church. Nor did his escape bother Klara unduly. Adolf was no joy to bring along. If not squirming in his seat, he would commence a contest with his stepsister to see who could succeed in pinching the other. On the sneak.

Yes, to be alone with Angela on Sunday morning allowed Klara to feel a little closer to her stepdaughter. If the truth be witnessed, she was also content not to bring Edmund along, nor to be obliged to hold Paula at her breast through the service, hoping all the while

that she did not wish to be fed. Today Alois had said he would remain with the two little ones. Klara could hardly believe such gen-
erosity. Was he softening? Was that possible? That was certainly
another question I might have to explore. But first I would speak
of Adi's excitement during this burning of the bees. His toes tingled, his heart shook in its chamber, he did not know whether to
scream or to roar with laughter. The ardors of living in Russia had,
however, left me a touch indolent. I did not, as yet, feel eager to
reenter the complexities of this particular six-year-old. My morale
was, as I have said, in fine shape, but I did not wish to set it to work
so soon. Indeed, on my return to modest duties in this region of
Austria, I did not mind that existence was simpler. Hafeld might
even be ready to offer its own revelations, and meanwhile, it allowed me to live with the subtlety of small tasks. I could, for example, witness a few changes in Alois' spirit. That alone was enough
to interest me.

For example, Klara had been mistaken. Alois was not softening,
not exactly. He had told her it was good for him to spend a little
time with the small ones every now and again, but the moment she
left, he put Paula in her trundle bed and told Edmund to stay in the
room and make certain she did not wake up. He knew Adolf would
go off by himself, and Alois Junior would be on the other side of
the hill with Ulan. Indeed, he was looking forward to being alone.
He wanted to meditate upon Der Alte's mishap. That event had
left Alois feeling cozy. A dire expectation was gone. He had always
expected to be the one savaged by the bees.

All through May, as the weather turned warm, Alois' recurring
fear had been that he would lose his colonies. He lived with a vivid
picture of himself up there, high in a tree, much too high, trying to
charm a maddened swarm back to their hive. The sad fact was that,
having eaten well through the winter, he felt as overstuffed as a
man who has crammed 250 pounds into a 200-pound sack.

Small surprise, then, if this Sunday he was ready to let his face
go slack, his stomach rumble, his sphincter break wind. There had
been too many weeks through the winter, and now even into the
spring, when he had become convinced he was going to fail at some

serious activity that would wipe out some important part of his self-esteem. If such an end once seemed unlikely because his vanity forbade it, that same energetic vanity (which he had constructed up from boyhood piece by piece, episode by good episode) now seemed to be fading. Where was his confidence? He had not gone to church on this Sunday, no more than any other. Of course not, not if he could help it. Yet he no longer knew whether he could continue to stay away. On this particular Sunday, he had even thought of accompanying Klara.

The thought was odious. To sit in a pew through the drivel! Such an act would wipe out his sense of himself as a man who does not shiver as others do. But possessing bees had scared the hell out of him. Might this last year have loosened the keystone of his pride? No one else he knew had ever been as ready to thumb his nose at bad omens. That was an achievement not common to any-one born as a peasant.

Yet, just a week ago, his hands had begun to shake while reading a story in his newspaper about the death of a beekeeper. The man had not recovered from an outbreak in a hive.

Looking to allay such fears, Alois even paid Der Alte a visit. This occurred while the old man was still in bed and at his weakest. Indeed, Der Alte burst into tears while describing his mishap. It left Alois with the same sense of cockeyed virtue that a younger brother can feel when he sees the older one cry.

Afterward, for a few days, Alois was relieved of his fear. He could not say why, but Der Alte's ill fortune had relieved his own dread. Now it was coming back. He had not felt right ever since Alois Junior had returned. He could not be such a fool, he told himself, as to live in fear of his bees because he was not at ease with his son. All the same, that could be the truth! Human beings were full of subterfuge. He had learned as much at Customs. He re-membered a woman who wrapped her gifts in the folds of her black lingerie. A good-looking woman. When caught by Alois, she was brassy enough to smile and say, "You are so smart. The other offi-cers were afraid to touch these private things."

"That," he told her, "is because most of my associates go to church. You did not have good luck this morning."

She laughed. He was tempted to let her off. Let her avoid the cost of the fine by smuggling him into her thighs. But he hadn't allowed himself. Serious rules he would not disregard.

All the same, the recollection kept him brooding about the nature of subterfuge. Back in the days when he could still enjoy a ride on a horse, there had usually been one or another steed who could rob some of his confidence, something in their gait—as if, should they choose, you would find what might as well be five legs under you rather than four. You wouldn't know a damned thing about how to control that kind of animal.

Yes, that was like Alois Junior.

On the other hand, he might be making too severe a judgment on his oldest son. Klara kept saying that Junior did not seem to be the same boy who had gone away to work for Johann Poelzl. Her parents must have been good for him. His manners were nice. He did not look to be judging you all the time. Before he had gone away, Klara said, he was like a friend who was warm to your face but would say something ugly so soon as you left. She had no proof, but she would swear that was how he used to be. Now there was something better about him. Maybe. He still spent too much time riding Ulan. Yet, as Klara also announced to Alois, she was ready to put up with that. Better to ride over the hill than to start flirting with his own sister.

"What would you ever know about such matters?" Alois asked.

"I don't," said Klara. "But when I was young, I saw things. In certain families. It is not something to talk about."

That she and Alois might have something larger and more private to talk about was not evident in her voice. She flushed only a little as she spoke.

This ability to wall up the most unpalatable facts about oneself will always elicit my unwilling admiration. I do not know if the inner construction of such a barrier is equal in difficulty, let us say, to scaling the Alps, but in any event, credit must go to the Dummkopf. He created the ban against incest—we certainly didn't—and then it became His secondary task to protect humans, should they ever do it, from remembering what they had done.

We lose certain advantages thereby. Most men and women are incapable of facing unpleasant truths. They have what can only be a God-given ability to conceal themselves from themselves. So I could appreciate how Klara was full of unadmitted worry over Alois Junior and Angela and never spent a moment pondering whether her husband was not her uncle but her father.

## 2

I, too, had been pondering the changes in Alois Junior. On the face of it, he had improved. If manners were a guide, he had become a reasonable imitation of a trustworthy and pleasant youth.

The devils I had left behind were now pleased to tell me that they had made a copy of a short letter Johann Poelzl had sent back with Alois Junior. It gave a definite and most decent opinion of the lad.

I could hardly trust the validity of the letter. For one thing, it was not the original but a copy made by the agent. That voided one of my talents—I can obtain a good deal of insight by no more than a glance at a person's handwriting. Many an undisclosed corner of the soul is revealed. Falsities stand out like acne.

As I have already indicated, the devils I had left in Hafeld had not been skilled. So they did no more than study Johann's letter (left in Klara's sewing basket) and make a copy. Possessed of more technique, they could have forged a facsimile and kept the original.

Bereft of the calligraphy, I had to content myself with the words.

**Esteemed daughter,**

**This I give to the boy. He will give to you. Your mother says he is good boy. She will cry for missing him. That is what she says.**

**Tell your esteemed husband. Alois Junior is good. Hard worker. Very good.**

**Your father,**

**Johann Poelzl**

I could have put in a request for one of our nocturnals in Spital to pass through Johann's thoughts on a milk run, but I decided to wait. He was a stubborn old man ready to repel any entrance into his mind, and I could learn as much as I needed to know about Alois Junior in Hafeld. The minor devils left here had, to my surprise, improved to some degree. Even without my surveillance, they were picking up our trade. One of them might soon be ready for lessons in dream-etching.

I will not, however, bother to describe them closely. At present, more than a century has passed, and former devils offer even less pleasure to memory than mediocre songs. While a man or woman's presence is closely related to their body, and so offers a multitude of insights, we devils are without salient personality except when it is necessary to dwell within some man or woman's body for the length of a project. Then we do have a presence and it is near to indistinguishable from the person we inhabit. I would say it bears no more relation to ourselves than a change of garment.

We enjoy a happier existence in the land of the dream. There—if we are ready to afford the expenditure—we can be anyone we wish. Some improvisations are brilliant. Indeed, if dreams dictated as much of human history as we desired, the Dummkopf would soon be the Maestro's retainer.

But we were nowhere near to such a point. Certainly not back in 1896. God was still the Lord of our immediate universe. Humans, animals, and plants were still His Creation. Nature, imperfect as it was and, on occasion, cataclysmic (due, I must repeat, to imperfections in His design), remained nonetheless in His command, that

far-from-faultless command. Only the night belonged in good part
to us.

Being most aware of this, the Maestro frowned upon self-
approbation. He let us know that devils were not to congratulate
themselves on the terrors they had initiated by nightmare. "Dreams
are evanescent," he told us. "Control of events belongs to the day."

Control of events? The Maestro was certainly keeping alive his
interest in the Hitlers of Hafeld, but when I looked to comprehend
why, his avowed high hopes for young Adolf Hitler made me wonder whether I could discern the Maestro's real interests. Our special six-year-old might be no more than one of a hundred or a
thousand prospects whom the Maestro was overseeing with no
more than the remote likelihood that they might yet become important to our serious intentions. Any estimate that my task might
be of major magnitude was obliged, then, to rise and fall more than
once in the immediate seasons ahead.

## 3

I have not described, and do not intend to list, the numerous
other activities, undertakings, and small explorations that the
devils under my authority were engaged in through those parts
of the province of Upper Austria (which includes Linz and the
Waldviertel). By now, they are of no interest.

History has, however, underlined the perspicacity of the Maestro's projections into the future, and so if I return in my understanding to the summer of 1896, it is with the strength of knowing
that one's work has been of significance: many a detail that is now
recalled was worthy of our attention.

I can assert, therefore, that Alois Junior was demonstrating his

considerable talent to charm whoever was in his immediate surroundings. For a time, he even succeeded in leavening the heavy
suspicion that emanated from Alois Senior's person, who, when he
was in an ugly mood, could come upon others like a wall of oncoming bad weather—an unsettling affect he had often used at Customs
while confronting a dubious tourist. Yet, such was the boy's charm—
a nice combination of youth, health, a touch of wit, and apparent
goodwill—that his father could not maintain this massive psychic
front for more than a few days. Moreover, Alois Junior was show-
ing some interest in the bees. He had many good questions to ask.

Before long, Alois Senior was beginning to feel a rare
happiness—he so seldom liked his children. Now he did. One of
them, at any rate. He even began to give Alois a few of his best lectures on beekeeping, and before long repeated all of his earlier
speeches to Klara and Angela and Adi, plus his monologues at
the Linz taverns, to which he could now add the newer ones at
Fischlham, where he played the resident expert from Hafeld. The
boy picked it up so quickly that Alois had to dip into more advanced knowledge of the sort he had ingested from reading apicultural journals. Finally, he was even presenting a few of Der Alte's
finer insights as his own, as, for example, the near humanity of the
bee, or the delicacy and high inspiration of their lives. The boy
kept taking it in, and he was deft when working with the hives. Senior began to dream of a future where father and son might add
colony to colony. This could become a true business.

One day he was feeling so proud of Alois Junior that he brought
him along on a visit to Der Alte. He had hesitated before deciding
on such a move—he certainly did not wish to be replaced as the
local expert in Junior's estimation. On the other hand, he was
proud of his association with Der Alte, so learned a man, yet ready
to treat him as an equal—that, too, might impress the boy.

The truth is that he was no longer uneasy over the beekeeper's
superiority. He had been fortified by the hour when Der Alte all
but wept in his arms. Moreover, he had again a practical need for
advice. His hives were full of honey. He had studied his manuals on

the technique of honey gathering, but he did not feel ready. In the old days, back at Passau and Linz, he used to make a botch of it. The honey he gathered was ridden with small chunks of wax, and—no matter his veil and gloves—he had received a few too many nasty bites where the cloth gaped on his neck and wrists.

Now it would be closer to a major effort. He could hardly sell the better part of this harvest if his product was not free of detritus. One dead fly was enough to spoil a sale if the customer saw it first!

So here he was seeking advice once more from the old goat. Yet now he felt more tolerant. It was amazing to Alois how little he was offended on this occasion by the aroma of the hut. Der Alte might know more about bees, but he, Alois, knew enough not to burst into tears just because something went all wrong.

He took Alois Junior with him, therefore, and Der Alte responded to the visit with warmth. He was happy not to be alone. His convalescence had dragged along and was sometimes as painful as a sharp light in the eye. His pride had drooped under the weight of all that was missing in his life. Hermits are not often ready to undergo intense self-examination. It hardly matters whether they are hermits protected by the Cudgels, or in service to us, or, very occasionally, unaffiliated—although this last is a feat, considering the loneliness, but in any event, such clients usually have to be taken at least once a year through a cleansing of their moods. For this last week, I had had to spend time on Der Alte. His spirit had fallen before the knowledge that he could not see himself in any way as a social leader—which had been the most intense of his early ambitions. He had no mate, no heirs, no real money. And his memory kept reminding him of men or women who had done him injuries which he had failed to pay back. Under it all was the heavy disappointment that he had not arrived at any of the powers and distinctions to which his intelligence should have entitled him. As is so often true of the depression that follows an unexpected accident, he saw this affliction as a judgment on himself.

I made a point of being present, then, during Alois' visit, for I wanted to improve Der Alte's mood. If a client's thoughts can be darkened when we wish to drive them down a bit, so too do we have the skill to lift a man out of a black mood for an hour or two, even—if it comes to it—provide a moment of joy. We do not want them to expire emptily. (Much better for us if they die young and in a rage.) Most of our old clients either cease to exist—no soul is left!—or are reincarnated by the Dummkopf, who does not like to give up on any of His creatures, large or small, wise or foolish—which may be one reason the world becomes more and more over-run by mediocrity.

The situation is, of course, never simple, since we, too, have to look to take what profit we can still extract from worn-out clients.

I was looking, therefore, to improve Der Alte's mood. Indeed, I was able to give him relief from his unhappiest thoughts so soon as Junior and Senior came to visit. I even connected him again to the notion that he was an attractive man. Vanity is always the human sentiment most available to us. Der Alte, therefore, felt powerfully attracted to Alois Junior. It was the first time in many years that he had felt the desire to make love to an adolescent.

After the introductions and the formal query about his health, they began to discuss the procedure. "Honey gathering! Of course! I can tell you about that."

In full form, intensely aware of the boy, Der Alte felt more than ready to launch into an exposition on the lesser-known aspects of the process.

"Yes," said my rejuvenated old fellow, "honey gathering is an art in itself. I am glad you have come to me on this day because, truly, able as your father has become in his short period here at Hafeld—a brilliant man, your father—nonetheless, the best of beekeepers have to learn what is virtually a new vocation when, after the long winter and a kindly, warm spring that fulfills our hopes, the larvae in our brood combs are now ready to hatch. That, if I may say, is a most pregnant moment for our vocation. The hives are teeming. The old bees are out on flights, and the youngsters are assigned to the innumerable tasks of housekeeping, one of which, for example, is to fill empty wax combs with honey and cap them with a fine, thin layer of wax. Specialists among the bees are given that assignment. Young Alois, it is equal to a miracle. Such workers are young, some are just ten days old, but already we may think of them as craftsmen. The layer of wax that covers each tiny comb has no more thickness than good stout paper."

Alois restrained himself from saying, "I know that already," and winked instead at Junior. He had told the boy to be prepared to listen. "When it comes to his bees, Der Alte can speak in full paragraphs. Sometimes it is full pages. All you need do is nod. I already know nine parts in ten of what he will say, but it is like fishing. Be patient, and you will get what you came for."

"So, yes," Der Alte now said, "the honey gathering, if not done properly and at the right time, can be a rude interruption of the work of the bees. The first question to ask oneself, therefore, is what will be the best hour to remove your honey from the hives?" He held up a hand as if to police his own exposition. "It is the late morning," said Der Alte. "That is definitely the best time. The hives are warm but not yet too hot. The worker bees are somnolent. I would go so far as to say that your little creatures might be taking a siesta at this time. They are, after all"—and he laughed—"*Italian* bees."

To be courteous, Alois smiled. So did Junior.

"Well, then," said Der Alte, "we take the great step. For that, I will have to lend you an empty hive body."

"Is it because we will have to transfer the bees who are in the honey chamber?" asked Alois Junior.

"Exactly," said Der Alte. "Your sense of anticipation is excellent. Your imagination is closely focused, I can see, on the particularities of this situation."

"Yes," said Alois Senior, "he is a bright boy, but if I may venture my opinion, there is no way to separate those honey-chamber bees from the honey unless one brings up a separator board."

"Of course," said Der Alte, "and so the first move, then . . . ?"

"Locate the Queen," said Senior. "That's one thing you taught me." He turned to Junior. "Yes, bees will panic when they do not know where their Queen is. To move them from one box to another, you also have to transfer her."

"Exactly," said Der Alte. "I have shown your father how to locate the lady. Then you must introduce a queen cage"—he took a little box from his pocket the size of a deck of cards. "With this, you will use a catching glass."

"Yes, my father has shown this to me. He even let me blow one of the Queens from the catching glass into the cage."

"That is a nice procedure," said Der Alte. "In a year or so, however, when you become as highly accomplished as I expect, you will dispense with the cage. You will be able to pick up the Queen with your fingers."

"Yes," said Alois Senior, "but don't try it in a hurry," and he made a gesture of slapping frantically at invisible bees, as if to remind Der Alte how this bold procedure could invite a disaster.

"Just yesterday," said Der Alte, "I moved three of my Queens into three separate hives. With my fingers. I could have used the catching glass. Undeniably, it is as your father suggests, a more cautious procedure. But I am like an acrobat who has taken a serious fall. There is no solution but to get up on that *verdammten* tightrope again."

Actually, Der Alte had gone back to the catching glass for these transfers, but as an experienced client, he was able to lie with whole assurance on any subject. His desire to elicit Junior's admiration was all the impetus he needed. First, however, Alois had to be neutralized.

"Your father," he now said to Junior, "has, as usual, gone to the heart of the matter. The Queen once removed, your bees will use the separator board to escape from the honey chamber into the brood chamber, for that is where you have relocated the Queen. How they will struggle with one another in their haste to use the exit and so be able to reunite themselves with their lady."

He smiled at Alois Junior. "Ah, to be young again and on the hunt for a young woman. In the old days, nothing could stop me. Would you say there is anything that might stop you?"

"Yes," said Alois Junior, "my father." All three laughed.

"You must listen to your father."

"I am prepared to," said the youth. He smiled warmly at Der Alte, as if to offer one concrete instant when they could feel nicely connected to each other. Before the air between them could take on such emphasis, however, Alois Junior made a point of adding, "I think you have confused me. Aren't all these bees little women?"

"Yes," said Der Alte, "in the technical sense, if we speak of their gender they are female, but, of course, they are not queens, so their generative organs are undeveloped. Consequently, they act like men. Some become guards. They defend all the gates in the hive. Some are warriors. Most of them are loyal, determined, hardworking. In that case, yes, they are like women, too. They live for the good of the hive. But they are like men when it comes to worshipping the Queen."

"This is all wonderful to hear," said Alois Senior, "but I am still waiting to get my honey out of the hive."

"In that case," said Der Alte, "I will give you the key."

"Timing," said Alois Senior. "You told us already."

"Yes, that is the general rule of thumb. But what is the secret to timing? It is to wait until you hear an unmistakable sound of happiness rising from the hive. Exactly so! When the honeycomb is full, and the bees know they have made good honey, why, they are ready to act like women again. They sing to each other. You must be able to recognize this sound. They sing in joy. On the morning after you have heard such a chorus of contentment, you must be ready to lead all these good bees through the exit in the separator board into the chamber where you have moved the Queen. Then, of course, the honey will be left ready and open to our invasion, if I may put it that way. But come, I will lead you outside. One of my hives is now singing this song of contentment."

I went with them to hear it. I do not know if I would have interpreted the hum that entered my ears in those words. The sound was unmistakably strong. It offered the rapt, intense sound of dynamos in an electrical plant, that elevating yet fearsome hum which comes into human ears whenever one form of energy is converted to another. So much is taking place. A dominion is being directed to enter another dominion. It is the sound common to many motors. "How much we have done," these motors could be murmuring.

Der Alte's last injunction was to put the honey chamber into a sealed box so soon as it was free of its bees. "Then you must take it indoors for the extraction. Into a good sealed room. I cannot emphasize this enough," he said directly to Alois Junior. "As you may not yet know, these divine creatures have two natures: total loyalty to their Queen, but whole greed for the honey itself. They will gorge on it anywhere they can find it, from any and all hives. So you must not attract any bees who may be out foraging. For that reason, extraction can never be attempted in open air. I repeat: it must take place in a sealed chamber."

# 4

Once given her instructions, Klara went to some pains by blocking up all the window- and doorsills to their kitchen with every rag at her disposal. She wore a white blouse and white apron for the occasion, and so did Angela. Alois Senior even gave up his cigar. For the family, that was, indeed, an event. But Der Alte had warned him, "Cigar smoke does pacify our bees. But when it comes to their honey, beware. A cigar must not be allowed to insinuate itself into the taste."

Luther was, of course, banished from the room. So were Adi, Edmund, and Paula, even if this occasioned a series of trips by Klara to the children's bedroom, each time removing the cloths piled up against the doors, then replacing them on return. Alois complained that she was protecting everything too much—he did not think one bee had gotten into the house.

Otherwise, the task went well. As each frame was taken out of the hive box, Alois Senior proceeded with the pride of a surgeon. He pared the wax caps from the honey cells by way of a tool designed to lift off the thin top layer of wax that closed off each cell in the frame. Since there were two thousand cells in each of the ten frames of the Langstroth box, and a cell was no wider in diameter than the fingernail of a child, one could hardly uncap them one at a time. That might have taken a week. Instead, Alois applied the separator knife to whole patches, stripping off swatches of wax an inch wide and from three to four inches long. To his eye, it was like a skin which he, the surgeon, had to remove, yes, no mean touch required to strip this wax without damaging the wax cells beneath. He was beginning to take pleasure in the job. He would have made a good surgeon, he decided. Out of the corner of his eye, he was looking to see if Alois Junior might also be admiring his command of the procedure.

The supposition that he had a talent for bodily operations had begun to warm his loins. A woman once told him that a surgeon of her acquaintance was one of the two best lovers she had ever had. Alois was the other. How he had enjoyed the remark. Of course. He had no fear of the flesh and neither did a surgeon—brothers under the skin!

After a time, nicely pleased with himself, he handed the decapping tool to Alois Junior, who mangled one swatch and then the next, but proceeded to get better at the job. Soon he was as deft as his father. This occasioned pride in Senior, and a touch of disappointment. To make it worse, Alois Junior said, "This is as good as scraping icing off a cake."

"Watch out for the cells," said Alois Senior. "Don't damage them with your big mouth."

Adi had by now been allowed into the room to watch, and Alois Junior extended the decapping tool toward his brother as if to say, "Want some?"

Klara reproved him on the instant. "Why are you offering your little brother a mouthful of wax? He could choke on it."

"No, no," said Alois Junior, "it is a legitimate offer. The wax has honey sticking to it." He nodded. "I do not think that Adi would be so silly as to swallow the wax."

When Klara glared at him, Junior proceeded to chew some himself, then extracted the residue from his mouth and nodded. Klara could only look away.

Soon the task grew more difficult—they had to strip another layer of wax from the back side of the tray, the frames having been installed on the vertical precisely so cells could be built on both sides of the glass surface. To remove the second surface took longer, however. Honey leaked from the front, and more from the rear. Soon enough, Klara had to take over. Before long, it was apparent that she had the cleverest fingers of all.

This work took a few hours. As each tray was uncapped, it had to be slotted into the honey extractor, where Angela was now turning the crank. With devotion, she followed her father's instructions. "Yes, yes, move slowly now as you start, yes, just as you are doing it. Look inside! The honey is beginning to come out of the combs. Keep it slow, yes. Don't speed up on that crank. Not yet. Slow, Angela, slow." (He could have been driving a cart while calling to his horses.)

It proved a strain. The more slowly Angela went, the longer it took for centrifugal force to fling the honey onto the metal sides of the extractor bucket down whose walls it would drip to a funnel. But when she sped up, too much wax flew off with the honey.

Before long, Alois Junior had to take over. There was silence in the kitchen as they listened to the murmur of honey dripping down the walls of the pail.

By way of a petcock at the bottom, the honey was then gathered in a basin. Klara was prepared with a coarse sieve and a fine one. But she held everyone back. It was absolutely necessary, she told them, that she and Angela spend another hour filtering the product through cheesecloth. Moreover, she was determined to save the wax as well. Beeswax had value. It could produce the finest grade of candles. So Mr. Rostenmeier had told her at the Fischlham store. Alois snorted. He could have told her that himself, he said.

Adi was the most impatient. He wanted honey, he wanted to gorge. Not even his mother would permit this, however. "Be patient," she said. "The honey has to settle."

"It is there," he cried. "It wants us to taste it."

"No," she said, "it is full of bubbles."

"I don't care."

"You must. Bubbles make honey uncomfortable."

"They don't," said Adi. "I know."

"You don't. Air," said Klara, "will be uncomfortable to the honey, just like gas would be on your stomach." She had no idea whether this might be true, but she hardly cared. It felt true. Besides, it would be good for Adi to wait. Patience could strengthen his character.

Tears came into his eyes. As was expected. Whenever he was denied, he was quick to weep.

"Think of this honey," she said to Adi. "It has gone through so much. Such a great deal. It was living in one place quietly and the bees were its friends. Now they are gone, and look at all that has happened. We have been shaking it and scraping it. Then we have been spinning it. Now the honey does not know where it is. Let it sit. We will wait. Tomorrow we can have the party."

## 5

No party took place the next day. Foam and bits of wax had collected on the surface of the honey. Klara scraped it off carefully, but insisted all the same on postponing the feast.

For one thing, Klara wanted to keep stirring the honey each day. She was convinced this was necessary. Whenever she returned to the kitchen, she stirred it for ten minutes or more and then dragooned Angela or Junior, despite their protests, to fill in for her.

They must, she told them, all work to keep their honey from be-coming hard. She remembered this from her childhood. Once in a while, she thought, a wife could see farther than her husband. Why not? God gives different gifts to everyone.

Finally, she declared the honey to be ready, and they had their party. Alois Senior considered inviting Der Alte, but Klara was quick to stop such a notion. "This is for the family," she said.

So they each took a spoon and stood in a circle, all but Paula, whom Klara held, and fed by way of her forefinger. The others licked their spoons. Instantly, they were ready for more. Klara had baked a sponge cake and offered slices dipped into their trove, but Senior and Junior and Angela and Adi just kept licking their spoons, yield after yield.

It was as if they were drunk. All of them. In separate ways, but certainly each and every one was having an exceptionally good time. For Alois, it was as special and highly particular as good French brandy—which he had tasted three times in his life. Yes, this honey was magical. It offered memories of Fanni, splendid memories he had not permitted himself to enjoy for years. That had been true heat. What a bitch! What a witch! Too bad. She had paid a great price. To die so young. Could it not be said that she had loved him too much? The thought of such an overabundance of love, excite-ment, and his old but so-successful treacheries toward Anna Glassl mixed well with the taste of the honey, yes, he might just as well be drunk.

And Klara, filled with notions of the panoply of God's gifts, thought again of a young fellow she had liked back in Spital when she was very young, even a year or two before Alois came to visit the farm, this uncle who would be her man for life. But the other fellow had been nice. They had held hands once, although she had never kissed him, not that. But this honey must have stolen into her heart because she realized now—so beautiful a memory—that she had been happy when she held hands with the rough paws of the farmer boy, happier than she had ever been with Alois. Such was life. One had to be careful. One could not live with honey every day. She was careful now to put down her spoon and eat the cake.

Alois Junior was thinking of Der Alte. It had been in the way the old man stared at him. Eyes so moist. The old man looked like he was ready to open his mouth and wet his lips and do the thing some of the younger boys back in Spital had done for him already. Once or twice. Then more than once or twice. The honey was telling him the truth. He had liked it. He had tried to get a girl to do it, but she had refused.

Now he remembered the older boys who had wanted him to do the same for them. One had even twisted his arm. When he yelled no, he wouldn't, this big fellow hit him in the stomach. He had been smart enough to throw up. That discouraged the big fellow. Now maybe he could enjoy something with Der Alte. It would get him ready for the girl he had in mind. Give her a ride on Ulan. Bareback.

Angela was off in her dream. The honey left her feeling nicer than she had ever felt. A sensation. So strong. She felt as if there were another person in her, someone new, someone good to feel. Was it right to enjoy anything this much?

If the question now exists, how is it possible for a devil like myself to enter the thoughts of this family when little Adolf is my only true client, I will give credit to the honey. We have among our gifts the power to invest many a substance with a trace of our presence. It takes no more. If we respect such a faculty, then that trace can, for a short period, enter the thoughts of a man or woman or child. This delicate link, carried off with finesse, can even be truth; I suspect that was why Klara kept stirring the stuff for those several days. It was as if she wished to step in as one more guardian against our inroads.

I did not spend time with Edmund and Paula. Before it was over, the boy would gorge too much and soil his pants, and the baby had a touch of colic. But that was later. At first, they kept smiling with such innocent glee that all the others were laughing at them.

Adi was the most interesting. As I anticipated, he went wild. The sweet had an effect on him equal to schnapps for Alois Junior on an empty stomach. So Adi made a point of giving sticky kisses to Klara and Angela, delighting in their cries and the panic with which they wiped his kisses off their mouths. Klara, particularly. To scrub her mouth was a reflex, but when she saw a hitch in Adi's laughter, as if he had been surprised enough by the detestation on her face to allow a tear to pop up in his eye, she caught the boy and kissed him with all the muscular intensity of a mother doing her duty, and Adi, not knowing whether he had been rewarded or further rebuked, crept up on Angela with a small gob of honey on his index finger.

Angela bellowed when it was entwined in her hair, and there was hatred in the sound. He had ripped her away from the sensations cavorting through her. But even as Angela was catching enough breath to scold him, Adi was prancing toward Alois Junior—who stopped him with a look.

Edmund remained. Adi left Edmund with so much honey on his head that the two-year-old dropped more caca into his pants, whereupon Adi went up to Klara, pointed at Edmund, and said, "Mother, I did not make messes like that when I was two years old. This Edmund, he is always dirty."

Thereby, he handed Angela her quick revenge. She was there on the spot to tell Klara what had happened, and proved so precise in her description that Klara began to scold Adi with words she had not used before, not to him. "This is a disgrace. Do you understand? It is a sin to be cruel to those who are smaller than you. How can you be so bad? God will punish you. He will punish all of us." She spoke with woe. She did not wish to spoil this splendid family occasion but must do it for the sake of the others, for Angela, and for poor little Edmund, dirty again. "How can you play such a trick?" she said to Adi. "Edmund loves you so much."

This time she actually did want to make Adi cry. Instead, she was the one with tears in her eyes. He—perhaps it was the honey—felt as important to himself as he had ever been in his six and a half years. He was enraged at these criticisms. He glared at Angela. He whispered to his thoughts, "I will never forgive her. That is a fact!

I will see her into hell!" And with it all, he was proud of himself. He had brought his mother to tears. "Let her cry for once. Not me. It is time for her to learn."

# 6

I must now describe the carnal act of Alois Junior and Der Alte. This is with some distaste. Be it understood, I am without moral judgments on these matters. Devils are supposed to be interested in every form of the bodily embrace, dedicated, casual, perverse, or, as the Americans say, *missionary*—"I got on top and whaled away." We are, of course, much more interested in sexual deeds that fall into no established fold. Routine practices are inimical to our purposes. First sexual encounters, however, are rarely to be ignored. We speak of them as *primes*. The stakes are larger. Few primes take place without some representative of the Maestro and the D.K. in attendance. Fucking—to employ that most useful, all-but-cosmopolitan, and near-onomatopoeic word, so close to the meats, body slaps, and fats of the occasion—is of real interest to both sides. Much can happen, and quickly. Old habits, whose presence in the psyche have become as heavy as old sandbags standing in place to bolster the trenches, can now be listed.

Small surprise, then, if we are free of moral judgment, and alert to fresh estimates. Will this particular joining weaken our position or enhance it?

I was repelled this time, however, by what took place. Der Alte, after a few habitual courtesies and social commonplaces designed to shield his excessive pleasure (and instant alarm) on seeing Alois Junior at his door—what if it all turned out a disaster?—soon came to recognize (given his decades of experience in these matters) that

Alois Junior had arrived for the precise gift Der Alte had dreamed of offering him ever since they met. "I am so glad you wished to visit," he repeated several times in the first few minutes, to which Alois finally replied, "Yes, here I am."

The hitching post was some fifty feet away outside, but Der Alte could hear Ulan swishing his tail. He knew enough not to spend one second more in conversation, but moved over to Alois Junior, knelt before him, laid his hand upon the boy's crotch. Whereupon—fierce jack-in-the-box—Alois Junior was on his feet, pants unbuttoned, and full of a happy, blood-filled organ, which he thrust at once into Der Alte's mouth—those yearning, long-unused lips.

It was during the next moments that I became displeased. If I am free of moral judgment, I am hardly void of good taste, and Der Alte demeaned himself. To say it straight, he slobbered over the boy, and spluttered raucously when Junior thrust a full discharge down his throat. Like a baby, Der Alte also peed in his pants. It was, in turn, his discharge—the best urination he'd had in months. Then he was all over Alois Junior with kisses, plus a variety of verbal endearments I will not repeat here. "You taste sweet, your heart is good" is perhaps the most manageable example to offer, and, of course, the most absurd, for Alois Junior did not have to be a client for me to perceive that his heart was cold. His first concern was loyalty to himself. Like all such very young men, he was filled with disgust for this quondam partner, and left as soon as he could.

That took a few minutes. He had no wish to be entangled for the best part of an hour with endearments that sat on his skin like spiderwebs. On the other hand, his practical nature kept him present long enough not to insult Der Alte directly. That could interfere with a return visit. Who knew? If he did not succeed in the next few days in convincing one particular farm girl he had in mind, then back he would come to this old pot. Alois Junior was the stuff out of which our best clients are made—at the age of fourteen, he already understood sex in a manner that was ideal for us. He would soon be adept at acquiring many a dominance by way of his priapic gifts. That, we can appreciate. So many of our clients have nondescript equipment. We never know when an erection will be there, ready to salute. That creates problems for us, although we can also manipulate whole or partial impotence into its own kind of effective instrument. For example, Adolf was to suffer from such a condition through adolescence, war, and his early political manhood.

Alois Junior was the opposite. Full of his father's blood, his natural interest was in women, except for what he considered their built-in trap. Girls, like women, were too attached to family responsibility. Boys, to the contrary, were right there—good for getting rid of the constrictions of the groin. And very nice to command a boy, or, better, a grown man.

Yes, he would have been perfect as a client. We would have enhanced his powers. He could have served us in so many ways. My instructions, however, were to leave him alone. The Maestro's eyes were for Adolf. I understood. It is disruptive to work with two clients in one family, and this is particularly true if they are apart in character. One devil, trying to tend to both, may be left at odds by their conflicting needs. But two separate devils overseeing two clients in one home can be worse. Envy might stir.

So I stayed away from Alois Junior. Soon enough, he did succeed in charming Greta Marie Schmidt, a strapping farm girl to whom he gave rides on Ulan. Before long, he had something like the same set of keys to her private parts that Alois Senior had had with Fanni when she was still a virgin. To use again one of my American vulgarisms (I confess to an unseemly pleasure uttering them), Junior knew Greta Marie from "asshole to appetite." He had no desire to steal her virginity—that was her well-cocked trap. Moreover, he did not really like her. She was a touch too crude. So he went back to Der Alte. Despite the full-grown odors of the hut, some of those occasions were full of libidinous novelty. Now that things had settled down, Der Alte offered languorous slides and inspired flutters of his tongue—all to the good for Junior, the pleasure lover, but, of course, once done, Junior could barely look at him. The youth was just as repulsed as I was by all that collaborative sobbing and gurgling. The sad truth was that Der Alte's tongue was preternaturally excited by the back door. Alois' buttocks began to feel like the portals to a bounteously endowed temple. He would wait until his pleasure rose high enough to be ready to explode, and then he would turn and give it all to the old boy's gullet. Afterward he stood still as a statue again, doubly disgusted by the recognition that his father, Alois, was hopelessly in awe of Der Alte. "How well he can speak," his father had said.

But Der Alte was so ready to serve himself up. So how was he, Junior, to respect Senior? All that awful, endless nervousness about his bees? Always seeking advice from Der Alte. Now that the family had had its feast of honey, here was his father worrying already about when to extract the rest of the product from the remaining two hives.

A near disaster was the upshot. I was not at all surprised. Alois Junior managed to leave one of those cherished hives out in the sun. For no good reason. Distaste for his father so deep he had hardly been aware of it.

## 7

His father came upon the hive, touched the box, felt the heat of the wood, but also recognized that the bees were not yet whipping about in too great a frenzy. He had come in time, and he carried the hive back to the shade.

*"What were you thinking, idiot?"* he shouted at Alois Junior.

The boy felt as if he had been pulled inside out by the power of his father's voice. The sound came with a thud, heavy as a blow. Adolescents can lose all sense of themselves when an unfamiliar punishment suddenly assaults them. That is because they are not only full of airs, poses, and witless shows of temperament, but, worse—at bottom, they do not possess a real age. In that instant, Junior ceased to be a youth of fourteen. Till then, he had seen himself as "Fourteen," a clear concept, stark in its outlines. But, like many another adolescent, he possessed the calculations of a twenty-year-old, while other corners of himself were as prone to self-betrayal as an eight-year-old caught in some foolishness. Like leaving a hive in the sun. At this moment, he actually felt full of tears.

He pleaded with his father. To his shame, he pleaded. "You have given me so much good information," he said. "So new and so stimulating, dear respected father." He slapped himself on the forehead. "I confess it may have been too much for my ignorant head. I made a mistake. I know that now. But I believed I was supposed to leave the hive in the sun, yes, for a few minutes—no more, I admit—so as to warm the honeycombs. It was so cold last night. For spring—so cold! I hope I did not make a terrible error."

He could hear the sound of his voice, sliding off every grip that he might keep on some semblance of manhood. So shrill! "You must forgive me, Father. My mistake is an outrage. I cannot apologize sufficiently."

He knew it was not enough. A massive weather front had come over Alois Senior, dark as the depths of suspicion. "Think of this, Alois," his father said quietly. "Our bees, all these bees, do their work by obeying the rules." Then he glared at Junior until the boy looked away. "They do not have patience with those who are weak or lazy. Or too selfish to remember their duties."

He took hold of Junior's chin. His eyes would not let go of the boy's eyes. He pinched him on the chin, his thumb and forefinger as direct as the claws of a pliers. But the pain rallied the boy. Der Alte had more respect for him, Alois Junior, than for this man, Alois Senior, who happened to be pinching him on the chin. The thought came into his eyes and remained in his expression. By the time it was over, Alois Senior had to recognize that the altercation had taken a good deal from him. Alois Junior had even dared to glare back.

If this bothered his sense of himself as a father, more was soon to come. Now it was Klara. She had received a letter from her mother that devastated all the uncertain confidence Klara had given earlier to her father's letter. So soon as she read her mother's words, she wondered how she could have thought for an instant that Junior had changed.

Of course, writing a letter was agony for Johanna. Klara knew that. From the age of nine, she had been the one to reply to the few letters that came to their house in Spital. Yet now, as if to emphasize the importance of this particular epistolary act, Johanna went on for a full page of the most painful halts and bumps. First she insisted on listing Alois Junior's virtues. He was so bright, very bright, she could say that to anyone. Good to look at, she would say that too. Junior even brought back old memories of his father, your husband, Uncle Alois, back then when your Uncle was so young, so attractive, a good young man, so responsible. All those years ago.

"Klara, I tell you," she now wrote, "I have to worry. What have we sent to you? Junior is wild. So wild, Klara, and we send him back to you. Had to, yes. Now Johann must hire another man for help. The new one is a drunk fool. We pay wages to this drunk. That is how much we lose by sending Junior back, but, Klara, this no-good drunk is better than Junior. We are not so afraid anymore."

Klara went to her sewing basket and took out the letter Johann Poelzl had written. Alois Junior had handed it to her on the day he arrived. She searched the top shelf of a cupboard to retrieve an old letter from her father, one she had taken the pains to wrap in a ribbon. It had carried his blessing on the birth of Edmund. Now, so soon as she looked at it, she knew the piece of paper Alois Junior had given her might be close to her father's handwriting but was not the same.

Klara did not say anything to Alois Senior. Not until well after dinner. There in bed, he had begun to complain about Alois Junior.

"I don't get good work from him," said Alois. "I speak to him, and he does not react to my satisfaction. He is off with the horse. I don't want to worry, but I do. He can get into trouble. He sees girls on the other side of the hill. In part, that can be my fault because of my conclusion not to raise potatoes this spring. Now there is not enough real work for him."

It was then that she told him about her mother's letter. He nodded. He merely nodded.

"What are you going to say?" she asked.

"I will think about it," he told her. "I must take my time. The next step could be of consequence."

She was infuriated. She could not sleep. There might as well have been a bug wandering in the bedclothes. If Alois was not ready to scold his son, she would have to. But she could hardly be ready for this. It was his son, after all.

On the following evening, not long before supper, Alois Junior began to act as if he now knew that there had been another letter. It is the best explanation I can offer for why he chose to break an egg on Adi's head.

The reason was simple. His girl, Greta Marie, had shown him a little more that afternoon of what she was at bottom—a dull cow. So the need for a new endeavor was in his fingertips. Something new. Having felt like smacking Greta Marie around, he now moved close to Angela. His sister was clucking again over her chickens, collecting each egg from each hen as if it were a gold ingot—plain, dirty, hen-stained eggs. So he took one out of her basket. Just to hear her scream. But when she did, he was ready to break the egg on her head. Only, he could not. She was his full sister—who else did he have? So he put the egg back. Nonetheless, this act cost too much. Yet here now was Adi, beside him, slunk up within reach, smelly little hyena. Right after coming back from his gallop with Ulan, he had seen Adi lying on the floor of their barn, screeching away, one more temper tantrum.

Junior lifted him off the barn floor, then forced him into a standing position. "Keep quiet," said Alois Junior.

"Try and make me," said Adi.

Alois Junior knew that the kid would go yowling to his mother. He always did. Adi had a mother—whereas he didn't. Therefore, he had to put up with the brat. It was a truce.

On this late afternoon, however, Angela was offering baby talk to her chickens, and Adi was leering at him. So safe on his side of the truce. "Try and make me."

Junior took an egg out of Angela's basket, smashed it on Adi's head, and took his time rubbing in the yolk and fragments of shell.

Adolf yowled. It was as if he had anticipated just this species of showdown. Now, all on his own, he proceeded immediately to squeeze his gummed-up hair long enough to coat his palm with some of the spattered yolk. Which he wiped on his shirt. When it did not leave a large enough stain, Adolf lifted another egg from Angela's basket—out came a yip from her!—and broke that all over his own head, face, and shirt, after which he caterwauled as loudly as if Alois Junior had kicked him in the shins. Then he ran from the barn to his mother. Vast screams, loud as catastrophe itself, could be heard.

Klara came running back, holding Adolf by the hand, her tirade begun before she reached them. She was trying to tell Alois Junior about the letter, but it spewed forth in no consecutive order. His lies, she told him, were worse than the filth left by pigs in a sty. "They have an excuse. They are pigs. You have nothing. You are a brute. You are a pig. You are nothing but filth." She could not believe her words. They were so strong. To her surprise, Alois Junior actually began to sob. In all of this, he had not had until now any real idea of how ready he had been to love her, and how ready she was to dislike him right down to the depths. Yes, secretly, he had thought she really did like him, yes, more than she did his father. Now he felt filthy. To his ego, this was equal to a bereavement. He could not bear it. Just as suddenly, his sobs were choked. By his will. He stopped crying on the instant, nodded formally, and strode away. He did not know where the world would take him, nor when, but he understood that he would not remain in Hafeld. He could not. Not for long. He must soon say goodbye to everyone and to everything here, especially to his horse. Or should he steal him?

This last idea proved too large for Alois Junior. Yet it was enough to know that, for the sake of his future self-respect, he would not leave until he was ready to strike back. That must come one way or another. Soon.

# 8

They were quiet at supper, even Paula, whom Klara kept on her breast. Alois Senior was certainly preoccupied. He had received a few more bee stings than the one or two or, occasionally, three, he was used to accepting on most days—that was part of the occupational hazard, no more. Tonight he not only had little to say, but hardly noticed that the others were silent.

He was waiting for bed. Lately Klara had begun to treat his bee stings and he was able to enjoy that. She was so adept. She was careful. She never pulled the stingers out clumsily. So he did not have to suffer the small bites of barbs left under his skin through the night. Done poorly, it could feel like a needle had been left inside. A tiny wound but a real one, ready to puff up. Sometimes it even felt personal, as if, from meanness itself, it refused to stop hurting. But Klara knew how to nudge the flesh where the stinger was peeping out and then coax it forth by soft pressure.

Now, when they went to bed, he was looking to have his pains cared for. Only, on this night, he had to wait. First she must describe all the mess that Junior had made, all that egg and shell. He did not care to listen. "*Ach,*" he said, "it breeds bad feeling if you always take Adi's side."

"What are you saying? Tell me of something good we can expect from Junior."

"No," he said, "you must listen to me. We are obliged to look for a balance. We must try. A good balance between these boys, and it will all quiet down. That is the secret."

A silence. It was followed by a deeper silence.

"I will try," she said at last.

Her instinct was to reduce this space between them. If she didn't, the difference would increase. But could she believe that her husband was right? Young Alois was behaving like Fanni. Only ten times worse than Fanni could ever have tried to be. Yet, was it possible? Had she left a curse?

They certainly had to live with poor omens for more than a few nights. Alois Junior kept giving a demonstration of his skills through these last days of June, doing just enough good work to justify his right to go off with Ulan. The boy was good at his duties, he kept the hive boxes clean, he knew when and where to move the trays. He was even able to locate the Queen and put her into a queen cage without using the glass trap. Like Der Alte, he could do it with his fingers.

Now, at the dinner table, his silences weighed on them. No member of the family crossed him these days, not even Alois Senior, but then, despite himself, he could feel sympathy for this son. He understood one side of young Alois so well. Riding Ulan, the boy must feel as handsome as an officer on one of the better streets of Vienna. But Alois also knew what was hatching beneath. If, at present, the horse came first, soon it would be all about girls. The father knew this as well as if sperm were stirring in his own good equipment. Those revelations! Nothing could be better than the moment when a woman opened her legs for you. That first time! If you had an eye for the little differences, you knew twice as much about her as you could learn from her face. Alois Senior would attest to that. The female organ! Whoever designed this form had certainly been sly about the job. (This was about as close as Alois ever came to admiring the Creator.) Such a wonderful array of meats and juices—such a panoply of flesh in miniature—this offering of archways and caverns and lips. Alois was certainly no philosopher, so he would not have known how to speak of Becoming (that state of existence when Being suddenly feels itself out in the open), but all the same, he could have given a tip to Heidegger. Becoming is, yes, exactly, when a woman opens her legs! Alois felt like a poet. How not? These were poetic thoughts.

Let me leave it at this: If Alois could have talked to his son, he would have had a good deal to tell him. But he would never venture to speak of these matters. Having been a guardian of the border, which is to say a policeman, he could not even trust his children. A good policeman had to live with trust as if he were handling a dangerous bottle of acid. Trust was teeming with risk. To offer your closest thoughts to others was to ask them to betray your counsel.

Still, if he could have spoken to young Alois, he would have been quick to inform him that there was nothing better than to be a young man interested in girls—he, the father, could tell him the best of stories if it came to that—"but, young Alois, I must impart this to you: Young women can be dangerous. Often, they are the sweetest angels, a few of them maybe, but it is not them you have to be ready to deal with. It is the fathers of these angels, or their brothers. It can even be an uncle. Once I almost received a beating from a girl's uncle. I was big enough, but he was bigger. I had to talk my way out of it. So will you. It is certain that you will know how to talk, young Alois, but that is an ability which only works in a good-sized town, or best of all in the city. Out here in Hafeld and Fischlham—not so good—country people can be difficult."

There was so much he would have told his son. If only they could have confided in each other. It made Alois sad. I must say, however, that it can certainly be construed as his fault. What could be closer to him than maintaining his authority?

So he would not be so generous as to offer the root of his advice. But if he had been able to, he would have told Junior: "Enjoy every woman you can, but be aware of the price. Especially in the country. Listen, young Alois," he would have said, "country people do not have enough to do with their minds. Their backs are strong, but their lives—year after year, it is the same. They are tired of being bored. So they start to think about the wrongs that have been done to them. I say to you, son, watch out! Do not get a girl in trouble. When the time comes, do not be too certain that you will be able to deny that you are the fellow who made her pregnant. Sometimes that does not work."

Alois lay in bed, drenched in perspiration. His son's drama unfolded before him with the power of a tragedy. He would have said to young Alois, "Do not take for granted the father of any girl you have had in the straw. Never insult a peasant who has too little to think about. Ten years from now, he will find out where you are living, and he will come to your door, and he will blow your head off with a shotgun. I have heard more than one story like that."

Since devils know to what extent men and women are able to conceal from themselves a clear view of their own motives, I soon understood that behind all this splendid advice to young Alois, the father was worried about his own safety, yes, Alois Senior felt as if it could be his own treasured buttocks that were exposed.

One evening, over a month ago, while having his beer in the Fischlham tavern, there had been talk which he dismissed at the time as idle, a bit of prattle about a fellow who lived on the other side of the tavern a few miles farther away from Hafeld. Two of the farmers in the tavern actually knew the man, and it seemed this fellow had spoken about Alois. Yes, more than once, they assured him, "He knows you, and he made it clear. He don't like you." They had laughed.

"I assure you," Alois said in all of his local majesty, "if I ever met this individual, I have forgotten it. His name means nothing to my mind."

Indeed, it did not, until the name came back to Alois during the middle of a sleepless June night. When he got up to look out their bedroom window, he was offered a moonlit view of silver fields, and thought of how happy these fields must be to lie fallow and not have to satisfy young potatoes grubbing down for more of the earth's riches. Alois, however, then made the mistake of looking at the full moon, and abruptly, the face of this fellow who had declared his dislike of Alois Hitler came back to him.

Good Lord! That fellow had been a smuggler, yes, he had caught him in Linz one day. Yes, he could remember now. The fool had been trying to take a vial of opium over into Germany. Alois could certainly recall the hatred in the man's eyes when he was caught. The vile look in his eyes had been offensive enough to tempt Alois to strike him, but such an act he considered entirely beneath himself. Certainly, he had not laid a fist on anyone while on Customs duty, not in years.

Was the full moon a mirror to one's memory? It was there before him now, and so clearly. He had not struck the fellow, no, but he had mocked him. "You are angry at me?" he had said. "Be angry at yourself. You are a fool. A measly test tube of opium buried inside a leg of ham. Even my first day on duty when I was eighteen, I would have caught you. That is the kind of fool you are."

If he was going to recall it properly, could it be that the smuggler had not begun to look back with hatred until Alois began to jeer at him? Smugglers do not hate you for catching them—that is part of the game—but do not mock them. How often had he said as much to young officers. "Have a little fun with a bad fellow, and he will never forgive you."

Alois suffered a night full of fear—the smuggler he taunted had received a year in jail. Now the man was free! Alois arose from a bed bereft of decent rest with the recognition that there was not going to be a hell of a lot of sleep for him until he got a new dog, a truly fierce hound. Luther was good for no more by now than yodeling at the moon on a night when nothing was happening. He needed a dog who would be ready for a lout stealing across the fields toward them with odium in his heart.

# 9

It so happened that the right dog was available. A farmer he knew was looking to sell a German shepherd. "He is the best of his litter, which is why I have kept him all these months and have fed him, this gross guzzler. Can you afford to labor longer hours? Because he eats all the time. That is why I will sell him to you for next to nothing. Maybe he will make you as poor as he has made me. Then I can laugh, and you will cry."

Good beer talk. Alois decided to buy the hound.

This was a good one, Alois could tell. When it came to dogs, he had always had a nice understanding. He could stare right into the eye of a fierce mongrel, yet because he felt a moment of love for the poor ugly old bastard, the animal would usually respond well. Alois could talk to dogs. If the beast growled a bit, Alois would say, "Oh, fellow, how can you speak like that to me? I like you, I approach you as a friend." And he even knew enough to bring his hand to the dog's mouth as a token of friendship. He had never made a mistake. The one time in a hundred when a dog was actually fierce enough to bite, Alois could sense that, too, and he would extend the forefinger and pinky of the near hand, his separated fingers directed to the dog's eyes like pointed horns, and the animal might keep up his imprecations, but he would not attack.

So Alois was delighted with this overgrown, six-month-old German shepherd who had the regal name of Friedrich. He would be fierce. Better still, he was a one-man dog. Let the children recognize that quickly. Let Klara complain. Let young Alois mind his business. He would be the only one to feed Friedrich. And he would change his name. From what he had heard, King Friedrich the Great had had a boyfriend, not a mistress. So maybe he was not so great. Besides, he was a German. To hell with honoring him. He would call the dog Spartaner. A warrior. Any ex-smuggler who had thoughts of coming to the farm in the middle of the night would not dare, not now, not with both dogs present. You could take care of Luther with a piece of meat and a cloth dipped in chloroform, but Spartaner would be there to attack you.

How Alois enjoyed the walk back over the hills. He let the dog off the leash early, threw sticks for the animal to return, taught him to stop and sit at command, although Spartaner learned all this so quickly that he must have been trained a bit already. No question, however, the dog was good. Alois found himself in such a fine mood that he almost wrestled with the beast. Indeed, he restrained himself only because it was too soon. Wonderful. Quick love between a dog and a man is close to a perfect event, he decided.

The animal did not cease grinning with an all-knowing, all-breathing tongue that lolled at the edges of his grin until they came in view of the farm. But now it was as if he realized, and all too abruptly, that there was a problem waiting right by the house.

Of course. It was Luther. Alois was ready to clap himself on the head for having been in such a state of blind certainty that he had not thought once of how these two dogs might get along on first meeting.

They didn't. They were terrified. Each was abominably afraid of the other, and each was sick with shame at his own fear. They nipped with their teeth at their own fur, clawed at newly discovered fleas beyond the reach of their bite, they barked at bees and then at butterflies, they ran in circles which did not overlap each other, they staked out territories with their urine.

Luther, while now an old dog, was larger than Spartaner, considerably so, but he was making the big mistake of lumbering around enough to tell the young dog what to capitalize upon.

As it transpired, they went to war two hours after this first sight of each other. The family rushed out in the yard to witness them rolling on the ground, their incisors as awesome as shark's teeth, blood on their faces and their flanks.

Alois, being the farthest away, was the last to arrive. He was also the first and only one to dive into the fray. He had no fear of either animal. He was too outraged. How did they dare to begin this? He had told Luther an hour before to shut up and sit down. This was rank disobedience.

He roared at them to stop. On the same impulse, he flung them apart with his bare hands. The sound of his voice was enough. They lay on the ground, half-stunned, breathless, two yards apart, show-ing open gashes on their noses and bloody fur at their throats. Spartaner kept panting as if the breath he needed was out there just beyond his tongue. Luther was ill within. The sum of his years had exploded. He looked at Alois with such pain and so full an expression that Alois could all but read what he said: "I have wor-ried about you and the safety of your house for all these years, and you yell at me as if I mean no more than that interloper you just brought in." Alois came near to petting him, and tenderly, but that would have spoiled his plans for turning Spartaner into a perfect dog.

As their wounds healed, Luther did not try to eat until after Spartaner had gorged himself. This regime continued even when Klara made a point of putting out separate bowls at a distance from each other. But Spartaner proceeded to gobble up the second bowl as well. It hardly mattered. Luther had lost his appetite.

Alois now decided what the next step must be. He would indeed have to dispose of Luther. Good old Luther was probably ready by now to lick the hand of the first thief who came strolling over in the middle of the night.

## 10

This was the second time that Adi had heard his father roar, once at young Alois for leaving that hive in the sun, and now again to shock the dogs into separation.

What mastery had been in his father's voice. What command of the situation! His father had leaped at two beasts entangled in one fury, blood flying from strings of saliva, yet his father had pulled them apart. So fearlessly! Adi was now in love with his father. Now when he went into the woods by himself—no small matter—Adi forced himself to try to be unafraid of the silence of these immense trees quietly muttering into the greater silence of the forest. There, shivering, Adi would work on the power of his voice. He would roar at the trees until his throat was sore.

I was delighted with him. I was beginning to see why the Maestro might be exhibiting this special interest. If, after Adi's best attempts to bellow, a few leaves did shift by way of a passing breeze, he was quick to decide that the power issuing from his throat had inspired the wind. And on so still a day!

Once he almost met his father in the woods, but I steered the boy away. I did not want father and son to meet. Not on this occasion. The father might have mocked the child for being so crazy as to shout at the trees, and the boy might have crept up behind his father and thereby would have witnessed the execution of Luther. I was looking to avoid that. The Maestro would be displeased if the shock proved disruptive. We looked to be the ones who would shape our clients, not events.

That afternoon became a long walk for Alois Senior and considerably longer for Luther. One of his hind legs had been infected by the battle. He limped, and after a few hundred yards, he began to hobble.

I think Luther understood what was awaiting him. While the Maestro must certainly possess the ability to monitor any thoughts that pass between humans and animals, he does not encourage us to exercise our instincts in this direction. Or, at least, not among the devils I work with. For that matter, I often feel painfully curious concerning all I do not know about the departments, outreaches, special services, zones, belts, salients, precincts, orbits, spheres, beats, and occult enclaves that the Maestro commands. Particularly this last—occult enclaves. For a devil, I know no more about the sinister than what I am instructed to use for effect in my work. The curses and spells which legend would have available to all devils are, actually, meted out to us as tools, and only when needed.

So it was not common for me to follow the thoughts offered and thoughts received that passed between Alois and Luther. All the same, I was at no loss to recognize that Luther knew his end was near and Alois, willingly or not, was fully occupied in thinking of how he would dispose of the dog.

To begin with, he decided he would not shoot him. He did own a shotgun and a pistol. The first would be too messy, and the second made him uneasy. It would dishonor Luther. Yes. Pistols were reserved for malefactors. Whether in cold blood or self-defense, a round from a pistol was not only impersonal, but a shattering end.

Let me remark that I was not surprised to read Alois' thoughts so easily. I was long familiar with the workings of his mind and so could often follow his conscious thoughts as adroitly as one connects the dots in a child's puzzle. He was not invested by me, yet I knew him better than many a client.

I think I may have developed or been granted a few exceptional abilities for this particular service. Adi might be my major assignment, but I had been granted some secondary powers on my return from Russia, enough, at least, to enter the father and mother with something like the clarity we possess for the humans we do own.

Alois' thoughts were, indeed, interesting on this occasion. He had decided that the only way to dispatch his old companion Luther was by the stroke of a knife directly into his heart. Poison would never do—worse than a pistol or a shotgun—wholly treacherous, and it might involve hours of pain. Alois did not know (or care that much) whether men and women had souls, but he was in no doubt about dogs. They did, and you had to be loyal to the soul of a dog. You would not blast him out of life with the reverberations of the bullet—what a shock to the soul!—no, it would have to be the incisive stroke of a knife, fierce and clean as the dog's heart itself in the moment when attachment to existence is severed.

Alois kept thinking these thoughts as he trudged through the woods, slowed and slowed again by the hobbling of the old hound, and soon there came a point where Luther sat down and refused to move and looked for a long time into Alois' eyes. I could swear that if he had speech at his command, he would have said, "I know you are going to kill me and that explains why I have been afraid of you all my life. Now I am still afraid, but I will not move further. Can't you see, I am losing the last of my dignity even as you insist on taking me further and further into the woods? I can no longer control my bowels and I do not want to keep pushing my legs on and on while they are covered with this filth, so here I sit, and you will have to lift and carry me if you wish to go further."

Alois blew his nose. He could see that the dog would not move. But they had not yet come to the ground he had selected for the deed. In his mind, he had chosen a small gully one half mile further along, where he could lay the carcass at the bottom of the divide and cover it with mud and leaves, then branches, and finally he would place a large hollowed-out branch over the body. If necessary, he would weigh it down with stones.

That had been Alois' plan. He had thought through every detail. He had liked the logic of such a burial—so much better than being choked by clods of earth, his dog was not a damned potato!— but now he saw that Luther would not move on. And he, Alois, regrettably, was no longer strong enough to carry him up and down this trail for the next half mile. Therefore, it must be here. After-ward, he would go back to the farm, get a pick and a shovel and dig a grave in this copse, which was, in fact, a green and decent place, enclosed by a half circle of trees and some scrub brush, yes, it could be done here. Poor Luther.

So Alois turned the sitting dog on his back, petted him, looked into his eyes, which had sickened in the last few minutes as directly and recognizably as the expression of any old creature whose liver is rushing to the grave ahead of him, a sad old face to be certain, and Alois unbuckled the flap of the sheath that held his hunting knife, laid the point of the blade at the center of the arch of Luther's rib cage, and pushed it in to the hilt. The dog's face con-torted, the sound of his expiring came out of him and it was hurtful to Alois' ear. For it was much more human than he had ex-pected.

Then the dog's face passed through many expressions. His look settled finally into the face it would hold for the first few hours of its death before all began to decompose. Luther now looked like a young dog again, and some indefinable self-esteem had returned, as if he had always been more beautiful than anyone had realized, and could have become a great warrior if it had been asked of him when he was young, yes, he did look like a warrior as his features composed into this near-final pride.

It was a better death than he had hoped for, Alois decided. He was pleased with his acumen, he had made the right choice, but all the same, he was startled by the changes he had seen in the dog's last moments, and he felt hollow.

Alois would live for six and a half more years, yet on this after-noon in the forest he passed a junction on the road to death. So he wondered afterward and often whether he was a better man or worse because of this commitment to dispose of Luther in person and take the pains to bury him carefully afterward.

# 11

In the course of a walk that Luther and he had been taking through the woods, the dog lay down to rest and died peacefully. That is what Alois told the family. Klara was the only one to suspect that more than this might have happened. For, on the same night, perhaps six hours after the dog's demise, Alois made love to her with a good deal of vigor. It was more than she had enjoyed in a while.

He had had a variety of insect bites from his second trip to the woods with pick and shovel to dig a grave for Luther. It had taken a while, therefore, to salve the bites and remove the stingers. By the time she completed her ministrations, they were both ready to make love. While she had no basis of comparison, she was ready nonetheless to think that there might not be another man of Alois' age, only one year shy of sixty, who was so vigorous, this Uncle Alois, her man, a good man.

They had an agreeable few nights. Alois was experiencing what can only be called a transformation. He was loving her. That event can take place in a marriage. Often, it is necessary. That is because most husbands and wives use so much of their time together in excrementitious exchanges. Indeed, that is often why they married in the first place. As the Maestro presents it, they needed to be able to exercise one or another petty cruelty at any moment to a dependable person who would be close at hand.

Yet even the worst marriage allowed one species of magic. The fierce upbraidings one would have liked to present to the world (but did not dare) could now be delivered through critical judgments on one's mate. All that spiritual excrement! In marriage, it is there to be traded back and forth, a practice which mediocre participants find much more to their need than trying to contain it fecklessly inside.

Ergo, marriage is a workable institution—especially for dreadful people. Of course, it can also serve men and women who may be seen as *average*, or slightly better than average. Like our Klara and Alois. And strange shifts into love do occur. Few of these reversals are permanent, but while they last, aeration is offered to what has been an airless union.

So we are always alert for signs of a fresh breath in the exudations of married people. We can use these turns to shore up the worst of marriages for a period—should that suit our purpose.

This was not the occasion here. The change in attitude was of their choice, and it caught me by surprise. Intoxicated by the full moon and the June air that came up at night from the fields, Alois lay beside her in a state of trust—he knew her fingers would make no painful mistake as she took care of removing each stinger. There were so many more of them these days, given this lush late spring, but she was deft, she was purposeful, and he was at peace beside her. For this little while, Klara became a presence he had never been able to know—a mother hovering over him.

Night after night, the ritual took place. He even grew so careless on occasion as to work without the veil. He was not seeking to be stung; he had, after all, acquired the skill to make fewer mistakes. Still, it is fair to say he did suffer a few needless attacks, but they enabled her fingers to play their delicate movements on his brow, the cheeks of his face, the meat of his hands.

Sometimes, Alois felt as if his brains were creaking. He was entertaining ideas he did not believe could belong to him. He actually began to consider whether the pain from these bites was a means of paying for one's sins. Just supposing—for in no other way was he ready to assume that he believed in sinning—but could it be that these little wounds were a way of accounting for bad things a man had done?

What a notion! Until the night that he had this thought, he had been enjoying decent sleep. It came from the knowledge that full-chested Spartaner was out there below occupying a new doghouse built for him on the day after Luther's death. That had been no small task, but necessary. Not only was a guard dog entitled to his own sense of shelter, especially in a new habitat, but Alois' handiwork had established close feelings between the hound and himself.

New ideas, however, can be full of paradox. Alois twisted in the discomfort of considering that guilt might be real. It gave too much dignity to all the weaklings who huddled in churches. They traveled around with a stone in their stomachs and a bigger one up their ass. But now, he did not know if he could scorn them any longer. For he had committed incest. If he had made love to all three of his stepsisters, that was not incest, no, not unless their father was his father. But had he not known that Johann Nepomuk was his father? Of course, he had always known it, although he had chosen not to. It had been the sort of thought he had always swept to the rear of his mind. Now it was in the forefront. Worse. If Klara was not the daughter of Johann Poelzl, then she had to be his child ("*Sie ist hier!*") That was a fact as sharp as the knife that had gone into Luther. God Almighty, what if there was a God who knew about things like this?

In common with most humans, however, he had the mental force to send such thoughts away again. He was not ready to relinquish the soulful pleasures that arrived each night in the wake of the needles removed from his flesh.

On such June evenings, his pains would resonate within. He did not look to divert these modest agonies by searching for happy thoughts. Instead, he was there, ready to accept the message that came to him from this mysterious province of pain. To Alois, it was a species of music, replete with new sensations for the mind and heart, full of its own clarity even as it spoke sharply, even with some cruelty to his flesh. He laid himself open to the soaring voice of each pain, as rich in amplitude as a choral group. In truth, he was exhibiting the saintliness of a sinner.

# 12

Too little is understood about these matters. Saintliness is present in everyone, even among the worst of the worst. While I would not characterize Alois in this manner, he was looking, nonetheless, to pick up a morsel of beatitude at small cost to himself. He did not know that offering one's skin to the rhapsodies of small torture is but another means of avoiding one's fears of divine retribution. Since he had come much too near, however, to a full acknowledgment of incest, his upsurge of saintly sentiments soon had to be altered. By morning, he was thinking like a policeman again. When an officer of the law detects a vice in himself, he knows enough to start looking for its presence in others. Soon enough, he began to worry about Alois Junior and Angela. Was there something unworthy going on in that quarter? He did not like the tone of the conflict that was developing between the boy and the girl over who could or should ride Ulan.

To the father's surprise, young Alois was not trying to keep total possession of the horse. To the contrary, he was offering to teach Angela how to ride. A danger sign. At the tavern, Senior had already picked up a few rumors about a girl named Greta Marie Schmidt—nothing to insult him or his son personally, but Junior had been teaching Greta Marie to ride bareback.

Now it was Angela's turn. She kept refusing. Junior kept teasing her.

"You are afraid to get on Ulan's back," he would say.

"I am not."

"You are. Admit it."

"No. It is simple," she said. "I do not want to get up on Ulan.

What for? If I learn, and am good at it, what then? You will still keep the horse to yourself. I will have to beg for rides."

"I will let you go on him as often as you wish. All day, if it comes to it."

"No. You will drive me crazy. I know you."

"This is an excuse. What you fear is obvious. You are afraid of being thrown."

"I am not."

"Yes, that is it."

Finally, she said, "Have it your way. I am afraid. So, why not? That horse will throw me, and I will break my neck." She was ready to start crying out of annoyance itself. "You are so very sure of yourself. You ride around wherever you want, but I know what will happen. I will get up on him and he will gallop. I will die of a broken neck."

"Never. Your neck is just as stubborn as you are."

"Oh, yes, you are very funny. But if I die, what will you care? You have girls all over the place. I hear about them. You are always kissing them, and then they kiss you back. But I am thirteen years old this week and I have never been kissed. So I don't want to die before I even know what that is like." Now she did burst into tears.

Alois Senior overheard this conversation. As he approached the barn, he was in time to witness young Alois' reaction. The boy was unable to stop laughing.

At this moment, Alois told himself that maybe it was for the best if the boy did spend all that time out there riding the hills, yes, better for all if he carried on with some farm girl, rather than fooling about with Angela.

Now Alois Senior began to wonder if the two had ever been together. Was it not likely that they had seen him approaching the barn? If so, this conversation—had it all been for him? Were they capable of such subterfuge? Why not? Their mother had been. Of course.

Over the next few days, Alois Senior tried to observe Angela closely. But he had spent too many years getting people to feel ill at ease through the intensity of his gaze. No surprise, then, if Angela was unsettled by her father's attention. She began to wonder why he was interested in her. At school, she had heard such stories. One girl had even been doing things with her father. Or so it was whispered. Ugh, disgusting, thought Angela, so very disgusting.

Now, whenever Alois Senior was near, Angela would slide around him, drawing her hips in toward her belly as if to make certain nothing brushed.

This upset Alois. She was too artful at keeping her distance. He certainly did not approve of female sophistication in girls as young as Angela. The manner, indeed, by which she drew in her hips. Where had she learned to do that?

Klara had no such concerns about Angela. It was Alois Junior who bothered her most. Since they could not send the boy back to the Poelzl farm, they must do something with him. After all, she had learned one simple lesson from life. It was that permanent situations were often not comfortable. A poor solution to a problem could sometimes prove better, therefore, than no solution. She had learned as much from her father and mother. If the Poelzl children kept dying, her parents had managed at least to love the few who were left.

While she could not even bring herself to like Alois Junior, and no solution was in sight, still she must decide upon one. Her husband was not going to plant potatoes again next summer. That was obvious. And putting in beets might prove just as unsuccessful. His bees, however, had been acceptable. Perhaps they could do something in that direction.

Klara fixed on this. An imperfect solution—to repeat her wisdom—was better than no solution. Idleness was equal to the boy riding horses up and down the hills and getting into trouble.

So she suggested to Alois that perhaps they should build a bee house where they could install ten or fifteen hives. A real business. That would keep them busy. And, she added, it would be good for Junior. Alois could make him a young partner. A small share of the profits could even go to him.

"Take him on as a partner? You don't even trust him. So you have told me again and again."

"I said all that, yes," she had to agree, "but I do understand your son."

"You do? I would say you make a lot of remarks. And they are contradictory."

"I understand him," she said. "He is ambitious. And he doesn't know what to do with himself. But I can see. He wants to make money. I will admit—for now, he is a little wild."

"He will always be wild," said Alois.

"Maybe so," she admitted. "But boys change. If we do nothing . . ."

"I must think about this."

The notion did appeal to him. Hitler and Son, Apiarian Products. If that crybaby, Adolf, and the snot-nose Edmund ever developed, it could be Hitler and Sons.

That would be down the road. But Klara was correct. They must do something to put the boy's ambition into focus. At present, he looked upon work as ignoble.

Alois went back to his books. Over the next couple of afternoons, he dredged up from his several tomes some of the history, culture, and ancient traditions of apiculture as a way of preparing to give a small lecture to the family. It would be designed for Junior, of course, yet not as elementary as his discourses in the taverns of Linz and Fischlham, but better, worthy of Der Alte.

He would tell about the endless strife between bees and bears in the Middle Ages. That, decided Alois, would make a good beginning. Give the family a taste of how even as recently as one hundred years ago, beekeepers would climb high trees to get to hives that bears could not reach. Then insert a little culture. "This was a common practice in northern Spain and southern France," he would tell Junior. "One has to know which trees to choose. I can tell you. They were alder and ash, beech and birch, and most certainly, honorable elm trees, maples as well, oak, and willows. Lime trees," he could hear himself declaring, "lime trees have always been great favorites for the bees and for us as well, even to this day. Such honey retains the finest aromatic traces of the skin of the lime. Yes," said Alois, addressing Alois Junior in his thoughts, "this love of the bee for the lime tree goes back to the very end of the Neolithic period, close to five thousand years ago. And the bees certainly knew how to build honeycombs in those days. North of here, up in Germany, they found one honeycomb recently, a fossil, that may have been larger than any man who ever lived. Unbeliev-able. An eight-foot-long honeycomb. They found it, yes."

He was prepared to give whole funds of new information at the midday Sunday dinner. Get into the Greeks and the Romans. Since he rarely spoke at such times, as if to rebuke Klara for spending the morning in church, the meal was generally consumed under the overarching profundity of his silences, but now it was his sense that a full exposition would impress Alois Junior, and a recital of the number of countries involved might be enough to stimulate his re-spect. He would have stories to tell about the Bassari in Senegal, the Mbuti of the Ituri forest, and the honey hunters in southern Sudan.

Yet, when it came to deploying such new erudition at the table, he decided to give the lecture up not too long after he embarked on it. Perhaps he had crammed too much knowledge into himself. Klara kept nodding with approval, but whether it was for his words or the apple strudel she had made, he could not really say, and An-gela kept nodding with an expression that spoke of schoolhouse miseries. The three younger children were half-asleep, and Alois Junior, who had shown a bit of interest, began to wilt.

Alois Senior had to contain his temper. It had gone wrong. He simply did not have the eloquence of Der Alte. "You," he said at last to Alois Junior, with an address as direct to the youth as a poke in the ribs. "You and me—let us go for a walk."

What a mistake to have given that lecture at a midday meal. It was obvious. When the boy was eating, he did not like to think. Could he be just like his father?

Alois did not take him far from the house, but sat him down on a bench near the hives and spoke instead about the money that they could make by working together. "It is even possible that we could bring in Der Alte. He has made hints. He would be happy to work with us. That leads me to believe we would have much the better of the bargain. In a few years, you could be a prosperous young man, yes, most prosperous. And let me say to you, good-looking young fellows like you are able to marry to advantage when it is seen that they are also able to make a fine living. We give it three years of hard work, and you will be sitting on top of a pretty good heap. Especially since you have a sharp sense of what is what. Believe me, you will be able to take your choice of some very good matches."

The afternoon sun was hot, and the boy was dispirited. Greta Marie had been unavailable that morning—she, too, had been in church with her parents, and so he had visited Der Alte, who on this occasion had been so greedy that Junior felt stripped of vigor. Der Alte's body odor was still in his nostrils. What a joy to work every day over the next three years with these two old men! Der Alte would be full of secret signals that his father might pick up, and it could be guaranteed that Alois Senior would find something to frown about every day.

This sweet talk was so full of fraud. Work for his father? Be a slave for three years? Too many good things were waiting. The moment he was ready, he would leave them and go to Vienna. The more abruptly, the better. He had not forgiven Klara for being so rude to him last week. No, he would never forgive that.

"Good and honored father," he said, "I appreciate your concern for my future. I, too, think about it, and often. I have come to certain conclusions."

"Yes," said Alois, "that is the first step to making a life for oneself."

"So true. You speak with the knowledge of your gifts. I can say that I am full of respect for them."

He had now arrived at the obstacle that stood between them like a fence. Yesterday, for the first time, he had taken a jump with

Ulan. It had been a hedge, and could have thrown both of them. But he had known. He had to take the jump. And he did. This was not the same, and yet in one way it was. He would have to do it again right now, by speaking up.

"Everything you say is so correct, Father, but . . ." He hesitated just long enough to repeat, "What you say is true for a person like yourself, who is not exactly like myself. I have other gifts. So I believe."

Alois nodded profoundly in order not to show his annoyance. "Perhaps you will disclose what these gifts might be."

"I would say I have a gift for dealing with people." His father nodded again. "When I think of what I will do in years to come, it will be to make my living that way. By dealing with people."

At this point, he chose to stare into his father's eyes. It was no mean feat, but he held the glance.

"Do you wish to say that farming is without appeal to you?" said Alois Senior.

"I must tell the truth. It is."

"But you wouldn't go so far as to say our little apiary has no appeal."

"I like the taste of honey. That is true. But I think I enjoy talking to people more than listening to our bees."

Now Alois dipped into his best reserve of wisdom. "Son, I am prepared to let you in on a secret that will save you a few years. Maybe more. One cannot charm people for long. Especially if you have nothing else to offer. People must respect you. If they do not, they will laugh with you, yes, they will sing with you, oh, yes, and then, poor boy, they will laugh behind your back. Hard work is the only basis for a solid continuing exchange between two serious people. A man who tries to get by on good talk is nothing but a fiddler."

"I respect hard work," said Alois Junior, "but not the kind that calls for being a farmer. A young man who works on the land all his life becomes, in my opinion, as dumb as the earth. That is not for me."

"I do not think you understood what I have said. It is not the earth I am asking us to use but the air. I am thinking of the little creatures who fly through the air. Plus Der Alte. Let me put him into our discussion. I see the most profitable use we can make of him."

"Father, with all respect, I cannot agree. You have said it yourself. He knows more on this subject than we do." The illumination that had come from vaulting the hedge with Ulan was with him once more. A direct sense of exultation. It was as if his blood not only insisted that he speak, but that he be ready to insult his father. That would be equal to taking your horse over a much bigger jump. "You must face it," he said, "we are not ready for Der Alte. He would rob us blind."

"What are you saying? Do you sneer at me as a beekeeper?"

"Well, you are always getting stung."

"That happens. In this work, it will happen."

"Yes, and for those who know how, they can say, 'Oh, I had a little accident today,' but for you, not so. You are full of bites. Always."

Now Alois lost his temper, that valuable but dangerous temper he was always ordering himself to keep locked within. Now there was no help. His temper was out of the gates.

"Boy," he said to his son, "you are not equipped to go out in the world. You have no schooling. You have no money. And you think you will be able to talk your way into money? That is nonsense. All you can know is how to get your farm girls to flap their tits at you and spread their legs. Why? Maybe they believe they will get lucky and pick up a husband as lazy as themselves. Maybe they will, and then I will have to look at grandchildren as ugly as your girlfriends, and you will have to work on her father's farm."

He had gone too far. He knew it. The fear he had been secreting was as loose by now as his temper. It had been a large mistake to speak his mind.

Alois Junior was infuriated. To speak of the children he might have as ugly—outrageous. "Yes," he said to his father, "I have seen you as a farmer. Your knowledge is outdated. Even Johann Poelzl, stupid as he is, knows how to farm. You don't."

"So, I am now stupid? You are the one to speak of such a matter when you flunked out of school. And then lied about it. What a stupidity! I have lived with this foul and rotten news for too long. I can come to only one conclusion. The only answer as to why you lied to us and tried to write a counterfeit letter is that you are indeed an idiot."

"Yes," said Alois Junior, "and you are different. You have beautiful children. Do you know why?" The boy's breath was coming so quickly that his voice went up in pitch. He was all but singing his way through the next words, "Yes, you find your women, you fuck them, and then you forget them. And my mother dies."

The father's reflex was faster than his mind. His fist struck Junior on the side of the head hard enough to knock the boy down.

# 13

If young Alois had been a client, I would have ordered him not to get up. His father would have been saddled with a guilt the boy could have ridden for a year. But since I had no control in this matter, Junior rushed at Senior, grabbed his legs, and, in turn, threw him to the ground. Turn for turn.

Knowing his life was at a crossroads, he made the error of helping his father get up. He had to. He knew an incommensurable terror in the immediate moment after upending him, for there was his father prostrate, looking like an old man. So Junior picked him up.

To be knocked down was bad enough, but to be assisted to his feet by a youth with an open pimple on his face and the beginnings of a ridiculous little brown mustache? Having sprouted but a few lank hairs, that mustache was an insult all by itself. He began to beat upon Junior until the boy fell to his knees, whereupon Alois kept pummeling him further even as his son lay on the ground.

Klara had come out of the house by now. She begged Alois to stop. She wailed. And that was just as well. For now, Junior did not move. He lay motionless on the ground and Klara kept screaming.

She believed she was shrilling for the dead. "Oh, God," she managed to cry out, "I cannot believe what You have allowed!"

I saw a rare opening. She was without her Guardian Angel—not a Cudgel near. Angels often flee from people who scream too loudly—they know at such moments how close the man or woman is to us, and they feel outnumbered. For devils rush in to attend such outcries. To add to the tumult, there was Adi giving vent to the most penetrating set of shrieks.

And Klara was vulnerable. I saw my moment. I touched her thoughts, I reached her heart. She believed Alois Junior was dead, and so his father would spend the rest of his days in prison. It was her fault, all her fault. She had told the father to get close to the boy, even when she knew better. Since the sum of her experience had told her that the majority of one's prayers to God were not answered, she prayed now directly to us, she called upon the Devil, she implored him. Only the pious can believe the Devil has such powers! "Save the boy's life," she implored, "and I will be in your debt."

So we had her for the future. Not as a client. She had merely ceded her soul to us. Unhappily, these changes are never whole and immediate. But at least we now had some purchase on her.

She was a true gain. So soon as Alois Junior began to stir, she was convinced that she had received our direct response. She felt the full woe of being responsible for a nonnegotiable oath. Unlike so many with whom we traffic, she was the essence of responsibility. In consequence, she felt a mutilation of her soul and was full of grief for the pains she must be rousing now in God. What a nun she would have made!

Our most significant gain was with Adi. He had seen his father beat young Alois into the ground. He had heard his father utter a groan remarkable for the fullness of its woe. Then as Junior began to stir, Adi saw his father stagger off into the woods, his stomach heaving and Klara's apple strudel now extruding from his nostrils. In consequence, unable to breathe, Alois felt as if he must evacuate a cannonball from his esophagus. The midday dinner was surging up and down in his gullet. But now, out in the woods, just so soon as his stomach ceased its heaving, he knew that he could not go back to the house. He needed a drink. It was Sunday, but he would find something in Fischlham.

That is time enough to spend on Alois Senior. My attention was for Adi. The boy had voided everything, urine, feces, food. He was half out of his senses with fear that his father would return and beat his head into the ground. I could not ignore so direct an opportunity to exercise a few skills. I would engrave this beating into Adi's memory. Again and again, I returned the same images to his mind, until—given his certainty that it would all be done to him as well when his father returned—I managed to brand his mind with a clear image of himself lying close to death from the beating his father had given him. He not only ached in his limbs, his head hurt. He felt as if he had just risen from the very ground where he had been beaten down.

In later years, at the height of his power, Adolf Hitler would still believe that he had received a near-mortal beating. On many a night during the Second World War, at Headquarters in East Prussia for the Russian front, he would tell the tale to his secretaries as they sat at table after evening mess. He would be eloquent. "Of course, I deserved a whipping," he would say. "I gave real trouble to my father. My mother, I recall, was distraught. She loved me so, my dear mother." He would remember himself as being just as brave as Alois Junior, yes, he had stood up to his father. "I think that is why he had to beat me. I must have deserved it. I said terrible things to him, words so awful I cannot repeat them. Probably, I deserved this good beating. My father was a fine, strong, decent man, one Austrian who was a real German. Still, I do not know that a father should ever beat a son so close to death—it was a little too close."

Yes, he could tell stories about his childhood to bring tears to the eyes, and pure sorrow to the hearts of all who listened. It had not come all at once, this immaculate bedrock of a lie I had fixed into those folds of the brain where memory is stored in close embrace with mendacity. My art was to replace a true memory by a false one, and that can be equal in its exactitudes to removing an old tattoo in order to cover it with a new one.

Moreover, this fiction would enable me to develop Adi's future incapacity to tell the truth. By the time his political career began, he was in command of an artwork of lies elaborate enough to support his smallest need. He could shave the truth by a hair or subvert it altogether.

Working properly on a client is, as I say, a slow process, and it took many a year to convert this particular scoring of his psyche into a full installation of well-layered mendacities. The grown man would have been ready to die in the belief that he was telling the truth when he declared that his father had almost pounded him to death. From time to time, I still took pains to reinforce the keel of this one absolute lie. It was worth it. For the Maestro often pointed to my work on this matter: "There is no better way to usurp the services of a high political leader," he would tell us, "than by this method. They must not be able to distinguish certain lies from the truth. They are of considerable use to us when they do not even know that they are lying, because the mistruth is so vital to their needs."

## 14

While the tavern in Fischlham served no drinks on Sunday, there was a house on the outskirts of town where you could buy a stein of beer in the pantry.

Alois had never visited this oasis before. It had been altogether beneath his notion of what a reputable retired official of the Crown might consider reasonable leisure activity, but this was one of the few times in his life when—and he had to keep telling it to himself—he had to have a drink. His knee throbbing from the first fall, his head aching from the explosive effects of his rage, and his heart sore, he had hobbled across the fields and by sunset had taken in close to a gallon of beer.

Nobody had to help him home. There were offers, but they were rejected—it was still early enough in the evening for the sky to retain some light. With a full sense of his own dignity, he made it up over the first hill out of Fischlham and almost over the second before he lay down in a pasture to sleep. He awoke a couple of hours later with his head not six inches away from a monumental cow flop the size of a derby hat.

His hair was clean. He had not rolled into it. If he had believed in Providence, he would have offered thanks, but it was just as well he did not, for by this time—it was after ten—decently rested by his impromptu slumber, he came up over the last hill and saw the embers of a fire not thirty feet from his front door.

There had been no wind that night, which certainly saved the house, but no more than ash remained of his three Langstroth boxes, nor any sign of bees except for those poor tens of thousands who had been roasted to a microscopic crisp. A startling sense of gloom was clinging to the walls of his home.

Klara met him. If she had been weeping, she was, by now, as crisp and dry-eyed as the husks of the hive colonies. An odor arose from the last black lees of the honey that was as harsh as a catarrh of the throat.

Alois knew. A part of his wife's heart had to have been soured forever by the fact that on this, the worst of all nights, he had found a way to drink enough beer to reek of it from six feet away.

Detail by detail, she told him all that had happened. The boy had ridden off on the horse and did not return until dark. They were all asleep, or pretending to be—she would admit that they by now felt afraid of him. He must have gathered together his clothing, tied it in a sack, attached it to the saddle of the horse, and gone off again.

Yet just half an hour ago, safe as they hoped themselves to be by now, Spartaner began to bay. He howled with such ferocity that she almost left her bed to see what was wrong. But then he made noise no more, just whined a little—like a puppy. And the horse neighed as young Alois rode off again. A minute later, the flames had begun. She had known almost at once what was happening. Adi, as alive as a deer in flight, kept running between the house and the beehives. "He has set them all on fire. With kerosene!" cried Adi. "I know. It is like it was before." And he was laughing as much as he was weeping, not certain whether this was a terrible event or another glorious act of incineration.

Klara and Angela had done what they could, which was to throw pails of water on the walls of the house closest to the flames. More than that would have required the presence of a man.

They had even heard the last sounds of Ulan's hooves as he trotted away. Nor would the boy be back. Had he left any way for himself to return? She did not think so. Before he left, he had poisoned Spartaner. The dog was dead by the time Alois came back.

# BOOK X

## To Honor
## and
## To Fear

# 1

A letter came in August. After that, they did not hear from Alois Junior again. In the course of a trip to Linz, Alois Senior learned that Ulan had been sold to a horse trader for half of his value, and that might be enough for Junior to live in Vienna until he could find work.

On many a late afternoon, Alois Senior would walk down the trail the boy had used on the night when he set out for the road to Linz. Senior would come to an old stump, now his favorite seat in the forest, and there he would listen to the birds.

At rest on the remains of what once had been a noble oak, he would mourn the bees he had lost, and dream that he had come back early enough on Sunday night to chase the horse and boy through the forest. This fantasy accompanied a long summer of mourning for all he could name as lost, and then he would grieve even more for what he could not name.

So the summer passed. He hired a man to assist him in mowing their pastures. He baled his cuttings and sold the hay in Fischlham. Having no hives to worry about, he had no fear of swarming, nor were there calculations to be made of how much feed to give in the after-season to the colonies, no further examinations of the health of the hives, no estimates as to how many old bees had died but were not yet replaced by newborn, no tremors at the thought of mouse invasions, no need to consider whether he should put up netting again to keep the birds away, nor a need to weigh his boxes or ponder whether enough pollen had been collected by the foragers to provide them with protein for the winter. There was no

Queen to locate. There were not even any Langstroths to repaint. He was done.

Sitting by the stump, there came an afternoon at the end of summer when the more caustic tastes of mourning finally passed through some vent of his mind, and he said to himself, "I am relieved that I do not have to worry anymore. I loved my bees, but their loss is not my fault."

At this juncture, I did not have to pay daily attention to the Hitler family. They would be in Hafeld until they left. I was hardly concerned. One of my developed instincts is to know when the humans under my study are ready to change at a good rate, as opposed to when they are virtually inert.

In truth, that is how we measure Time. Except for those occasions when the Maestro assigns us to arenas where history can be shaped, we live reflexively. We, too, are in need of fallow periods. For me, the quiet summer of the Hitler family went by like sleep. I tended a little to other clients.

Alois, meanwhile, was marooned in the pall of a long and lackluster meditation. He was worrying to a modest degree about the value of the farm. If he were to sell it, could the price match what he had paid? Or would a potential buyer recognize the beginnings of neglect? That became the focus of his attention. Nothing, he decided, can be more subtle than the onset of neglect. While he did feel more relaxed than in many a year, it did nag at him that he was leaving all too many chores to the women—certainly those which did not call for a man's strength. He did nothing with the vegetable garden. He thought of buying a new dog; instead, he examined the paint on poor dead Spartaner's doghouse and decided it was not yet ready to peel in the summer heat.

They did not seem to need a new dog. With young Alois gone, he did not have to entertain any fears of an irate father skulking in the neighborhood. No parent of Greta Marie Schmidt was likely to appear on the doorstep—he could give thanks that that particular young lady was not pregnant, for if she were, he would by now have known all about it. And the smuggler who lived on the other side of Fischlham hardly entered his thoughts. Somehow, that phantom of a malefactor also seemed far away.

Senior's real worry was that he might become habituated to idleness. Even a few minutes spent in doing nothing at all had once been guaranteed to annoy him. Now he felt a little too contented by the drift of a cloud or, for that matter, a curl of cigar smoke.

Such peace could prove expensive. A farm that remained unworked—no matter how tidy one kept the house, the barn, and the yard—might never look right. Not to a potential buyer. A small part of Alois continued to run uphill in his sleep. It was as if his un-planted fields were reproaching him.

The economic facts (which he calculated over and over on sepa-rate pieces of paper using separate stubs of pencil) were that he and Klara, no matter how careful they might be with expenses, would sooner or later be obliged to spend more each quarter than his pension.

So there might come a time when he would have to decide that it cost too much to go to his miserable tavern in Fischlham. That would double every indignity. He had to recognize a fact. He was missing Linz. There, at least, you could drink with intelligent peo-ple. What it all came down to was that they must sell the farm. He knew it would not happen quickly. These days, the less work one did, the longer it took for anything to get done. Moreover, very much against his will, he was beginning to feel remorse about Alois Junior. What an ungovernable emotion! Was it incumbent upon him as a father to forgive his son? Yet what if Alois Junior was also full of remorse? He could not bear the thought of that boy alone in a poor room, sitting on a mean cot, his eyes full of tears.

He might as well have had an amputated forearm whose nerve endings remained alive. Alois Senior began to think again of Hitler and Sons, Apiarian Products. Because he had to invest no real be-lief in the idea, the dream, perversely, was sweeter than before.

He even brought it up with Klara. If she had felt at a good and considerable distance from her husband all summer, if she could not forgive him for being such a helpless drunk on that terrible night, nonetheless, her sense of duty still prevailed. "If you want him back, if you truly want him back, I will not stand in the way." That is what she said. That was what she felt obliged to tell him. She even felt a sense of shame, for her quick hope was that they would not find him.

No such drama was going to develop, however. A letter without a return address came a few days later from Vienna, a vile letter. "You killed my mother." The phrase was repeated several times. Then the letter declared that the son would yet be famous, and the father would twist in his grave.

Alois could not believe what he read. The rest was worse. "You were a terrible farmer, and the reason is clear. You are, as I happen to know, half-Jewish. No wonder you cannot be a farmer." And there were so many misspellings in the letter that out of a sense of shame for his son, Alois Senior had to write it out all over again before he felt able to show it to Klara. As he wrote, his hand shook badly, but the original, with its ink blots and errors of syntax, was abominable. And to think that the boy had always been able to speak well.

All the same, these awful words had to be shown to Klara. Alois Junior could only have received such rank ideas by listening to Johann Poelzl. That pious hypocrite!

Klara, however, kept the discussion well away from Poelzl. She only said, "I did not mind that thought so much. I used to think this was your reason for not going to church."

He was indignant. "It did not bother you to believe you had a husband who was half-Jewish?"

"How could it? Alois, you have always said that a man who hates Jews is uncultured. So, I knew. It is not appropriate to hate Jews. It is a sign of ignorance."

"But that does not make me Jewish."

He had a headache, sudden and fierce. Old memories of the earliest taunts at school now came back. When he was six years old. Of course. That had been the talk in Strones and in Spital.

"It never bothered you to think I was half-Jewish?" he said again.

"No. I was always so worried about our children. I wanted them to be able to live." She could not keep her eyes from watering—not with these recollections at the root of her tear ducts. "So I was glad to think you were part Jewish. I thought maybe that could give a little fresh blood to our Adolf and our Edmund and Paula."

"But I am not at all Jewish," he said. "We must be clear about this. Old Johann Nepomuk once told me who I am. I am his son. I am your real uncle, yes."

"He told you? He said such words?" She knew her grandfather Johann Nepomuk well enough to understand that he could never utter such a speech. Not in that way—not so directly.

"He," said Alois, "suggested this information to me. He did state that he knew who my father was. And then he said, 'This man was not Jewish.' He did not have to say more. It was clear. There was only one way he could know. So that was that. The next time a boy called me a Jew, I gave him a good poke in the face and broke his nose. That was one fellow who was left with an ugly mug." Alois began to laugh at the recollection. Then he laughed even more, as if to signify that he was not heartsick. "And all these years you thought the opposite?"

She nodded. She hardly knew whether to be relieved or disappointed. She had always felt excitement sneak into her at the thought of being wed to a man with such blood. Jews did forbidden things in bed. That she had heard. Maybe Alois and she had even done these same forbidden things—was that not so? And Jews were reputed to be intelligent. That she had also heard. Now she was truly confused.

Alois, thinking of Johann Poelzl, could have boiled the old bird for soup.

# 2

The reader may recall that when I presented myself as the narrator of this novel, I appeared as an SS man. Indeed, I was one. Over that period in the late 1930s, I was installed corporeally in a particular SS officer named Dieter. At a price to myself, I lived and functioned within him. I can say that we do not engage in total investiture unless the stakes require it. For our personal cost is direct. One has to relinquish the stimulation of living in more than a single consciousness. Demonic power is thereby reduced. One has become a simulacrum of a human.

So, as Dieter, I did make inquiries in Graz in 1938 about Hitler's grandfather. The way I learned, however, that the true father of Alois was Johann Nepomuk came by information I had once received directly from the Maestro, which, of course, meant that I was not in a position to name my source. In Special Section IV-2a, we were obliged, as in any other Intelligence organization, to be credible at least among ourselves, and so the only way to explain to Himmler what the origin of my information had been was to fabricate the story. While I knew that Hitler was not Jewish, I would not have been able to convince Heinrich Himmler of such a fact without revealing my source. So, to make it credible, I needed to use a means of information gathering with which Heini was familiar—human witnesses.

Of course, it was not quite that simple. I did not know the truth to a certainty back in 1938 so much as I sensed that once I had known it—which is a way of saying that the Maestro must have concluded long ago that he had to close down the memories of his devils if he wished to keep order in his share of the world. Nonetheless, I would warrant that the memories we are not encouraged to recall are still there to serve, no matter how muted, as our guides.

I mention this condign matter because the question whether Jewish blood was present in Alois has reared up so suddenly.

He was in a fury. His rage at Johann Poelzl would soon subside into what would be no less than a lifelong detestation—his heart would lift on the day that Poelzl died—but his fury against Alois Junior rose up again.

For that matter, his conversation with Klara had stimulated such an inner storm that he could not stay in bed. For the first time in all the years they had lain side by side, near to each other or not, he now had to get up on this night, dress, pace the floor, try to sleep on the couch, try to sleep on the floor, and succeeded, of course, in keeping both of them awake.

Klara knew she would have to pay. "Don't say a word," she told herself. "Do not touch this subject ever again."

While I cannot speak with the authority of those devils who are doctors of medicine, I will say it is possible that the cancer which would end Klara's life in 1908 could have taken a step forward on this miserable night.

Too much had happened to her at once. She had lost possession of a long-cherished idea. Because of the certainty that all her children with Alois were one-quarter Jewish, she believed that her last three had been provided with more opportunity to stay alive. If she had one notion about Jews (and she could not really say she had ever met a full-blooded Jew), it was that no matter what their faults might be, and she had heard the most awful stories from friends and relatives, even from storekeepers, the truth was also obvious—those Jews knew how to survive. To be so disliked, yet still be among the living. Some were even rich! Klara had always been impressed, therefore, in absolute privacy with herself—whom could she talk to about this?—that she did have three living children, saved in good part by their Jewish blood.

If Gustav and Ida and Otto had all died much too soon, she could attribute that to her side of the family. But Adolf had survived, and then Edmund and Paula, over whose health she prayed every night.

Now her confidence was breached. If the three remaining children continued to live, it would not be because of some preservative in their veins. There would be no such advantage.

A large reason not to sleep. What was worse, she was ashamed of her cowardice. How could she have accepted the idea that Alois Junior should be invited back? Lying there, listening to Alois Senior thumping the floor with his body as he lay down, she was soon suffering her own rage. It was shocking. She could not believe what she was telling herself. If it was possible, yes, she would kill Alois Junior. Only, she knew she could not. She would not ever. But the effort to repel such a fury throbbed in her heart, which is to say, in her breast, with such force and such detestation that, yes, it is possible—this could have been the night when the breast cancer which would yet burn with hell's pains in her chest might have begun. Since the answer is not easily available, I prefer to return to Alois trying to sleep on the floor.

The immensity of his rage on this night was that he had betrayed himself. That spoiled all the joy which is also implicit in rage, a notion too infrequently considered. Rage, after all, can offer the same nourishing sense of self-righteousness that is available on more ordinary occasions to the most hypocritical of churchgoers. The core of such pleasure is never to be angry at oneself, only at others. Yet, here, on this night, Alois was infuriated at the cost of his own deeds.

If Junior had turned out badly, it was his fault, his fault alone. By such a light, he was among the worst of human beings, a weak father. He had spent his life obeying orders, and then enforcing them in the Customs service, he had revered Franz Josef, a gallant, great, and good king who embodied hard work and discipline. His guardianship of his own nature had become a species of homage to Franz Josef. Yet he had implanted none of this sense of respect in

Alois Junior. Was that because he did feel guilty about the boy's mother? Yes, he had treated Fanni badly, so badly that he could not be stern with her offspring. That had been a lack of discipline in himself.

It took every hour through the darkness of this night for his rage to subside. It was not until the first light of morning—a dim light that came with shrouds of rain at dawn—that he was able to speak from one part of his mind to the other, and so could issue a few orders on what his future conduct with Adi must become. He was not going to make the same mistake he had allowed with Junior.

## 3

Now, whenever he wished to bring Adi to his side, Alois would whistle. It was a fine drill of a whistle, sharp enough to hurt the ear. Nor did he reduce the intensity when the boy was within reach. In the tavern, Alois was now fond of saying, "If you are raising a son, do not let go of the whip. I speak from experience."

More than once, Alois said to Adi, "Time and sacrifice were wasted on your older brother. You, Adolf, will not waste my time."

Adi was paralyzed with fear. I had to wonder how the final effects of this could serve our purposes. We certainly know how to use humiliation and self-abasement as a tool when working with manic-depressives. If we look to drive a client into a violent act, a series of humiliations can stir the subject into oscillating too fast between the poles of his depression and his mania. Soon enough, there is an eruption.

I did not see why we needed anything so drastic here at so early an age. The Maestro was, however, not urging me to restrain Alois, and the father was drenching the boy's spirit with wretchedness. Adi was being given more than a hint of the anguish that attaches itself to the onset of ineradicable melancholia.

These are established means for seeding suicide. So I could not know what ultimate purpose the Maestro had in mind. The boy was delicate enough for it to go wrong. What a disaster, and for so little.

Yet the Maestro often surprised us by such moves. He was often ready to take bold chances with the lives of our clients. There were occasions when the Maestro, entertaining an ambitious future for a young client, would be ready to encourage such parental domination and, at times, incite it. I think he saw it as still another species of inoculation against future emotional crises.

Naturally, these gambles could also make for future instability. Once we implant a deep humiliation in a proud client, we also set ourselves the task of converting such a wound into a future strength. That can prove equal in difficulty to converting a coward into a hero. Yet, when we succeed, when the psychic abyss of a would-be suicide is transmogrified into promontories of ego, an immense gamble has succeeded. The once-humiliated wretch has now acquired the power to humiliate others. That is a demonic power and is not acquired easily. Nonetheless, I would not wish to exaggerate. Adi was, at this point, far from being altogether reduced. He did show some talent for pleading his case before Klara.

"Mother," he told her, "my father now looks at me as if I am always guilty."

She was aware of this. The whistle had become a needle into her own ears as well.

"Adi, you must never say that your father is wrong," she told him.

"But what if he might be wrong?"

"He does not wish to be. Perhaps he makes a mistake."

"What if he is very wrong?"

"It will not remain that way." She nodded. She did not know if she believed what she said next, but she said it nonetheless. "He is a good father. A good father always realizes sooner or later that he may have been going in the wrong direction." She nodded again, as if to oblige herself to believe such words. "There can be a moment," she said, "when the father recognizes that he, too, can be in error." She put her hand to the boy's face as if to cool the fever in his cheeks. "Yes," she said, "he hears his own words and realizes that they are not correct. So he changes."

"He does?"

"Absolutely. The father changes." She spoke as if this had happened in the past. "He changes," she repeated for the third time, "and now there is order in what he says. Now it goes in a good direction. Because he is ready to change. Do you know why?"

"No."

"Because you were able to tell yourself that you would never cause him confusion. You would not do that, because he is your father." She held Adi by the waist and looked into his eyes.

Klara had been the first in the family to recognize (and she was still the only one) that Adi could be spoken to as if he were ten or twelve years old. "Yes," she now said, "it is best when there is no confusion in the house. So you must never accuse your father. That might cause him to feel *weiblich*. And for him to feel weak is very bad. You cannot expect him to admit that he has a weakness."

At this point, she began to speak of *die Ehrfurcht*. To honor and to fear. Her mother had used the word when speaking of Johann Poelzl. He was, she had all but said to Klara, a hardworking but very unlucky farmer—who in the family did not know that?—and yet she had always treated her husband with *Ehrfurcht*, as if he were an important and successful man. "That is what my mother taught me, and I now tell it to you. The word of the father is the law of the family."

Klara said this with such solemnity that the boy felt it come into him as holy strength. Yes, someday he would have a family and all who were in it would honor him and they would fear him. At this point, his need to urinate became pressing. (This phenomenon always afflicted him in these years whenever he was on the point of developing large and happy thoughts about himself.) In the midst of his mother's peroration, he almost had an accident but did not—not if he was going to believe that in the future he would receive his share of *Ehrfurcht*.

"Yes," she said to her son, "the word of the father must be law. Right or wrong, one cannot argue with his word. You must obey him. For the good of the family. Right or wrong, the father is always right. Otherwise, all is confusion."

Now she referred to Alois Junior. "He did not have *Ehrfurcht*," she said. "Promise me that will never be said of you. Because now you are the oldest brother. You are important. That boy who used to be your brother is as good as dead."

Adi's body was wet. His perspiration might as well have been illumined by sacred light. Just so complete was the importance of this sentiment. I entered his thoughts long enough to tell him, "Your mother is correct. You are now the oldest brother. The younger ones will honor and respect you."

Yes, Adi understood, and nightly I worked upon his mind until this concept became a mental certainty equal to one of those well-paved avenues of the mind that are always ready for heavy mental traffic. On many a night I would tell him again and again that Alois Junior was separated forever from the family.

Alois Senior was of no small aid to me. By December, he wrote a new will. It stipulated that in the event of his death, the son named Alois was to receive no more of the estate than the minimum prescribed by law. "The smaller the better," he added. Since the act of drawing up a will reengaged all of Senior's long-developed sense of proper official procedure, he also added: "This is stated in the full recognition of the seriousness of such an act by a father. In my years as a Chief Customs Officer for the Crown, I warrant that I became most familiar with the responsibility that must always be seriously attached to such grave decisions."

Whereupon, having completed the rewriting of his will, he whistled for Adi and read portions aloud to him.

# 4

Alois' decision to write a new will came after he knew that he would be able to sell the farm. The buyer had been referred to him by Herr Rostenmeier, who had even offered good advice to Klara.

"Dear Frau Hitler," he told her, "your farm will only find a buyer for one reason—because it looks good. Is that not exactly why your husband bought it in the first place?"

"I will not say that has to be untrue," said Klara. (For her, this remark was equal to flirting with Herr Rostenmeier.)

"Yes," he said, "it is good you recognize this. I believe you will be able to sell your property to people who are less experienced at farming than yourselves, but"—he held up a finger—"more well-to-do, not so? You must have the patience to wait. Soon enough, one of these comfortable people will come along. And when he does, you must please send him to me. I will be your friend. I will know how to answer all the questions that are asked."

The wealthy house hunter did arrive, did like the look of the house and the land, knew even less about the pitfalls of husbandry than had Alois, and the sale took place. If the price presented no real profit, neither did Alois suffer the loss he had feared. The finality of the transfer even convinced him that any dream of living out his last days on a farm could be put to rest together with any hopes that the oldest son would yet bring him some reason for pride. No, it was now up to Adi. He was not nearly so lithe nor strong as Alois Junior, nor nearly so good-looking, but as bright, perhaps, and obedient. He was certainly obedient. Whistling for him had become a pleasure. The response was quick.

In his heart, however, Alois Senior did keep the equivalent of an old photograph. There still were nights when he would sit on the oak bench and muse again about the Langstroth box he had built for himself. He would pat the seat as if to recall the sound of the slap he used to give that wooden box in the old days, yes, a nice and solid slap to stir up his bees.

That is far down the road. History (for those who have lived in it for as long as myself) is seldom recalled as all-fascinating. It is such a bed of lies. That is the only reason I could recommend the life of a devil to would-be aspirants. We know so much about how it happens, how it really happens. Who could ever wish to lose such riches? Yet it is not inconceivable that this is exactly what I have done by revealing my relation to the Maestro. Perhaps the perversity of our diabolical natures does bear some relation to that curious human nature, which forces its way into existence between the hazards of urine and excrement yet will later dream each night of a noble life.

# BOOK XI

## THE ABBOT AND THE BLACKSMITH

# 1

In the summer of 1897, after the sale of the Hafeld property, the family moved to the Gasthof Leingartner in Lambach, and there they would live until the end of the year. Having left behind the responsibilities of the farm, Alois began his true retirement, which occasioned a few small but surprising changes. He had, for instance, no interest in the cooks and maids at the Gasthof. Worse, they seemed to have no interest in him. Nor did he mind it.

I would even say that Alois was temporarily content. Since that could affect our purposes in regard to Adolf, I kept a close eye on Senior's modest activities. To my surprise, he took a proprietary interest in the medieval flavor of Lambach and so enjoyed walking down its streets. The town had a population of no more than 1,700 people, but it could boast of a Benedictine monastery founded in the eleventh century, and a church, Paura, that had been built in the shape of a triangle, with three towers, three gates, and three altars. I must say Paura had the strangest effect on his thoughts.

Alois had begun to wonder whether, hundreds of years ago, he had had a previous life here. Was he feeling some shadowed hint of an earlier existence? He did not dismiss the notion. He could have been a medieval knight. Why not? It would certainly account for his boldest qualities as a man. *Der Ritter Alois von Lambach!*

If it be asked once again how I can be aware of such a reaction when Alois is, after all, not my client, I will reiterate that on occasion we can enter the thoughts of humans who are closely related to one of our charges. Alois' meanderings about reincarnation were available to me, therefore, and he had come to quite a conclusion. Most people, he decided, could not believe that they would ever cease to exist.

I must say that for Alois, this was a stimulating thought. Reincarnation might well be conceivable, and if so, then he, Alois, must have been one hell of a licentious knight. Such a possibility put him into an excellent mood. New ideas were exactly what he needed. They kept you out of the quicksand of growing old, he now decided.

# 2

The imperative he put upon himself to entertain fresh thoughts may account for the reception Alois gave to Adi's desire to join the children's choir at the Benedictine monastery. Klara could hardly believe her husband would say yes. She had, for that matter, come close to warning the boy not to ask, but then asked herself: What if God wanted Adi to be in that choir? She was not about to interfere with what might be the Lord's purpose.

So young Adolf, spiritual hat in hand, did approach Alois and managed to say that the monks told him he had a good voice. With his father's permission to stay after school, he could rehearse.

If it would be asked why Alois was amenable to allowing any son of his to study with monks and priests, his answer would have been ready. "I have made careful inquiries," he would have said, "and these Benedictines conduct the best school in Lambach. Since I wish Adolf to do well in life, I have decided to send him there no matter what other objections I choose to retain."

Adi took to the school. Soon enough, he was seen by the monks as one of their best pupils, and he knew it. In turn, Alois was delighted with his marks. The boy was not only taking twelve required subjects but was receiving the highest grade in each course, which was more than enough to leave Alois in a benign mood.

"Let me tell you," he said, "when I was young, I, too, could lay claim to a good voice. It was a gift from my mother. She was once the soloist in the parish church at Döllersheim."

"Oh, yes, Father," said Adi. "I remember how well you sang on the day we first came to Hafeld from Linz."

"Yes," said Alois, "the old ditties did come back. Do you remember the one that upset your mother?"

"I do," said Adi. " 'She kept saying, '*Ach*, not for the children!' "

They laughed. The memory prompted Alois to sing the same lines.

*He was the best I ever had,*
*Together through good and bad,*
*The drum called us to fight,*
*He was always on my right.*

*A bullet flew toward us,*
*Meant for him or meant for me?*
*Into his life it tore,*
*At my feet a piece of gore.*

Alois laughed and so did Adi. They remembered. That was when Klara had cried out, "No, not for the children!"

Now Alois' voice grew even more resonant.

*My friend, I said, I cannot ease your pain,*
*But in life eternal we will meet again,*
Mein guter Kamerad, mein guter Kamerad.

Alois now declared in a voice made husky by the song, "Yes, I will give permission. That is because I have come to believe in your future possibilities. You are to be rewarded for the excellence you have shown in your new school."

To himself, Alois was thinking, "Of course, I will not encourage him to go too far on this path. No need to end as a sickly priest."

Adi, however, was wondering whether he might, one day, become a monk, or better, an Abbot. He loved their black habits, and his image of heaven quivered in the light that came through the rose windows. The boy was ready to weep before the power of "Grosser Gott Wir Loben Dich":

*Holy God, we praise Thy Name,*
*Infinite Thy vast Domain,*
*Everlasting is Thy reign . . .*
*Fill the Heavens with sweet accord,*
*Holy, Holy, Holy Lord.*

While he sang, I was encouraging him to believe that he might rise supreme over all these monks and hold authority in one hand and mystery in the other. Indeed, he had a model. The Abbot of this monastery was the most impressive man Adi had ever encountered. He was tall, his hair was silver gray, his expression was elevated. To Adi, he was as handsome as a king.

One time, alone in the room at the Gasthof that he shared with Angela, he lifted her darkest dress off its hook and draped it around his shoulders as a species of vestment. Then he stood up on a stool. He knew he must speak in a low voice or he would be overheard in the hallway, but he felt full of the sermon he had heard at Mass, as well as the prayer addressed to St. Michael the Archangel that he repeated every day. Now he was absorbing these sounds and relishing the moment when he would be alone in the forest speaking to the trees.

First he felt impelled to voice the sermon that had preceded the prayer. "These fires of hell," he said, "will reach into every pore of your body. They will melt your bones and your lungs. A terrible odor will arise from your throat. The stench of the body will be heinous. This is the fire that will never end."

He staggered as he stood on the stool. The force of the words had left him giddy. He had to take a breath before he could utter the prayer.

"Thy Glorious Majesty, we supplicate Thee to deliver us from the tyranny of the infernal spirits, from their snares, their lies, and their furious wickedness—O Prince of the Heavenly Host, cast into hell Satan and all evil spirits who wander through the world seeking the ruin of souls, Amen."

He felt most excited. I did my best to encourage him to believe he was receiving a sign from above. But then to spoil it all—were other forces present?—he proceeded to have the first real erection of his young life. Yet he also felt like a woman. It must have been the odor of Angela's dress. So he threw it away from him and jumped down from the stool, even kicked the dress before he picked it up, sniffed it again, and was abominably disturbed. He still felt like a woman.

It was at this point that he knew he must do what other students were doing. He had to feel equal to them. He must start smoking. He had been breathing the fumes of Alois' pipe since he had been an infant, and he detested the smell, but now he had to feel male again, purely so. No more of this half and half.

### 3

Over the entrance to the monastery was a large swastika carved into the stone of the arched gate. It was the coat of arms of a previous Abbot named von Hagen, who had been Abbot Superior in 1850, and von Hagen must have enjoyed the propinquity to his own name—a hooked cross was called a *Hakenkreuz*.

Not too much, I hasten to add, should be made of this. Von Hagen's swastika was subtly carved, and so offered no striking sug-

gestion of the phalanxes yet to march beneath that symbol. Nonetheless, there it was, a hooked cross.

On his ninth birthday, Adolf was alone and smoking a cigarette
in the archway. He was not alone for long, however. The meanest
of the priests under whom he studied, a prelate notorious among
the students for his stealthy tread, came by to catch Adolf in the
act. The cigarette (a twist of Alois' pipe tobacco rolled into newspaper) was immediately seized and stomped upon by the cleric. He
had all the frenzy of a man who is squashing cockroaches.

Adi was ready to weep. "It is possible," he now heard, "that the
Devil has entered into you. If so, you will die in great misery."
Then he gave an evil smile. He was summoning the powers of
anathema he had collected over the years.

So soon as Adolf was able to speak, he said, "Oh, Father, I knew
it was wrong. I detested it always. I will never go near to tobacco
again."

At that moment, however, he had to run down to the grass beyond the stone steps of the entrance, where he immediately threw
up. The execration of the priest had presented such aridity of soul
that Adi could not breathe. The long nose of the man seemed as
malignant as his lips and they were as thin as a knife edge. All the
while, in the midst of suffering such a whole set of atrocious feelings, Adi was already calculating how to seek forgiveness from the
Abbot. He knew he would be sent over to that august office so soon
as he stopped vomiting.

Before the Abbot, he burst into tears again. He had the inspiration to say that he did not want this abominable act to interfere
with his longing to become a priest. How much he wished to re-
pent, he declared. When he was done, the Abbot even said, "Well,
someday you may yet make a fine man of the cloth."

The sincerity in Adi's voice resonated with the full inspiration of
an outright lie. His one taste of anathema had been sufficient. He
was now disabused forever of the thought of becoming a priest.
Only his admiration for the Abbot remained intact.

By the measure of my endeavors, it had been a profitable day.

Given the many clients I was overseeing in that part of Austria, I cannot claim to have been always in the right place at the best moment, but on this occasion I was. Our mean-spirited cleric—small surprise!—happened to be one of my finest clients in Lambach and had of course been alerted to take a quick stroll over to the gate where von Hagen's hooked stone cross was emblazoned.

# 4

I will say that Adi's veneration of the Abbot was retained, but only as an echo of that early infatuation. His hatred of the priest with the long nose did not diminish, and so the memory of the moment when Alois gave him permission to sing in the choir was all but gone. In any case, the recollection would soon have lost all warmth, since it had also become obvious that his father favored Edmund. Once, after Adi had given him a good shove, Edmund dared to poke back. "Don't you touch me," he said. "I am just as good as you are."

For that remark, Edmund was hit hard enough to encourage him to wail with all the power of his four-year-old lungs.

When Klara descended, Adi said, "Alois Junior always used to hit me. Nobody ever cared about that."

Alois now loomed overhead. "You had your mother to protect you from Junior," he said. "I remember. She was on your side always. Even when you were in the wrong. This used to upset your brother very much, and maybe I did not pay enough attention!"

Alois chose, therefore, to give Adi a spanking. It was stinging to the boy's backside but without real force. Alois still lived in fear of the anger with which he had belabored Alois Junior once the youth was on the ground.

These quarrels between Adi and Edmund resounded through the inn, and Klara was thereby embarrassed. The innkeeper and his wife were, however, content with the rent provided by the Hitlers and made a point of treating Klara with the greatest respect, even trying to give her the illusion that she was a notable example of a fine, middle-class lady. Klara was not about to believe them. Klara knew better. She told Alois that the family needed to find more space at a lower cost.

She had also decided that Angela was much too old to keep sharing a room with Adi. Indeed, Angela had complained that one of her best dresses had dusty shoe-prints all over it—that had to be her brother's doing. Klara decided not to accuse him. He would deny it. The true problem remained; they had to move. Nor was Alois opposed. Adi's quarrels with Angela had been getting on his nerves. One time, he had said to Klara, "You wish me not to give him a good one, but he's very trying."

"When children fight," said Klara, "it can be the fault of both."

"Well, I am not about to put her on my knee."

With true perturbation, Klara said, "Of course not."

"In any case, it is the boy. I repeat: I find him trying."

Klara now decided to tell Alois about the day Adi was caught smoking. In the hope that Alois might feel sympathy, she said, "Adi needs kindness. He needs that so much. After the Abbot forgave him, Adi told me, 'I didn't know a big grown man could be so kind.' Alois, he needs a kindness from us."

Alois shook his head. "No," he told her, "already you are his slave. I think it is all to the good that he started smoking. In time to come maybe he will like tobacco and even become a real guy." At which point Alois laughed until he began to cough.

Klara thought, "Yes, one tough guy, full of phlegm."

It could be said that Klara was beginning to have a few private thoughts. For years, she had felt that such private views might not be suitable for a good wife. Now, however, she had begun to entertain a secret project. She had come to the conclusion that it would be good to buy a nice house, but she knew Alois was not yet ready.

Instead, she would have to go along with his decision to move to the unused upper floor of a nearby grain mill. That would be considerably cheaper than the inn and would offer a good deal of space. Moreover, Angela would have her own room. Let her begin to enjoy some of the opportunities that Klara had never had. Later, once they owned a house, whether in this town or another, she could hope that Angela would yet be married to a fine young man. And for the present, she certainly deserved to have her own room. Such a good stepdaughter.

So Klara put up with Alois' desire to move to the mill. There would be endless work, but Angela was done with school and ready to take on her part of the task. Early in the winter of 1898, they did rent a floor, therefore, on the upper story of the grain mill. Its owner, one Herr Zoebel, kept four mules to activate the grinding wheel. To add to this clamor, there was also a blacksmith shop at the rear worked by a big fellow named Preisinger. Living on the floor above would be a war against dust, but Klara was not unhappy. Angela was always ready to be Klara's maid, or a devoted younger sister, or a devoted friend. That left Klara free to enjoy some time alone with Paula.

# 5

From Paula's infancy, there had not been a morning when Klara did not whisper to her, "You will be so beautiful."

But now, although not yet two years old, Paula seemed a little backward.

Alois did not notice. He loved to dandle Paula on his knee. He was ready to dream of a time when this child would be the loveliest young lady in town. Her wedding might even be an event.

But on a given day, after a visit to the town doctor, Klara came home with the news that their daughter was developing too slowly.

The doctor's remark had not come as a surprise. Klara had certainly been concerned. At two, Paula could not use a spoon without spilling most of the contents, whereas Edmund had been able to manage the trip from the soup bowl to his mouth not long after he was a year old. At two, he could dress himself, even begin to wash himself. Paula could not. She would lie in her cot with her good friend, the rag doll, hugged to her breast.

Long before he was two, Edmund knew the words for arms, legs, fingers, and toes. Paula would giggle, but knew none of these words. During the doctor's examination, she was asked to stand on one foot but could not keep her balance. Now, she looked blank when the doctor asked her, "What do you do when you are tired?"

Klara tried to help by saying, "Sleep," but the doctor was annoyed. "Please, Frau Hitler, no help," he said.

"Yes," Klara now told Alois, "he even says she is retarded."

"He doesn't know what he is talking about."

"Alois, it could be true." Klara began to weep.

Alois fell into a depression. His old gifts of perception, so skilled at spotting a smuggler across a Customs shed, were now addressed to examining Paula's smile. It seemed to him that her eyes were much too vacant.

An ugliness of mood descended upon the family. When Alois would go on his walk, Adi would look to badger Edmund. To Klara, that was intolerable. She would snap at Adi, then feel disloyal. The truth was that Edmund had become the bright light of the family. Having grown out of his runny nose and dirty pants, he had become a charming four-year-old, as full of future promise—in Klara's opinion—as a prince, and it had all happened since they left Hafeld. Edmund did have the sweetest smile, and the funniest face. Klara had to laugh at the expressions he offered, so wise, so comical, and sometimes so outrageous. He was a good little boy and a scamp, all in one. But Adi was reacting badly. He had formed the habit of sticking a leg out just far enough to trip his little brother whenever Edmund ran by. Edmund, however, would not complain, just get up and keep running up and down the floor of the loft.

It would have bothered Klara even more if she had been aware of Adolf's secret desire. It was to hit Edmund as hard as he could and not be punished for the act. Alois, Klara, and Angela were always carrying on about how blue were Edmund's eyes. Yet his own eyes, Adolf decided, were a nobler blue. Besides, Edmund's face looked squashed together. How he would have liked to squash that face a little more whenever his parents called his little brother cute.

Edmund was always receiving praise for the concern he showed for Paula, whereas Adi felt that he had been the first to see how Paula was not too bright. He could have told them, but no, his mother and Angela were impressed instead with how much Edmund loved his little sister.

Klara was even glad that the big, sweaty blacksmith, Preisinger, was down there in his shop hammering away because Adi liked him and stayed there a good deal. That was better than trying to keep watch on him when he would sit outside her kitchen waiting for Edmund to run by so he could stick out his leg and trip him one more time.

# 6

At this time I had to move from Austria to Switzerland, and was active in Geneva for the next month overseeing the transmogrification of a petty criminal into an impassioned assassin.

Given the variety of clients I was developing in the environs of Linz, I had to return to Austria more than once to take note of their condition and so was able to stay close to events at the grain mill in Lambach, but I will not speak of those matters until I tell a little about my assignment in Geneva. To those readers who are, by now, wary of these expeditions, I can promise that this time I will not be absent from young Adolf for more than an interesting chapter or two.

Moreover, a few pages of the text to come will quote Mark Twain, even if he was never my client—I would not have dared to make that attempt! In truth, if such a possibility had existed, the Maestro, given his admiration for great writers, would probably have looked to explore such a seduction on his own.

In the event, Twain, a most complex man, was not considered suitable material. Some of his associates were, however, and so I knew enough about his activities to respect the passion with which he wrote about the assassination of the Empress Elizabeth in Geneva on September 10, 1898. Married in 1854 to Franz Josef, she had long been considered the most beautiful and cultivated queen in Europe. Her favorite poet, for example, was Heinrich Heine. What added to the lady's exotic status was that after the double suicide in 1889 of her beloved son, Crown Prince Rudolf, and his young mistress, Baroness Vetsera, the Empress dressed only in black. That tragedy, known to all of Europe as "Mayerling," was an event in which I had played no small part. Indeed, that may have been why I was chosen to shepherd Luigi Lucheni around Geneva after he had been sighted as a putative assassin.

"He's a dreadful piece of work," the Maestro said, "but made to order for us. A most unbalanced little malefactor. He sees himself as a serious philosopher and is sincere in his belief that only the most exceptional individual deeds will leave a lasting influence on the public. So, go to it!"

I worked with Luigi Lucheni. I expanded the gaseous irresolutions of his psyche, then compressed such inflammable vapors until they were as focused as a blowtorch. Assassins need many quick magnifications of their ego if they are to be ready at the murderous moment.

I did not fail. Lucheni, an impoverished young man, chose to become an anarchist after he came to live with the Swiss. In Geneva, he found revolutionaries who accepted him, at best, with misgivings. His fellow Italians chose to call him *il stupido* (which doubled the daily compression of his furies). It was of help to me that he was being ridiculed by those whom he had expected to applaud him. "Convince them by way of your actions," I kept counseling. "You are here among us to take the life of someone who is very high among the oppressive classes."

"Who is this person?" he asked.

"You will know when the person is pointed out."

Poor Empress Elizabeth! She was so proud and so poetic that she allowed only a few bodyguards to escort her when she was on vacation. Even then, they had to stay at a remove of ten paces from her person. It did not matter that strangers were bound to approach. Invariably, it would be a tourist asking for an autograph. So, as she stood by herself on a promenade along the banks of the Rhone, Lucheni came up, took out a sharpened rat-tail file, and thrust it into her heart.

He was immediately apprehended, his quarters were searched, and his diary examined. All the world soon knew that he had written: "How I would like to kill someone—but it must be someone important so it gets in the papers."

He might have chosen Philippe, the Duke of Orléans, who was present in Geneva then on a visit, but so was the beautiful Sisi—Empress Elizabeth. Sisi, I knew, would count for more. Even as I had led the anathematic priest by his long nose to the gateway where Adi was smoking, so did I direct Lucheni to Empress Elizabeth.

If it is discomforting to the reader that I usually present myself as a calm observer, capable of a balanced narrative, and yet am also able to abet the most squalid acts without a moment of regret, let it not come as a surprise. Devils require two natures. In part, we are civilized. What may be less apparent on most occasions is that our ultimate aim is to destroy civilization as a first step to obviating God, and such an enterprise must be able to call on one's readiness to *do what it takes*—a fine expression I picked up years later from a minor client who worked on a film crew.

In any event, the immediate effect of the deed was exceptional. I will, however, leave that description to Mark Twain himself.

# 7

The author was then at Kaltenleutgeben, a small Austrian town forty miles from Vienna. By way of the failure of his investment in a new linotype machine, Twain was bankrupt.

So he left his home in Hartford, Connecticut, and traveled through Europe giving popular lectures for fees large enough to pay off many of his debts. Resting in Kaltenleutgeben when the murder of Elizabeth occurred, he wrote the next day to a friend: "This murder will still be talked of and described and painted a thousand years from now."

I cannot begin to speak of the elation with which I read those words. My own opinion of the importance of the deed had now been confirmed by a master of prose. Indeed, Twain was so powerfully affected that he soon composed an essay full of the incomparable flow of his language. Although, for a myriad of reasons too labyrinthine to catalog, he chose not to publish it. I, however, came into possession of these pages by way of one of his servants.

*The more one thinks of the assassination, the more imposing and tremendous the event becomes. . . . One must go back about two thousand years to find an instance to put with this one. . . . "The Empress is murdered!" When those amazing words struck upon my ear in this Austrian village last Saturday, three hours after the disaster, I knew that it was already old news in London, Paris, Berlin, New York, San Francisco, Japan, China, Melbourne, Cape Town, Bombay, Madras, Calcutta, and that the entire globe with a single voice was cursing the perpetrator of it.*

*. . . And who is the miracle-worker who has furnished to the world this spectacle? All the ironies are compacted in the answer. He is at the bottom of the human ladder, as the accepted estimates of degree and value go; a soiled and patched young loafer, without gifts, without talent, without education, without morals, without character, without any born charm or any acquired one that wins or beguiles or attracts; without a single grace of mind or heart or hand that any tramp or prostitute could envy him; an unfaithful private in the ranks, an incompetent stone-cutter, an inefficient lackey; in a word, a mangy, offensive, empty, unwashed, vulgar, gross, mephitic, timid, sneaking, human polecat. And it was within the privileges and powers of this sarcasm upon the human race to reach up—up—up and strike from its far summit in the social skies the world's accepted ideal of Glory and Might and Splendor and Sacredness! It realizes to us what sorry shows and shadows we are. Without our clothes and pedestals we are poor things and much of a size; our dignities are not real, our pomps are shams. At our best and stateliest we are not suns, as we pretended, and*

*teach, and believe, but only candles; and any bummer can blow us out.*

*And now we get realized to us once more another thing which we often forget—or try to; that no man has a wholly undiseased mind; that in one way or another all men are mad and one of the commonest forms of madness is the desire to be noticed, the pleasure derived from being noticed. . . . It is this madness for being noticed and talked about which has invented kingship and the thousand other dignities. . . . It has made kings pick one another's pockets, scramble for one another's crowns and estates, slaughter one another's subjects; it has raised up prize-fighters and poets, and villages' mayors, and little and big politicians, and big and little charity-founders, and bicycle champions, and banditti chiefs, and frontier desperadoes, and Napoleons. Anything to get notoriety; anything to set the village, or the nation, or the planet shouting, "Look—there he goes—that is the man!" And in five minutes' time, at no cost of brain, or labor, or genius, this mangy Italian tramp has beaten them all, outstripped them all, for in time their names will perish; but by the friendly help of the insane newspapers and courts and kings and historians, his is safe and will thunder all down the ages as long as human speech shall endure! Oh, if it were not so tragic, how ludicrous it would be!*

I rushed to present this to the Maestro. I do not know that I had ever taken myself so seriously before. I knew that I was, at last, an actor in history.

He was scathing. "I may value great writers," he said, "but look how Mark Twain exaggerates the event. It is hysterical. One thousand years! Sisi will be forgotten in twenty."

I did not dare to ask, "Does the event serve no large purpose?"

My thoughts were heard. "Oh," he said, "it's a bit of help. But you, like Twain, are much too impressed by mighty names. They count for so little once they are gone. I'd like to clean the snobbery out of you. It's not the name. Only an exceptional client that we develop ex nihilo—or virtually ex nihilo—can affect history to our advantage. But for that, we have to build him up from first brick to the last. Killing Sisi offered no such value. It will not be conducive to ongoing social unrest. Khodynskoe is still serving us, whereas knocking off Sisi? I tell you that if I were a gourmet picking a perfect peach off the tree, I might be able to enjoy a few minutes of gastric excellence. That would be analogous to the pleasure we can take because of your nice work with Luigi Lucheni. But you must not lose your sense of measure." Here, he did smile.

"There was one nice moment," he said. "Our great author did recover his good sense on the last paragraph."

Twain had also written:

> *Among the inadequate attempts to account for the assassination, we must concede high rank to the many which have described it as "ordained from above." I think this verdict will not be popular "above." If the deed was ordained from above, there is no rational way of making this prisoner even partially responsible for it, and the Genevan court cannot condemn him without manifestly committing a crime.*

"Yes," said the Maestro, "when it comes to being aware of us, that good fellow, Mark Twain, must have been so near to saying 'ordained from below.' Thank God, he didn't!"

How the Maestro could laugh on these rare occasions when he felt merry.

# 8

I had, as I related, been at a distance from Lambach until after the assassination, and by then the Hitlers no longer lived in the grain mill nor even, indeed, in Lambach. They had moved to a larger town (Leonding, pop. 3,000) which, at first, was much to Klara's satisfaction, for it was the result of her subtle manipulation of Alois. That was novel. It had taken her years to begin to understand how to manipulate her husband. God-fearing, she did not like to use calculated tactics. Until they lived at the mill, it never occurred to her that she might make Alois jealous.

Indeed, Klara had never been able to believe that she was worthy of her husband—he was still so preeminently an uncle. But, at last, she came to realize that he might even need her. Even if he did not love her in large measure, he did need her.

Armed at last with this thought, she was able to recognize that Alois might be old enough by now to feel jealous. She, in turn, so long as she broke no Godly injunctions but merely bent them a bit, might, yes, might, make Alois jealous enough to wish to move away from the mill.

This possibility resided in the form of the big, soot-covered man on the ground floor, the blacksmith, Preisinger. Fascinated by him, Adi often spent hours at a time watching him work and listening to him talk. She could hear their voices even as she worked in her kitchen on the floor above, and the sounds that came up were curiously engaged with those she made—the splash of water from a pail to a basin seeming to be answered by a few ringing blows on an anvil.

She knew why Adi was eager to be with the blacksmith. The man worked with fire. That was exciting, even if she was not about to ponder why fire pleased her so. If she had known since childhood that God was everywhere, well, so was the Devil. As long as one did not oblige oneself to follow every thought, then the Devil could have no access. God would be there to protect your ignorance.

So it was enough for her to understand that Adi would be full of a sense of mystery as he watched the blacksmith heat a piece of iron until it was white-hot, at which moment another piece, also white-hot, could be attached. Out of such melding would come more complex joinings ready to become useful tools— for everything from forging carriage axles to mending broken ploughs.

Soon enough came an occasion when she had a reason to visit below. The water pump in her kitchen needed a repair on its cylinder. The crack was soon mended, but to her surprise, she stayed a little longer and talked with the blacksmith. Then he invited her to come back whenever she would like a cup of tea.

To her amazement, this big bull of a man, this Preisinger, had nice manners. He not only treated her with the greatest respect, but he could also speak well, considering that he was as uneducated as herself. He did not brag, but did leave the impression, which she found most agreeable (even as she had once had just such sentiments about Alois), that he was a person of natural importance. She could hardly believe how pleasing it was to listen to him as she sat in the one good chair of his shop while Adi stood beside her close to transfixed.

Preisinger's trade was not only engaged with farmers in the area, and occasionally with travelers whose horses were having trouble with a shoe, but, as he explained, many merchants in the area depended upon him for odd repairs. Moreover, he could diagnose many an equine ailment. "I have been able to act, Frau Hitler, as a veterinarian. Yes, I can say that. Because sometimes I have to know more than the vets."

"Can you really say that?" asked Klara, and blushed at her own straightforwardness.

"Frau Hitler," answered Preisinger, "I have seen valuable animals hobbled to where they could barely walk. And for a simple reason. The veterinarian, however good a fellow he might be concerning other animal diseases, did not know as much about a horse's hoof as was necessary."

"I suppose that is true," said Klara. "You have had so much experience."

"Young Adolf will tell you. There are market days when I shoe as many as twenty horses, one after another. No stopping."

"Yes," said Klara, "how much work must come rushing in when there is ice on the ground."

To which he answered, "I see that you understand these matters."

Klara had to blush.

" 'Give me a better grip on the ice,' " Preisinger now said. "I hear that every winter. Over and over. Once, on a freezing day, I had to shoe twenty-five horses, and every one of those farmers was asking me to hurry up."

"Yes, but Herr Preisinger would not agree," said Adolf. "He told me, 'Speed is speed, yet one nail gone wrong, and that horse will never trust you again.' " Adi's cheeks were flushed. He could not tell Klara what else the blacksmith had confessed. "Young fellow," Preisinger had said, "there were nights when I couldn't sit down because I had the horse's name on my behind."

"The horse's name?" Adi had asked.

"His hoof. I can recognize horses by their hooves."

"You can?"

"Old Clubfoot. Old Crookedhoof. What name would you like? I will find it for you on my backside."

He had laughed, but then, seeing that Adi was bewildered, Preisinger was quick to add, "I am joking. Only joking. But a good blacksmith knows that you can get kicked for your trouble."

"How often does that happen?" the boy asked. He was so obviously seeing the event in his mind that Preisinger decided to remove himself from such images.

"No longer," he said. "Now it is not even one time a year. In this work, you have to be very good or you don't last."

With Klara, Preisinger preferred to discuss how he might compound his own special caulk for the hole left by old nails—he was proud of the various kinds of problems he was ready to solve. While he spoke, she looked at the occasional imprint of horseshoes on his dirt floor, there in the dark dust on the earth floor. She certainly did like this man. She could share his pride in the sea anchor he was making for a rich man—no, no ordinary problem, an anchor—one had to be certain there were no weaknesses between the ring, the stock, the crown, the flukes, the palm, and the shank. She did enjoy the sound of such words. "The palm and the shank," she repeated.

After her third visit in two weeks, Preisinger insisted on returning upstairs with her one morning to collect all her knives, which he then proceeded to sharpen in his smithy. Afterward, he refused payment. What impressed Klara most was that his work clothes might be black with soot, yet he moved with such a sense of where he was that no detritus was left in her clean kitchen.

Then, on a Saturday evening when he must have known Herr Hitler would be off to the Gasthaus for his beer, Preisinger came by on a visit, dressed in his Sunday shirt and suit. That caused no little perturbation in Klara (and in Angela), but he, too, was uncomfortable and sat on the edge of the sofa.

Yet Klara would look back on this occasion with satisfaction. That was because when Alois returned, he was even more disturbed than his wife at the sight of Preisinger installed on their sofa, huge hands clamped together in his lap. While the blacksmith departed soon after, he did bow to Klara and manage to say, "Thank you for your invitation."

Alois waited until he and Klara were alone in their room.

She was contrite. "No, I didn't invite him." She shook her head as if to tumble a few bits of memory back into place. "Well, yes," she then said, "I suppose I did." She had been courteous, merely courteous. Adolf had been spending so much time down below with Herr Preisinger that she thought it would be polite to make a suggestion, no more, that Herr Preisinger visit them for her strudel. But only on some day or other. She had not specified. It had not been a true invitation.

"And did you serve him strudel?"

"Well, I had to. Does one offer a guest nothing?"

"A guest?"

"Well, a neighbor."

On it went. Afterward, she never knew how much of all this could have been planned. She would deny such a possibility. Yet, not two days later, Alois informed her that he had sent a letter to a friend in the Customs House at Linz inquiring whether real estate was available in Linz or nearby. "I am bored here," he told her. "The noise from below is becoming intolerable."

A week later, an answer came. There was a fine little house at a good price in Leonding, not too far from Linz.

Klara and Alois knew that they would buy that place before they even went to look. Each was full of the same determination, if for altogether opposite reasons.

# 9

This would be all I need to narrate about Preisinger (since they would never see him again after the move), but I cannot leave the man without speaking of one of his final conversations with Adi, now that he knew Klara would soon be gone.

Preisinger had fallen in love. Needless to say, it could not be love with lively hope for the outcome, yet all the same, he had felt a sympathetic quickening in her. Conceivably, it could in time become a legitimate match. Her husband was certainly getting old. So Preisinger, full of his own hard-acquired dignity, was desolate when he heard that she and the boy would soon be gone.

He acted, therefore, in the only way he could. He took the liberty of offering up the depth of his working philosophy. The boy might be only nine, but by Preisinger's estimate, there was true eagerness to know more.

"Why is iron so strong?" Preisinger asked, and replied to his own question. "Because it is in its spirit to be strong." He paused. Any further exposition would depend on the boy's reaction to what he would next be told. "Every material," Preisinger said, "has a spirit which is its own. Some spirits are strong, some are gentle."

Young Adolf did not reply but chose to nod. Preisinger decided to proceed. "Grass," he said, "will bend before every wind. It is ready to give way to any foot that steps upon it. It is the opposite of iron. Even so, iron ore can be found deep in the same earth where grass grows above. And, once this iron ore is smelted you can make it into a scythe. A scythe is there to cut the grass."

"That is so interesting," said Adi, with real enthusiasm.

"Yes. You do not step on a piece of iron. Iron will hurt any foot that does not show respect." Preisinger's breath grew heavy with the ardor he felt for his subject. "That is because iron ore, once it has passed through the hottest fire, will turn into a unique material."

"Unique?" the boy asked.

"Unlike any other. Unique."

"Yes, that is so." The boy paused. He hesitated to ask his question, then did. "What is a will of iron? How is that made?"

Preisinger was delighted. "Think of how hot a fire must be to call out the will of iron that is in the ore. Iron is strong against every force except the one that made it into iron. I will say that I have felt such a force within myself."

Adi was agog with the incandescences necessary to create a will of iron. He even made the mistake later that night of trying to explain what he had been told to Angela and to Edmund. Alois, however, happened to overhear and roared with derision. "The mark of a truly stupid man," he announced to Klara, "is that he takes his own occupation so seriously that he comes to believe it is superior to others."

Nonetheless, Preisinger's discourse on the will of iron was to prove of considerable use to Adi after he received his first serious whipping. The spirit of restraint Alois had been looking to develop came to an end on a given night when Adolf was playing soldier in the woods and continued to stay out long after dusk. Normally, as evening approached, Alois had only to whistle and Adi would race upstairs from Preisinger's shop or come whipping back from the nearby woods. Indeed, if he did not arrive soon after the echo of the first whistle, Alois would put him over his knee and give him one rousing slap on his behind. In secret—he would hardly admit it to himself—he liked the feel of Adi's buttocks.

On this evening, however, the light that lingered in the forest proved too exciting. It was night before the boy came through the door.

Alois had been brooding over Paula's condition—just that day she had been trying to jump up and down in place (which, the doctor had assured Klara, would be a sign of development) but the child soon gave up. Despite Alois' coaxing, she would not try again. Then, Alois had to whistle for Adi. When the interval became too extended and he had to whistle again, Alois decided it was a willful insult and proceeded to give him a genuine whipping.

Full of Preisinger's precepts, Adi took an oath. He would live with whatever came down. He would fortify his will of iron. Even as the first blow fell, he was issuing orders to himself to fortify such determination by biting his lips.

Tears stood out in his eyes but he would not allow himself to cry. Even as he was being belabored, Preisinger's mighty biceps oscillated before his eyes. Let his father injure himself against a will of iron.

# BOOK XII

## EDMUND, ALOIS, AND ADOLF

# 1

Since Leonding was only five miles from Linz, Alois could feel that he was near again to the active life of a real city, a longing he had not allowed himself to indulge in Hafeld or Lambach. For Klara, however, the house would have been more attractive if it had not been situated across the street from the town cemetery. On the other hand, this was the only reason they could afford it.

For compensation, the village church was near, and their new home sat within its own garden bordered by maples and oaks whose limbs had grown into such artful shapes that a godly spirit must have been present. So Klara decided.

Nonetheless, Klara feared the move to this Garden House—as indeed it was called. Part of the uneasiness came, I would warrant, from her friendship with Preisinger. He had aroused an interest that ought to belong only to her marriage. Now, on these streets of Leonding, many of the townspeople had faces sly enough to suggest that they knew quite a bit about these treacherous sides of life. While she had certainly lived in any number of more sophisticated places—Vienna, when she kept house for an old lady, in Braunau with Alois, and then Passau—she had never looked for anything larger than her duties or her family. Now she might be ready for more. Not permissible! So, for a time, forays to town were restricted to visiting the shop of Josef Mayrhofer, who not only owned a fine grocery but was a fine man and the Mayor of Leonding. There she bought vegetables two or three times a week, and always dressed neatly for the occasion. She was friendly to Herr Mayrhofer, but invariably would say, "I can't stay. There's so much work waiting for me."

She was of course still living with the conviction that she had given herself over to the Devil on the night when she thought that Alois had just killed Alois Junior. She could see the boy on the ground again and remembered her vow, "Oh, Devil, save him, and I will be yours!"

All the same, she was attracted to Mayrhofer. He was more worldly than Preisinger, and that could prove tempting. She kept telling herself that she must not ruin a good man.

I was witnessing a comedy. I knew nothing would happen. Mayrhofer happened to be as proper as Klara. Moreover, he and Alois had already formed a quick friendship. Alois was drawn to a man smart enough to be Mayor, and practical enough to own a prosperous store. In turn, Mayrhofer respected Alois' years of service in Customs, particularly his promotions. Before long, they were drinking together at the tavern.

Nonetheless, a subdued flirtation stayed alive between Mayrhofer and Klara, and I continued to enjoy it because Mayrhofer, a man of honor, by his own measure, could not smile too often when Klara was near. Along with all else, he had a jealous wife. So Klara was doubly content to leave well enough alone. Alois had told her that the woman was a shrew and always pointing her finger. "These women who come to the store every day," Frau Mayrhofer would repeat, "are just waiting to throw themselves at you." Indeed, Mayrhofer confessed to Alois that years ago, he did have a small affair. Just one. Then his wife found out. His life had been a misery since. In turn, Alois was wise enough not to tell his new friend that in this regard, his own life might have been more agreeable.

At first, they drank only in the local tavern, but Mayrhofer soon confessed that given his position as Mayor, the premises were a little too raw for his office. After some deliberation, he even invited Alois to a *Buergerabend*, an evening for the town burghers. That was an occasion which took place on four separate evenings each week. The members could attend regularly or rarely, but it was an opportunity for substantial individuals to exchange opinions.

These gatherings, explained Mayrhofer, rotated among the best four inns of Leonding and were held for the sole purpose of good talk with good prosperous company. The object, as Mayrhofer explained tactfully, was not to get drunk but to enjoy conversation. In fact, he did murmur that they had had a few tipplers who were not asked to come back. "We did it politely—as much as possible, under the circumstances—but it is essential, Alois, that a man must never appear to be even a hint *unbalanced* on these occasions. Merriment is certainly acceptable, but good manners are paramount."

"I have to agree," said Alois. "That is always the essence of fine and decent company."

So Alois was introduced, and went through the considerable tension of sitting in with the local gentry. He most certainly did not get "unbalanced," and he did return several times a month to keep up his friendship with Mayrhofer, who would not even go to the tavern any longer because of one dreadful occasion when a drunken lout tried to insult him. The malcontent had been told to leave by the tavern owner, and did, but the place was spoiled for the Mayor.

During the day, Alois now spent his time working in the garden or at his new beehive. He had purchased one Langstroth box, and to it added only a modest population. As he explained to Mayrhofer, "Some honey for my family's use and gifts for friends—no more than that. At Hafeld, I used to feel so dominated by these little creatures. They are a force larger than oneself."

"So is the Mayoralty," replied Mayrhofer.

Soon enough, Alois grew impressed by the Buergerabends and purchased a book of Latin quotations. Retaining the phrases was a treacherous enterprise, however. His greatest problem these days had been boredom. Now he had discovered its loyal assistant—poor memory!

The greatest counterbalance he found against the long stretch of eventless afternoons at home was to play with Edmund. The little boy was more charming at four years of age than any of his other children had been, and Edmund stayed so close to him at the beehive that Klara had to make a little veil and sew up white pants to go with a white shirt and white gloves. Klara protested: "The boy is too young." But Alois insisted, and so the two were out at the hive a great deal.

Before long, Alois had fallen in love again, a charming love, indeed, for he knew it was bound to be his last true romance. He adored Edmund. It was not only because his little son was so clever but that he was, in addition, tender and sweet. "If I had ever met a woman so perfect, I would have married her for forever," he would repeat to himself as a joke. He did like humor that was bifurcated. He could picture the look of woe on Klara's face if he ever told her this, and yet he also laughed at his own tenderness—for the boy and for Klara, too. So much of all that was good in her (which he was never about to acknowledge) was in Edmund too. As Alois measured it, the boy had his father's intelligence and his mother's capacity for loyalty. A fine balance.

Yes, so bright. And Edmund loved the bees. He did not even squeak too much when some of the sluggards crawled over his gloves on their way back to the hive entrance. Once he even received a bite inside the glove but kept from crying, so soon as Alois said, "We must keep this a secret. Your mama won't let you play here again if she knows."

"No, Father," said Edmund, "she will listen to you."

"It could cause trouble," said Alois.

"That is true," said Edmund and sighed. "Too bad," he said, "it hurts. I would really like to cry."

At which they both laughed.

Back in the house, they would play Customs. Alois even put on his old uniform (although he could hardly button the waist) and they pretended that Edmund was trying to smuggle a valuable coin past a border inspector.

"Why is my coin so valuable?" asked Edmund.

"Because it was owned by Napoleon," said Alois. "He used to keep this guilder in his pocket."

"He did not," said Edmund. "You are teasing me."

"No, I am not. It is part of the game."

"I like that."

"Yes, but just you try to hide that coin from me."

"How will you get it back?"

"I will tickle you. Then you are bound to confess."

"I won't," said Edmund, giggling already, and stepped into the parlor closet to hide the guilder. Struggling beneath the coats hanging from the rack, he wedged the coin into the cuff of his boot. That way, he did not have to undo the laces.

When he came out, Alois stared at him with a fair share of the malevolence he used to direct at suspects who were being interviewed.

"Are you ready to confess?" he asked.

Edmund was hardly frightened. He began to giggle.

"Very well. Since you are so insolent," said Alois, "I will pat you down," and proceeded to tickle him under the arms until Edmund dropped to the floor in a puddle of helpless mirth. "Stop it, Daddy, stop it!" he cried out. "I have to pee."

Alois desisted. "But you are not ready to confess."

"That is because I am not smuggling anything."

"You are. We know. We have information that you have Napoleon's coin."

"Try and find it," said Edmund, and began to giggle again.

"Oh, I will find it," said Alois, and pulled off Edmund's boots, shook them, then watched the guilder fall out. "You are under arrest now," he said.

Edmund was furious. "You cheated," he said, "you cheated. You did not obey the rules."

"State your case."

"You said you would only tickle, but you took off my clothes."

"These are not your clothes," said Alois, picking up a boot. "Clothes are garments. This is footwear."

"You changed the rules."

Alois made a face. "That," he said in a deep voice, "is what we like to do in Customs."

For a moment, Edmund was uncertain. Then he began to laugh. Alois laughed so hard and so long that, once again, he began to cough, which, at first, was fine—he could clear some phlegm—but his coughing did not halt for many seconds, and then came a minute of paroxysms which brought Klara over to the parlor from the kitchen. Alois rolled his eyes at her and took a tentative breath. Had he come close, he wondered, to a hemorrhage of his lungs?

Edmund began to weep. "Oh, Papa!" he cried, "you must not die, you must not," and the sound of his voice numbed the response of his parents—he had seemed so certain of the outcome.

"Papa, I know you will not die," he now said in amendment. "I will ask God to forbid that and He will listen. I pray to Him every night."

"I don't pray," Alois almost said. Still cautiously in balance from the reverberations of this attack, he could not speak but did shake his head at Klara. These pious women were the real smugglers—to steal across the border of a young boy's mind, especially when he was so bright. Someday Edmund might be an esteemed professor, or even a legal eminence in Vienna, and yet his mother had to offer this religious pap, good oats for horses.

All the same, Alois was not yet ready to correct her. Religion was necessary, perhaps, for the very young. For now, he would leave it at that. There was so much beauty, Alois decided, in the boy's love for his mother and, yes, most certainly, his father.

Up in his bedroom with the door locked, Adolf took his revenge on the sounds of laughter he had to hear from below. He chose to masturbate. The image he held in his head was a picture of Luigi Lucheni that he had seen in the *Linzer Tages Post*. It was the assassin's small mustache, fixed to his upper lip just below his nostrils, a dark little daub of a mustache. That certainly excited Adolf. Once, at a time when he and Angela had still been sleeping in the same room, he had caught a glimpse of her pubic hair just as it had begun to manifest itself, no more than a patch of dark down, and Luigi's postage stamp of a mustache was close in resemblance.

The combination had to excite him—that small peekaboo into

Angela's privacy, so much like the mad murderer's upper lip. He grew twice as excited when he heard his father coughing away like still another maniac.

# 2

On one of his occasional visits to the Buergerabends, Alois decided to speak. This was after listening to the "Atheist-in-Residence," a member who delighted in assuring all the others that "I am the only brave man in our ranks. I feel blessed. That is because I do not have to believe in God." To Alois' critical eye, he was a scrawny chap, though a long-invested member—his grandfather had been one of the founders of the society. Nonetheless, it did seem that the man had little else to offer. So Alois decided to speak up. He declared that each intelligent human had to decide for himself whether the Deity did exist, but he, for one, was certainly opposed to the sanctimony of all those pietists who would run to church at every drop of rain in their lives. He would attend on one day only of the year and that was the Emperor's birthday. "In my opinion, it is Franz Josef who is to be celebrated. Especially now, after Sisi's death."

He soon discovered that he was dealing with a class of people who had a special attitude about such matters. While they did seem to exhibit some distaste for unseemly devotion in religion, they were still churchgoers.

If Alois had been a client, I could have alerted him. To be privately superior to religion is a privilege of the upper classes, but they do see going to church as the keel to preserving social life in common people.

One of the older gentry did reprove Alois' views, therefore, by saying, "I would agree that I would not wish to be counted among those who become overenthusiastic about every last Saint's Day observance. So often these rites are no more than a haven for unhappy women. But let us recognize that without religion, we would suffer chaos. It is the most dependable deterrent to madness in all of world history."

Alois was ready to take up the argument. "Nonetheless, good sir," he said, "permit me to suggest that religion does offer its own varieties of madness. I could offer as examples such highly immoral Popes as"—he knew the list—"Sixtus IV, Innocent VII, Alexander VI, Julius II, Leo X, and Clement VII. Simony was their daily practice, and a cardinal's hat was waiting for every one of their illegitimate sons. Yes, good sir, I would declare that it was madness to exhibit such an excess of corruption."

He sat down, pleased that there was at least a modicum of courteous applause, but he had to recognize that the recognition was formal—each speaker would receive, at worst, some minimal response. Nonetheless, a chill had come upon the room. He had been too outspoken. It made him decide, most unhappily, that he should not return too quickly to the Buergerabends. Indeed, when he did come back, he chose to be silent.

All the same, these evenings were diversions. The gentry certainly knew a lot about high styles of living. They were so knowledgeable about antique collecting and spoke of interesting innovations that would soon be available in indoor plumbing and electric lighting. Again he was obliged to feel the insufficiency of his own experience.

No surprise, then, if at the Buergerabends he thought often of the young officers for whom he made boots when he was working in Vienna, dreaming all the while of a beautiful young woman who would put together exquisite ladies' hats before sharing his bed in the evening. Now, on the way home from a Buergerabend, a wealth of pity could pass through him for what had never come to pass.

Let me suggest that if the intensity of such compassion is enough to charm the heart of a saint, that is because self-pity is able to reach the finest operatic heights. It is indulged, however, at considerable expense to oneself. Alois was paying too much. His dreams at night had begun to bother him. He had now developed the fearful intuition that sleep was a marketplace where the dead could return in order to remind you of your personal debt to them. So he thought of Johann Nepomuk and his mother, and then he had to brood over his two dead wives. What if they met in this marketplace of sleep? What if they came to agree with each other concerning their former husband? He would then be facing a cabal. "That might even be more dangerous," he told himself, "than for two of a man's former mistresses to become friends."

One of the gentry had made that remark at the Buergerabends, and it occasioned the heartiest burst of laughter. Of course, the fellow was an old roué from one of the best families in town. Alois had enjoyed those words enough to make them his own, and even served them up at the tavern. He had to notice that the louts laughed at this with as much gusto as the gentry. How unfair that this joke should now plague his dreams!

# 3

Adolf liked the new school in Leonding. It was a short walk from the Garden House, and less strict than the monastery. While he was, once more, an excellent student, he could hardly wait each day for school to end. The Kumberger Forest outside Leonding was full of wooded draws and small caves where one could prepare an ambush. He began to recruit schoolmates to join the battles, and they had a few encounters in the late afternoon, although the major event every week was reserved for Saturday morning, when there would be wars between white settlers and Indians.

Not all of his recruits wanted to be white settlers. That was because a redskin could steal up on a settler from behind, get an arm around the other boy's neck, and declare, "You are scalped." Then they could run back to their dens in the forest. Adolf was even scalped once, but he declared it illegal. "You do not attack leaders," he said. "Indians believe in the vengeance of the war gods. So they do not attack high officers like myself. They do not dare. A terrible vengeance would fall on them."

He even took Edmund along, Edmund, who was now five years old and certainly the youngest to participate. Nonetheless, the older kids liked him, even if Edmund could hardly be of service when attacks began. Still, Adolf liked having him alone in the forest. He could command Edmund then, which, of course, he was not able to do at home, where Klara would protect Edmund, Angela would protect him, and Alois certainly did.

Adi could remember that they had once used to safeguard him from Alois Junior, but that had been justifiable. Alois Junior had even planted a turd on the end of his nose, whereas he didn't do such things to Edmund. But he did giggle at the thought that if he could do it, what a joy it would be to hear Edmund scream. Once, out in the forest, he even poked Edmund in the back with a stick and told him it was a hornet, which, of course, Edmund mentioned to Klara. He knew it was not a hornet.

The story worried her. Was Adi's animosity worse than Alois Junior's had been? Yes, she decided, worse. Adolf and Edmund were blood brothers.

By now, Adi was having trouble with one kid who gave promise that it might end in a fight. He had never had a fistfight, he had always known how to avoid them, but now he took a vow that he would not allow anyone to humiliate him. He would do what was necessary, even if that meant he had to do it with a rock in his hand. Visions came to him on the edge of sleep. He saw this boy he truly feared staring at him with a blood-spattered head. Could that happen?

Then an episode occurred which ended these wars for the

rest of the winter. On a day when no one felt warm enough to hide motionless in ambush, a trooper declared that he was able to start a fire by rubbing twigs together. The others jeered, but Adolf said, "If you can make a real fire, then I give you the order to proceed."

The boy did. Once the fire was lit, all went off to find fallen branches dry enough to burn. Soon the fire was not only blazing but ready to advance into the surrounding brush. Since there was no water handy, they tried to stomp it out, but smoke kept rising into the sky.

They quit the fire. One by one, they ran until they were a quarter of a mile away. Adolf began to explain to the others, all twenty-odd, that they must not tell anyone.

"Yes," said Adolf, "if any one of you tells about this fire, we will all have to pay for it. And then we will look to find out who was the one who told. And there will be consequences. A brave soldier does not betray his comrades."

One by one, two by two, they left the forest. By now, the fire had grown to a size visible enough to bring firemen, water wagons, and teams of horses out from Leonding.

On the way home, Edmund said that he had to tell one person, their father. "If you do," said Adolf, "I will be severely punished. And you, too, will have to pay for it."

"I do not believe that," said Edmund. "Our father would never permit that. So don't you try to hit me."

"It is not me you have to fear. It is everybody else who was there. They will be punished, and then they will be waiting for you. All of them. If necessary, I will be the one to let them know that you can't keep your mouth shut."

"I have to tell our father."

"What did you promise?"

"I have to tell him about anything that bothers me."

"All right. That is all right for all other matters. But not this. I tell you, the other boys will beat you up. I will not be able to protect you. In fact, I won't even want to!"

"I feel sick."

"You are nothing but a snot-nose. Go throw up."

Alois, however, had his own suspicions about the fire. Once they reached home, Alois held Edmund on his lap and looked tenderly into his eyes. Before he could ask a question, however, Edmund threw up again. Alois decided to let it go. He was convinced that Adolf had had something to do with the blaze, but Edmund's life could become a misery if he forced him to talk about it.

Moreover, there might be repercussions. If he knew for certain that Adolf was one of the malefactors, it would be expected of him, as a father and a good citizen, to inform the authorities. Once he did, however, they could hold him responsible for the costs of bringing out the fire wagon. So Alois wiped Edmund's spew off his own shirt and hugged him tenderly. He also made a point over the next few days of not looking Adolf in the eye.

# 4

In school that winter, Adolf's class read a book by Friedrich Ludwig Jahn that spoke of a force powerful enough to shape history. That cetainly did remind him of the blacksmith. This force would depend on the presence of a "Führer cast of Iron and Fire." Then came a sentence that brought tears to Adolf's eyes: "The people will honor him as a savior and forgive all his sins."

Of course, the class had also been offered Kant and Goethe and Schleiermacher, but Adolf felt these authors showed too much respect for reason. That bored him. His father, for one, was always speaking of the virtues of reason. "Human nature is undependable," he would tell his family. "What enables stable societies to work is the power of the law. It is the law, not the people." He looked around at the supper table and decided this should be of interest to Adolf. "It is legal constitutions that are needed, Adolf, constitutions that are constructed by the finest people. Then reason can do its work with the respect it deserves."

Adolf preferred Friedrich Ludwig Jahn. He had decided that reason could be treacherous. It was like the sirens that swim in the Rhine and lead you to your death. Even while you drown, they sing sweet songs. Personal strength was of more importance. That would take care of your sins. Such small flaws would be incinerated by the heat of your effort.

He certainly rejected Goethe and Schiller. Their humor annoyed him. It was too personal—as if they were much too pleased with what they were saying. Not serious enough, Adolf decided. The other two, Kant and Schleiermacher, he simply could not read. After Jahn, his highest pleasure came from the fairy tales of the Grimm brothers. That had also been assigned to his class. Those were good stories, and deep! He delighted in acting them out for Edmund, who might be too young to read but was always ready to listen. He explained to Edmund that the Grimm brothers had written these tales so children would know how important it was to obey their parents and their older brother and sister. Then he spoke of one story called "The Girl Without Hands": "This is about a father who has been ordered by the Devil to cut off the hands of his young daughter." When Edmund shrieked at the thought, Adolf spoke in the voice of the father, explaining it to his daughter. "I don't want to do this, dear daughter. But I must. These are orders. It is not for me to question orders that have come down to me from a very high authority. So I must obey."

"What does the daughter say?" Edmund asked.

"Oh, she is obedient. Very obedient. She says, 'Father, do with me what you will. For I am your child.' Then she puts her hands right up on the chopping block. Her father picks up a big cleaver and he does it."

"That is so awful," said Edmund. "He chops off her hands?"

"With one whack! But she lives happily ever after."

"How?" asked Edmund.

"Her father takes care of everything." Adolf nodded. "I could tell you a worse story, but I won't."

"Tell me."

"It is about a girl who was so disobedient that she died."

"What did she do?" asked Edmund.

"It doesn't matter," said Adolf. "She was disobedient. That is enough. They bury this disobedient girl, and what do you think? It is hard to believe, but she remains disobedient even after she is dead. One of her arms keeps poking up out of her grave right into the air."

"Is she so strong?" asked Edmund.

"The Devil is helping her. What else—that is the way it happens. So when her relatives see that arm up in the air, they come out to her grave and try to push it down again. They can't. You are right. The arm is too strong. So they start to cover it with a mound of dirt. But her arm knocks the dirt away. Then her mother goes back to the house and picks up a heavy poker from the fireplace. When she gets back to her daughter's grave, she starts beating on that disobedient arm until it is broken. That way, it can be folded back under the dirt. So the girl is able to find some rest."

Edmund was shivering. He was crying and laughing at once. "Would you do something like that to me?" he asked Adolf.

"Only if you should die and I would see your arm popping out from your grave. Then I would have to do it to you. I certainly would."

"Oh," said Edmund, "I don't like that."

"It does not matter what you would like. It would have to be done."

"Tell me one more story."

"It would take too long. I'll just give you the end: It's about a queen who boils a child to death. Afterward, she eats the body."

"Do you have to be a queen to be able to do something like that?" asked Edmund. "Isn't this so?"

"Yes, probably. Especially if it is your own child that you are boiling." Adolf nodded profoundly. "But nobody can take these matters for granted."

"My mother would never do that to me."

"Maybe not our mother, but I cannot say what Angela would do."

"Oh, no," said Edmund, "Angela would never do something like that to Paula or to me."

"Don't be so certain."

Edmund shook his head. "I know you are wrong."

"Do you want another story?"

"Maybe not."

"This one is the best," said Adolf.

"Is it truly the best?"

"Yes."

"Then maybe I don't want to hear it."

"It's about a young man who is ordered to sleep with a corpse. In time to come you, too, may have to sleep next to a dead man."

At this point, Edmund shrieked. Then he fainted.

Unfortunately for Adolf, this last conversation was overheard by Angela. She was standing in the doorway shaking her head. Adolf had time to think that his luck was foul.

Angela patted Edmund's face until he could sit up. Then she went to tell Klara.

His mother no longer called him Adi, certainly not on any occasion when she had to scold him. "Adolf, this was dreadful. You are going to be punished."

"For what? Edmund loves the stories. He kept asking me for more."

"You knew what you were doing. So I am going to tell your father. I have to. He will decide on your punishment."

"Mother, this is not something to bring Father into."

"If I don't tell him, then I will be the one who must look for a real punishment. And maybe I will. Maybe I will buy you no present at Christmas."

"This is so unfair," said Adolf. "I try to entertain my kid brother. But he is a brat."

"Do you accept what I say? No gift for Christmas?"

"Yes. If you think that is fair, I have to accept. But, Mother, please, look into your heart when the time comes. See if you will still see me as guilty then."

Klara was furious. This was even worse. He was so certain that she would change her mind and buy him a good present after all.

That evening, therefore, she did tell Alois.

His father had no doubts. He gave Adolf a severe whipping. It was the worst since they moved into the house in Leonding. But this time, Adolf was determined to make no sound at all. He thought of Preisinger all the while. He stiffened his body.

Alois was beginning to feel as if he had Junior back on his hands. Another criminal to deal with! That excited more rage.

Between each blow, Adolf thought of how Alois Junior had run away. It was the one memory he could use to make no sound. He could be and must be as strong as Alois Junior. If he did not cry, then his own strength might become great enough to justify whatever he might yet want to do next. Strength created its own kind of justice. He called upon the force of command that had been near to him after the fire in the forest. He had ordered them all then never to speak of it, and they had obeyed. Yes, he had been full of fear then, but he had called on his force of command. Then he had lived for days in the fear that someone would talk. He could hardly know it, but I had been with him through that turmoil, and I was with him now. Adolf's confidence was so fragile that, metaphorically speaking, I had to maintain his ego at full erection. (Egos are prey to the same weakness that erections exhibit when unsure of what comes next.)

So, yes, I was there to monitor the whipping of Adolf, and fortify his resolve. If it was most important to him that he not weep, I had to be ready to diminish the intensity of Alois' blows whenever the boy might break. Equally, I was ready to increase his father's force, whenever it flagged. There were moments when Alois' fear of overstraining his heart was in direct opposition to my desire to salt Adolf's will. Let his hatred for Alois become intense enough to serve many an uncommon purpose ahead.

Nonetheless, balance is crucial to our activities. Equally, I could not allow antipathy to his father to become excessive. Immense hatreds in childhood that find no dependable outlet have to make a client unstable. While high imbalance was acceptable in Luigi Lucheni, that would not do for Adolf. We had put in too much effort on the boy. We did not care to have to deal with a future too full of errant impulses and blind rages. Indeed, one product of this heavy whipping was bound to be detestation of Edmund. That made me uneasy. Edmund had remained in such a sorry state after hearing the tales of the Grimm brothers that Klara tried to lull him to sleep with lullabies. Adolf, lying in the next cot, felt as bruised thereby as if he had fallen out of a tree. Indeed, his feelings became so outraged by Klara's apparent indifference to him that he decided to run away. Right there, lying on his cot, he so decided—aching bones and all. He even made a point of telling this to Edmund after Klara left the room.

"It is all your doing," said Adolf. "So I must go."

Immediately, Edmund leaped out of bed and ran to tell his father. Yet, when Alois came up the stairs to collar the potential runaway, Adolf said, "It's a lie! My brother is always telling lies. This one I will not forgive him for. This lie is atrocious! I'll get him for this!"

"You'll get him, will you?"

Alois was not ready to give another beating. His arms were aching more than Adolf's back. Still, he was sufficiently concerned to lock the boy in a room on the ground floor whose only window had bars. Alone, Adolf tried to squeeze his way through. It was too tight. He soon discovered that his pajamas seemed to make the difference. Their buttons kept getting caught on the bars. So he took them off, rolled them up, put them outside the bars, and, stark naked, attempted to wriggle through once more.

He was so overheated with the fury of his righteousness that he did not feel the chill of the open casement window nor hear the sound of his father's boots returning to the room. Only at the sound of the door unlocking did he pull away from the bars, seize a tablecloth, and wrap it around himself. Alois, entering, the brass key still in his hand, took in the situation, and roared with laughter. He yelled for Klara until she came through the door. Then Alois pointed to Adolf and said, "Look at the toga boy, our Toga Boy!" Klara shook her head and left the room. That roused Alois to a full harangue: "So you were trying to run away. I tell you, it would not be such a loss. All the same, I forbid it. Not because I would miss you, Toga Boy. I would not. I forbid it because I would have to call in the police to tell them you are missing, and they might put me in jail." Alois knew this was an outright exaggeration, but he was full of masterly scorn. "How your mother would weep! Her son is lost and her husband is in prison. Shame has come upon the Hitler family! All because of Toga Boy!"

Adolf had stood up to the whipping, but now he was in tears. My work on his ego had suffered a loss.

What soon made it worse is that Alois came back into the room, roared with laughter, and said, "I have just stepped outside. It is so cold tonight that you would have been back in two minutes knocking on the door. It is not so good to have a bad temper, but it is worse to be a fool."

# 5

A few weeks later, Alois awoke worrying whether Alois Junior had been a product of too many beatings. Next day, while walking with Mayrhofer, the subject came up once more. Alois declared that he never engaged in corporal chastisement. (He even said to himself, "Oh, you are lying like a thief.") But Mayrhofer's good opinion was crucial to him. So on he went: "I never strike my kids. I must admit, however, that I do bawl them out frequently." How could a parent not? "Adolf," said Alois, "is the one I scold the most. He can be a miserable urchin. Sometimes I say to myself, 'I'll bash him yet.' " Alois said that on purpose. It would serve as an explanation if it were ever to come out that he had been whipping him.

In truth, however, it was becoming more difficult to grab hold of him. The boy had a way of sliding and turning, a product perhaps of his skill at the war games. Usually, he succeeded in getting away from Alois after one off-centered slap on the rump. And for those times when his father did manage to turn him over his knee, there was now no great arm left to give the whipping. How sodden was Alois' heart on such occasions. It had become more enjoyable to call him Toga Boy. Alois even kept the mockery in play until Adolf reacted by coming down with an attack of measles.

Such a connection may be, of course, too simple. In Leonding, at this time, others his age were also in bed with the disease. While it was certainly contagious, Adolf may, in effect, have been made vulnerable by the ongoing misfortunes of recent events. His army ceased operations after the fire in the forest. Now the jeers about

Toga Boy rankled his skin. The worst news, however, was to hear that Der Alte had died. An obituary had even appeared in the *Linzer Tages Post*, such news forwarded all the way from Hafeld, but then, the event could be seen as sufficiently unusual to be worth a description in newsprint. By the time his body was found, Der Alte had been in a sad state of decomposition. "Such," observed the *Post*, "is often the fate of lonely hermits." To make matters worse, the unfed bees had perished in the cold. How many must have kept beating their wings until the end!

Adolf was in silent mourning.

Alois, however, retained enough sour feeling about Der Alte to be rewarded now with a keen trace of pleasure—a most unseemly reaction. To compensate—he hardly knew why—he did buy Adolf an air gun for Christmas. It was a solid gift, ready to pump out pellets with enough power to drop a squirrel or a rat, and so would prove its value to the boy, but not as yet. Alois had the impression that his son might even be crying in his sleep. He did look frightful in the morning. Then he came down with the measles.

Klara kept the house in a rigid quarantine. No one was allowed to visit Adolf in the hitherto-unoccupied maid's room on the second floor. Only Klara, wearing a gauze mask, would tend to him, and she would wash her hands afterward with antiseptic.

He had a rash, he had red eyes, he was not allowed to read, he suffered boredom, he complained endlessly to his mother yet was almost glad when she left the room. The odor of the antiseptic she brought with her was near to intolerable.

It proved, however, to be a mild case. The white spots on his tongue and in his throat disappeared after a few days and his rash lessened, but his disquiet increased. He was obsessed with how filthy he felt. Was that not exactly the way they all thought of him? Diseased and therefore filthy. He worried about where Der Alte might be now that he was not only dead but had been left alone to rot.

# 6

A last word about Der Alte might be fitting. Adolf still hoped that Der Alte, rot or not, was on his way to heaven. Such a sentiment in my young client disconcerted me because I was hardly certain we had carried the old boy over to hell in high style. In truth, I do not know much about hell. I am not even certain it exists. The Maestro has kept us, after all, in enclaves. We are not supposed to know what we do not need to know.

To keep up our morale, therefore, we are reminded constantly of how much cosmic pretension there is in human affairs. We are frequently brought back to Nietzsche's immortal remark "All priests are liars."

"How could it be otherwise?" the Maestro says. "The Dummkopf is not about to open His secrets to individuals distorted enough to choose the ministry or the priesthood in order to dominate gullible audiences with their self-serving descriptions of how the Lord will reward their belief when they die. Priests are, indeed, liars. They do not know a thing about the highest matters. Nor, for that matter, do any of you."

Leave it then that I knew nothing of the final destination of Der Alte. I do suspect he was the sort of long-term client that, by the end, we are often obliged to ignore. Certainly his use for us had dissipated. So it is possible that he was ready to beseech heaven to grant him final acceptance. Who knows? Given the few hints I can use, I would suppose that the Dummkopf does accept some of our clients for reincarnation. As I have mentioned, the Maestro is not vigorously opposed to this. "Let us have the pleasure of picking up this piece of small fry once more if the Dummkopf is so foolish as to give Der Alte another opportunity to pump up his vanities."

Throughout his illness, Adolf not only thought of Der Alte but even more often wished that the misery of his measles would visit Edmund. Then, after Adolf recovered, Edmund did come down with a severe case. I will save the reader a detailed description of the turmoil that *reverberated*—that is the word—through the Garden House as Edmund's condition worsened. His face swelled. He became incoherent. The doctor warned the family that he might yet suffer from encephalitis.

In their bedroom, Alois knelt beside Klara, and they began to pray for Edmund's life. Alois even said, "I will believe in God if Edmund is spared. May I die if I do not obey this vow."

We will never know whether Alois would have been true to such an oath. Still, he did say, "God, take my life, but spare the boy."

Then, Edmund died.

Prayer can be a perilous expedition for those who pray. We, for example, have a power—which is expensive to call upon—that enables us to block even the most essential, heartfelt, and desperately important prayers, and we exercise such powers when the stakes demand it.

Cheap prayer, on the contrary, we encourage. We see all that as adding to the Dummkopf's Fatigue, to the Dummkopf's Indifference. Cheap prayer wearies Him. Cheap patriotism enrages Him. (Cheap patriotism is, after all, one of our most useful provenances.)

The point is that despite Alois and Klara's prayers, blocked or not, Edmund did die on February 2, 1900. I even felt as if I were one of the mourners. Edmund was the first child for whom I had entertained so curious a set of sensations as love (or at least a wholehearted liking sufficient to explain the warmth that inhabited me when in his presence). I had not been certain of what I was feeling. I only knew that Adolf was not ready to contemplate his brother's death (for, indeed, he had a secret to bury as direct and powerful as the arm that protruded from the grave), and I was not ready to contemplate it either. I, too, had been culpable.

# 7

On the day of Edmund's funeral Alois told Klara that he would not go. He could not even give a reason. He stood there like a pillar of stone.

Then he began to weep. "I cannot control my feelings today," he said. "Would you have me make a spectacle of myself in church? A church that I hate?" For the first time in their marriage, she raised her voice in anger. "Yes," she said, "this church that you hate. But I go to it for peace. For a little consolation. I am able to speak to our Gustav then, and to Ida and Otto, and now"—it was her turn to burst into tears—"to Edmund."

They did not quarrel. They wept together. She said at last, "You must stop being so hard on Adolf. He is now the only hope left for you to have a good son. Why must you beat him into the ground?"

Alois nodded. "I will make a promise," he said. "That is, if you will stay here with me today. For I cannot go to the funeral. I am not able to keep myself together." Before he could finish speaking, he was weeping again. He hugged her. "I need you," he said. "I need you to stay with me in this house." He had never said that to her before. He could hardly believe he was saying it. "Yes," he declared, "I will take a solemn promise. I will not strike Adolf again."

It is a mistake to characterize a husband and wife who are in pain, but I cannot resist remarking that in my experience, few marriages exist where a vow is not countermanded by a secret covenant.

Yes, that is our Alois. He has already told himself, "No, I will not strike Adolf again unless he does something awful," but then,

Klara was not of one piece either. Not now. She was beginning to wonder if it was the fate of her family to be destroyed. Indeed, she was not ready for the funeral. This once, let God pay attention to her.

So Klara told Angela that she must represent the family. "If people ask, just say that your parents are stricken. This is true," said Klara. "I don't trust myself to go, and your father cannot. I have never seen him weep before. He is near to out of his mind. Angela, it is so terrible for him. I cannot leave the man alone. I must not! So today, you will act as the woman of the family. For today at least, you must be the woman."

Angela said, "You have to go to church with Adolf and me. It will be a scandal if you don't."

"You," said Klara, "are much too young to worry about scandal. Tell them we are ill. That has to be sufficient."

"Will you stay here at least, will you promise to stay in the house?" asked Angela. "I am afraid he will want to go out. He will want you to bring him to the tavern. He will get drunk so it doesn't hurt so much. You must not leave the house."

"It depends on your father."

"You are his slave."

"Silence yourself!" Klara said.

So to Adolf's surprise, he and Angela went to church by themselves. When asked for a reason, all Angela said was, "Before we go, you must take a bath. You smell awful again."

## 8

Alone with Alois, Klara could not bear to think of each and every death in her family. It was not only her children, but the deaths of her brothers and sisters. "Cannot God have mercy?" she asked herself. She felt a frightening exhaustion, as if she were standing in an old house and the floor was falling apart and she had no interest in saving herself. She was tired of believing that the fault must be her own.

I have to admit that I was tempted to approach her, but I knew this would be refused by the Maestro. What, after all, could be gained by looking to pick up a client like Klara? We could put the Cudgels in disarray for losing her. But what labor there would be to train so new and difficult a client.

Indeed, I soon recognized that Klara was having no more than a rebellion, which is common among pious people. Piety can also serve as a wall to keep the pious from recognizing how profoundly angry they are at God—this God who has failed to treat them by what they see as their proper right. Since this illicit wrath is usually submerged in pestilential waters of modesty, they do not make sterling clients for us, although, in the event, we do use some. Pious people can derange those in their family who are less pious. Repetition kills the soul.

On this long day, Alois felt so savaged by the loss of Edmund that he had to look into the long-buried recollections of his incest. Were he and Klara polluted people? If so, Edmund might be better off dead. Again he wept.

When, at one point, Klara began to have second thoughts and

said, "Maybe we should go to the church after all," he was gripped
with fear. "For me to break down in public?" he repeated. "That is
worse than death." Now Klara asked herself, "What is wrong with
weeping in church when one's heart is broken?" She began to wonder. Was Alois evil? Was she? What of the vow she had taken when
Alois Junior seemed lifeless on the ground? Perhaps it was better,
yes, actually better, that they stay away. For evil people to attend a
funeral might hurt the departed. Slowly, over that long day, as they
remained at home, she felt an awful flush in her breast. Was this a
fury directed at God? She, too, was now afraid to go to church. Yes,
how could one ever dare to bring such fury into a holy place? That
would be like taking another vow of allegiance to the foul one.

## 9

At the funeral, Adolf heard none of the words. His head was
ablaze. In the hour that Edmund died, Alois had said to him,
"You are now my only hope."

"Yes," Adolf said to himself, "it is true, my father used to see Edmund as the only hope. That is what he really was saying. But
actually, he hates me. He thinks I was cruel to Edmund."

Yet Adolf refused to agree that he might have mistreated Edmund. "It was no more," he told himself, "than the way Alois Junior used to treat me." All too soon, however, he began to feel full
of dread. How deep and unrelenting might be the anger of the angels!

In the days just before he came down with measles, he had taken
Edmund for a walk in the woods. He was still uneasy about the fire
and so he remained concerned over Edmund's loyalty to him. He
picked up a twig on the path and scalped his brother by drawing

the stick in a circle across his forehead, above the left ear, under the back of the head, and then above the right ear, before returning to the forehead. Then Adolf said in a most vibrant voice, "Now I own all. Your brain is mine."

"How can you say such a thing?" said Edmund. "That is stupid."

"Don't be a fool," said Adolf. "Why do you think Indians wanted scalps? It is because it is the only way to own the person just captured."

"But you are my brother."

"It is better that your brother owns your brain than some stranger. A stranger could throw it away."

"Give it back to me," said Edmund.

"I will when the time comes."

"When will that be?"

"When I tell you."

"I don't believe you. I don't believe you own anything. My brain feels the same."

"Oh, you will see a difference. You will feel headaches. They will bother you. That is the first sign."

Edmund was ready to cry, but he did not. They walked home in silence.

Now, in church, Adolf's heart was beating in time, step by step, with the strides they had taken on returning from the woods.

He was also feeling a most peculiar pain from this recollection. It was in his heart and was as sharp in sensation as a splinter driven under one's fingernail.

He told himself not to think about Edmund anymore. Not on this day. Indeed, he prayed to God to be able to cease thinking of Edmund. With my help, he succeeded to some degree, as much as one can remove most of a splinter under the nail. The fragment that remains, however, has now become a root ready to offer its own discomfort. So the memory festered in his heart.

It was his turn now to be ready to weep. He thought of how Klara used to call him "*ein Liebling Gottes.*" "Oh," she used to tell him, "you are so special." That was true, he told himself. ("God's own Beloved.") He had not been like Gustav and the others. Perhaps he had been selected by Destiny. He had survived.

I could see the extent of the reconstruction that lay before me. I would have to restore him once more to what he had felt when he was three and his mother had adored him.

Now he felt that his mother was ready to abandon him, just as she had abandoned Edmund. Why, then, must he feel so guilty? Let her be the one to feel the pain. She had pretended to love Edmund and yet she was not here in church. How awful. So unfeeling!

# 10

E ven as brother and sister came away from the grave, some mourners began to pay attention to Angela, who was embarrassed by knowing how red-faced she had become. How could she avoid that? She was trying to speak of how terrible were her parents' feelings. "It is so frightful a day for them—they are both in bed. They are too weak to move." On she went, embarrassed yet excited to be the center of this occasion.

Once they were alone, however, and could walk off into the forest, Adolf did say, "Why do I know that my mother will not come to my funeral?"

Angela berated him: "Klara is the finest person I have ever known. The kindest. No one is more good! How can you say something like that? She is suffering for your father. He loved Edmund so much!" And when in payment for this remark, Adolf looked venomous, she added, "As well he should. Edmund was a beautiful child. I cannot say that of you. Even on this day of your brother's funeral"—she had to repeat it!—"you still have an unpleasant body odor."

"What do you mean?" he answered. "I took a bath. You know that. You even forced me to. You said, 'Going to the funeral, smelling as you do? Get into the tub,' and I told you it would take too long to boil the water. What did you care?"

He had had to use cold water. It had been a splash and a wipe, no more. Maybe he still did smell. "No," he said now, "I forbid you to speak that way to me. I do not have an unpleasant odor. I did take a bath."

Angela said, "Bath or no bath, Adolf. You just may not be a very good person."

He was so furious with her that he stepped off the forest trail into the unpacked snow. She, just as angry, followed him. The moment they were out of earshot of any person who might have been at the service, she yelled at him so loudly that he ran off, "Not a good person! An awful one! You are a monster!"

Alone in the forest, Adolf began to have fears of his own death. It was so cold in the snow. He was recalling the look of terror in Edmund's eyes as he listened to the tales of the Grimm brothers.

When Angela caught up with him, they walked home silently to find that their father now had a red and swollen face. He turned to Adolf and said, "You are now my life." He embraced him and began to weep all over again. How false were his words, thought Adolf. His father still believed that Edmund was the only hope. He could not even pretend that anything else was true. "I hate my father," Adolf told himself once more.

## 11

Several nights after the funeral, I prepared a dream-etching for Adolf. An angel told him that his cruelties to Edmund would yet be justified. Why? Because Adolf's life had been spared in infancy. There was a special purpose yet to come. He need only remain loyal to every command he received from above. In this manner, he could escape any and every ordinary death. He would yet become God's gift to the people, fierce as fire, as strong as steel.

It was a carefully worked-up dream, but I had to ask myself whether such a belief was being implanted too soon. It did suggest that he would live forever. Of course, that is not at all impossible to believe. There is good reason why it is difficult for any man or woman to picture their own death: The soul, I would offer, does expect to be immortal. To a degree, this may even be true. Many humans, after all, are born again. I would not wish to suggest that this is by way of the passing hand of a priest or by a reverend as one is submerged in the river, no, they are born again through reincarnation. The Maestro has told us that this is part of a conceptual scheme developed by the D.K. "He does see Himself as the Divine Artist. Of course, He is also a blunderer—so many of His creations are botched. A good many are disasters which He then proceeds to plow back into the food chain. That is His only means of keeping His multitudinous, mediocre, and often meaningless spawnings from choking the existence of the rest. Yet, I will admit, He is dogged. He is still looking to improve His previous creations." As the Maestro describes it, the Dummkopf is bound to try to improve even His most unsatisfactorily developed humans. And that is why few men and women really believe that they will cease to exist. They would say it aloud if not for their fear of appearing ridiculous. Indeed, their real anxiety is that the new life, because of the ways in which they wasted the last one, might bring them closer to the heat of the Dummkopf's Wrath, yes, closer than in their previous existence. One's new situation in life might reflect how badly the last life was lived. So the rebirth could offer a pure example of living hell. While the Maestro does not impart such answers to us, I am convinced that there is a region in the unconscious of every human being where belief does exist that one is immortal.

This conviction of personal immortality can cause us considerable difficulty. Many of our men and women, particularly late in life, come to the conclusion that if they atone for their sins, they will be reborn. That does play havoc with hitherto dependable clients. They are not, after all, completely unbalanced on this certainty. No matter how abominable and unrepentant are a few of the humans chosen by Him to be born again, he probably does feel there is something exceptional present even if it failed to develop properly last time out.

At this point, I began to wonder whether the Maestro might even have a covert influence in the D.K.'s councils. It is, obviously, too large a question for me, but the Maestro does seem to know which of our clients have been chosen for rebirth. Yet to speak of this with greater authority, I would have to know how the D.K. envisions the future of His Creation. Is it comparable to the ruthlessness of our Maestro? Is ruthlessness indeed a necessary passion among these divine forces?

# 12

A few months after Edmund's death, Klara began to have fearful thoughts. Was it possible that Adolf's attitude to Edmund had been more than cruel? Was it even unforgivable? Angela told her again that when the brothers played together she had overheard Adi terrifying Edmund with fairy tales from Grimm, the very worst ones.

From her bedroom window, Klara could see Adolf shooting at rats while sitting on the cemetery wall. She would flinch each time she heard the popping sound of the discharge. For her, the air gun was equal to an ugly voice. She felt as if she could hear disaffected spirits coming up to her from the cemetery. When someone is not a client, we can still exert some small influence on them, and in this case, I certainly did not wish Klara to be pushing Adolf more deeply into his depression, so I did lay atmospheres upon her sleep in which I suggested that Adi was not evil, but suffering terribly. This technique is available to use on any mother who retains some love for her child. Over a period, therefore, the situation did improve. Once again, Klara came to recognize the need to change Alois' feelings. As she told her husband, the boy's dreadful mood was beginning to affect his marks at the little school in Leonding. The explanation had to be that he was mourning for Edmund. "But he is also afraid of you," Klara dared to say. "He hates disappointing you. Alois, you must become again a kind man to your son."

Those were heartfelt words, but they only succeeded in reminding him of Edmund. Adolf, alas, was not Edmund. All the same, he nodded.

"I will do what I can," he said. "Sometimes my heart slams shut like a door."

Once aroused, however, she was not about to close off her own feelings. She must find a way to be near again to Adolf. His heart could also shut like a door. But she had noticed that Adolf was most impressed with the new year, 1900. "Adolf, this will be your century," she told him. "I know it. You will do wonderful things in time to come."

He did feel important that she spoke in such a tone, but he hardly knew whether to believe her. How could it be his century? At this point, he felt incapable of accomplishing anything of high worth. So he nagged her. "Is it really so?" he kept asking. At last, her tongue slipped enough to uncover the truth. "You are the one I must love," she said. He brooded over her phrasing. He was aware for the first time that women were not there just to love you because that was their duty. Instead, they could offer love that was real or provide a substitute that was less dependable.

Here the Maestro intervened. "Do not," I was told, "encourage any undue interest in women. Let him remain fearful."

# 13

On late overcast afternoons in early spring, when there was a fog, and the odors of moss and mold rose from many a tombstone, Adolf would sit in the damp of the low cemetery wall and wait in the dusk for rats to come out. When they faced to the west, their eyes would shine in the sunset, even in a clouded sunset, and so would offer sharp targets. When he was able, however, to hit one with his air gun, he did not feel up to approaching the corpse. It was too close to evening for him to be ready to step off from the low wall onto the cemetery sward.

Early morning, however, before he was off to school, he would pass by, and if no dogs or cats had been ready to reconnoiter the graveyard at night, and the cadaver of the rat was still intact, he would inhale a first hint of the aroma of carrion. That stirred his mood. He would wonder whether comparable changes had taken place in Edmund's flesh.

Even by spring, he did not feel ready to go back to the forest. He kept to his perch on the cemetery wall.

In turn, I had decided not to discourage Adolf's guilt. Indeed, this instinct was soon corroborated. While the Cudgels were partial to guilt, since they were invariably looking to increase all impulses to atonement in their clients, we usually chose to calcify guilt, leave it, so to speak, bone-dry. While that did raise the risk that we were narrowing future possibilities for the psyche, I had to be ready to lift Adolf out of his depression before it grew extreme. Depression can descend into aberration. On many an evening, Adi sat on the cemetery wall wondering what he would do if Edmund's arm were to rise suddenly out of the grave. Would he run? Would he attempt to talk to Edmund? Would he ask for forgiveness? Or would he pelt the limb with his air gun?

All through the winter, the spring, and the summer of 1900, the memory of Edmund's illness remained like a deadweight on his chest.

It was not hard to discern the reason. Adolf still possessed some funds of conscience. Even as self-pity is the lubricant we use most often to smooth the entrance of the heart into uglier emotions, so does conscience become our antagonist. The Cudgels whip people into shape by way of conscience. We, in turn, when dealing with the most advanced of our clients, do our best to extirpate conscience altogether. Once accomplished, we then proceed to build up a facsimile of good conscience, ready and able to justify most of the passions that the Cudgels seek to repress: greed, lust, envy—no need to list the sacred seven. The point is that when this substitute is properly developed by us, our clients' ability to justify ugly acts is strengthened. We have then succeeded in releasing conscience from the shameful memories that obliged it to develop in the first place. I can add that we are most successful when the all-but-emptied remains of the old conscience are stubborn enough to vie with one's new sense of detachment, and so are felt to be a useless scourge, an enemy to one's well-being. Of course, serial murderers who take pride in their daring have usually succeeded in banishing all conscience. A corollary to this is the benefit we gain from war when a soldier grows conscienceless. Our work is then simplified. It is calm periods that call upon the skills of advanced devils like myself. I will say that it is not at all routine to convince a man or woman to slay another. Left to their own estimate, they worry that murder may be the most selfish of acts. Primitives certainly know this to be true. When ready to sacrifice an animal for one of their feasts, they are wise enough to ask forgiveness before cutting the throat.

In turn, I was now ready to fortify Adi's sense of the power that murder can offer the murderer. Of course, he was too young for our most developed techniques, but I did work up a dream-etching where Adolf became a hero in the Franco-Prussian war of 1870. This entailed the suggestion that he had been there in his previous life, almost two decades before he was born in 1889. It was not difficult to bring him to believe he had massacred a platoon of French soldiers who had made the signal mistake of attacking his lonely outpost. Of course, such a dream-etching was gross, but it did prepare a base on which to lay more sophisticated impulses later. By itself, however, the Franco-Prussian dream-etching was naught but a wish fulfillment, and their effects are most temporary.

May I say that we knew all about wish fulfillment long before Dr. Freud had anything to say on the matter. Our approach to human psychology must of necessity go further. Indeed, we smile at the superficiality of so many of Freud's analyses. That is his fault. He wanted nothing to do, after all, with angels or demons and was willfully determined not to recognize the engagement of the Dummkopf and the Maestro in large or small human matters.

On the other hand, a small portion of praise can still be given to the good doctor for his delineation of the ego. That concept has become one of the tools by which humans have become almost as adept as we are at assessing shifts of self-worth within.

Be it said that the state of Adolf's ego had become the focus of my attention. It would do no good to keep raising his estimate of his own worth if, at the same time, he was terrified that he had helped to kill Edmund. Because he did not wish to believe it, he most certainly did feel guilty, and the worst of it was that I hardly knew the answer. Had he, or had he not?

The facts were simple—which is to say that the deed was clear, but the consequences were not. On a morning when Angela was working with Klara and Paula in the garden and Alois was out for his walk, Adolf found Edmund playing alone in the room that they had shared until Adolf's illness.

Adolf walked over and kissed Edmund. Simple as that. I must admit that I was impelling him. If, personally, I certainly did feel something comparable to affection for Edmund, there was little I could do about it in this situation. In those days, I was not prepared to defy an order given directly by the Maestro.

"Why are you kissing me?" asked Edmund.

"Because I love you."

"You do?"

"I love you, Edmund."

"Is that why you scalped me?"

"You must forget that. You must forgive me. I think that is why I caught the measles. I was so ashamed of myself afterward."

"Is that true?"

"I think so. Yes. And that is why I must kiss you again. That is the way to give you back your scalp."

"You do not need to. I have no headache today."

"We cannot take a chance. Let me kiss you again."

"Isn't that bad? You have had these measles?"

"Between brothers and sisters, yes, it could be bad. But not between brothers. It has been established medically that brothers are able to kiss even when one has measles."

"Momma said we must not. We are not supposed to kiss you yet."

"Momma does not understand that it is all right between brothers."

"You swear?"

"I swear."

"Let me see your fingers when you swear."

Adolf was impelled most definitely by me then. He held up his hands, fingers outstretched. "I swear," he said, and kissed Edmund repeatedly, a boy's kiss full of slobbering, and Edmund kissed him back. He was so happy that Adi did love him after all.

Edmund came down with the measles. And the disease proved fatal. We were responsible for his death. Or we were not. I knew no more than Adolf. Night after night, therefore, a new platoon of French soldiers were massacred in Adolf's sleep. I had decided to distract him with one wish fulfillment after another. Taken each by each, they would produce no large effect, but quantity does change quality, as Engels once wrote to Marx, and so I believe my work would have had its desired effect if there had not been separate problems with which he had to contend. Otherwise, I think Adolf might have been ready eventually to move his psychic strengths over to the rigorous belief that murder offers power to a murderer.

# BOOK XIII

## ALOIS

### AND

## ADOLF

# 1

Adolf Hitler's readiness to exterminate humans in the gas chamber was obviously not at this time, in 1900, an active longing. If I speak, therefore, of a year like 1945, it is to make no direct connection to the months after Edmund's death. Wholly guided in those years by the Maestro, I was looking to do no more than intensify some early sense that he might yet become a high agent of the gods of death. That did allow him to believe that his own end would not be like others. Of course, I had no real expectation as yet of the dimensions to come. I would have done the same for Luigi Lucheni if he had been my client when he was young.

I do find it interesting, however, that close to the last few months of his life, Hitler did wish to be cremated. The meanest aspect of his life had always been his body, but by then, late in life, his soul—by any but our measure—was more befouled than his torso. Of course it is also true that when one has become an overseer of death who holds the power to liquidate masses of people, one is also in great need of a very hard shell to the ego in order to feel no intimate horror over the price to one's soul. Most statesmen who become successful leaders of a country at war have usually risen to such eminence already. They have installed in themselves an ability not to suffer sleepless nights because of casualties on the other side. They now possess the mightiest of all social engines of psychic numbification—patriotism! That is still the most dependable instrument for guiding the masses, although it may yet be replaced by revealed religion. We love fundamentalists. Their faith offers us every promise of developing into the final weapon of mass destruction.

If these are personal conclusions, I must also warn the reader that the Maestro detests large thoughts in his minions. He speaks of such ideas as "your vapors." He reminds us to return to matters within our competence.

I think by the end Hitler may have been weary enough to share this sentiment. In 1944, one of the worst years of his life, with the war going badly, the Führer, out at his underground retreat in East Prussia—the Wolfschanze—would try to relax by telling his secretaries old anecdotes over dinner. He would relate how his father, on many a night, would lay a whipping on him. But, as he assured his secretaries, he had been brave, yes, just as brave as an American Indian under torture. Never had he made the smallest sound. The ladies were regaled with these tales of his heroism. By then, being much more aged than his actual years—fifty-five—Adolf was ready to enjoy the advantages of old age. He delighted in receiving the admiration of women without having to pass through the anxiety of deciding whether he should consider copulating with them. His sexual spirit, so wholly unlike Alois', had never committed itself to seeking the glories or perils of new fornication. (The fear of embarrassment was prodigious in Adolf, and we looked to keep it that way.) An earthly companion was by now not in the least necessary to our aims.

Of course, the story he told the secretaries was a shameless exaggeration. On occasion he would even speak of two hundred blows delivered to his bottom by his father's arm.

Once, in the late 1930s, talking to Hans Frank, he said, "When I was ten or twelve I had to go late at night into this stinking smoke-filled tavern. I made no attempt to spare my father's feelings. I went right up to the table where he sat staring at me doltishly and I shook him. 'Father,' I would say, 'it's time for you to come home. Up you get.' And often I would have to wait for a quarter of an hour or more, pleading and scolding before I could get him to his legs. Then I supported him home. I never felt so horribly ashamed. Hans Frank, I tell you, I know what a demon alcohol can be. Because of my father, it was the bane of my youth." Indeed, he told the story so well that Herr Frank even repeated it in the course of the Nuremberg trials.

## 2

Actually, Alois happened to be drinking less. He did not dare to take too much. The fact that Edmund would not be there to greet him in the morning was unendurable. He felt as if he had consumed a bowl of ashes in his sleep.

On many an evening, he also needed to be alert because he was going to the Buergerabends. The gentry might be more cultivated than he was, but their company was able to lift him for a little while out of his worst moods. Without such elegant diversion, he would have had to spend his night brooding on the young one's death. And so he became a regular and was often present all four nights a week no matter which inn had been chosen. If, in the beginning, he had been stiff in his entrances and departures, the condition was eased by the quiet compassion he was receiving. A general courtesy met him when he entered. Many offered their warmth when he left. "This is the good side of the gentry," he told himself. At Customs, he had always seen them as chilly in their manner except when they had something to hide.

What also impressed him was that one of the members often present at these Buergerabends was a rabbi named Moriz Friedmann, who had been a member of the Austrian District School for eighteen years. Alois could see that most of the members were respectful of Friedmann, and this certainly helped to reinforce his notion that humankind could be divided into those who were cul-

tured and those who were not. If a Jew could be acceptable to
a Buergerabend, he told himself, then so could a peasant born
into the lowest circumstances, yes, a child born illegitimately to
a woman who slept on straw in an abandoned cattle trough. No,
he was not about to drink too much on these evenings. Adolf
never had to bring him home drunk. Given the decent welcome
the Buergerabends gave him now, he concluded that he had a right
to belong in their society because he, too, like Rabbi Moriz Friedmann, was a special individual. Something like six hundred Jews
were living in Linz at this time, which, given a population of sixty
thousand, meant that there was one such man or woman in one
hundred. Most of these Jews came from Bohemia and were actually
not as crude as one would expect—so he would have told Klara if
she had not supposed he was Jewish. Indeed, many of them were
assimilated. They didn't walk around in old caftans smelling of
stale places. Many were professionals or manufacturers, and many,
like Moriz Friedmann, had honorary federal posts. So, yes, they
had come from the outside and so had he.

By now, Alois felt (just like Mayrhofer) that the town tavern was
too raw. Given his grief, the loud voices could bring him close to
tears whenever he thought of Edmund. Besides, he'd drink more at
the tavern. What an unmanly sight it would be if he broke down
there.

## 3

Adolf entered middle school in September of 1900, close to
eight months after Edmund's death. Provided he was able to
pass all his grades over the next four years, he would be out by his
fifteenth birthday. His preference, he declared, was to attend the

Gymnasium, with its curriculum focused on the classics and art, rather than the Realschule, where emphasis would be given to practical disciplines.

Alois and Adolf had discussions concerning this. Sometimes Klara would sit in the room, sometimes not, but the point at issue was the Gymnasium. Adi felt he could work there to good effect. His talent, he declared, was for art. Looking to put Alois in a compliant mood, he added that he was also ready to study the classics. Alois was scornful. "The classics? Are you serious?"

Klara spoke. "Our boy is upset. Naturally, that affects other things."

"I can appreciate some of his unhappy thoughts," said Alois, "But what you say is neither here nor there. I see no use in trying to enter the Gymnasium. He is not going to prove acceptable." He chose to look into Adolf's eyes. "Since you seem unable these days to spell German correctly, how, in the name of what your mother calls the Good God, will you do anything with Latin or Greek?"

At this point, Alois chose to speak to him in Latin. Not to test him, but to mock him. "*Absque labore nihil,*" said Alois.

"And what does that mean?" asked Klara sharply. How cruel of Alois! He made a show of lighting his pipe, pulling smoke in slowly, then releasing it at leisure before he said, " 'Without labor, there is nothing.' " He nodded. "That is what it means." He exhaled the smoke with small cultivated puffs. "I would say that certainly applies to schooling. In the Gymnasium, students must master their grammar. In Latin and in Greek. Both! Those are fine knowledges to acquire. It would give you superiority over others for the rest of your life. But there is nothing without proper labor, and that school, Adolf, is not for you. Nor do you require courses in Ancient History or Philosophy or Art. In very few of them do I believe you would excel. It is better for you, in my opinion, to go to the Realschule. Not only is their practical teaching what you need, but I can help you to get in." (He was thinking of Mayrhofer's assistance.) "The other one is out, no matter what efforts I put forth. One look at your spelling will be all it takes."

Alois knew that he could ask members of the Buergerabends for recommendations to the Gymnasium, but to what end? Doubtless, that would not suffice. He would lose so much more than he could gain, and to no point or purpose. He sighed.

# 4

A dolf's life would now change for the worse. Linz was five miles away and twenty times larger than Leonding. A trolley car was available once an hour, but Klara expected him to walk, and it was a long hike across fields and forest before reaching the Realschule.

Each morning, he would be reminded in one or another manner by his father, his mother, or even Angela that he was the only son left, and the family must be able to count on him. Before long, he loathed the Realschule. It was a forbidding edifice on dark days. Gone was the pleasure he had taken at school in Hafeld, in Lambach, and in Leonding, where he would excel. Now the halls were ready to share his gloom. He thought often of the day when Alois, weeping over Edmund's death, had nearly suffocated him with the force of his embrace, all the while repeating, "You are my only hope." Such hope was reeking of tobacco. Would the atmosphere even listen to such a lie? This recollection, so full of misery and mistruth, was now attached to the portals of the Realschule.

His classmates, for the most part, came from prosperous families. They carried themselves differently from the farm boys and town boys he had known for the last few years. So he did not believe his mother when she told him: "Your father is the second-most-important man in Leonding. And the first, the Mayor, Mayrhofer, is his good friend."

He doubted that their importance reached to the outskirts of Linz. Why, the Mayor, who, according to his mother, was the most important man in Leonding, also sold vegetables in his store—a most elevated Mayor! Adolf had not been in the school for a day before he felt uncultivated. In recess, he overheard two students speaking of the merits of the opera they had been taken to by their parents the night before. That was enough to give him pause, and he had to wonder what they might say about him. "This Hitler, he has to walk all the way here from Leonding." Yes, on rainy days, he could take the trolley, but only if his parents gave him the pfennigs to afford it. An outlander! So many of these boys from Linz had never even seen Leonding. They assumed it was mud-ridden. And then he could hardly stay after class and make friends when he had to plod back to the Garden House. His mock wars in the forest had become possible now only on Saturday. There was no time to train troops.

Before long he was overcome again with the old question. Was he responsible for Edmund's death? Once more, he chose to talk to the trees. But the conversations had become orations. He inveighed against the stupidity of his teachers and the stale aroma of their clothing. "They are earning a pittance," he said to a stately oak. "It is obvious. They cannot afford to change their linens. Angela should smell these teachers. Then she would respect her brother!" He had other topics. To an old elm, he declared, "It is supposed to be an advanced school, but I can say that it is a stupid place. It is uncouth." He could hear the leaves murmuring in assent. "I have decided to devote myself to drawing. I know that I am excellent at capturing every detail of the most interesting buildings in Leonding and in Linz. When I show these drawings to my parents, even my father approves. He says, 'You are an excellent draftsman.' But then, he must spoil it. He also says, 'You have to learn more about perspective. You have not found the right size for the people who walk in front of your buildings. Some could be eight feet tall, others are pygmies. You must learn to draw bodies to scale. The people must be in proportion to the size of the building and to their distance from it. Pity, Adolf, that you cannot get this right, because your drawing of the edifice, taken by itself, would be an excellent sketch.' "

Of course, half praise from his father was worth more than all of Klara's loving approvals. It proved his point. Art was worth pursuing, not scholarship. "Scholarly work," he told the next grove of trees, "is pretentious. That may be why my teachers show a lack of interest in my possibilities. They are snobs. They dance disgustingly over boys who come from rich families. The air of this school, therefore, has become intolerable to me." What he did not tell the trees is that the only students who would have anything to do with him during recess happened to be the ugliest kids in class, or the stupidest, or the poorest.

He believed in the wisdom of these old trees. They seemed as wise to him as full-grown elephants.

Some mornings he would dawdle and so be obliged to take the train from Leonding to Linz. That bothered Klara. It was not a large expense but it was unnecessary when the sun was out. She had a gnawing sense of loss whenever money was disbursed heedlessly. Coins spent in such a manner fell into a well that was dry at the bottom and so made an awful clatter.

Still, on those many mornings when he did have to walk, his route would take him across fine old meadows and he soon became interested in the forts on the way, particularly after he learned that these crumbling towers were left over from the earliest years of the nineteenth century, when the Austrians had lived in fear that before long, Napoleon was bound to march his armies across the Danube. So they had built these watchtowers. One morning, thinking of the workers who had put them up, and the soldiers who had inhabited them, he became so excited that he had an ejaculation. Afterward, he was languid, but joyous. He was, of course, very late for school and was sent home with a note for Klara to sign. She did not know whether to believe him that he had missed the train.

# 5

There was an irony of which Adolf's schoolmates were not aware. Far from being a mud-ridden town, Leonding did have an upper class and they were regulars at the Buergerabends. The subtle differences of status between these members began to intrigue Alois and became a small diversion from his grief. Such surcease could not, however, last for long. He knew that he must continue to descend into his sorrow, step by step, and all the while he encountered such confusion that he had to wonder if his mental balance was in question.

It was not always fearful. In time, he began to feel as if he might recover from the death, perhaps regain his strength. Only not altogether. Not ever. There remained a hole drilled through his heart.

Nonetheless, these evenings did help. He needed to hear witty conversation. These were the smartest and best-educated people he had ever associated with socially, and that warmed his need to believe that he, too, was a man of sophistication. On one night, for example, he listened with high attention when one of the gentry, obviously possessing a comfortable, even superior knowledge of wine, remarked in passing, "The British call this hock. But that is only because the Riesling they like so much comes from Hochheim." Alois had learned to give a self-satisfied nod, as if each bit of culture just gained was already in his possession. One night Silvaner was served in oddly shaped bottles called *Bocksbeutel*. A round of laughter followed. *Bocksbeutel* meant "Ram's Testicle." Alois' mood lifted sufficiently to wonder whether he should speak up. Who could know more about rams' testicles? Hadn't he once owned a well-endowed pair? Ask the ladies. But he did not dare to speak. He knew the difference between himself and these gentry. They, for the most part, were able to stay in bed after the sun was up. So they could eat and drink well into the evening. If it came to it, they could go on to midnight. Even when he was younger, he had rarely reached such an hour unless he happened to be in a new woman's bed. Sad to say, he might just as well have been a common laborer going to work with a loaf of bread, some liverwurst, and a jar of soup. He could see these gentry, now in their retirement, getting up to have a light breakfast—Eggs Benedict!—and then a fine cigar. Often in the late afternoon, such people could enter their carriages and drive into Linz with their wives in order to have a five o'clock tea at the Hotel Wolfinger or the Drei Mohren, founded in 1565. There they would listen to violins. What did he know of that? Yes, it would be a rare late afternoon when he would have five o'clock tea at the Drei Mohren or in the lobby of the Wolfinger. As he told Klara, these were the men of Leonding with the most elevated idea of themselves.

"Forget about Mayrhofer," he told her. "He's a fine fellow, but these people come from very old families, the kind who have six courses for dinner. I have heard of as many as eight."

Klara remarked, "I could do that for you."

"No, my dear, no," he told her. "I am not even considering such a venture. Because the secret is you can't offer fancy recipes unless you have Meissen china or proper wineglasses."

"Proper wineglasses?" she asked. To her surprise, she was in some pain listening to him.

"Yes," he said, "they give a ring if you flip your finger on them."

Indeed, he was invited to one of those dinners. He went alone. Klara stayed home to take care of the children. When he came back, Klara remarked that perhaps they should invite these people to their home.

Alois replied, "They have indoor plumbing. Their bathroom is not an outside shed. The door to their bathroom does not have a hole cut into it in the shape of a quarter-moon. Our new friends, if they were such, would look upon such conditions as . . . *droll.*" He had never used the word before. "No," he went on, "we cannot have guests of that sort. What could I say when they ask, 'Where might I find the water closet?' Do I tell them, 'Don't mind the hole. Nobody will peep!'?"

# 6

On the last day of January, five months after Adolf had begun his studies at the Realschule, Klara was requested to come to the school.

Afterward, on the trolley, her eyes shut tight to control her tears, Klara did not know whether she had the courage to tell Alois that Adolf's report card was dreadful.

Indeed, when Alois did learn on the following evening, it came after what was now the second-worst morning of the year for him, the first of February. He was trying to be ready for the anniversary of Edmund's death on the next day, February 2, and in the course of walking through Leonding, ready to think of nothing, he encountered Josef Mayrhofer. The Mayor then suggested something most unusual. Rarely did he leave his shop in the care of his assistants unless as Mayor of Leonding tasks were awaiting him in Town Hall, but now he proposed that they go to the tavern for a drink.

Once there, they spoke of the oncoming weight of this first anniversary—good men in the grip of sorrowful emotions. Then Mayrhofer did something he had never done before. He said: "You must promise not to punish the messenger."

Alois replied with confidence, "You would never be the bearer of ill tidings," but already he could feel stirrings in his chest.

Mayrhofer said, "I must ask, do you have an older son who shares your first name?"

Alois seized the Mayor's forearm so hard that he bruised it. Mayrhofer freed himself with an unhappy smile. "Well," he said, "you have punished the messenger already." He held up a hand. "Enough," he said. "I have to tell you—a report came through today that circulates through the district. Your son is in prison."

"He is? For what?"

"I am so sorry. It is for theft."

A low guttural sound came forth. "I cannot believe it," Alois said. But he knew it was true.

Mayrhofer said, "You can visit him should you so desire."

"Visit him?" said Alois. "I don't think so." He was full of sweat, and on the edge of losing his good manners.

"The hardest thing I ever had to do in my life was to disavow my oldest son," he managed to put together. "Mayrhofer, you understand, we are such a good family. My wife and I have been careful to raise them properly. But Junior was the bad apple in the barrel. If I had not disavowed him, the other children would have suffered. And now the three who are still alive"—he caught himself, he did not sob—"will turn out very well indeed."

That evening, at Klara's insistence, Adolf had to show his report card to Alois. Now, witnessing the expression on Alois' face, she felt as if she had betrayed her son.

In tones sufficiently somber to pronounce the onset of war, Alois stated: "I gave a vow to your mother. It was at her request. I said that I would never whip you again. That was a year ago. We were thinking of the tragedy in our family. But now, you can be certain, I will break my vow. That is the only course to take when the vow has been dishonored by the person most protected by it. Come! We are going to your bedroom." Once more, he was holding his temper. It broke, however, so soon as he took off his belt.

At the first lash, Adolf told himself, "I will not cry out!" The blows were, however, so severe that he began to shriek. Alois had never used a leather strap before. It felt as if a tongue of flame was at the end of it. All the boy could think was that he did not wish to die! Indeed, he did not know what would destroy him first—this scourge upon his buttocks or the shock to his heart. At that moment, his father, seriously winded, stopped, pushed Adolf off his knee, and said, "You can stop crying now."

Alois went into his own depression—to live as long as he had and now feel no confidence in the poor remains of his male line.

# 7

Adolf was suffering true torment. He had dared to show his drawings to the art teacher. He had assumed the submissions would be chosen at once and would dominate the cork wall reserved for students. He had even meditated on how to phrase some quietly confident response to the praises he would receive. These fine moments would compensate for the poor marks on his first report card.

I can admit that I affected the result. While Adolf had talent, it was nothing remarkable—I could see at a glance that he would never be an artist of large promise. (Young Pablo Picasso, for example, was already by 1901 a young man in whom we were most interested.) By contrast, young Adolf Hitler produced drawings just good enough to tack to the cork wall.

"Prevent this," was the instruction I received from the Maestro. "The last thing we need is one more artist full of sour spirit at his lack of large recognition. I say it's better to put him into a real slump."

I was in position to accomplish this. Adolf's art instructor was one of our clients. (Indeed, he bore a close resemblance to the mediocrity described by the Maestro.) By way of an altercation I developed between him and his wife, I gave him a fearful headache. Adolf's work was seen through the light shafts of a migraine. None of the drawings were selected.

He could not believe it. In that hour, he withdrew forever from the idea that he would ever look again for success in school. He would learn to live on his own.

Of course, he would not, like Alois Junior, leave home, no need for that. Toga Boy still brought sweat to his back. No, he would continue to live among others while developing, unbeknownst to all, a will of iron.

He continued to do poorly in school. The report card of his first full year, which he handed over to his father in June, showed a failure in two courses, Mathematics and Natural History. Poor Alois. He could not muster the energy to give Adolf a beating.

That summer, knowing that he would have to repeat his first year, Adolf was equally depressed, but did manage to tell himself (with my assistance) that he comprehended the art of learning better than other students. He had the secret. He would retain only the essentials. Students were too ready to busy themselves with endless memorization of nonessential details. They were just like the teachers. They could only recite lists and categories. They were bores. They squawked like parrots. They acted as if they were truly intelligent whenever a teacher approved of what they said. They were the ones who got the good marks.

He was considerably above such concerns. So he told himself. He was interested in the core of each situation. That was the valuable knowledge. So he would not subject his mind to the methods others used. That could only reduce the power of his mind.

It was imperative to cheer him up. His best amusement these days had become his power to tease Angela. Physically, he was, at last, her equal in strength. So whenever she criticized him, he called her a "stupid goose." For Angela, this was a dreadful term. She would even complain to Klara. She hated geese. She had seen them landing in the town pond, and to her, they were filthy. Angela had watched these geese as they crowded up on the banks, leaving their droppings behind them. She was, she told herself, more like a swan.

I did allow Adolf one fantasy where he proceeded to imagine himself a teacher at the Realschule, dressed in elegant style, clear voiced, incisive, and regarded with admiration for his wit.

> ADOLF: Here is the essential, young men. Do not try to remember all the facts of every historical event. I would say instead: "Protect yourself. You are swimming in clouded water." Most of the facts you have memorized are no better than debris which contradict other facts. So you will be in a state of confusion. But I can rescue you. The secret is to retain essentials. Select only those facts which clarify the issue.

# 8

On a lively night at the Buergerabends, one speaker, a portly man, offered the thesis that railway travel had affected long-established social relations. "Our sense of the world," he declared, "has been turned inside out by the railroads. The king of Saxony, for example, is not in favor of such travel. As he put it recently, 'The laborer can now arrive at his destination on the same train as a king.' This is equal to saying that men who are well-off no longer travel more rapidly than the lower classes. Social disharmony could be an eventual consequence of all this."

Another member stood up to say, "I agree with my distinguished friend that many of these so-called improvements are of dubious value. Pocket watches are certainly a prime example. In these days, anyone can buy a timepiece at a reasonable price. Yet I still recall an era when it was a privilege to carry a fine watch. A person in one's employ had to take note of the fine quality of your watch and chain. They would leave your presence respectfully. Now any roustabout can pull a piece of shoddy out of his pants and declare that his piece keeps better time than yours. Do you want to hear the worst of it?—sometimes that is true."

Laughter followed this remark. "No, gentlemen," the speaker went on, "a cheap watch can be more accurate in this matter than our family heirlooms, which, after all, are cherished because they have been with us for so long."

One evening, the lecture was on dueling scars. That left Alois wistful. He listened with full attention to varied opinions on the best location for the wound. Should one desire the left or right cheek, the chin, or the corner of the lips? He did, however, chime in toward the end by remarking that when he was a young officer in the Customs service, many of his superiors bore those scars and "we did respect them." He sat down flushed. His remark had contributed little.

On another occasion his feelings were hurt by a young sportsman (with a prominent dueling scar) who entered into a long conversation with him. The first auto tour from Paris to Vienna had recently passed through Linz, and the man with the dueling scar not only owned a motor car but had been in the race.

Earlier on this same evening, the sportsman had enlivened a debate over the question of whether it was sensible to purchase an automobile, and the back and forth of oratorical heat stimulated fiery comment. Those who were opposed to motor cars spoke contemptuously of the dust, the mud, the uproars, and, worst of all, the fumes.

The sportsman replied, "Yes, I know—these infernal machines are awful to you, but I happen to like the fumes. For me, they are an aphrodisiac."

This remark was received with hoots and howls. He laughed, "Say what you will, the fumes do offer a hint of debauch." At which he dared to sniff his fingers. Groans and laughter were the response of the company. "You can rest content with your carriages and your stables," he went on to say, "but I like traveling at high speeds."

"Oh, that is much too much!" someone called out.

"Not at all," the speaker told him. "The sense of danger is welcome to me. I am stimulated by the roar of the engine. The attention of those many pedestrians who used to admire a fine horse and carriage is now offered to the virtues of my iron monster. I see it out of the corner of my eye even as I rush by."

Alois was certainly impressed by this rich sport, who capped his argument by saying, "Yes, to drive a motor car does offer some peril. But it is also dangerous to rein in a maddened horse. I would rather risk my neck in a motor car than shatter my bones in an overturned coach. Or sit behind some old nag of a beast who secretly loathes my guts."

How they roared at that! Nothing worse than such a horse.

Later, when the debate was over, the speaker chose to engage Alois in a quiet conversation whose concealed agenda soon became evident, since he chose to ask more than a few questions about Customs procedures. Alois was offended. Brilliantly full of himself at the podium, the man was now obvious in his motive. "You sound as if you are going to cross a few borders," Alois remarked.

"Indeed I am," said the Sport. "But it's the English I am thinking about. They say the English can be the worst." He made a point of speaking in profile, so that Alois might be properly impressed with the dueling scar on his left cheek.

It was a good jagged cicatrix, perfect for a man as handsome and self-possessed as this fellow, but work in Customs had offered its own sagacities, and so Alois could distinguish a genuine scar occasioned by the saber of a dueling partner hacking through the padding on your face and thereby leaving a bona fide laceration from a self-created dueling scar worked up by some ambitious toad looking to charm the ladies. A fellow like that would use a razor to open a wound on his face and then embed a horsehair in the gap.

That could build the scar up into a welt high enough to dignify the rest of his career.

When well done, such a scar might appear to be authentic, but Alois had already decided that this fellow had almost certainly used a horsehair. The scar did sit too perfectly on his face.

So Alois said no more in return than, "I expect we are still just as good as the English if it's a matter of spotting some joker who looks to bring precious objects into Austria without paying duty. *Celer et vigilans*," added Alois. "That used to be my motto." It was a happy prevarication—he had happened to memorize the saying just that afternoon. *Celer et vigilans*—quick and watchful. That ought to give the fellow some pause.

"*Numquam non paratus*," answered the Sport, to which Alois could only smile.

His first act on returning home was to look up the meaning. "Never unprepared." An old wrath came back to him for a moment. How he would like to get his hands on this man in a Customs shed.

All the same, Alois was feeling expansive at dinner. The excitement of the discussion was still with him, and as he recounted his final observation on the dueling scars, Adolf did listen avidly. Someday he would have his own motor car. Perhaps, even, his own dueling scar.

# 9

To Adolf's surprise, there came a night when Alois did take him to the opera. This event—they were to hear *Lohengrin*—had come about by way of an improvement in his report card for February of 1902. Due to his previous failure, the first half of his second year had been a repeat of the first half of the first year, and so he did receive a passing grade in every course. There were even favorable comments on his diligence and conduct. This occasioned Alois to declare, "A good sign. Once you allow conduct to be your first concern, the rest has been known to follow."

Alois was easing up on his demands. He had been ill. Two months earlier, in December of the previous year, 1901, he had had influenza, which frightened him. Once again he felt an overbearing need to be able to improve this recalcitrant son.

So, in early February, soon after the second anniversary of Edmund's death, Alois decided to try once again to come a little closer. Having noticed that Adolf listened with intense interest whenever the conversations at the Buergerabends were described, he was also pleased to see that Adolf would read all the newspapers that were brought home. Indeed, by virtue of a few remarks Adolf offered at the family table, Alois knew that some of his son's fellow students (obviously from the more well-to-do families) did talk in recess about operas they had attended. Alois decided it was time to take the boy.

It came as no surprise that Alois was also ready to speak derogatively of the Linz opera house. "To Linzers," he told Adolf, "this opera house is a splendid building, but if you have spent time in Vienna and know, as I do, a true opera house, you would find the performance here not so impressive. Of course, coming from Hafeld and Lambach or even Leonding, I expect that you will think you are hearing high opera tonight. And, indeed, Linz has obtained the right to call itself a city and be proud of its opera house. Nonetheless, tonight will be in no way equal to Vienna. Adolf, if you prove successful in a career, then someday, perhaps, you will live in Vienna. That is when you will truly enjoy the heights of musical pleasure."

Alois was pleased with the speech. He had come to the point in his life where he felt that if much else was diminishing, the ability to express himself with the well-rounded criticisms of a true *Buergerabender* had certainly developed.

So Adolf was taken to hear his first Wagner in a second-rate opera house. And despite his father's comments, he was more than once enthralled. If he sneered at the entrance of the great swan who was towing Lohengrin's boat onstage to rescue Elsa (for Adolf could hear the squeak of the boots made by the two men installed inside the swan), he was overcome by Elsa's aria of welcome to Lohengrin. "I see in splendor shining, a knight of glorious mien. . . . Heaven has sent him to save me. He shall my champion be."

Tears came to Adolf's eyes. Tomorrow, he would mingle among the students who spoke of operatic performances they had attended. During intermission, therefore, he listened to the comments of the most impressive-looking operagoers. "How fastidious of Wagner," said one such man to another, "that he uses the violins and woodwinds rather than allow himself to be trapped by the harp. Wagner knows his celestial sounds. It is as if he is the first to have discovered them. Violins, oboe, bassoon, yes, but away with the harps."

Yes, thought Adolf, he would repeat this tomorrow at school.

Alois, in turn, was off on his own meditation. Brooding over the skill of the upper classes, he decided that they had a foundation for their good fortune. They knew how to obtain proper installations for their sons in the army, the church, or the law, and thereby could continue to be proud of the family achievements. Yet why conclude that he was not as good as them? Granted, he had started from a low place, but he was ready now to live with their point of view. They understood that the oldest son, able or not, must still be ready to fulfill the destiny of the family. That was not only true for the army and the church but could include government officials as well. Some bureaucrats, after all, did become ministers of state. If that had not been the case for him, not when a man had to start at the bottom of the ladder, still he felt entitled to one certainty. If he had had these advantages of birth, he would have made a fine minister. Now, should Adolf ever become a man worthy of respect, he would also be in position to rise above his father's achievements. Listening now to this music, so true to his elevated mood, so vaulting, so ambitious, so bold, Alois allowed himself to shed in the dark a few happy tears upon a well-spent life, and these sentiments were now so finely mingled with *Lohengrin*'s final sounds that his palms were red from the applause he gave to the company of this second-rate opera house.

Adolf, however, was not ebullient. Given the power of the last chords, he soon plummeted from a high and splendid mood into his familiar despondency.

I would say this is one of our basic problems. We have more than our share of clients who can rise high into the intoxications of their private dreams but then plummet down to the ugliness of their real condition. So we have to calm them. Even as he was soaring into the empyrean with Wagner, the downfall of his confidence was commencing. Wagner was a genius. Adolf had come to that opinion instantly. Every note spoke to him. But could he say this was also true of himself? Or was he not a genius after all? Not next to Wagner.

# 10

Going back to Leonding on the last trolley car, Alois was no happier than his son. Now that he had given Adolf the gift of *Lohengrin*, he must find a way to present the bill. Would the boy feel ready to accompany him on a visit to the Customs House? For months he had been contemplating each and every reasonable occupation for Adolf to pursue and had come to the conclusion that Customs remained the best choice. It would, at least, be comparable to entering an esteemed profession from a good family.

Whenever conversation moved in that direction, however, Adolf would speak of becoming an artist. Alois would then suggest, "You can do both. Without question, you can do both. Have I not done more than one thing in my life?"

Well, there was the boy nodding in gloomy resignation, as if it was obligatory to keep paying homage to a father's repetitions. In time, Alois had ceased speaking of the Customs service. The meager results left him feeling liverish.

Yet the slight improvement in Adolf's marks did remind Alois that a father must not fail to pick up any hint of a positive change in an adolescent son. Another effort must be made, therefore, to give the boy a worthy life. He would get him to come along on a visit to the Customs House.

On a given night, therefore, Alois gave one of his monologues at the family table and felt that the spirit of the Buergerabends now enabled him to display more rhetorical gifts than ever. "There is one fellow in our club who keeps saying, and I must agree it is an interesting opinion, that the gap between the wealthy and the poor is being diminished."

"Is that so?" asked Klara, wishing to come into the conversation.

"Absolutely. We've had fine discussions on this matter. It is due to our railway system. You can be rich or you can be poor—no matter! You travel at the same high speed. Oh, I tell you, and you, children, pay attention to this, you, Angela, and you, Adolf. Remember this prediction: The cities are going to expand, and there will be money everywhere. I've heard talk in these evenings at the Buergerabends of peasants, people so poor that—I will use an expression you are now old enough to understand. There are people so poor that"—he had to whisper the next—"they use their hands to wipe themselves."

"Oh, Daddy!" screamed Angela.

Alois could not resist. "And then they scrape their fingers in the dirt."

To which Angela could only scream again, "Oh, Daddy! Oh, Daddy!" but she was laughing at how ready he was to be disgusting, and yet how well he knew her. It was true. He knew how to make her laugh.

"Oh," said Alois, "that was the way it used to be. But now some of these once-impoverished people are smart enough to know what is coming. I even hear of peasants who are sharp enough to sell their holdings to the men who are planning to build factories in those places just so soon as the roads come in. And the roads will come. Yes," he said, "everything is racing forward, and even the peasants are in this race. But you, Adolf, with your intelligence, well, I've come to the conclusion that you are potentially a very intelligent young man, and will yet be cultured. So I would look to warn you. These changes in society are going to alter the nature of the work we do. Education is coming, and it will take over everything. Even fools will be able to read and write. Of course, it is also important that not everybody become so well educated that we lose all distinction of what it means to be called Herr Doktor. Adolf, if you study hard at your school, yes, it is only the Realschule not the Gymnasium, nonetheless, you will be able to go on and become an engineer, may it be, and they will call you, once you get your Ph.D., yes, that will be the day for you and for all of us, for then you, too, will be called Herr Doktor. I can tell you I would have liked to have been addressed in such a way and thereby enjoy even a higher level of respect in the community than I do now." He held up his hand. "Although I certainly do not complain. Not at all. But if I had been Herr Doktor, your mother would have been called Frau Doktor even though she has never seen the entrance gates to a university." At this point Alois laughed and Klara turned red. "Yes," said Alois, "it is possible that your interests may turn to business. In my day that was not possible for someone with my origins. But now is not like it was when I was young. Now maybe your gift will be for commerce or technology. And yet, I do not really see you as an engineer or a businessman because there is one fault with all such success—you have no time to yourself. A businessman has no peace. He takes his work home with him. So does an engineer. What if his bridge collapses?" Alois paused, took a deep breath, and remarked: "If you should ever decide to work in Customs, your evenings and your weekends will always be there, open to your choice. You will be able to work at your art."

Despite all, Alois was having his effect. Such talk left Adolf with a nervous stomach. But that was because he was no longer certain whether his father was absolutely a fool or might have to be listened to. If the latter, then there could be some most miserable choices ahead and nothing but awful people to live and work among. What if he was not destined to be a great artist or a great architect? What if he was no Wagner? There was one thing that could be said for Customs, and his father had made the point—he could have a separate life after work.

So they went to the Customs House. Despite all of Alois' locutions, the visit did not succeed. The worst of it was that they entered into the main accounting house, where the clerks were at work. An unhappy smell came up from the general collection of middle-aged bodies gathered together under gas lamps with eye-shades on their foreheads. Naturally, his father would not mind such aromas. When young, he had made boots and had to sniff officers' toes during the fitting. No, he, Adolf, would not spend his life in a mausoleum full of the old smells of old men sitting on top of each other like monkeys in their cubicles.

After the visit, Alois made another attempt. "So many of my colleagues," he said, "are now fine friends. Should I choose to, I can visit good people all over Upper Austria, men still in Breslau and Passau, yes." Adolf was wondering where they all might be. He had rarely seen anyone come to visit, not even Karl Wesseley, often mentioned as his father's best friend. But Alois went on: "There are so many benefits, yes. The pensions, the time that is there for yourself. I can tell you, security plus a good pension enables a man to avoid all misery after he retires. He does not have to worry then about not having enough funds. Nothing, I warn you, Adolf, creates more discord in a family than lack of money. That is why our family does not have ugly arguments. There is no need for that."

Since this speech was at the dinner table, Angela could not help herself. She was thinking of the sudden departure of Alois Junior. No ugly arguments! How could her father speak that way? Passing behind his back, she stuck out her tongue. Klara saw this, but said nothing. It would be bad enough when Alois came to realize that his fine talk would go for nothing. Indeed, she was correct. As the months went by, Alois gave up the idea of the Customs House. His son was not going to follow decent advice. But it did spoil many a mood.

His spirits picked up, however, on hearing of a fine bargain in the neighborhood. A small coal merchant who lived nearby needed to sell a load to pay off some debts. Since customers were all too few in summer, Alois was able to make a very good deal for the coal.

He chose, however, to ignore Klara's advice. She told him to hire an assistant to help with the task of getting all that coal down to the cellar bins. He also ignored her second suggestion that he use Adolf. He did not wish to share labor with the boy—they were bound to have a dispute.

Still, Klara's suggestions did bear some weight. Having succeeded in purchasing the coal at half price, he tried to bargain with the seller. "I expect you," he told him, "to bring it down to the bin," at which point the dealer replied, "Oh, you rich fellows. You are always ready to keep us poor. No, sir, I cannot carry your coal down for you. Not at the price you reduced me to." So Alois decided to do it himself. "I may not be as rich as you think I am," he told the man, "but I am certainly stronger than I look."

Ergo, he toted a half ton of coal down to the bin. It took two hours up in the sun and down in the dust of the cellar. Once the job was completed, he keeled over with a hemorrhage.

## 11

For the weeks following Alois' recovery, Adolf would hear wonder in his mother's voice at how much blood had issued from Alois' mouth, and if he could not quite admit it to himself, he regretted that he had not been present on that occasion.

For that matter, following a suggestion from the Maestro, I encouraged Adolf to brood upon the matter, and he was soon illuminated by a concept. Blood possessed magic. It could be shared by a people. When he looked at the strongest and most handsome boys in his class, he tingled in those places his groin usually reserved for the forest. When blood charged to his penis, it was blood that he possessed in common with fellow students.

I, of course, was free of attitude on this matter. I was ready to work with Austrian clients who, like Adolf, believed in German blood, but I could be just as effective with Orthodox Jewish clients who believed in the supremacy of their blood. I could also work, and very well indeed, with Jewish clients who were Socialists, or with German Socialists, although that called for being comfortable with intellects whose emphasis was on the air and the spirit—all of those invisible currents and gases where enlightenment and the security of un-bloody worldviews might be found. And, of course, I also worked with clients who were Communist and would not have called themselves Reds if they did not, in their fashion, believe in blood. We were always able to improve on the beliefs which our clients held. Once established in their prejudices, we could move to alter their certainties. Often we would intensify the hatred such clients felt for all that was opposite to them in other humans.

# 12

After recuperating from the hemorrhage, Alois gave Adolf no more beatings. Sometimes when Alois thought the boy was becoming too sure of himself, he would threaten a whipping, but the warning had lost all drama.

At the Buergerabend on the night before New Year's Eve of 1903, the members allowed themselves a bit more to drink, and Alois could feel how disturbed was the mood. In the last few weeks, a Capuchin Monk named Jurichek had been invited to preach in St. Martin's Church, where he would deliver his sermon in the Czech language as a means of collecting money for a proposed Czech school. Some members at the Buergerabends began to complain (most incorrectly as it turned out) that before long there would be a Czech invasion of Linz.

Alois was uneasy. "If a Czech uprising takes place," he did say, "it could mean the end of the Austrian-Hungarian Empire. Yet," as he would also murmur, "my best friend is a Czech."

He almost recounted a discussion with Karl Wesseley, who had passed by on a business trip from Prague to Salzburg. "We Czechs," Wesseley had argued, "offer more loyalty to the Emperor than you Austrian-Germans who would dissolve the Empire in a moment if you could just link up with the Prussians."

His brief visit left Alois in a state of confusion. Contradictory remarks were now being voiced by him at the Buergerabends. It was as if the loss of blood had also loosened his tongue. First he would find himself on one side of an argument, then the other. Finally, he was attacked by one of the oldest gentlemen in the club.

Unfortunately, this fine elder also proved to be a hint unbalanced. "Herr Alois," he said, "you have been so totally opposed to our poor little local priest, who wants to invite poor Czechoslovakian workers to come to free food kitchens when they are hungry. That does make you sound like you are a pro-German. 'Get rid of these dirty Czechs,' it seems you are saying. But I cannot follow you. Your best friend, you tell us, is a Czech. Dear Herr Hitler, I hesitate to say this, but I must attribute your confusions to the one affliction we are all in danger of approaching these days. That is premature old age. You are not an old man, not as old as I am, but, my esteemed fellow Buergerabender, I must warn you that confusions, if not promptly cleared up, can swallow good intentions." And abruptly he sat down, as if to apologize for having gone too far.

Unhappily for Alois, the old man had not been inaccurate. Since the lung hemorrhage, Alois had lost exactly that clarity of which he had been so proud. Now many of Alois' thoughts seemed to come into his head for no better purpose than to proclaim the opposite of his previous remarks. Indeed, Alois had confessed as much to Wesseley on the last visit, after which he sighed and said, "I like talking to you. In my opinion, you are as deep as the sea."

"Alois, tell the truth. Have you ever seen a large body of water?" asked Wesseley.

"Beautiful lakes I have seen, and plenty. That is enough." He paused. "I feel as if I am living in the desert."

A couple of nights after the old member's tirade, Alois kept remembering how some of the Buergerabenders had been nodding their heads in agreement. And Alois did keep hearing the old man's voice: "You say that we give too much to the Czechs, but then I hear you tell us that to be against the Jews and the Hungarians is antagonistic to good culture. Where is the focus of your thoughts?"

In the course of that upbraiding, Alois had felt so weak that he could not summon enough vigor to stand up and leave the room. Then he found the strength. Not often did members walk out of the Buergerabends in such an abrupt manner, but on this occasion it became imperative. Be damned to how weak he felt.

He was furious. It seemed undeniably clear to him that he had only been tolerated at the Buergerabends. Did they laugh among themselves at remarks he had made? Was it like that? Had he been their resident fool?

It gave him a fearful headache. Four days later, on January 3, he was dead before noon.

# BOOK XIV

# ADOLF

# AND

# KLARA

# 1

On the morning of January 3, 1903, Alois was not feeling too well, and so on his daily walk through Leonding he decided to stop at the Gasthaus Steifer for a glass of wine. To cheer his mood, he called upon an old memory.

Once, in Customs, many years ago, he had come across a box of cigars whose seal had been carefully removed, then repasted. He could discern as much by a thin welt of cement at the edge of the stamp. Thereupon, the box was opened for examination and revealed a diamond hidden under the cigars. He was even tempted to pocket it. The smuggler—a well-dressed traveler—was ready to make any arrangement if he was not charged. Alois, however, was afraid of a trap. Moreover, he was proud of his honesty. He had never indulged in such chicanery. If, on this occasion, he was tempted—the gem did look to be valuable—still, he turned it over to the authorities. That certainly helped to advance his promotions.

He had used this recollection more than once as a tonic to his spirits, but now, at the Gasthaus Steifer, he did not capture the pleasure he expected on the first sip of the wine. Instead, to the consternation of the few Saturday-morning drinkers present, he collapsed. His last thought was in Latin: *Acta est fabula*. He said it aloud and passed out, proud to have remembered Caesar's last words: "The play is over!"

Now the innkeeper and his assistant carried him to an empty side room. The waiter was ready to run for a priest, but the tavern owner said, "I don't think Herr Alois would want one!"

"Sir," asked the waiter, "can one be certain in matters like this?"

The innkeeper shook his head. "All right, get him."

But it developed that their patron was dead before the priest came in, dead from a pleural hemorrhage, which a doctor declared soon after.

Klara ran up with the children a few minutes later, and Angela began to sob. She was the first to see her father's body. Laid out on the table, he looked made of wax. Adolf burst into tears. He was terrified. He had dreamed of his father's death for so long that when the waiter came rushing to their house, Adolf did not believe the news. He was certain his father was merely pretending to be dead. That would be his father's way to rouse a little sympathy from the family. Indeed, even as they hurried through the streets to the Gasthaus, Adolf remained convinced. Only when he saw the body was he overcome. He wept loudly and without cease. His immediate necessity was to conceal every last wish he had had for the demise of his father. It was as if the more he wept, the more might God believe he did mourn the loss. (That he was certain of God's interest in him was now a keystone of his vanity—one of my major contributions.)

On January 5, the day of the funeral, he wept in church. By now, however, it had become a labor to force these tears forth sufficiently to impress the men and women who might be staring at him. I, in my turn, had to convince him that God was not angry at him. In consequence, I was presenting myself once again as his guardian angel. While we can, on occasion, alleviate fear of the Lord by increasing our client's sense that the Power Above does love him, it is a tricky task, since the better we are at it, the greater grows the risk that the client will react with sufficient piety to attract the attention of the Cudgels, and they in turn will be particularly vindictive toward us because we dared to imitate them.

Indeed, on one occasion when I played at being a guardian angel for another client, one of the Cudgels threw me down a flight of stone stairs. It may be hard to conceive, but spirits can also take a damaging fall. Since I was not corporeal at the time, there was no flesh to bruise but, oh, what a pummeling to my inner presence! Steel and stone are harsh materials when they come in contact with the Spirit. That is why prisons are built of steel and stone.

Let me not digress, however, from the funeral. I had to prepare Adolf to deliver a good many facsimiles of grief. We were certainly facing a demand altogether different from that first burst of tears when he saw his father dead. Now, in order to come forth with a few sobs, he had to uproot bits and pieces of memory from the few good conversations he had had with Alois. It helped that he had used to admire (if grudgingly) the way his father could speak. But that might not be enough to prime the dry well of so impoverished a sorrow. At last, he chose to think of the day when they went to Der Alte's house for the first time. He was able to bring forth tears at this recollection, but it was for Der Alte's death.

So the weeping, while in full view of everyone in church, did have to live with ongoing inhibitions. His sobbing pinched off each time he had a memory of Alois' body at the Gasthaus Steifer, and he was able to cry in earnest only by thinking of how awful it had been for Der Alte to die alone and not be found for weeks. Given these impediments, he was often close to hiccups.

Klara sat close to Adolf on this occasion, but her maternal sensitivities, never wholly removed from telepathy, had her soon thinking of bees. She remembered how she would talk to the Langstroth boxes in Hafeld on evenings when Alois was at the tavern in Fischlham. Now she wondered whether she might even leave a wreath on the empty beehive that still remained at the back of the house in Leonding. Alois' last little hive had only given them a small return of honey, but back in Hafeld, following the old customs of Spital and Strones, she had made a point of talking to the beehives and would relate to them what was going on in the family. During her childhood she had been told that it was bad luck not to speak to your bees. They expected such attention. But if you ever were so unlucky as to see a swarm alight on a dead plant, why, then, a member of the family was bound to die.

When Alois had started the new hive in Leonding, she had told him about this practice and asked if he would like her to talk to them. He laughed. "I can see the point if it's a real bee house of the sort Der Alte had. When there's a large investment," said Alois, "one would not wish to endanger it in any manner. So, of course, a few superstitions cannot hurt, and how can one say it will not help? But, if you insist, give a real speech to the bees and tell them all there is to know about us. They will look to pass such gossip on to the newspapers," and he had laughed heartily at his own joke, enough for her to regret telling him.

She remembered how, just six months ago, Alois had cursed bitterly when his hive had swarmed away. That had been the end of the venture in Leonding. The unhappy dream he had had in Hafeld six years ago that his hives would desert him had been realized instead in the summer of 1902.

Now, at the funeral, a half year later, she was convinced that this flight of his bees had helped to bring on his lung hemorrhage. She knew. He had been afraid to climb the tree onto which they had swarmed. Indeed, he knew in which tree they had installed themselves but pretended he didn't. Yes, she knew. That was because he did not feel able to climb a tree. So, to make up for that, he had chosen to carry the coal all by himself down to the cellar. So foolish an act! His disappointment with Adolf, his heartbreak concerning Paula—no, she must not dwell on any of this, not for a moment. Nor dare to think of Edmund! She blinked back bottomless grief. One must weep properly at a funeral, and she wanted to scream.

The priest's eulogy proved acceptable. She had chosen not to tell him how irreligious was her husband, even as she knew he must have heard many a rumor. All the same, this priest now offered a dignified description of Alois' service to the Empire. That, said the priest, could also be God's desire.

Later, after the funeral, as people came to visit at the Garden House, Klara tried to convince herself that Adolf's grief was real. Once again she chose to decide that he had loved his father. It was just that both of them had lived too much in their pride, and such pride was bound to turn into animosity. They were men. Anger was natural to them. But beneath was love. Such love could not be expressed easily. In years to come, however, wisps of grief were bound to wander through Adolf's soul, grief possessing all the tenderness of a mist. So she had decided.

While this funeral took place on an icy day, and the roads were glass, the trees were bare, and the skies dark, virtually everyone they knew in Leonding was there, as well as his colleagues from the Linz Customs office. Karl Wesseley had come all the way from Prague. He spoke to Klara for a little while and said, "Oh, we used to tease each other unmercifully, Frau Hitler, and how we laughed. Alois, as you know, loved his beer, and I had my preference for wine. 'You are nothing but an Austrian,' I would tell him, 'so you drink beer like a German, but we Czechs are cultured enough to enjoy wine.' We certainly joked. '*Ach*! You Czechs,' he would then say to me, 'You are cruel to grapes. You stamp all over them with your dirty feet and then, when the poor things are feeling very sour from such mishandling, you add sugar and pretend to be connoisseurs. You sip your sour juice and sugar and try not to make a face. Beer, at least, comes from grain. Its feelings are not so tender.' " He laughed as he told her. "Your husband knew how to talk. We had fine times together."

Mayrhofer mentioned the frightful day when he had had to tell Alois about Junior's incarceration. "Dear Frau Hitler," he said, "I wake up at night and upbraid myself for having been such a messenger."

The *Linzer Tages Post* also carried an ad.

*Bowed in deepest grief, we, on our own behalf, and on behalf of all the relatives, announce the passing of our dear and unforgettable husband, father, brother-in-law, uncle, Alois Hitler, High Official of the Royal Imperial Customs, retired, died Saturday, January 3, 1903, at 10 o'clock in the morning in his 65th year, suddenly fell peacefully asleep in the Lord.*

In the cemetery, Alois' stone carried his photo protected by a glassed frame, and beneath was the following inscription:

HERE RESTS IN GOD
ALOIS HITLER
HIGHER CUSTOMS OFFICER AND HOUSEHOLDER.
DIED 3RD JANUARY, 1903, IN HIS 65TH YEAR.

Adolf decided that his mother was a criminal hypocrite. She would honor her husband's memory, yes, indeed! "Rests in God," indeed! All that was left of his father was his picture resting in a frame set on the headstone in the cemetery, the glass in the frame ready to protect the photograph from the wrath of the weather, Alois' hair close-cropped, his small eyes standing out, just as beady as a bird's, and his Franz Josef sideburns. Yes, here was a man who had served his Emperor, but how could anyone say he was resting in God?

Klara, however, was warmed by a notice the *Linzer Tages Post* gave to the funeral:

> *We have buried a good man—this might we say of Alois Hitler, Higher Collector, Retired, from the Imperial Customs Service, who was borne here to his final resting place today.*

She was so proud of the notice. It was not an advertisement. The paper had done it on its own, the paper with the largest circulation in Upper Austria. She read this item over and over. The lines brought back each moment of the funeral. She could picture Adolf weeping once again, and felt considerable comfort. To herself she said, "He did love his father, after all," and she had to keep nodding her head to sustain the thought.

# 2

Each year, Klara would receive a pension from the government that came to half of Alois' annual salary. In addition, other monies would be paid to the children so soon as they turned eighteen. The total would be enough to keep them comfortable.

Even Adolf had to recognize that Alois' remarks about security in a family did make some kind of sense. He certainly would not have liked to go to work at this point.

There were other compensations. Attending the Realschule for the second half of his third year, Adolf could see that a number of the students were less unfriendly. Was this due to the death of his father? Free of Alois' wrath, he also felt more comfortable with his studies, and soon became more ready to talk back to his teachers, particularly one unhappy middle-aged instructor who was there to conduct religious instruction for several hours each week.

Adolf decided this instructor must be the poor relative of somebody who had had enough influence at the school to procure him the job. Herr Schwamm was sad and dank, so there he was, teaching religion.

During recess one morning, Adolf heard one of the students telling others about a medieval churchman, St. Odon, who was the Bishop of Cluny. "I have a brother who studies Latin," the boy said, "and he gave me my first lesson: *'Inter faeces et urinam nascimur.'* " So soon as this was translated, Adolf was shocked, then thrilled. What strong language! True force! He was aroused enough to dare to go to the Anatomy Museum in Linz once school was out. He managed to get in by lying about his age and so was able to see a penis and a vagina, both modeled in wax, as well as a few full-sized naked men and women, also in wax. The Latin kept pulsing through his mind. To be born between piss and shit! That was what he had always supposed. Sex was filthy.

On the other hand, his description of the visit made him more popular with some of his classmates, who asked again and again for the details. This encouraged him to bait the teacher, so he made a point of uttering the phrase that came from the Bishop of Cluny. Herr Schwamm pretended not to understand. Already a few of the boys were tittering.

"Latin cannot be slurred," stated Herr Schwamm. "The manner by which you try to declaim these words lacks all authority."

Adolf replied, "Then I must speak in German." He frowned, he swallowed, he managed to enunciate, " *'Zwischen Kot und Urin sind wir geboren.'* "

Herr Schwamm had to wipe his eyes. They had filled with tears. "I have never listened to such filth before," he managed to state, but then hurried out of the classroom. Adolf now enjoyed thirty seconds of bliss. Boys who had ignored him all year were pounding him on the back. "You're a real guy," he was told.

For the first time in his life, he received a standing ovation from the class. One by one, they rose to their feet. But then two monitors came in to escort Adolf to the principal, Herr Dr. Trieb.

"If it were not so close to the end of the year, and if our school had not worked so hard to improve your consistently poor grades, I would be ready to expel you," said Herr Dr. Trieb. "Under the circumstances, I will choose instead to assume that the death of your much-mourned father may have been a factor in your un-speakable behavior. So I accept your presence in school for another semester provided there is no continuation whatsoever of this be-havior. You will, of course, apologize to Herr Schwamm."

That proved a curious meeting. Herr Schwamm taught Adolf an unforgettable lesson. It is that one knows nothing about a person until a weak man's strength can be observed.

Herr Schwamm was wearing his best suit on this occasion, and he spoke to the point. He did not try to look into Adolf's eyes yet was able to say in a tone more severe than he could muster in class, "We will not discuss the reason you are here. Instead, I will insist that you read aloud the following prayer." Whereupon he presented a text to Adolf. In full capitals, the words had been written out on a page of good linen paper.

FULL GLORIOUS MAJESTY, WE SUPPLICATE THEE TO DELIVER US FROM THE TYRANNY OF THE INFERNAL SPIRITS, FROM THEIR SNARES, THEIR LIES, AND THEIR FURIOUS WICKEDNESS— OH, PRINCE OF THE HEAVENLY HOST, CAST INTO HELL SATAN AND ALL EVIL SPIRITS WHO WANDER THROUGH THE WORLD SEEKING THE RUIN OF SOULS. AMEN.

"Do you know to whom this prayer is addressed?" asked Herr Schwamm.

"Is it not addressed, sir, to St. Michael the Archangel?"

Of course! That was one prayer Adolf knew well enough. At the monastery in Lambach, he had repeated it every morning after Mass. Moreover, he still retained an image of himself teetering on a stool, Angela's dress draped over his shoulders. "Yes," he replied, "the prayer, sir, is to St. Michael the Archangel," and he even felt an echo of his first erection. Schwamm was a Lutheran and so would not know that if this prayer had once possessed extraordinary force for Adolf, it was by now familiar. He had little fear as he read it aloud. Indeed, his voice resonated with force.

The short speech Herr Schwamm had prepared concerning these fires and perils of hell now seemed nugatory. Indeed, he felt a most unhappy inadequacy once again before this young and sullen student, just one more repetition of unhappy outcomes. So little turns out as one expects.

He offered a few phrases to the effect that he was pleased to recognize "a sober side in you, young Hitler," and stopped before he began to stammer.

"I apologize most abjectly for my actions yesterday, Herr Schwamm," Adolf replied, and was not in the least abject.

Herr Schwamm felt himself close to tears once more. He maintained his composure by making a modest gesture of dismissal.

Once on the other side of the door, Adolf was in a fury. These hypocrites should be dragged to see the wax vagina at the Anatomical Museum.

Indeed, he was preparing the speech he would give to his fellow students when they surrounded him at recess to find out what transpired.

"Well," he would say, "I certainly held my own with poor old Schwamm."

It was a late afternoon in March when he came out of school, but he initiated a snowball fight with a few of his new friends and they kept at it until twilight. He kept repeating a phrase, "Optimism, fire, blood, and steel," and was immensely pleased that the three students on his side in this impromptu and ice-cold test of battle repeated it. So far as he knew, the phrase had not come from a book but had sprung from his throat: "Optimism, fire, blood, and steel!" (Was he repeating words I had given him? I cannot always remember every inspiration I have offered to each client.)

Leave it that Adolf did pick up his volume of Treitschke when he reached home and soon proceeded to memorize the following words:

> God has given all Germans the earth for a potential home, and this assumes that there will come a time when there will be a leader of all the world, a leader to serve as the embodiment, the incarnation, the essence of a most mysterious power which will tie the people to the invisible majesty of the nation.

He thought of this passage often in months to come. Could he believe it? Was it true? There were all kinds of Germans, and some, he decided, were as spineless as Schwamm. Still, he used this long sentence as a rallying cry to himself when in the rigors of one more battle in the woods. He hardly knew what it meant, and yet he kept repeating the words to himself. Nothing that he would read over the next four decades would live for him with such certainty. We devils have known for a long time that a mediocre mind, once devoted entirely to one mystical idea, can obtain a mental confidence well beyond its normal potential.

By late spring of 1903, his war games took on other complexities. Sometimes, on Saturday afternoons, there were as many as fifty boys to a side, and Adolf was introduced, willy-nilly, to logistics. Each army now had to deal with its wounded and its prisoners. Even as Adolf had been seen (until recently) as a minor presence in his school, so was he now, by full contrast, a generalissimo in the forest. Indeed, he was forever pronouncing new battle codes, then changing his own rules. On a given Saturday he would decide that once a man was captured, the only choice was to put him in prison or kill him.

Then he had to recognize that the latter could end many battles too quickly. Where could the dead soldier go but back to his house? So now, serious discussions arose about the length of time required for incarceration. Should it be for thirty minutes, or an hour? And who could keep track? It had to be a separate time-keeper, loyal to neither side. (They ended by choosing the one boy who owned a pocket watch.) Then Adolf had an inspiration. A prisoner could gain his freedom more quickly by becoming a spy. Or he could refuse all offers and stay in prison, but that choice was not often taken. Adolf was aware that captured men soon get bored.

School ended in June. The previous summer, spent at the Garden House, had ended with Alois' first hemorrhage. Now, in the summer of 1903, the family put all that might be needed into two huge trunks, and Klara, Angela, Adolf, and Paula traveled to Spital, where Klara's sister Theresa lived. There they spent the summer. When Alois was alive there had been no question of returning. He could never bear to go back. It reminded him of the cattle trough in which his mother used to sleep. By now, however, the farmer Schmidt, married to Theresa, had a holding large enough to put up all who were in the Hiedler-Poelzl clan. The farm came to no more than the land, the house, the sheds, the outbuildings, and the animals, but Schmidt was a hard worker, and he had managed, by the measure of Spital, to make it profitable. With several fields to work, and woodlands to harvest for nuts, he was ready to use all the labor Klara could offer. "It'll be good for her sorrow that she's here to work it off," he said.

That summer, unlike other members of the family, Adolf did not work. He played with the younger farm children once their afternoon chores were done, and he tried to teach a few war games, even if his recruits were tired enough to fall asleep at their stations.

For most of the day, protected by Klara, he spent his morning and early afternoon reading or drawing, after which he would wander into the woods to search for new military positions. On one occasion he was asked to join in the field work, but Klara declared that he must do no labor at all, considering the ongoing trouble with his lungs. She even told her sister Theresa that since she did not wish him to do any labor, she would pay for his food. That proved acceptable.

After the summer, Angela was going to marry a man named Leo Raubal, who worked as a notary in a bank. Adolf did not enjoy the sight of him. Whenever Raubal would visit, he would tell his future brother-in-law, "Your lungs are not as bad as you claim, isn't that the truth?" and this was enough to leave Adolf in a cold fury. Where could Raubal have picked up such an idea if not from Angela?

Nonetheless, Adolf could see one positive element in this marriage—his own financial condition would improve. There would be a larger share of pension money for him once his big sister was gone from the household. Of course, Angela was hardly bewitched by her situation. She was entering into marriage with a man she didn't adore, but a man, nonetheless, who was available. So Klara's grand plans for Angela's future had come to little. If Angela was ready to accept such a marriage, Klara was not only disappointed but surprised. She was also furious with herself. She could not forgive herself. She had created no social life for Angela. The family lived in the Garden House, a fine place for a young girl to receive company, but Klara had not known how to make the right kind of friends for that. When it came to meeting strangers and impressing them with your charm, and the possible size of a dowry, well, she and Angela had both been much too shy. Raubal turned out to be the best that was available.

As far as Klara was concerned, this man was lucky to steal her stepdaughter. It was virtually a crime. Angela was entitled to much more. Raubal wasn't even healthy in appearance.

What Klara did not know was that Angela had been living with a guilty secret. She had never stopped pining for Alois Junior. She knew that Junior would never come back, but in the course of these seven years of absence, she had transmuted him into a perfect young man. She remembered how handsome he had been on Ulan. She was certain, of course, that if she and Alois Junior were still to-

gether, she would never take one improper step, but all the same
she might now allow her brother to dismount from his horse and
kiss her. Even after the family moved to the Garden House and
Angela had a room to herself, she still kept, carefully hidden, a
photograph of her brother taken by an itinerant photographer on
a fine warm day in Hafeld. Alois Junior had been proud to obtain a
picture of himself standing by his horse. Indeed, he had taken Ulan
out of the stable and led him up to the view camera.

Angela had stolen that picture. It had been her way of paying
Alois back for the times he had teased her when she refused to
mount Ulan. When the photo disappeared, she had to swear to
Alois Junior that she had no idea where it might be. "I say this on a
stack of Bibles," she had said.

"Where are these Bibles?" Alois Junior asked.

"In my mind. They are there. You can trust me."

She did not mind that he was suffering just as much as if he had
lost a gold watch. He deserved to suffer for the way he had teased
her. So cruel!

Angela still kept this photo hidden, but, as the date of her marriage neared, she became more concerned about the carnal redolence that remained in her heart for this innocent—yet maybe not
so innocent—attachment to a fading sepia portrait. Finally, she
came to the cruel recognition that the picture had to be destroyed.
(Otherwise, Leo Raubal was bound to find it sooner or later.)
So, on a night when she was unable to sleep, in a small but most
private ceremony, she tore up this small piece of her past and in the
dark of early morning put the scraps in a small bowl, set a kitchen
match to them, and wept silently as bits of the photograph turned
to black.

After the wedding, Adolf was bothered by thoughts of how ugly
must be the acts that Angela and Leo were performing in bed.
Adolf had seen the groom's phallus one time when they urinated
side by side in a field, and thought it was nothing agreeable to look
at. Now Leo was rubbing it in and out of this supposedly sacred
passage between Angela's two unmentionable holes—how disgust-

ing! His thoughts came to a halt when he recognized that his father and mother were no different from the newlyweds. How awful was this secret that all men and women had to keep silent about.

4

By May of that next year, 1904, in addition to earning another mediocre set of marks, Adolf failed French. A make-up exam would await him in the fall. He did receive a passing mark, but the principal remained unforgiving about the episode with Herr Schwamm. If Adolf Hitler wanted to enter his last year in a Realschule, the principal declared that it would not be at Linz. In retaliation, Adolf said to himself, "I will never allow this school to insult my intelligence again."

Klara solved the problem by sending Adolf to a town called Steyr, fifteen miles from Leonding. It was there that he could finish his Realschule studies. Given the pension, Klara could afford to rent a room for Adolf rather than be obliged to pay for his travel back and forth every day by train. So, from Sunday night to Friday afternoon, Adolf stayed with a woman who was also boarding four other students. It was Frau Sekira's duty to see that her boarders were reasonably well fed and did their homework. Indeed, she was motherly. Adolf always addressed her in a formal manner and then was off to his own small room, where he would spend his time reading and drawing. His marks in the Steyr Realschule were no better, however, than in Linz, and by the end he even failed French once more. In the fall of 1905 he would have to face a makeup exam in order to graduate.

Over the next summer, Klara took Paula and Adolf back to Spital, but in September he traveled to Steyr again for his French test.

This time he passed and so received his graduation certificate. In celebration, he and some of the new roomers at Frau Sekira's house decided to have a party. One of the boys had brought four bottles of wine from home and was generous enough to share them. "My father said that it is good to make a pig of yourself once a year. That is just what my father said. Do it once, not twice." They all applauded the absent father.

The students stayed up late that night and by the end, Adolf declared, "I am as drunk as my father ever was," and fell asleep on the floor. In the morning, he could not find his certificate of graduation. It had been in his pocket but now it was gone. Since he would be going home later in the day, he had to have something to show to his mother. She would never believe that he earned his degree if he could not present the certificate. Trying to put together an explanation, he wondered whether he could tell her that on the train he had unfolded this precious piece of paper in order to enjoy looking at it, but since it was a warm day, he had also opened the train window. With no warning, a gust of wind carried it off! Yet, now as he stepped outside to clear his mind, he recognized that such a story would not suffice. It happened to be a cold day.

Preparing to say farewell to Frau Sekira, he did mention his troubles. Frau Sekira suggested he not attempt to deceive his mother. "That is so inadvisable," she said. "If your story is accepted by her, you will then feel so very guilty. And if your mother does find out, it will be worse."

Over the previous school year, she had been no more than a woman who served him food every day and changed the sheets once a week. Now she had become a rare and thoughtful human being. In misery, he asked, "What should I do?"

"Oh," she said, "tell them the truth at school. They might be unhappy but they will certainly give you a copy."

So Adolf went back to a school he thought he would never see again, and the Rector kept him waiting. It was, after all, a day of registration. Yet, when the Rector did let him in, it was to open a locked closet and take out a heavy paper bag. After which he said,

"Your certificate is here. It has been torn into four pieces. You will soon see its condition." Now the Rector stared at him. "It is one thing for a student to celebrate his graduation when he is pleased that he passed a makeup examination. At last he can allow himself to think that perhaps he has taken a valuable step toward his future. It is, however, another matter, Herr Hitler, to enter into a bout of intoxication that ends in despicable acts." He shook his head. "I can see by the absence of recognition in your face that you do not even have a recollection of the low act you chose to indulge."

This was now becoming equal to standing before the long-nosed priest who had caught him smoking. "Sir, what have I done?" he managed to say. "Be so good as to tell me."

"My dear Herr Hitler, I will be exactly so good as to tell you. You took this document and left your filth on it!" His hands shaking with disgust, he passed the bag over to Adolf. Then he said, "I cannot bring myself to believe that any student in our school could have committed such a bestiality. You would do well to fear that you will go through life never learning to govern perverse impulses. Shall I write to your mother? No, I will not. She is probably a good woman who does not deserve such a stinking embarrassment. Instead, you are to swear to me that from the moment you leave this office, I will never have to see your face again. Just be certain that you do not open the bag while you remain within the walls of this school."

Adolf nodded. By now, he could remember. Yes, he had taken the certificate and wiped his ass with it. The moment came back. He had been feeling so endowed with inner grandeur! How his drinking mates had applauded. His ass was now superior to all that scholarly nonsense.

What made it worse was that he had to wonder how the Rector had found out. There was only one explanation. One of the four students with whom he had been drinking must have turned it over to him. But who would that be? He did not want to find out. Such a confrontation could add to his shame. What if the perpetrator was one of the two fellows bigger than himself? That was most likely.

Back at Frau Sekira's, he spent a long time at the washbasin cleaning the certificate, and drying it. Then he pasted the pieces onto another piece of paper. Now he would have evidence that he had passed his exam. For Klara, he would come up with some explanation.

"Oh, Mother, the more I looked at it, the more did I realize how much you sacrificed for me, and how little I had understood. I tore it up to keep from crying like a baby." Yes, thought Adolf, that will take care of that.

He had to keep wondering, however, which of the students had been the traitor. It could have been all four! He decided that he would never drink again. "Liquor is for traitors," he told himself. He kept sniffing the document to make certain that it now smelled of talcum powder.

I have to remark that no event since Alois' death had come so near to breaching Adolf's sense of personal importance. I had built, however, such a protective palisade around his vision of himself that even this episode did not become a disaster.

## 5

Klara wept with love when she heard why the certificate had come back to her in four pieces.

"It is even more valuable to me this way," she said. "I will be proud to put it into a frame."

That was the hour when he decided that the ability to lie with art was a skill to be esteemed and, indeed, they had a lovely evening, mother and son. With Paula soon asleep, they sat side by side on the sofa and reminisced over old times, when he had been two and three.

That was a special occasion. Over the previous year, coming back from Steyr each weekend, he had certainly grown weary of listening to Klara speak of Alois. In her mind, the old man was now to be remembered as a pillar of their Empire, a profoundly dedicated Civil Servant. His long-stemmed clay pipes were set up on the mantelpiece, each installed in a special holder. The family gospel took it for granted that Alois had given a blessing to Adolf. It was a blessing to have a father who, in his career, had climbed the equal of a mountain.

I was ready to tell him as much myself. These days, I looked to implant one notion into his thoughts. It was that Alois had given Adolf the opportunity to start from a higher place than his father, and so he could become a most prestigious individual. I cannot say whether Klara or myself had the larger influence concerning this matter, but these thoughts became so embedded in Adolf's brain, that by the time he wrote *Mein Kampf* nineteen years later, in 1924, he would speak of Alois in eulogy:

> *Not yet thirteen years old, the little boy he then was, buttoned up his things and ran away from his homeland, Waldviertel. A bitter resolve it must have been to take to the road into the unknown with only three Guilders for traveling money. By the time the thirteen-year-old was seventeen he had a long time of hardship. Endless poverty and misery strengthened his resolve with all the tenacity of one who'd grown "old" through wanton sorrow. While still half a child, this seventeen-year-old youth clung to his decision and became a Civil Servant. Now there has been realized the promise of the vow to which the poor boy once had sworn, not to return to his native village until he'd become something.*

# 6

To improve her economic situation further, Klara sold the house in Leonding, and the family moved to an apartment in Urfahr, just across the river from Linz. During the day, Adolf rarely left these new premises. He did not see any profitable way to enter the ranks of the employed. For that matter, he had no desire to work for others. Besides, he did feel a touch consumptive— enough to keep Klara in a whole state of in-held terror. Would he, like Alois, die of a lung hemorrhage? It was not difficult to persuade her that at this point it would be unwise to look for a career. As he presented it to her, he would be seen one day as a great painter, a great architect, or quite possibly both. Staying at home for the present, he could still amplify his education: He would read and he would draw. He did not need to say more. After five years of suffering the rigors of the Realschule, he was certainly able to enjoy his new life on Humboldtstrasse in Urfahr. His mother paid the bills and Paula cleaned the bathroom. He grew a mustache. He rarely stepped out into the sun. Only in the evening did he take a stroll across the Danube from Urfahr to Linz in order to walk by the opera house. Klara had bought him new clothes, and he ventured out in a good dark suit, wearing a dark overcoat and a black fedora while sporting a silver-handled cane, his most treasured possession. He would be seen, he believed, as one of the young gentry of Linz. Every glimpse he caught of his reflection in store windows confirmed this effect.

His need to stay in the house during the day was matched only by his love of the dark. Not all of the clichés concerning the Devil

are false. Most humans do not begin to appreciate the depth of the
general assumption that what is commonly condemned as Evil does
indeed seek the dark. For good cause. The night is more open to
evocation.

Klara was, of course, taking great pride in his appearance. She
knew that once he was feeling ready, opportunities would open. He
was not only a most unusual boy, but probably needed this kind of
leisure for the present.

Adolf's style of masturbation had also altered. His practice in
the forest had been to spew all over the nearest leaves. (He loved
leaves and he loved spewing on them.) Now, locked behind the
door to his room, he kept a handkerchief at the ready. Yet, before
he would allow his thoughts to lift beyond his control, he would
practice holding his arm in the air at a forty-five-degree angle for a
long time. He would think of the times in the Realschule bathroom
when he had demonstrated this prowess to other students. They
might have their two testicles and he only one, but he could keep
his arm erect on high, and they could not. Of course, there were all
too many other occasions when the general interest had been in
another direction. The boys had collected around the urinals in
order to compare the size of their genitals. It had been a curious
occasion. They were always afraid a teacher might barge in. Erections were lost, therefore, with great speed before the smallest sound, and so Adi's ability to hold his arm high was no more
than another distraction. Now, in his room, he found, however,
that he could maintain his erection even while his arm was raised.
Thoughts of the great variety of personal equipment he had seen
among the students were enough to keep him full of hearty remembrance.

One flaw remained, however, in his present life. That was Angela's husband, Leo Raubal. He could not speak to Adolf without
droning into his ear, "Fellow, you have to start earning your living.
You will keep feeling unwell until you do. I think that is because
you are depressed by the thought that all your relatives in Spital
think you are a good-for-nothing. We know that is not true, but

you have to give up your present occupation, which consists of doing nothing."

Adolf would walk out of the room. Angela would be full of dismay. How rude he was to her husband! Klara, hearing it all, would be silent, but that was only out of respect for Angela. This oaf, Leo Raubal, was, after all, her dear stepdaughter's husband. Therefore, she would not cause trouble. She would not be a mother-in-law to create trouble for a young married couple. That might be even worse than having to listen to your son being scolded by this new son-in-law, who had much too exaggerated an opinion of the worth of his advice. To herself, Klara declared, "Adolf is not a loafer. He does sit at home, but he works so hard when he draws. Besides, he has no need to drink, and he doesn't smoke. That is not a loafer. He does not waste his time. There are no bad girls he likes to see. No girls I must worry about. Maybe he will yet become a great artist. Who is to know? Who is to say? He is so serious. When he is alone and working, he is so strong and so proud of himself. He is full of the knowledge that he, too, will amount to something. To that degree, he is just like Alois. Or, maybe more so. Alois wanted too many things at once." And again, she repeated, "Adolf does not waste time with girls. There are no bad girls in his life."

Nor would there be. Not for a long time. She would have done better to worry about love affairs yet to come with men and boys, some of them even with bad men.

Since Klara saw Adolf by now with all the love of her heart, she was hardly the sort to ponder what might be in his head when he masturbated. Indeed, how could she guess? There was no evidence. He was careful to rinse out his handkerchiefs. No, she did not know that while stroking himself, coming closer and closer to being shot out of his own cannon, he would wonder whether there was any connection between his refusal to work at Customs and his father's last hemorrhage. If so, that would make two people he had scalped in real life: Edmund and Alois. And this thought, in concert with thoughts of the Realschule students at the urinals, so excited his fast-increasing compressions that he could hold them no longer and presto! it was over. It was over, and he was happy, and he was exhausted by how much had been churning within.

# 7

Years later, a girl who went to Paula's school often saw her walking with Klara. Until recently, this girl had lived on a farm, but now almost every weekday she would watch Klara take Paula all the way to school before saying goodbye with a kiss. Nothing like that ever happened to the farm girl. Her mother had always been too busy. So it did not matter to the girl that Paula was backward in class and had been left behind—the farm girl envied her all the same. A mother's love, she decided, must be as sweet as honey.

Indeed, we are there to enjoy it as well.

# THE
# CASTLE
# IN THE
# FOREST

In the beginning, I said that my name was D.T., and that was not wholly inaccurate. It had been a nickname for Dieter while I was occupying the body and person of an SS man, an installation that did not terminate until the end of the Second World War. (At which time Dieter did have to get out of Berlin in a hurry.) That, in brief, is how I came to be at the edge of an uproar on a field where a celebration was continuing through the night. A concentration camp had just been liberated by American soldiers on the very last day of April 1945.

Installed in a small cubicle, I was being interrogated by a psychiatrist, Captain in rank, assigned to the U.S. division that had captured the camp. Given the tumult of the last few days, he had been issued a .45 and it now lay on the table near his hand. I could see that he was not comfortable with the weapon, but then he was a doctor and not practiced in sidearms.

The name tag on his lapel was Jewish and, needless to say, he was unhappy with what he saw.

A pacifist by temperament, this Jewish officer had done his best to withdraw from the worst of these surroundings—which is equal to saying that he was looking to flee from some most offensive human odors. Rank effluvia certainly accompanied the former prisoners' cries of joy. Indeed, it was sufficiently pestilential for the American to order me, his only available opposite number, to remain with him in this office. There, after midnight, I gave answers to his inquiries.

As alone with each other as two souls out in the ocean on a rock

not large enough for three, I confess that I played with his sentiments. It was a time of defeat for me. I was nearly out of games.
The Maestro had just relieved me of service. "For now, fend for
yourself," he said. "I will be moving our operations to America and
will call on you again once I have come to a few determinations as
to what we are ready to do over there."

I did not even know if I could believe him. Rumors were
rampant among us. One devil had even dared to suggest that the
Maestro had been demoted.

This possibility—if it was true—suggested that there were ele-
vations and depths to the Maestro's domain that were altogether
beyond my comprehension. So I acted as humans might—I chose
not to think about it. I thrust myself into another game altogether.
I decided to play with this Jewish psychiatrist by pretending to
explain the worldview of those among whom I had served. I elabo-
rated on the psychological ventures we Nazis had taken into un-
charted regions.

I was not without effect. Dieter had been a charming SS man,
tall, quick, blond, blue-eyed, witty. To give a further turn to the
screw, I even suggested that he was a troubled Nazi. I spoke with a
fine counterfeit of genuine feeling concerning the damnable ex-
cesses that were to be found in the Führer's achievements. Outside the room, former inmates were rampaging up and down the
parade field. Those who still had the strength to give voice were
screaming like loons. As the night went on, this Jewish Captain
could not endure his situation. Sequestered in the depths of the
average pacifist—as one will invariably discover—resides a killer.
That is why the person has become a pacifist in the first place.
Now, given my subtle assault upon what he believed were *his* human
values, the American picked up his .45, knew enough to release the
safety, and shot me.

I can say that I have had to vacate a body more than once. So I
did move on. I traveled to America. I spoke to the Maestro. He did
remark, "Yes, that Jewish Captain showed the way. We will invest
in Arabs and Israelis both!"

Upon which he wished me good luck and I was left to fend for myself in America. That is another story but less interesting, I fear. The figures, including myself, are smaller. I am no longer part of history.

All that remains to discuss is why I have chosen this title, *The Castle in the Forest.* If the reader, having come with me through Adolf Hitler's birth, childhood, and a good part of his adolescence, would now ask, "Dieter, where is the link to your text? There is a lot of forest in your story but where is the castle?"

I would reply that *The Castle in the Forest* translates into *Das Waldschloss.*

This happens to be the name given by the inmates some years ago to the camp just liberated. Waldschloss sits on the empty plain of what was once a potato field. Not many trees are in sight, nor any hint of a castle. Nothing of interest is on the horizon. Waldschloss became, therefore, the appellation given by the brightest of the prisoners to their compound. One pride maintained to the end was that they must not surrender their sense of irony. That had become their fortitude. It should come as no surprise that the prisoners who came up with this piece of nomenclature were from Berlin.

If you are German and are possessed of lively intelligence, irony is, of course, vital to one's pride. German came to us originally as the language of simple folk, good pagan brutes and husbandmen, tribal people, ready for the hunt and the field. So it is a language full of the growls of the stomach and the wind in the bowels of hearty existence, the bellows of the lungs, the hiss of the windpipe, the cries of command that one issues to domesticated animals, even the roar that stirs in the throat at the sight of blood. Given, however, the imposition laid on this folk through the centuries—that they be ready to enter the amenities of Western civilization before the opportunity passes away from them altogether—I do not find it surprising that many of the German bourgeoisie who had migrated into city life from muddy barnyards did their best to speak in voices as soft as the silk of a sleeve. Particularly, the ladies. I do not include long German words, which were often a precursor to our technological spirit today, no, I refer to the syrupy palatals, sentimental sounds for a low-grade brain. To every sharp German fellow, however, particularly the Berliners, irony had to become the essential corrective.

Now, I recognize that this disquisition leads us away from the narrative we have just traversed, but then, this is what I wish to do. It enables me to return to our beginning, when Dieter was a member of Special Section IV-2a. Needless to remark, it is my hope that we have come a long way since. If the act of betraying the Maestro does not succeed in obliterating me, perhaps I will be able to go back someday to a further account of my share in the early career of Adolf Hitler, up even to the late 1920s and the beginning of the '30s, because in that period, Adolf had the love affair of his life, and it was with Geli Raubal, Angela's daughter. Geli was full-bodied, good-looking, and blond. Hitler adored her. They had the most perverse relations. As a high subordinate, an accomplished piano player and socialite named Putzi Hanfstaengl, was to put it, "Adolf only likes playing on the black keys."

In 1930, Geli Raubal was found dead on the bedroom floor of the chamber she occupied along one wing of Hitler's apartment on Prinzregentenstrasse in Munich. She had been shot. Either that, or she had killed herself. This answer was never established. The immediate business was, of course, wholly covered up.

Nor can I satisfy myself in regard to this question. Shortly before the event, I was relieved of my continuing assignment to Adolf Hitler. The Maestro had decided that the Führer-to-be was now of sufficient importance to be guided by a presence higher than myself. Indeed, I suspect it was the Maestro who replaced me. In any event, I never learned more about Geli's death. An absolute silence was the only emanation from that event. Three years later, Hitler and his Nazis were in power, and I was then assigned to enter the body of that good SS man Dieter. I confess that I could not forgive the Maestro for my demotion, which is perhaps the best single explanation of what led me to write this book.

There could, however, be another motivation. One theme does

return. Can it be that the Maestro, whom I served in a hundred roles while holding to the pride that I was a field officer to the mighty eminence of Satan, had indeed deluded me? Was it now likely that the Maestro was not Satan, but only one more minion—if at a very high level?

There was, of course, no answer to be received, but the question may have encouraged the seed of my rebellion to take root.

If this leaves the reader with new discomfort—not even to know now whether it was Satan's words that were reported or no more than the sardonic insights of one more intermediary—I will confess that I remain enough of a devil to feel no great sympathy. What enables devils to survive is that we are wise enough to understand that there are no answers—there are only questions.

Yet is it not also true that one cannot find a devil who will not work both sides of the street? So I must admit to a surprising degree of affection for those of my readers who have traveled all this way with me. I have come so far myself in offering this narration that I can no longer be certain whether I still look for promising clients or search for a loyal friend. There may be no answer to this, but good questions still vibrate with honor within.

*Acknowledgments*

To my fine assistants, the late Judith McNally and Dwayne Prickett; to my good friend and archivist, J. Michael Lennon; to David Ebershoff, my editor, and to Gina Centrello, my publisher, for their ready cooperation and sharp insights; to Jason Epstein for his generous perusal of an earlier draft; to Holly Webber and Janet Wygal for excellent copyediting; to my good friends Hans Janitschek and Ivan Fisher for their readings of the manuscript; to Elke Rosthal for lessons in German; to my wife, Norris, and my nine children for the warmth they offer to my life; and to Andrew Wylie and Jeff Posternak, my keen and formidable agents.

# Bibliography

Some of the books listed in this bibliography have been given an asterisk for their historical or thematic relevance to *The Castle in the Forest*. It should be unnecessary to add that the other works cited also enriched many a fictional possibility. Those titles to which an asterisk is attached did provide me, however, with a bounty of factual and chronological references that a novel in this form can never ignore. With all else, character is sequence.

—Norman Mailer

Anderson, Ken. *Hitler and the Occult.* Amherst, NY: Prometheus Books, 1995.

Armstrong, Karen. *The Battle for God.* New York: Ballantine, 2001.

Binion, Rudolph. *Hitler Among the Germans.* Dekalb, IL: Northern Illinois University Press, 1976.

Brysac, Shareen Blair. *Resisting Hitler: Mildred Harnack and the Red Orchestra.* New York: Oxford University Press, 2000.

* Bullock, Alan. *Hitler: A Study in Tyranny.* New York: Bantam, 1961.

* Bullock, Alan. *Hitler: A Study in Tyranny* (abridged edition). New York: Harper Collins, 1971.

* Bullock, Alan. *Hitler and Stalin: Parallel Lives.* New York: Knopf, 1992.

Burleigh, Michael. *The Third Reich: A New History.* New York: Hill & Wang, 2000.

Cocks, Geoffrey. *Psychotherapy in the Third Reich.* 2d ed. Somerset, NJ: Transaction Publishers, 1997.

Colum, Padraic. *Nordic Gods and Heroes.* Mineola, NY: Dover, 1996.

Crane, Eva. *The World History of Beekeeping and Honey Hunting*. London: Routledge, 1999.

Crankshaw, Edward. *Gestapo: Instrument of Tyranny*. Reprint. Cambridge: Da Capo Press, 1994.

Erikson, Erik H. *Young Man Luther*. Reprint. New York: W. W. Norton Co., 1962.

Farago, Ladislas. *After Math: The Final Search for Martin Bormann*. New York: Avon, 1975.

* Fest, Joachim C. Translated by Richard and Clara Winston. *Hitler*. New York: Harcourt Brace Jovanovich, 1973.

Fest, Joachim C. Translated by Bruce Little. *Plotting Hitler's Death*. Reissue. New York: Henry Holt, 1996.

* Fest, Joachim C. Translated by Ewald Osers and Alexandra Dring. *Speer: The Final Verdict*. New York: Harcourt, 1999.

* Fulop-Miller, Rene. *Rasputin: The Holy Devil*. New York: Viking, 1928.

Gallo, Max. *The Night of Long Knives*. Reprint. Cambridge: Da Capo Press, 1997.

Gilbert, G. M. *Nuremberg Diary*. Reprint. Cambridge: Da Capo Press, 1995.

* Gobineau, Arthur de. *The Inequality of Human Races*. Reprint. New York: Howard Fertig, 1999.

* Goebbels, Joseph. *My Part in Germany's Fight*. Reprint. New York: Howard Fertig, 1979.

Goldhagen, Daniel Jonah. *Hitler's Willing Executioners: Ordinary Germans and the Holocaust*. New York: Knopf, 1996.

Goodrich-Clarke, Nicholas. *The Occult Roots of Nazism: Secret Aryan Cults and Their Influence on Nazi Ideology*. New York: New York University Press, 1985.

Goodrich-Clarke, Nicholas. *The Occult Roots of Nazism*. 2d ed. New York: New York University Press, 1992.

* Grimm, Jacob. *Teutonic Mythology*. Vols. 1, 2, 3, 4. Reprint. Mineola, NY: Dover Publications, 1966.

Gun, Nerin E. *Eva Braun: Hitler's Mistress*. New York: Meredith Press, 1968.

* Haffner, Sebastian. *The Meaning of Hitler*. Cambridge: Harvard University Press, 1979.

Haffner, Sebastian. *The Ailing Empire: Germany from Bismarck to Hitler*. New York: Fromm International Publishing Corp., 1989.

* Hamann, Brigitte. *Hitler's Vienna: A Dictator's Apprenticeship*. New York: Oxford University Press, 1999.

* Hanfstaengl, Ernst "Putzi." *Hitler: The Missing Years*. Reprint. New York: Arcade Publishing, 1994.

Heidegger, Martin. *An Introduction to Metaphysics*. New York: Doubleday, 1961.

* Heidegger, Martin. *Being and Time*. San Francisco: Harper Collins, 1962.

Heiden, Konrad. *Der Fuehrer: Hitler's Rise to Power*. Boston: Houghton Mifflin Company, 1944.

Heston, Leonard L., and Renate Heston. *The Medical Casebook of Adolf Hitler: His Illnesses, Doctors, and Drugs*. New York: Stein and Day, 1979.

* Hoess, Rudolph. Translated by Steven Paskuly. *Death Dealer: The Memoirs of the SS Kommandant at Auschwitz*. Amherst, NY: Prometheus Books, 1992.

* Hoffmann, Heinrich. *Hitler Was My Friend*. London: Burke, 1955.

Iliodor, Sergei Michailovich Trufanoff. *The Mad Monk of Russia, Iliodor*. New York: The Century Co., 1918.

Irving, David. *Goebbels: Mastermind of the Third Reich*. Horsham, West Sussex: Focal Point Press, 1996.

Janik, Allan, and Stephen Toulmin. *Wittgenstein's Vienna*. New York: Touchstone/Simon and Schuster, 1973.

* Jenks, William A. *Vienna and the Young Hitler*. New York: Columbia University Press, 1960.

* Jetzinger, Franz. Translated by Lawrence Wilson. *Hitler's Youth*. London: Hutchinson of London Press, 1958.

* Jung, Carl. *Memories, Dreams, Reflections*. New York: Pantheon, Random House, 1963.

Kaufmann, Walter, translator and editor. *Goethe's Faust*. New York: Doubleday, 1961.

Kelley, Douglas M. *22 Cells in Nuremberg*. New York: Greenberg, 1947.

Kershaw, Ian. *The Hitler Myth: Image and Reality in the Third Reich*. New York: Oxford University Press, 1987.

* Kershaw, Ian. *Hitler: 1889–1936: Hubris*. New York: W. W. Norton, 1998.

Kershaw, Ian. *Hitler: 1936–1945: Nemesis*. New York: W. W. Norton, 2000.

* Kersten, Felix. *The Kersten Memoirs 1940–45*. Reprint. New York: Howard Fertig, 1994.

Kirkpatrick, Ivone. *The Inner Circle*. London: Macmillan & Co., 1959.

* Kogon, Eugen. *The Theory and Practice of Hell: The Shocking Story of the Nazi SS and the Horror of the Concentration Camps*. New York: Berkley Publishing, 1950.

* Kubizek, August. *The Young Hitler I Knew*. Boston: Houghton Mifflin, 1954.

Langer, Walter C. *The Mind of Adolf Hitler: The Secret Wartime Report*. New York: Basic Books, 1972.

Levenda, Peter. *Unholy Alliance*. New York: Avon, 1995.

* Longgood, William. *The Queen Must Die!: and Other Affairs of Bees and Men*. New York: W. W. Norton, 1985.

Lukacs, John. *A Thread of Years*. New Haven: Yale University Press, 1998.

* Lukacs, John. *The Hitler of History*. New York: Knopf, 1997.

Macdonald, Callum. *The Killing of SS Obergruppenfuhrer Reinhard Heydrich*. New York: The Free Press/Macmillan, 1989.

* Machtan, Lothar. *The Hidden Hitler*. New York: Basic Books, 2001.

* Maeterlinck, Maurice. *The Life of the Bee*. New York: Dodd, Mead and Co., 1919.

* Mann, Thomas. *Dr. Faustus*. New York: Knopf, 1948.

Manvell, Roger, and Heinrich Fraenkel. *Heinrich Himmler*. London: Heinemann, 1965.

Maser, Werner. *Hitler: Legend, Myth & Reality*. New York: Harper & Row, 1971.

Massie, Suzanne. *Land of the Firebird*. Blue Hill, ME: HeartTree Press, 1980.

May, Karl. *Winnetou*. Reprint from the 1892–93 ed. Pullman, WA: Washington State University Press, 1999.

McLynn, Frank. *Carl Gustav Jung*. New York: St. Martin's Press, 1996.

Melzer, Werner. *Beekeeping: A Complete Owner's Manual*. Hauppauge, NY: Barron's Press, 1989.

* Milton, John. *Paradise Lost*. New York: Signet, 1968.

* Mironenko, Sergei, and Andrei Maylunas. *A Lifelong Passion: Nicholas and Alexandra: Their Own Story*. New York: Doubleday, 1997. The letters in Book VIII were taken from this source.

Moeller van den Bruck, Arthur. *Germany's Third Empire*. Reprint. New York: Howard Fertig, 1971.

Mosse, George L. *The Crisis of German Ideology*. New York: Grosset & Dunlap, 1964.

Mosse, George L. *Nazi Culture*. New York: Schocken Books, 1966.

Mosse, George L. *Toward the Final Solution*. Reprint. New York: Howard Fertig, 1978.

Mosse, George L. *Toward the Final Solution*. Reprint. New York: Howard Fertig, Inc., 1985.

Mosse, George L. *The Crisis of German Ideology*. Reprint. New York: Howard Fertig, 1998.

Mosse, George L. *The Fascist Revolution*. Reprint. New York: Howard Fertig, 1999.

* Newman, Ernst. *The Life of Wagner*. Vols. 1–4. New York: Knopf, 1946.

*The Nibelungenlied.* Translated by D. G. Mowatt. Mineola, NY: Dover Books, 2001.

* Nietzsche, Friedrich. *Beyond Good and Evil.* New York: Random House, 1966.

* Nietzsche, Friedrich. *The Birth of Tragedy and the Case of Wagner.* New York: Random House, 1967.

* Nietzsche, Friedrich. *The Genealogy of Morals and Ecce Homo.* New York: Random House, 1967.

* Nietzsche, Friedrich. *Thus Spoke Zarathustra.* New York: Penguin, 1978.

Nietzsche, Friedrich. *On the Genealogy of Morals.* New York: Oxford University Press, 1996.

* Nietzsche, Friedrich. *Human, All Too Human.* Lincoln, NE: Bison Books/ University of Nebraska Press, 1996.

* Nietzsche, Friedrich. Walter Kaufmann, ed. *The Portable Nietzsche.* New York: Penguin, 1982.

Noakes, J., and G. Pridham, ed. *Nazism 1919–1945: Vol. 1, 1919–1934.* Exeter: University of Exeter Press, 1983.

* Noll, Richard. *The Aryan Christ: The Secret Life of Carl Jung.* New York: Random House, 1997.

Nolte, Ernst. *Three Faces of Fascism: Action Francaise, Italian Fascism, National Socialism.* New York: New American Library, 1965.

* Payne, Robert. *The Life and Death of Adolf Hitler.* New York: Praeger Publishers, 1973.

Posner, Gerald L., and John Ware. *Mengele: The Complete Story.* New York: Dell, 1986.

Radzinsky, Edvard. *The Rasputin File.* New York: Anchor Books, 2001.

Ravenscroft, Trevor. *The Spear of Destiny.* York Beach, ME: Samuel Weiser, 1982.

* Rosenbaum, Ron. *Explaining Hitler: The Search for the Origins of His Evil.* New York: Random House, 1998.

Rubenstein, Richard L. *After Auschwitz: Radical Theology and Contemporary Judaism.* Indianapolis: Bobbs-Merrill Co., 1966.

* Salisbury, Harrison E. *Black Night, White Snow: Russia's Revolutions 1905–1917.* New York: Doubleday, 1978.

* Schellenberg, Walter. *The Schellenberg Memoirs: A Record of the Nazi Secret Service.* London: Andre Deutsch, 1956.

* Sereny, Gitta. *Albert Speer: His Battle with Truth.* New York: Knopf, 1995.

Shirer, William L. *Berlin Diary: The Journal of a Foreign Correspondent, 1934–1941.* New York: Knopf, 1941.

Shirer, William L. *The Rise and Fall of the Third Reich*. New York: Simon and Schuster, 1960.

Showalter, Dennis E. *Little Man, What Now? Der Sturmer in the Weimar Republic*. Hamden, CT: Archon Books, 1982.

Sichrovsky, Peter. *Incurably German*. New York: Swan Books, 2001.

* Smith, Bradley F. *Adolf Hitler: His Family, Childhood & Youth*. Stanford: Hoover Institution Press (Stanford University), 1967.

* Smith, Bradley F. *Heinrich Himmler: A Nazi in the Making 1900–1926*. Stanford: Hoover Institution Press (Stanford University), 1971.

Snyder, Louis L. *Hitler's Elite: Nineteen Biographical Sketches of Nazis Who Shaped the Third Reich*. New York: Hippocrene Books, 1989.

* Speer, Albert. *Inside the Third Reich*. New York: Macmillan, 1970.

Speer, Albert. *Spandau: The Secret Diaries*. New York: Macmillan, 1976.

* Stein, George H., ed. *Hitler*. Englewood Cliffs, NJ: Prentice-Hall, 1968.

* Sturmer, Michael. *The German Empire (1870–1918)*. New York: The Modern Library, 2000.

Taylor, Telford, introduction and editor. *Hitler's Secret Book*. New York: Grove Press, 1961.

Toland, John. *Adolf Hitler* (vol. 1). New York: Doubleday, 1976.

Tolstoy, Leo. *The Death of Ivan Ilych*. New York: Signet, 1960.

Tolstoy, Leo. *Anna Karenina*. New York: Viking, 2001.

* Trevor-Roper, H. R., ed. *Hitler's Secret Conversations (1941–1944)*. New York: Farrar, Straus and Young, 1953.

Trevor-Roper, H. R., ed. *The Bormann Letters*. London: AMS Press/ Weidenfeld and Nicholson, 1954.

* Trevor-Roper, Hugh. *The Last Days of Hitler*. Chicago: University of Chicago Press, 1992.

Trotsky, Leon. *My Life*. New York: Pathfinder Press, 1970.

Vassilyev, A. T. *The Ochrana*. Philadelphia: Lippincott, 1930.

Viroubova, Anna. *Memories of the Russian Court*. London: Macmillan, 1923.

von Frisch, Karl. *The Dance Language and Orientation of Bees*. Cambridge: Belknap Press of Harvard University, 1967.

von Lang, Jochen. *Hitler Close-Up*. New York: Macmillan, 1969.

von Lang, Jochen. *The Secretary. Martin Bormann: The Man Who Manipulated Hitler*. New York: Random House, 1979.

* Waite, Robert G. L. *The Psychopathic God: Adolf Hitler*. Reprint. Cambridge: Da Capo Press, 1993.

Warlimont, Gen. Walter. *Inside Hitler's Headquarters 1939–45*. New York: Presidio Press, 1964.

* Weitz, John. *Hitler's Diplomat: The Life and Times of Joachim von Ribbentrop*. New York: Ticknor & Fields, 1992.

Wilson, Colin. *Rasputin and the Fall of the Romanovs*. New York: Farrar, Straus and Co., 1964.

Wykes, Anton. *Himmler*. New York: Ballantine Books, 1972.

* Youssoupoff, Prince Felix. *Rasputin*. London: Jonathan Cape/Florian Press, 1934.

Youssoupoff, Prince Felix. *Lost Splendor*. Reprint. Chappaqua, NY: Helen Marx Books, 2003.

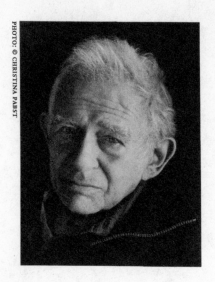

NORMAN MAILER was born in 1923 and published his first book, *The Naked and the Dead*, in 1948. *The Armies of the Night* won the National Book Award and the Pulitzer Prize in 1969; Mailer received another Pulitzer in 1980 for *The Executioner's Song*. He lives in Provincetown, Massachusetts.